"These guys are persistent. I'll give them that."

"Which means we can't go to the next ranger station. They'll be waiting for us there." If they weren't already. Vincent couldn't take the chance. Not after Shea had risked her life to save his. He'd promised to get her to New York to fight for her son, and he had no intention of failing her again. "We have to go deeper into the woods. North. They won't be looking for us there."

"Every minute we spend out here is another chance we don't make it out of these mountains." Wide eyes searched his face. "If we head north, we'll just be saving the guys with the guns the trouble when we die out here from exposure."

"We have to take the risk. Otherwise, they'll shoot us on sight. I need you to trust me."

SURVIVAL
ON THE SUMMIT

NICHOLE SEVERN

&

MELINDA DI LORENZO

Previously published as *The Line of Duty*
and *Trusting a Stranger*

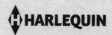

H HARLEQUIN®

ISBN-13: 978-1-335-42481-5

Recycling programs
for this product may
not exist in your area.

Survival on the Summit

Copyright © 2021 by Harlequin Books S.A.

The Line of Duty
First published in 2020. This edition published in 2021.
Copyright © 2020 by Natascha Jaffa

Trusting a Stranger
First published in 2015. This edition published in 2021.
Copyright © 2015 by Melinda A. Di Lorenzo

This edition published by arrangement with Harlequin Books S.A.

For questions and comments about the quality of this book,
please contact us at CustomerService@Harlequin.com.

Harlequin Enterprises ULC
22 Adelaide St. West, 41st Floor
Toronto, Ontario M5H 4E3, Canada
www.Harlequin.com

Printed in U.S.A.

CONTENTS

Nichole Severn writes explosive romantic suspense with strong heroines, heroes who dare challenge them and a hell of a lot of guns. She resides with her very supportive and patient husband, as well as her demon spawn, in Utah. When she's not writing, she's constantly injuring herself running, rock climbing, practicing yoga and snowboarding. She loves hearing from readers through her website, nicholesevern.com, and on Facebook, Facebook.com/nichole.severn.

Books by Nichole Severn

Harlequin Intrigue

Blackhawk Security

Rules in Blackmail
Rules in Rescue
Rules in Deceit
Rules in Defiance
Caught in the Crossfire
The Line of Duty

Tactical Crime Division

Midnight Abduction

Visit the Author Profile page
at Harlequin.com for more titles.

THE LINE OF DUTY

Nichole Severn

This one's for you! You made this series possible, and while this might be the last book of the origin series, Blackhawk Security isn't finished yet!

Chapter 1

He had a lead.

The partial fingerprint he'd lifted from the murder scene hadn't been a partial at all, but evidence of a severe burn on the owner's index finger that altered the print. He hadn't been able to get an ID with so few markers to compare before leaving New York City a year ago. But now, Blackhawk Security forensic expert Vincent Kalani finally had a chance to bring down a killer.

He hauled his duffel bag higher on his shoulder. He had to get back to New York, convince his former commanding officer to reopen the case. His muscles burned under the weight as he ducked beneath the small passenger plane's wing and climbed inside. Cold Alaskan air drove beneath his heavy coat, but catching sight of the second passenger already aboard chased back the chill.

"Shea Ramsey." Long, curly dark hair slid over her shoulder as jade-green eyes widened in surprise. His entire body nearly gave in to the increased sense of gravity pulling at him had it not been for the paralysis working through his muscles. Officer Shea Ramsey had assisted Blackhawk Security with investigations in the past at the insistence of Anchorage's chief of police, but her formfitting pair of jeans, T-shirt and zip-up hoodie announced she wasn't here on business. Hell, she was a damn beautiful woman, an even better investigator and apparently headed to New York. Same as him. "Anchorage Police Department's finest, indeed."

"What the hell are you doing here?" Shea shuffled her small backpack at her feet, crossing her arms over her midsection. The tendons between her shoulders and neck corded with tension as she stared out her side of the plane. No mistaking the bitterness in her voice. "Is Blackhawk following me now?"

"Should we be?" Blackhawk Security provided top-of-the-line security measures for their exclusive clientele, including cameras, body-heat sensors, motion detectors and more. Whatever their clients needed, Sullivan Bishop and his team delivered. Personal protection, network security, private investigating, logistical support to the US government and personal recovery. They even had their very own profiler on staff to aid the FBI with serial cases. The firm did it all. Vincent mainly headed the forensics division, but he'd take up any case with Shea's involvement in a heartbeat. His gut tightened. Hard to ignore the quiet strength she'd kept close to the vest when they partnered together on these past few cases. It'd pulled him in, made him want

to get to know her more, but she'd only met him—and
every member of his team—with resentment. Not all
Anchorage PD officers agreed with the partnership between the city and the most prestigious security firm in
Alaska. Officer Ramsey led that charge.

He shoved his duffel into the cargo area as the pilot
maneuvered into his seat. The small plane bounced with
the movement. The cabin, he couldn't help but notice,
filled with her scent. "I'm not here on Blackhawk business. I've got…personal business to take care of in New
York. You?"

"I have a life outside of the department." She hadn't
turned to look at him, her knuckles white through the
taut skin of her hands as she gripped the seat's arms.
The plane's engine growled at the push of a button, rotors sending vibrations through the sardine can meant to
get them halfway to New York in one piece before they
switched to another aircraft to make the rest of the trip.

"You guys ready?" the pilot asked. "Here are your
headsets."

Hell, Shea was so tense as she took hers, she probably thought the wrong gust of wind could shoot them
out of the sky. She closed her eyes, muscles working
hard in her throat. The tarmac attendants removed the
heavy rubber blocks from around the plane's wheels,
and they slowly rolled forward. Every muscle down her
spine seemed to further tighten.

Something inside him felt for her, forced him to
reach out to offer assurance. Vincent positioned the
headset over his ears, then slid his hand on top of hers.
Smooth skin caught on the calluses in his palms, and
suddenly those green eyes were on him. In an instant,

her fingers tangled with his. Heat exploded through him, the breath rushing out of his lungs as she gripped on to him as though her life depended on it.

Pressure built behind his sternum as the small passenger plane raced down the runway, then climbed higher into the sky. His back pressed into the soft leather seats, but his attention focused 100 percent on the woman beside him. On the way her skin remained stretched along her forearm revealing the map of veins below, on the unsteady rising and falling of her shoulders when she breathed. Snow-capped mountains disappeared below the windows, only reappearing as the plane leveled out high above the peaks mere minutes later. The pilot directed them toward the mountains, but the pressure hadn't released from his rib cage. Not when Shea was still holding on to him so tightly. He raised his voice over the sound of the engine. "I'm going to need that hand back sooner or later."

"Right. Sorry." Shea released her grip, then wiped her palm down her thigh, running the same hand through her curly hair. Her voice barely registered above the noise around them. "You'd think five years on the job would give me a little more backbone when it came to planes."

"There's a difference between facing the bad guys and facing our fears." His hand was still warm from where their skin had made contact, and he curled his fingers into his palm to hold on to it for as long as he could. "At least there was for me."

She slid that beautiful gaze to his, the freckles dusted across the bridge of her nose and onto her cheeks more pronounced than a few minutes ago. "You were with

NYPD's forensics unit for nine years before you came out here, right? Can't imagine there's much that scares you anymore."

She'd be surprised. Her words slowly sank in over the engine's mid-frequency drone, and Vincent narrowed his attention. She'd looked into him. There was no way she could've known how long he'd worked forensics by simply searching for him on the internet. NYPD records weren't public information. Which meant she'd used her access through federal databases. Out of curiosity? Or something else? His attention darted to his duffel bag. He'd booked a private passenger plane out of Merrill Field for a reason. The SIG SAUER P226 with twelve deadly rounds of ammo in the magazine was currently nestled in his bag. He'd worked with Officer Ramsey before. The background check the firm had run on her when Blackhawk had need of the department's assistance on past investigations hadn't connected her with anyone from his past. But what were the chances that she of all people had ended up on this flight? "Someone's been doing their homework."

"All of you Blackhawk Security types are the same. You take the law into your own hands and don't care if you jeopardize the department's cases. You run your own investigations, then expect officers like me to clean up your mess. You're vigilantes, and you endanger the people in this city every time you step out of your downtown high-rise office. So, yes, I've done my homework. I like to know who I'm being forced to work with." She pinned him to his seat with that green gaze, and the world disappeared around them. "And you...you were a cop. You used to have a conscience."

Vincent clenched his back teeth against the fire exploding through him. He leaned into her, ensuring she couldn't look away this time. "You have no idea—"

The plane jerked downward, throwing his heart into his throat. The engine choked, then started up again. He locked his attention out through the plane's windshield. His pulse beat loudly behind his ears. The rotors were slowing, grinding. He shouldn't have been able to track a single propeller if they were running at the right speed. Gripping one hand around his seat's arm, he pressed his shoulders into the leather and shouted into his mic. "What the hell is going on?"

"I don't know." The pilot shot his hand to the instrument panel. "We're losing altitude fast, but all of the gauges check out." Wrapping his hand around the plane's handheld CB radio, the pilot raised his voice over the protests of the engine. "Mayday, Mayday, Mayday. Merrill Field, this is Captain Reginald, a Robin DR400, Delta-Echo, Lima, Juliet, Golf, with total engine failure attempting forced landing. Last known position seven miles east of Anchorage; 1,500 feet heading ninety degrees." Static filled their headsets. "Can anybody read me?" The pilot looked back at his passengers. "The controls aren't responding! I'm going to have to try to put her down manually!"

Vincent pressed his hand to the window and searched the ridges and valleys below for a safe place they could land. Nothing but pure white snow and miles of mountains. Jagged peaks, trees. There was no way they'd survive a forced landing here. There were no safe places to land.

"No, no, no. No! This wasn't supposed to happen."

The panic in Shea's voice flooded his veins with ice. She grabbed her backpack off the floor from between her feet and clutched it to her chest. Fear showed brightly in her eyes a split second before she was thrown back in her seat. She clutched the window. "This wasn't supposed to happen."

The engine smoked, and the plane jerked again. Vincent slammed into the side door. Pain ricocheted through the side of his head, but he forced it to the back of his mind. They were losing altitude fast, and dizziness gripped him hard. They had to get the engine back up and running, or they were all going to die. He couldn't breathe, couldn't think. Double-checking his seat belt, Vincent locked on Shea's terrified features. *This wasn't supposed to happen.* The mountain directly outside her window edged closer. "Watch out!"

Metal met rock in an ear-piercing screech. The mountain cut into the side of the plane, taking the right wing, then caught on the back stabilizer and ripped off the tail end. Cold Alaska air rushed into the cabin as luggage and supplies vanished into the wilderness. The plane rocked to one side, the ground coming up to meet them faster than Vincent expected. He dug his fingers into the leather armrest, every muscle in his body tensed.

The pilot's voice echoed through the cabin. "Brace for impact!"

He reached out for Shea. "Hang on!"

The sky was on fire.

Red streaks bled into purple on one side and green on the other as she stared out the small window to her right, stars prickling through the auroras she'd fallen in

love with the very first night she'd come to Anchorage.
Rocky peaks and trees framed her vision, and every cell
in her body flooded with pain in an instant. A groan
caught in Shea Ramsey's throat, the weight on her chest
blocking precious oxygen. Her feet were numb. How
long had she been unconscious? Her hands shook as she
tested the copilot seat weighing on her sternum. Closing her eyes against the agony, she put everything she
had into getting out from under the hunk of metal and
leather, but it wouldn't budge.

The plane had gone down, Vincent's shout so loud in
her head. And then… Shea pushed at the debris again as
panic clawed through her. They'd crashed in the mountains. The pilot hadn't been able to reach anyone on
the radio. Did anyone even know they were out here?
She couldn't breathe. Tears prickled at the corners of
her eyes as the remains of the plane came into focus.
Along with the unconscious man in the seat beside her.
"Vincent, can you hear me?"

His long black hair covered the pattern of tattoos
inked into his arms and neck as well as his overly attractive face. His Hawaiian heritage and that body of
a powerful demigod had tugged at something primal
within her every time she was forced to work alongside
him in the field, but she'd buried that feeling deep. He
shouldn't have been here. The pilot had told her she'd
be the only passenger on this flight. She hadn't meant
for the Blackhawk Security operative to get involved—
hadn't meant anyone to get involved—but she'd been
so desperate to get to New York. That same determination tore through her now as the plane jerked a few
more inches along the snowbank. Out Vincent's win-

dow it looked like they'd crashed at the base of a steep cliffside, with nothing but sky and snow in every direction. A scream escaped her throat as the cabin shook. One wrong move would send them down the short slope and over the edge.

"Shea." A groan reached her ears as Vincent stirred in his seat. Locking soothing brown eyes on her through the trail of blood snaking through his left eyebrow, he pushed his hair back with one hand. "That…did not go as I expected. But we're okay. It's going to be okay."

Was he trying to convince her or himself?

"I can't…breathe." Understanding lit his bearded features as he noted the seat pressing against her chest, and in that moment, her body heat spiked with the concern sliding into his expression. Memory of him holding her hand during takeoff rushed to the front of her mind. Vincent pushed out of his seat, and the plane slid another couple of inches toward the cliff. She closed her eyes as terror ricocheted through her. "No, don't!"

"Shea, look at me." His featherlight touch trailed down her jaw, and she forced herself to follow his command. He stilled, bending at the knees until her gaze settled on his. Her heart pounded hard at the base of her skull but slowed the longer he stared at her. "I'm going to get you out of here, okay? You have my word. I need you to trust me."

Trust him. The people he worked for—worked with—couldn't be trusted. None of them could. Blackhawk Security might help catch the bad guys, same as her, but at the cost of breaking the law she'd taken an oath to uphold. They didn't deserve her trust, but the pain in her chest wouldn't let up, was getting worse, and all she could do was nod.

He moved forward slowly, and Shea strengthened her grip on the metal crushing her. The only reason the seat hadn't killed her was because of the padded backpack she'd clutched before the crash, but how much more could her body take? The plane was shifting again, threatening to slide right toward another cliff edge. They'd survived a crash landing from 1,500 feet. What were the chances they'd survive another? Vincent crouched beside her, the plane barely large enough to contain his hulking size. Although the gaping hole at the tail end helped. "Hey, eyes on me, Officer. Nowhere else, you got that? I'm going to try to get this thing off of you, but I need you to focus on me."

Focus on him. She could do that. She'd spent so long trying not to notice him while they worked their joint investigations, it was a nice change to have permission for once. Pins and needles spread through her feet and hands as cold worked deep into her bones. The back of the plane had been separated from the main fuselage, and the bloodied windshield had a large hole where she'd expected to see the pilot in his seat. They were in the middle of the Alaskan wilderness, and temperatures were dropping by the minute. "You're...bleeding."

"I've survived worse." He skimmed his fingers over hers, and her awareness of how close he'd gotten rocketed her heart into her throat.

"Worse than...a plane crash?" How was that possible? She'd read his service records, thanks to a former partner now working for the NYPD. Vincent Kalani had been assigned to the department's Detective Bureau's Forensic Investigations Division, collecting and analyzing evidence from crime scenes for close to ten years. Until suddenly he wasn't. There was nothing in those files about an injury in the line of duty. In fact, it was as though he'd simply disappeared before signing on with Sullivan Bishop's new security firm here in Anchorage.

"I think I've got this loose enough to move it. You ready? I need you to push the seat forward as hard as you can." Vincent handled the leather seat crushing her chest. "On my count. One, two, three." Together, they shoved the debris forward, and Shea gasped as much crisp, clean air as her lungs allowed.

"Thank you." The pain vanished as he maneuvered the hunk of metal to the front of the plane, and a panicked laugh bubbled to the surface. Because if she didn't have this small release, Shea feared she might break down here in front of him. The ground rumbled beneath them, and she stilled. The plane hadn't moved. At least, not as far as she could tell. So what—

Another shock wave rolled through the fuselage, and she tightened her grip around the backpack in her lap. "Vincent…"

Fear cut through the relief that'd spread over his expression. "Avalanche."

Shea twisted in her seat, staring up at the ripples creasing through the snowbanks high above, her fingers plastered against the window. Strong hands ripped her out of her seat and thrust her toward the back of the plane. Adrenaline flooded into her veins, triggering her fight-or-flight response. The plane tilted to one side as they raced toward the back, threatening to roll with

their escape. Cargo slid into her path. Her boot caught
on a black duffel bag, and she hit freezing metal. The
rumble was growing louder outside, stronger.

"Go, go, go!" Vincent helped her to her feet, keeping
close on her heels as the plane shifted beneath them.
With a final push, he forced her through the hole where
the tail end of the plane was supposed to be, but they
couldn't stop. Not with an entire mountain of snow cas-
cading directly toward them.

Flakes worked into the tops of her boots and soaked
through her jeans. She pumped her legs as hard as she
could, but it wouldn't be enough. The avalanche was
moving too fast. She was going to die out here, and everything she'd worked for—everything she'd ever cared
about—wouldn't matter anymore.

"There!" Vincent fisted her jacket and shoved her
ahead of him. "Head for that opening!"

Trying to gain control of the panic eating her alive
from the inside, Shea sprinted as fast as several feet of
snow would let her toward what looked like the entrance
to a cave a mere twenty feet ahead of them. Her fingers
ached from the grip she kept on the backpack, but it was
nothing compared to the burn in her lungs. A rush of
cold air and flecks of snow blew her hair into her face
and disrupted her vision, but she wouldn't stop. Couldn't
stop. Ten feet. Five. She pumped her free arm to gain
momentum. Sweat beaded at the base of her neck. They
were going to make it. They *had* to make it. Glancing
back over her shoulder, she ensured Vincent was still
behind her, but the plane had already been consumed.
Snow started to fall over the cave's entrance in a thun-

dering rush, and she lunged for the opening before it disappeared completely.

And hit solid dirt.

She clutched the backpack close to her chest, as if it'd bring any kind of comfort.

Within seconds, darkness filled her vision, only the sound of her and Vincent's combined breathing registering over the rumble of them being buried alive. She reached for him, skimming her fingertips across what she assumed was one of his arms, but the padding of his jacket was too thick to be sure. Dust filled her nostrils as she fought to catch her breath. Silence descended, the wall of snow and ice settling over the cave. "You saved my life."

A soft hissing sound preceded a burst of orange flame. Shadows danced over Vincent's features, his battle-worn expression on full display in the dull flame of the lighter, and a hint of the awareness she'd felt when he'd held her hand during takeoff settled low in her stomach. Faster than she thought possible, he hauled her from the floor and pinned her against the wall of the cave and his body with one hand, her pack forgotten. "Tell me why you were on that plane."

His body pressed into hers. Shadowed, angry angles were carved into his features, unlike anything she'd seen before when they'd worked together. Shea pushed at him, but he was so much stronger, so much bigger. "Get off me."

"Before we crashed you said, 'This wasn't supposed to happen.'" He increased the pressure at the base of her throat, simulating the crushing debris he'd pulled off her chest mere minutes ago. "There was no reason that plane should've crashed unless it'd been sabotaged. You know something, and I'm not letting you go until you tell me who sent you after me—"

Turning one side of her body into him, she struck his forearm with the base of her palm and withdrew her service weapon with her free hand from the shoulder holster beneath her jacket. She aimed center mass, just as she'd been trained, but kept her finger alongside the trigger. "Touch me again and I won't hesitate to shoot you. Understand?"

He backed off, easing the blood pulsing in her face and neck.

"Nobody sent me after you, whatever the hell that means." In the dim light of the flame, Shea swallowed the discomfort in her throat as though that would make it easier to breathe, but she wouldn't lower her weapon. "I was on the plane because I need to get my son back."

Chapter 2

"What do you mean get him back?" Shea had a son. Of all the cases they'd worked together, neither of them had revealed more than they'd had to, but a son? Why hadn't that come up in her background check? How hadn't he known, and why did the thought of her creating life with another man tear at the edges of the hollowness inside him?

She lowered the barrel of her service weapon an inch, but kept the gun raised. Like the strong, stubborn, suspicious police officer he'd come to know. He shouldn't have pinned her against the wall, her sultry scent embedded now in his lungs. But more than that, he hadn't meant to intimidate her. Hadn't meant to drive a larger wedge between them than already existed. "My husband—my ex-husband—he…" Swiping her tongue across her bottom lip, Shea shifted her weight between both feet, but her gaze softened in the little bit of flame they had left. "He took Wells from me."

The muscles down Vincent's spine hardened with battle-ready tension. Rage, hot and fast, exploded through his veins. Her son had been taken. He could only imagine the hurt, the fear she'd had to live with this entire time, and she hadn't said a word. Every cell in his body urged him to find the bastard responsible and make him pay, to bring her son home, but there was nothing he could do for either of them right now. Sympathy flooded through him, and he raised his hands in surrender, the lighter clutched between his thumb and palm. "You can put the gun down."

One second. Two. She lowered the gun to her side but didn't holster it. Pressing her back against the cave wall, she slid to her haunches and collected the backpack she'd held on to so tightly during the flight. "Why do you think the plane was sabotaged? Flights go down all the time. It could've been an accident—"

"Because of the pilot," he said. "He reported the gauges were fine, but the engine had stalled. My guess is someone tampered with the fuel tank. Maybe replaced the fuel with some other kind of liquid. The gauge would've read full, but the engine can't run without gas."

"I didn't sabotage the plane." She nodded absently. "But I might know who did."

"Let me guess. Your ex." Hell. He'd been dispatched to enough domestic cases over the years to understand the lengths some guys went to keep their girlfriends or wives from escaping, but bringing down a plane? Kidnapping a child? Vincent forced himself to breathe evenly. Any evidence that someone had messed with the plane was gone, buried as deep as if not deeper than they were at the moment. No way to confirm Shea's ex-husband—or anyone else—was responsible, but he wouldn't discount the possibility that her being on that plane wasn't just a coincidence. "Tell me about your son."

"Wells?" Her lips tugged into a weak smile as she holstered her weapon under her jacket. Dark patches of water stained her jeans, and he realized she must be freezing right about now. The sun had already started going down when they'd woken up in the wreckage. So they'd have to make camp here tonight, get a fire going once he mapped out the rest of the cave. Maybe there was another entrance that hadn't been buried during the avalanche. "He's…a handful. Unlimited energy, great negotiation skills, even though he's not old enough to talk." A laugh escaped as she pushed her long dark hair over her head, but her smile disappeared as quickly as it come. "I found out I was pregnant a couple months after Logan and I got married. We were both so excited to be parents, but then…then everything changed." Shadows hid her expression as Shea wiped her palms down her jeans and stood. "My ex was able to convince a judge to give him temporary custody of our son after the divorce, but I have to fight for him. Logan has been doing everything he can to keep me from seeing Wells. Sending threatening messages, having me followed, but I never thought he'd bring down a plane to keep me from getting to the custody hearing. That he would try to kill me."

Whoever was behind this had almost succeeded, too.

"That's why you were headed to New York." Hell. And they'd just crashed in the middle of the Alaskan wilderness. Vincent gripped the lighter in his hand; her gaze blazed in the dim light. They'd barely escaped with their lives and had been trapped in this cave under who knew how many feet of snow. As far as rescue coming, the tower had no idea they'd gone down, and their pilot had gone missing. Maybe had even been buried in the avalanche after getting thrown from the crash site. Vincent had taken leave from Blackhawk for the next week and a half. No one would know he hadn't made it to New York. As far as his team was concerned, he was going back home to Hawaii. So he and Shea…they weren't going anywhere. "Did you file a complaint with the police department?"

She hesitated, bottom lip parting slightly from the top, then shut down the slight hint of retreat as she leveled her chin with the cave floor. "I'm a cop. I can protect myself."

"If you can connect the messages and stalking back to him, you'll have a stronger case, but you already know that." Hell, she advised the same protocol when dealing with domestic violence victims on the job. Which meant she wasn't telling him the whole truth. Closing the small distance between them, he admired the way she held her ground, the way she locked her back teeth and flexed the muscles along her jawline as though to prove how strong she was, how capable and driven. And damn, if that wasn't one of the sexiest things he'd ever seen. "As of right now, we have to assume no one is coming to save us, but I'm going to do everything in my power to get you to that hearing."

"How? We're literally trapped inside a mountain under several feet of snow, our pilot is missing and the plane is gone." Shea ran her hands along the cave wall, shadows consuming her from head to toe. "Unless you have a couple shovels in that bag of yours and something to keep us from freezing to death, we're on our own."

"Then that'll have to be enough." Vincent knelt beside the duffel of supplies Blackhawk Security operatives were required to carry, no matter the situation. Couple bottles of water, a day's worth of emergency food, first aid kit, change of clothes, space blanket, lighter, small bundle of kindling, anything portable they—or their clients—might need to survive the harsh temperatures of Alaska. He unpacked his SIG SAUER from the side pocket and checked the magazine in the flame of the lighter.

"Why are you helping me?" Her voice wavered as chills rocked through her. Shea attempted to warm herself by folding her arms across her chest, but her clothing had already been soaked through. The only thing that'd keep their bodies from sinking into hypothermia was a fire—and each other. "We're not exactly friends. We work together occasionally. Nothing more."

"Either we survive together, or we die alone. I don't know about you, but I prefer the former." He dug a flashlight from the bottom of the bag and let the lighter's flame die. Sweeping the beam over her, he studied the glistening wall at her back. Alaska was known for its gold and silver mines, but a handful of precious metals weren't going to keep them warm. "Night's already falling, so we're not getting out of here until morning. We need to search the cave and find a spot to build a fire. Only problem is ventilation. If we don't find the right spot and we light a fire, we'll—"

"Suffocate." She turned away from him, following the flashlight's beam up along the cavernous openings above them. "My brother was an Eagle Scout. I helped him with a lot of his merit badges."

"So what you're saying is you're going to be the one to make sure we don't die." Hauling the duffel over his shoulder, he ignored the pain spreading up his leg and treaded deeper into the cave. Blood trailed down the inseam of his pants and into his boots. Freezing temperatures had already worked deep into his muscles, slowing him down, but the addition of the sliver of shrapnel from the crash threatened to bring him to the edge. They had to find a place to camp and get the fire going. Only then would he worry about his leg. "Now I feel safe."

Her laugh curled around him from ahead, echoing off the bare walls of the cave, a deep, rich laugh he'd never heard from her before. What he wouldn't give to witness the smile accompanying the sound, but she'd already moved a few paces ahead of him, weapon drawn once again. Caves like this were perfect for wildlife native to these mountains. Bears, wildcats. They couldn't be too careful. "Don't get your hopes up. I wasn't paying that close attention."

A smile tugged at one corner of his mouth. Of all the people who could've stepped foot on that plane, the second passenger had to be Shea Ramsey. Intelligent, driven, beautiful. She'd pulled at something inside him the moment she was assigned to assist one of Blackhawk's past investigations, a need he hadn't thought about since waking up in the middle of the crime scene he was supposed to die in.

Darkness intensified his other senses as they felt

their way deeper into the cave, his awareness of her—
of the way her jeans brushed together at the apex of her
thighs, of how her hair fell across her back—at an all-
time high. A rush of cold air hit him square in the face,
and he dragged the flashlight beam along the ceiling.
There. A small opening about thirty feet up that hadn't
been covered in snow. Big enough to provide ventilation for a fire. Studying the ground around them, he
kicked loose rocks and dirt away from the area. "We
can build a fire here."

Shea rubbed her hands together in an attempt to
warm herself, but it wouldn't be enough. Not out here.
"Shouldn't we be looking for a way out?"

"We're not going anywhere tonight." Vincent
dropped to one knee, unpacking the lighter and small
bundle of kindling from his bag. Within a minute, a fire
snapped, crackled and popped. They'd been exposed to
the coldest temperatures Mother Nature had to offer,
and the twigs wouldn't last all night. He straightened,
tearing his jacket from his shoulders, then lifted his
soaked T-shirt over his head. "Do you want to be the
big spoon or the little spoon?"

He couldn't be serious. Of all the members of the
Blackhawk Security team, Vincent Kalani ranked first
on the people she fought to avoid in the field, with the
firm's private investigator, Elliot Dunham, in a close
second. Didn't matter that they'd crash-landed in the
middle of the mountains and had to conserve body heat.
She'd freeze to death before considering stripping out
of her wet clothing in front of him. She attempted to
control nervous energy in her gut, her chest still ach-

ing from where she'd been pinned against her seat in the plane. Vigilantes didn't follow the laws she'd sworn to uphold. And she didn't trust him. "I'd just as soon spoon a bear."

Heat drained from her neck and face as Vincent turned toward her. Intricate tattoos stretched across valleys and ridges of muscle all along his arms, up his sides and across his chest, and his question fled to the back of her mind. Her mouth dried as she studied him, studied the scars marring the designs along his shoulders when he laid his wet clothing on the ground to dry. So many of them. Curiosity urged her to close the distance between them, to run her fingers over the waves of puckered skin to see if they felt as soft as they looked. Did the scars stretch down his back, too?

"Considering where we are, that can probably be arranged. Although you might not live long enough to enjoy it. At least I don't bite. Unless you ask me nicely." His voice was gravelly. Vincent locked dark brown eyes on her, shadows dancing across his expression. Straightening to his full height, he suddenly seemed so much... bigger than he had before. He wiped his hands on his T-shirt as he approached with supple grace. "Got something you want to ask me, Officer Ramsey?"

She'd been staring. Taking a step back, she tried to gain control of her expression and the rush of emotions flooding through her. "I didn't realize you'd been injured."

"Yeah, well, there's a lot you don't know about me." He turned away from her, dark hair falling over powerful shoulder and back muscles. "Or my team."

She had to give him that.

"Can I..." She swiped her tongue between her lips. His heated gaze snapped to her mouth, and a rush of awareness chased back the tremors rocking through her. Her fingers tingled, but she wasn't sure if it was from the sensation returning to her hands or something more. Something that had nothing to do with hypothermia and everything to do with the man standing a few feet ahead of her. "Can I touch them?"

"What?" He lowered his hands to his sides, shock evident in the way he narrowed his eyes on her, in the way his voice dropped into dangerous territory.

Oh no.

"I'm sorry. I..." Shea blinked to clear her head, the spell broken. Her mouth parted. Had she really asked him if she could touch his scars? What the hell was wrong with her? "I didn't mean—"

"Nobody's ever asked me that before," he said. "Most people avoid them."

Most people? As in previous lovers? The fire crackled beside them. Her heart threatened to beat out of her chest as sympathy pushed through her. She'd understood the feeling of rejection all too well toward the end of her marriage, and the sudden urge to connect with Vincent reared its head. Or maybe she'd ignored her own needs for too long. She swallowed around the tightness in her throat. Nothing would happen between them. Not even if they were the last two people on earth. Swiping her suddenly damp palms on her jeans, she shook her head and stared into the fire. "I shouldn't have asked."

Vincent unzipped his duffel bag and dumped the contents onto the cave's floor. "We need to inventory our supplies and rest up."

Right. Because they were trapped inside a mountain with no tools to get them out, no rescue on the way and no communication to the outside world. She tugged her phone from her jacket pocket, chilled by the damp fabric. Still no bars, and the battery had already lost half its life with the dropping temperatures. Damn it. Her long curls slid over her shoulder as she settled on a large rock within the flames' glowing perimeter. Guessing from the size of the fire, it wouldn't last through the night, and she closed her eyes in defeat. Shea locked her back teeth against the truth. Without Vincent, she wasn't getting to New York. Hell, she wasn't even getting out of this cave. "We're going to have to cuddle, aren't we?"

"Only if you want to survive the night." He separated his supplies into piles, then handed her one of the clear plastic containers with a red lid from his pack. Food? "Look at it this way, at least I'm not a bear."

Not the kind that would put her in immediate danger, anyway. The container emitted a slight warmth through to her numb fingers. Out here, clean water wouldn't be a problem with the dozens of feet of white snow, but food? They'd be lucky to find an animal who hadn't gone down for the winter. Even then, the only weapons they had were their sidearms. Not overly effective against larger prey, and too many risks involved using them. They might miss, wasting their ammunition, or the sound could trigger another avalanche. But this... "You brought food with you on the plane?"

"My mom makes sure I don't go anywhere without a couple containers of her homemade meals. Makes me lunch every day." A wistful smile tugged at his mouth as he pried the lid from his own container. Using his fingers, he scooped up a bite of rice and tilted his head back as he dropped it into his mouth. "Blackhawk requires all of its operatives to carry supplies, but we don't know how long we're going to be out here. We'll need to ration out our food and collect some water in the morning."

Aromas of raw fish, mangoes, cucumber and soy sauce tickled the back of her throat, and her stomach growled in response. Poke. One of her favorites. Shea couldn't remember the last time she'd eaten. As soon as she'd gotten Wells's location from the same former partner at the NYPD whom she'd asked for Vincent's service record, she'd packed a couple days' worth of clothes and toiletries and jumped on the first flight out of Merrill Field. Vincent was right. They didn't know how long they were going to be stranded out here without help, and she wasn't stupid enough to turn away a filling meal when the opportunity presented itself.

She unsealed the container, crusted blood staining her knuckles from the crash, and shifted the fleshy muscles in the backs of her legs to get comfortable on the rock beneath her. Tears burned in her lower lash line at the offering, but she wouldn't let her weakness show. She'd survived the lowest point in her life by clawing her way out, fought to prove she could be the mother Wells deserved by seeing doctors, therapists, committing herself to the job. She wouldn't break in front of Blackhawk's operatives, least of all this one. But damn it, why wouldn't he fit inside the box she'd created for him at the back of her mind? Why couldn't he just be the lawbreaking investigator she'd made him out to be instead of a fellow survivor offering her half of his provisions? He had no reason to help her. "You don't have to share your supplies with me."

"Like I said, we survive together or we die alone."

Dark eyes studied her as he withdrew a fresh long-sleeved shirt from his bag and threaded his arms through the sleeves, but Shea knew he wouldn't find anything in her expression. She'd mastered locking down her feelings months ago, learned from her mistakes. The minute she'd lost Wells to her ex-husband in the custody battle, she had nothing left inside, and old habits died hard. "I don't know about you, but I don't plan on dying out here."

Neither did she. Splitting the amount of food he'd given her in half, Shea ate as much as she dared and saved the rest for their next meal. There was nothing more for them to do tonight. Maybe in the morning, with the sun higher in the sky, they'd be able to navigate their way through the rest of the cave. Until then, they'd have to save their energy. Because this nightmare was far from over.

Vincent unpackaged a silver space blanket with his teeth, tearing through the plastic before smoothing out the fold lines. The material reflected the fire's brightest flames. "Put your jacket close to the fire so it can dry while we still have enough kindling. Do you have any other clothes in that bag?"

"A couple days' worth." But nothing that would hold up against temperatures hitting twenty below. Unlike him, she hadn't prepared for their plane to crash in the middle of nowhere. "Do you always carry around an entire arsenal of gear, or were you on your way to a survival expo?"

"No. It's part of my contract with Blackhawk." His laugh echoed through the cave, deep, rumbling, warming her in places she'd forgotten existed. Could be she'd ignored her own needs for too long, or the fear of dying alone without ever seeing her son again had hiked her body's systems into overdrive. Whatever the case, she'd hold on to it as long as she could. To prove she could still feel something. Vincent maneuvered around the fire, space blanket in hand, before taking position on the ground with his back to the nearest wall. A defensive habit she recognized in soldiers and cops who'd been on the job for too long. "Every operator has to be prepared to protect and assist our clients, no matter the situation. Sometimes that includes plane crashes in the middle of the damn mountains."

"I guess that makes me lucky you were on that plane, too." He'd saved her life. And no matter how much it pained her to admit it, she'd never forget it. Shrugging out of her coat, she laid it flat at the base of the rock she'd taken up, her arms suddenly exposed to the frigid cold. She'd lived in Anchorage most of her life, her parents moving her and her twin brother to the last frontier when they were only toddlers after her father's career in engineering took a sharp dive. She knew how deadly the cold could be. Wrapping her arms around herself, she settled into the thin layer of dirt coating the cave floor in front of him, lying on her side to face the fire. Exhaustion, muscle soreness and his close proximity triggered tension down her back. Then increased as he shifted closer, but she couldn't ignore the heat he provided. "I still have my gun, Kalani. Don't think I won't use it if you get handsy."

Another deep laugh reverberated through him, fighting to break apart the knots down her back from behind. "Wouldn't dream of it, Officer Ramsey."

Chapter 3

She was asleep in his arms.

They'd survived the night despite losing their main source of heat, their bodies keeping each other warm. Her curls caught in his beard, and Vincent pulled his head back. His right arm had fallen asleep with the weight of her head on him, but he reveled in the feel of her body pressed against his. When had he wrapped his free arm around her waist? Sweat built at the base of his spine, but he didn't dare move. Not when the woman in his arms fit against him so perfectly, a woman who hadn't turned away from his scars in shock and disgust as so many others had.

They couldn't stay here. Someone out there had possibly brought their plane down, and there was a chance whoever had would scour these mountains to ensure they'd finished the job. Whether it was Shea's ex-husband as she believed or someone from his past, he had no idea. But he'd find out. The fact that his flight had taken a nosedive in the middle of the Chugach mountain range right after he'd had a break in the case couldn't be a coincidence. Maybe, after everything she'd already been through, Shea Ramsey had simply been in the wrong place at the wrong time. Maybe his past had finally caught up with him. No way to confirm unless they found the plane. And to do that, they had to get out of this damn cave.

"Please tell me it was all just a dream. I'm going to open my eyes, and none of this will be real." Her sleep-frogged voice caused the hairs on the back of his neck to stand on end, and it didn't take much to imagine waking to that voice anywhere else but on the floor of a snowed-in cave. Dangerous territory. He had a job to do—a case to solve—and no matter how driven, pragmatic and sexy as hell she was, he couldn't afford to lose his focus. There were too many lives at risk. She lifted her head, untangling herself from the circle of his arms, and pinned beautiful jade-green eyes on him. Swiping her hair out of her face, she sat up, clothing mostly dry, and shoved away from him. "Ugh. No such luck."

"Good morning to you, too, Freckles." Cool air rushed over his exposed skin without her added body heat. Vincent straightened, locking back the groan working up his throat at the pain in his leg, and reached for the jacket he'd laid out the night before. Dressing, he stood, stretching the soreness out of his back as Shea grabbed the single roll of toilet paper from their pile of supplies and wandered farther into the cave, out of sight. He grabbed one of the food containers they'd rationed last night, downed a handful of rice and fish, and started packing. This early in the year sunlight only lasted six hours at most. They had to get moving if they were going to prove the plane had been sabotaged and try to contact rescue. Footsteps registered off to his left, and he nodded toward the food he'd saved for her. "Eat up. We don't have much time to find the plane."

"10-4." Shea finished off the container, handed it back to him, and shrugged into her coat and pack. Ready in less time than it took most of his team to prep for tactical support. For a woman who'd woken up with a piece of debris crushing her chest in the middle of the wilderness, she'd taken their situation better than he'd expected. No questions. No complaints. Impressive. Then again, Shea had been trained in all kinds of high-level circumstances just as he had with the NYPD. Hostage negotiation, standoffs with gunmen, dangerous pursuits, interrogations and more. Everything about her was impressive. But last night, he'd seen a different version of her from the cop he'd gotten to know over the past few months, the cop he'd gotten to admire for her sheer professionalism. She'd given him a glimpse beyond the emotionless mask she'd secured during their joint investigations, and, with her guard seemingly back in place, Vincent found himself wanting more.

"Have you ever patched a pair of jeans before?" He shifted his injured leg toward her, barely enough light coming through the opening above them to make it visible. The pain had dulled overnight, but blood was still oozing into his pant leg. If he didn't get the wound taken care of before they trekked through the snow, it'd become infected.

"What?" Those mesmerizing eyes of hers caught sight of blood. In an instant, she closed the distance between them, crouching in front of him. Down on one knee, she framed the wound in the side of his thigh with both hands, and every cell in his body sang with a rush of electricity. "How long were you planning on keeping that to yourself?"

"I need you to remove the shrapnel and stitch the wound, if you wouldn't mind," he said. "I'd do it myself, but it's at an odd angle. There's a needle, thread and some rubbing alcohol inside the first aid kit in the bag."

She pulled the kit from his duffel and located the medical supplies. Washing her hands with the alcohol, she handed the bottle to him to do the same to his leg. Stinging pain raced down his leg a split second before Shea came back into focus. Hesitation flared in her expression as she turned back to him, the box of sewing thread and needles in her hand. "Any color preference?"

"Black is fine." The breath rushed out of him as she tore the hole in his pants wider, her fingers icy against his skin. Metal on rock resounded through the cave as she tugged the piece of shrapnel from his muscle. In minutes, Shea had cleaned and stitched the wound and secured a fresh piece of gauze over the injury. Couldn't say she wasn't efficient. "Thanks."

"Any time." Cleaning her hands once again, she packed the supplies and handed him a roll of duct tape to patch the hole in his jeans. Out here, exposure would kill them faster than anything else, especially if the wind had picked up overnight. "Now let's get the hell out of here."

They moved farther into the cave, systematically

following piercing rays of sunlight to find an opening big enough for them to escape. So far, nothing. A combination of cold humidity and staleness dived into his lungs as they moved, but not enough to choke out Shea's familiar scent, and he couldn't help but breathe a bit deeper. Columns of stalactites and stalagmites were closing in on both sides of the path ahead. They'd already spent too long trying to find an opening, but if they couldn't venture any farther, there was no way they were getting out of here before they starved.

"I think there's an opening up ahead." Her words vibrated through him with the help of the bare rock walls narrowing in around them, pushing him harder. The stitches in his leg stretched as Shea half jogged toward the largest pool of sunlight they'd come across so far. Her bright smile flashed wide as she turned back toward him, and his heart jerked in his chest. From the sight of her happy or from their discovery, he didn't know—didn't care. They'd found an escape.

Melting ice dripped onto his shoulders from above as they passed into the outside world, exposed skin tightening at the sudden change in temperature. Vincent pulled his T-shirt over his mouth and nose as his lungs ached from dropping temperatures. The plane had gone down on the north side of the peak, and this entrance to the cave sat on the west. They'd have to navigate to the other side in several feet of snow and treacherous heights to get to the crash site. Climbing and hiking had been one of his passions over the years, but it'd been a long time since he'd been in the mountains, and he sure as hell hadn't climbed in this much snow. They'd have to take this one step at a time. A gust of wind blew snowflakes in front of them, whiting out his vision for a moment. Hell. Without getting to the plane, they couldn't contact his team or confirm his suspicions. They'd die out here. Which meant they didn't have a choice. Not if they wanted to survive. "I need you to take my hand. Follow in my footsteps, got it? It's the only way we're going to be able to do this."

"Okay." Nodding, she interlocked her fingers with his, gripping him tight as he took the first step. His boots disappeared into the sea of white, but he hit solid ground. Slowly he led them alongside the peak, his back to the mountain, Shea close on his heels. Each step brought them closer to the curve of the rock. The wind threatened to unbalance them, but right now, they had all the time in the world. Nothing existed outside of the small pocket of reality they'd created between the two of them. Nothing but the next step. She'd expressed her distrust with the Blackhawk Security team—more than once—but in this moment, she was relying on him to keep her alive, to get her back to her son. He wouldn't fail her.

"Almost there!" The howling wind whipped his words away. The sudden pain in his leg buckled his knee, and his foot slid beneath the snow. Her short-lived scream echoed in his head as she clenched his hand tighter. He righted himself before he slid down the mountain and pulled her in close. Sweat built between their palms. His heart threatened to beat out of his chest as he reevaluated their plan. They were in this—100 percent—and they couldn't give up now. They followed the curve around the northwest corner of the mountain, and the wind immediately died. Crystalized puffs of air formed in front of his mouth as he took in the sun glittering off the tumble of snow that'd buried them beneath the rock. Without thought, he brought her into the circle of his arms as relief coursed through him. Neither of them would've survived the night without the other. He might've helped save her life during the avalanche, but without her, he wouldn't have made it this far.

Her body stiffened beneath his touch, and he instantly backed off. Right. They didn't know each other, not really, but it was the way her eyes narrowed on a single point over his shoulder that triggered his internal warning system. She nodded, his name on her lips barely a whisper over the wall of wind howling through the trees. "Vincent."

He turned to see what she'd locked onto.

The plane's hull had been cleared, leaving it bare to the elements.

"Is that…?" Disbelief tinted her voice as she fought to catch her breath and stumbled into him. "How is that possible?"

Vincent released her and unholstered his weapon from beneath his coat. Thick trees impeded his view of the surrounding area, and his instincts prickled with awareness due to the fact that they were clearly out in the open. Vulnerable. "Because someone's already been here."

They weren't alone.

"The pilot could've survived." Shea ducked deeper into her coat that wasn't nearly as thick as it should've been out here. She'd added a few more layers beneath, but the wind chill had dropped temperatures well below freezing. Her ears burned without anything to stop the cold from seeping in, the numbness in her toes and cheeks spreading. Her fingers tingled with pins and needles as Vincent released her hand, and she flexed them into the center of her palms inside her gloves. They'd made it back to the crash site, survived the night. Only they weren't the only ones. "He could still be out here. Maybe hurt."

There'd been so much blood on the windshield, she couldn't imagine their pilot would last long out here on his own, but there was a chance. If he was able to get to what was left of the plane's supplies, he could've staved off hypothermia for a little while longer. But then why not stay with the plane and wait for help?

Vincent shook his head as he circled around the plane's remains, attention on the ground. He kept a wide perimeter as though studying a scene and was trying to keep evidence contamination to a minimum. Out here, though, it wouldn't be long until the winds and the fresh snow buried it all over again. "I count at least four sets of footprints here."

"A rescue team then." Shea didn't dare let the hope blossoming in her chest settle. No one from the tower had answered their Mayday call, and they would've heard a chopper or another plane searching the area by now. Wouldn't they?

"No one brings down a passenger plane without good reason. Wouldn't get as much attention as a commercial flight, and there's no guarantee anyone would see the crash or find us out here." He reached through the shattered front window into the cockpit and tugged something free, and her stomach wrenched. The handheld radio wire had been cleanly severed from the device. Not a rescue team. Which meant... "Whoever unbur-

ied the plane was looking for something. Or someone."
His massive shoulders rolled beneath his coat, snow
sticking to his dark beard. "Which means one of us,
including our missing pilot, could be a target for the
people who did this."

No. No, no, no, no. Shea stumbled back a few feet,
snow working into the tops of her boots. This was crazy.
The adrenaline from the crash had worn off and now
her wild theory about Logan didn't make sense. Her ex
wouldn't hire a team of men to ensure she never made it
to New York. They hadn't ended their marriage on the
best of terms, but to outright want her dead because she
hadn't signed her parental rights away crossed a line.
There was no way he'd do that to Wells. Despite the
bitterness she'd held on to for the past few months for
Logan leaving her, for moving Wells across the country,
she had no doubt he loved their son. Her ex wouldn't
risk losing the one thing that mattered to them both.
"Logan wouldn't do this. He doesn't have the funds
to hire anyone to sabotage a plane or a motive to want
me dead. I'm not trying to take Wells from him. I just
want to see my son."

Vincent dropped his duffel into the snow and ducked
into the side door of the plane, where one of the wings
had been torn clean off by the rocks during their de-
scent. "I've known people to kill for a lot less."

Unfortunately, so had she. More recently, while
working a case with Blackhawk's private investigator,
Elliot Dunham, and a woman Shea believed to be a
murderer. In the end, the real killer had left a trail of
bodies for fear he'd lose everything if news he carried
the warrior gene found in his genetic makeup went pub-

lic. She'd been the arresting officer on that case, forced to work beside Vincent Kalani at the chief's orders, to prove Elliot's client had been framed. So many lives taken for the sake of holding on to a reputation.

It hadn't been her and Vincent's first case together, but she'd done everything in her power since then to ensure it'd be their last. The way her breathing changed when he studied her, the way her heart rate picked up pace when he neared, even how every muscle down her spine seemed to relax when she caught his clean, masculine scent... Working cases with him had helped her break through the fog that'd cut her off from her family, friends and coworkers, made her feel things she hadn't felt since before giving birth to her son. But it wasn't enough to convince her he and his team were above the law.

A hunk of metal landed beside her boot, pulling her back into the present. Her ears rang. Terrifying memories seared across her brain as Vincent tossed more debris into the snow, and she focused on pushing one foot in front of the other to aid in whatever search he was navigating. Didn't matter they'd been stranded together or that they'd be partnered together on future cases between the department and Blackhawk. She wouldn't give in to the desirable impulses carving at the hollowness inside. Not with him. "What are you looking for?"

"The black box is gone." Vincent pulled free of the hull and dusted snow and dirt from his jacket before turning to her. Solid exhales formed in front of his mouth as he ran a hand down his beard. He slammed his fist into the side of the plane, and she flinched as the sound bounced off the peaks around them. "All the emergency supplies are missing, too. Probably sucked out the back with the rest of the cargo when the tail ripped off." His shoulders heaved with his overexaggerated breathing before he locked dark brown eyes on her. "What we have won't last more than a day, two at most."

"Then we need to try to get out of here on foot. West." Her gaze slid to the black duffel bag at his feet, and she threaded her arms through her pack, bringing it around to her front. Shea dropped to her knees and consolidated everything into the one bag. Easier to carry than the duffel but would leave one person without supplies if they were separated. In less than a minute, she slung it back into place, fingers gripped around the straps, and faced him. They could switch off carrying the supplies to conserve energy and camp for the night when it got dark. Leaving the plane was a risk. What if someone in the tower had heard their distress call? What if the footprints did actually belong to a rescue team? What if they were making a mistake? They were lost some where in the middle of the Chugach Mountain range, with mountains surrounding them in every direction. Any attempt to head out of here on foot increased their chances of hypothermia, frostbite, starvation, getting lost, any number of possibilities that could end with their deaths. But Shea had to get to her son. And she wasn't going to let anything—anyone—else stand in her way. "The only way we're getting out of here is if we work together."

One step. Two. Vincent closed the distance between them, and she swallowed the urge to back away. To prove he didn't affect her. He brought his gloved hand up, setting his fingers at the back of her neck. Ice clung to where his gloves touched her exposed skin, but in that moment, she could only focus on the pressure building behind her sternum. "And here I thought you've been avoiding having to work with me."

She could still smell him on her. A mixture of something spicy and wild. Every time she moved, she resurrected the scent, but it was even more powerful now that he'd breached her personal space. An overwhelming sense of calm spread down her back and across her shoulders. Shea opened her mouth, not really sure how to respond—

A gunshot exploded from above.

The reaction was automatic. Her vision blurred as she slammed into him, and they fell into more than three feet of snow together. His hands wrapped around her arms to pull her off him as reality set in. They were out in the open. Vincent brought his head up, scanning the surrounding area a split second before he tugged her to her feet. Adrenaline surged through her as they headed for the closest patch of trees, his injury making him limp, her lungs on fire. The pack slowed her down, but she wouldn't ditch it with the possibility they'd have to keep running.

She skimmed her gloves over rough bark and doubled over to catch her breath. Searching up through the branches of the large pine, Shea watched for movement, listened for another shot—anything—that would give them an idea of what they were up against. She swiped her hand across her runny nose. "These mountains carry sound for miles."

"The shot sounded like it came from close by." His weapon was in his hand. His lighthearted expression she'd gotten used to since they'd crashed faded into a stone-cold wall of unreadability, as though he'd tear any threat apart with his bare hands. Vincent Kalani had served New York City as one of the best forensic investigators in the country, but in that moment, he'd become one of Blackhawk's vigilantes. Powerful. Dark. Dangerous. "But that doesn't make me feel any better, either."

"We need to go." They couldn't stay here. No telling if the team who'd unburied the plane had fired that shot or if they were here to help at all. Whatever the case, Shea wasn't interested in finding out.

A twig snapped from behind, and she spun, unholstering her weapon in the same move. She took aim as Vincent maneuvered in front of her, as though he intended to use himself as a shield to protect her. Her breath shuddered through her, the cold stiffening her trigger finger as they studied the shadows in the thick line of pines. Branches dipped and swayed, and the tension Vincent had chased back a moment ago climbed into her shoulders once again.

A man stumbled from the tree line, and she tightened her grip on her weapon. Black slacks, graying hair, white button-down shirt. Blood spread from the injury in the center of his chest and from a deep laceration on his head. Locking his gaze on Shea, the man collapsed to his knees and reached for her as he fell forward.

She lunged, catching their missing pilot before he hit the snow. Her gun fell from her hand as she laid his head back and studied the fresh bullet wound in his chest. She tugged her glove free with her teeth and set her fingers at the base of his neck. The breath rushed out of her. She looked up at Vincent, at a loss for words. It was too late. "He's dead."

Chapter 4

There pilot was dead, they didn't have any way to contact the Blackhawk Security team, and there was at least one gunman closing in. He and Shea had to get the hell out of here.

They trudged through knee-deep snow as fast as they could between the trees, but the downward angle of the mountain threatened to trip them up with every step. His boot slid against hardened ice beneath the powder, but Shea kept him from rolling down the hill, one hand wrapped around his arm and the other around the tree closest to them. They'd had to leave the pilot where he fell. No time for a proper burial. Not with a killer possibly on their trail. He'd had basic medical training on the job, but it'd been too late. Someone out here had sabotaged their plane, cut their chances of communicating with the outside world, and already killed a man. Hell, he didn't even catch their pilot's name. The longer they stayed in one spot out here without moving, the higher the chance the cold would seep into them. Hypothermia was real. And it was deadly.

"Are we going to talk about what happened back there or pretend someone didn't just kill our pilot?" Her voice cut through the deafening silence around them. "At the crash site you said one of us might be the target of whoever took down the plane." The mountain blocked most of the wind, but an attractive red coloring spread over the freckles speckling her cheeks all the same. Her shallow breathing made her words breathy. "Why was that your first theory? Why not a terrorist attack or simple engine failure?"

"Our focus needs to be on surviving right now. Not theories." Vincent slowed his pace to give her a chance to catch her breath and take some weight off his injured leg. Scooping a handful of fresh snow into his mouth, he cleared the stickiness building under his tongue. A headache pulsed above his eyebrow where he'd swiped dried blood away. Must've gotten hit by something during the crash. Although he couldn't remember what it was. There were any number of reasons someone would've wanted to take down their plane. Any number of reasons they could be targets. In reality, too many to count. But none of them mattered out here. They'd left the safety of the cave out of necessity, but they wouldn't last long once night fell. They had to keep moving. He continued down the incline, but the lack of her familiar breathing said Shea hadn't followed.

"What aren't you telling me?" she asked.

Vincent turned back toward her, gravity pulling at

one side. Pressure built from her intense questioning gaze, as though she were trying to read his mind to get the answers she deserved, and damn, he found himself powerless to the fire in her eyes in that moment. Powerless to her. "There's a chance this has to do something with the last case I was working for the NYPD."

She kicked up loose powder as she closed in, those mesmerizing green eyes still locked on him. "What case?"

Sense returned in small increments. He hadn't told anyone—not even his team—what'd happened that night. For good reason. The more people he got involved, the higher the risk to their lives. Then again, maybe he'd already sentenced Shea to death by getting on that plane.

"Doesn't matter." He stared out over the expanse of trees, rock and snow—miles of it—to escape the sickening clench in his gut every time those memories rushed to the surface. Vincent had fled to Anchorage and joined Blackhawk a year ago for one reason: to move on and to forget. Only now, with the discovery of a partial fingerprint from Internal Affairs Bureau Officer Ashton Walter's death scene, he couldn't hide from the truth any longer. Someone had killed two members of his forensic unit the day of the fire in an attempt to cover up the evidence left behind, but he'd survived. Now he was going to find out why. In any other circumstance, he would've had a lead on who'd tampered with the plane by now and possibly been able to connect the dots, but out here, with nothing but a day's worth of food, a first aid kit and a handgun, he was useless.

"Unless we find shelter for the night, none of this is going to matter."

Shea moved into him, never breaking eye contact, so close he could count the freckles across the bridge of her nose. A bruise marred perfectly light olive skin across her left cheek, one he hadn't seen before now, as she drew her eyebrows inward. It was a small price compared to what could've happened when they'd crashed but still twisted his insides. If the people he'd suspected of killing that IAB officer had found him, Shea would be nothing but collateral damage to them. His fingers tingled with the urge to trace the dark outline of the bruise. Or was it frostbite finally settling in? She set her hand over his coat, directly over his heart, and his body temperature spiked. "Whatever you're hiding, it might've already tried to kill us." Her hand fell to her side, and he went cold as she pushed past him. "Just remember that in case we don't make it through the night."

He spun after her. "Shea, I—"

Bark splintered off the tree he was holding on to with a crack as loud as thunder, and Vincent fell forward. Her eyes widened a split second before he collided with her, then they were both falling. The gunman had caught up with them. Their surroundings blurred as they rolled down the incline, each clinging to the other. Momentum and gravity ripped her from his hands. Ice worked beneath his coat as he rolled, and all he could do was wait for the ride to end. Pain cracked down his spinal column what felt like hours later as he slammed into a large boulder. His head snapped back into rock, his ears ringing, but he forced himself to push to his feet.

Couldn't stop. His vision wavered as Vincent stumbled forward. "Shea."

Where was she? Had she been hit?

The world righted itself, shouts echoing off the cliffs around them. He reached into his coat for his weapon but found only an empty shoulder holster. Damn it. He must've lost the gun when he'd rolled down the mountain. He'd tumbled at least one hundred feet. It could be anywhere. Snow clung to his hair and beard, and he shook his head to clear the haze holding tight. His heart threatened to beat out of his chest. "Shea!"

"I'm here. I'm okay." Movement caught his attention through the thick branches of a tree a few yards to his left seconds before her five-foot-three frame filled his vision. Relief swept through him at the sight of her, drawing him closer. Shooting her hands to his arms, Shea leaned on him, hiking his blood pressure higher, but he didn't have more than a few seconds to revel in the sensation. Her attention shot up the hill as shouts echoed down, and she sank a bit deeper on her back foot. She unholstered her weapon, fixing her index finger over the trigger through her gloves. Snow fell from the backpack of supplies and the ends of her hair as they took cover. "They're coming."

Determination and something he couldn't quite put his finger on pulled her shoulders back as she took aim. She was prepared to fight, but she couldn't hide the fear in her eyes.

"Listen to me. I need you to run. Don't look back. Don't wait for me." He'd hold them off. At least until she found cover. Crouching, Vincent scanned the trees, senses on alert. They didn't have much time before the shooter or shooters caught up with them. "I'll distract them as long as I can."

"From the sound of those voices, we're outnumbered and outgunned." Shea widened her stance as the shouts grew closer. Brilliant emerald-green eyes narrowed on him, and his breathing slowed, as though his body had been specifically tuned to hers over the past twelve hours. "I'm not leaving you to face them by yourself. Survive together or die alone, remember? We're going to figure this out, but right now, we need to live until we can get that chance."

A bullet ripped past them, and Vincent automatically shielded himself behind the closest tree. They were pinned down. Any movement on their part would expose them to the next shot. They needed a distraction. These trees were thick, and the team on the other side of those guns had to be tactically trained. No way he and Shea could take them out with only the sixteen rounds from her weapon. "Toss me the pack."

She switched her weapon to her other hand before throwing their supplies at his feet. Another shot tore through the bark mere inches from his shoulder, and he dropped to the snow as Shea returned fire. Once. Twice. "I've got fourteen rounds left."

The shots reverberated through him and off the rocks surrounding them. He wrapped his grip around the flare gun he'd taken from the small case beneath one of the plane's seats. One shot. That was all he needed. Arching around the tree, he homed in on the dark clothing set against white snow about thirty feet above then took aim at the brush the bastard was using for cover and pulled the trigger.

The flare hit the dried tinder, catching it on fire within seconds. Black smoke billowed between them and the gunmen. The flame wasn't designed to last long. They had to move. "There's our chance, Freckles. Go!"

Shea took off, Vincent close on her heels, down the mountain. Muscles burned in his legs, the stitches in his thigh protesting every time he pulled his boot free from the powder, but he wouldn't slow down. Not until he got her the hell out of this mess. Another round of gunfire exploded from behind but never found its target. He pushed himself harder, careful to keep Shea in front of him as they sped down the incline in an effort to protect her from the next bullet.

The distraction had done its job, giving them enough time to put distance between them and the tactical team, but it wasn't permanent. Whoever'd sent those gunmen wanted something—or someone—and if they were anything like him and his team, they wouldn't stop until they got it.

She couldn't take another step.

They'd been wandering through the wilderness, running off pure adrenaline, but Shea had nothing left to give. Her feet and hands had gone numb more than an hour ago, her lungs burning with every inhale. Ice crusted to her hair and eyelashes. One more step. That was all she had to focus on, but she couldn't do it. She leveraged her arm against the nearest tree for support. They were still miles away from civilization, with no idea where they—

She saw the glimpse of dark blue in a land of white, brown and green. Straight ahead, topped with inches of snow, surrounded by a clearing of pines. But... She didn't dare breathe. Was it real, or had hypothermia already set in? Was this her body's final attempt to survive by giving her false hope? Her mouth barely moved to form his name, the muscles in her jaw aching from the cold. "Vincent?"

"I see it," he said, and everything inside her released. "Looks like a ranger station."

A sob built in her throat. She collapsed into the powder as relief coursed through her, but Vincent was there, pulling her upright. Before she had a chance to protest, he swept her over his shoulder in a firefighter's hold. She couldn't imagine the amount of pain he must've been in with her added weight, admired him for making it this far with his injury, but he held her tight. His steps were strong, evenly paced, as he hiked over uneven rocky terrain leading to the ranger station.

"I've got you." His words vibrated down his back and into her chest, and she believed him. Just as she'd believed he would do everything possible to give her a chance to get to safety when the bullets had started flying, even at the cost of his own life. But she hadn't been able to leave him. Not when she'd taken an oath to protect and serve. Not when... Not when he'd gone out of his way to save her life after the crash. To keep her warm when their fire had gone out. To share his supplies when they both knew there was only enough food for one of them.

She had no reason to trust him, other than neither of them would make it out of here on their own, but the bitterness she'd clung to on the plane seemed stupid now. The edges of her vision darkened as he lowered her feet to the ground, but she failed to keep her balance and fell back.

But still, he was there. Even with his dark Hawaiian complexion, color had drained from his face, a thin layer of snow and ice clinging to his beard and exposed skin, but he hadn't complained once. Hadn't let her give up. Vincent tore his glove from one hand, the other centered on her lower back as he helped her sit. When had he gotten her inside? "Hang on, Freckles. Stay here while I try to get the heat going."

He disappeared deeper into the station, her gun in his hand.

Shea gave in to gravity, falling back on a single twin mattress shoved into the corner of the main room in the station. The National Park Service had cabins like this all over the mountains. They were used as shelters for backcountry hikers who hadn't been able to escape bad weather or for support for rangers circulating through the area for their shifts. Which meant they'd hiked into a national park. They weren't lost anymore. Seconds slipped by in silence. Minutes? She had to get up. Had to find Vincent and make sure he hadn't succumbed to hypothermia. Because without him, she wasn't going to ever see her son again.

Stinging needles exploded through her hands, and Shea forced her eyes open. Haloed by a warm, orangish glow from behind, Vincent centered in her vision. He rubbed her hands between his big, calloused palms. He'd pulled her boots and jacket free, layering her in a thick quilt she hadn't realized kept the tremors in her body at bay until now. She must've fallen asleep. Or passed out. She wasn't sure which she preferred, but the truth was, she knew she was lucky to be alive. "You saved my life again, didn't you?"

"We saved each other." He massaged heat and pressure into her hands, then her wrists and arms, a known technique for combating hypothermia to get the circulation in her body going again, but it was more than that. There were no visible signs of frostbite on her fingertips and toes, yet he hadn't stopped touching her. Dark brown eyes studied her from head to toe, the sensation so raw it felt as real as physical touch. Or was that the lingering effects of the cold-induced delirium? "I'd have a bullet in my back if it weren't for you tackling me like an NFL linebacker."

A small laugh bubbled past her lips. The past few hours of memories played back as he continued rubbing small circles into her arms, and the warmth he'd generated drained. Them finding the plane unburied, the pilot stumbling from the trees with a fresh bullet wound in his chest, the destroyed radio. It all fit with Vincent's theory. Someone had sabotaged the plane, then hired a team to ensure no one had survived the crash. But who? Who would want either of them dead? "Why is someone trying to kill us, Vincent? What happened on your last case?"

His strokes slowed, then he pulled away altogether, and her stomach jerked in protest. Running one hand through his hair, he leaned back in his chair. "My forensic unit was called to the scene of an officer-involved shooting back when I worked for the NYPD. An Internal Affairs investigator named Ashton Walter. He'd been killed in the warehouse district, but the medical examinor couldn't give us anything solid to identify a suspect, even with small amount of evidence my team collected—or wouldn't. The victim had been looking into a handful of unsolved homicide cases I brought to his attention after my commanding officer shot down my suspicion the killer had to have been familiar with crime scene procedure and forensics. According to her, Walter wasn't supposed to have been in that area and had most likely gotten involved in something he shouldn't have, but nothing I recovered from the scene supported that theory."

"You think he was killed because he was looking into your unsolved cases?" Her heart jerked in her chest. That amount of guilt could crush a person from the inside, even someone as insightful, intelligent and innovative as Vincent.

"Officer Walter was a good guy, good investigator. He had a wife and a kid on the way at the time. Brass couldn't prove their corruption theory, and Homicide was instructed to close the case." A disbelieving laugh rumbled through him. Vincent crossed his arms over his heavily muscled chest, gaze distant as though he wasn't really seeing her in front of him. Shadows danced across his expression from the single lantern he must've lit while she'd been unconscious, hiding his expression, but she caught the soberness in his words. "So I convinced a couple techs from my team to take another look at the scene on our own. I just…" His thick brows furrowed over the bridge of his nose, those dark eyes centered on her, and the crash, the gunmen, everything disappeared for the briefest of moments. "I couldn't let it go. I was trained to follow the evidence, but the place had been wiped clean before we'd gotten there. There was no evidence to follow, and less than two minutes after we arrived on scene someone knocked me unconscious. Next thing I knew, the entire place and everything in it was on fire. Including me."

Her breath shuddered out of her, and Shea wanted nothing more than to reach out to him, but any kind of sympathy from her paled in comparison to what he'd already been through. "That's how you got your scars."

"I got out." He nodded, pressing his shoulders into the back of the chair. "But the other two members of my team didn't."

"I didn't realize..." What? That he wasn't the only one with a guilty past? That the Blackhawk Security operative she'd built in her mind over the past year wasn't the man sitting in front of her? Swallowing around the tightness in her throat, she pushed to sit up and swung her legs over the edge of the bed. In her next breath, she leaned into him, wrapping her arms around his neck, and held him. She didn't know what else to do, what else to say. The feel of him against her chased back the final tendrils of ice in her bones. Ducking her forehead into the tendon between his neck and shoulder, she breathed his earthy, masculine scent deeper. Until she couldn't take one more single sip of air. "I'm sorry."

The air around them shifted as Vincent threaded his arms to her lower back, holding her against him, and she gave in to him at that moment. Didn't matter she'd promised herself to keep her distance, not to get attached to the man she was so determined to hate. They'd survived a plane crash together, outrun an avalanche and fought off a team of gunmen after someone had killed their pilot in cold blood. She needed this. Right now, she needed to feel something.

Shea turned her head upward, planting a small kiss against his jawline, and pleasure unlike anything she'd ever felt before immediately shot through her. She and Logan had done what all married couples were supposed to do. They'd conceived Wells together, but this... This was different. She slid her mouth along the veins in Vincent's neck, smiled as his breathing shallowed, and a tremor shook his mountainous shoulders. *This* was unfiltered physical want. What *she* wanted. Something she hadn't let herself give in to for so long.

She'd traded her own path for the things others expected from her most of her life. She'd joined the Anchorage PD after her twin brother had been killed in the line of duty to carry on the family blue blood. She'd married the boy next door at her mother's insistence that she move on after the funeral. She'd gotten pregnant after Logan had convinced her a baby would fix their problems. She'd given everything to live up to her friends' and family's expectations and had been the only one left with the consequences afterward.

Vincent's beard bristled against her oversensitized skin as she framed his face with her opposite hand. Logic battled desire. They were practical strangers, believed in wholly different ideals. Not to mention someone had sent a team of gunmen to hunt them down, but, in this moment, none of that mattered. It was only the two of them here.

Now it was her turn to be happy.

Chapter 5

"Shea..." Damn, she felt good, her lips pressed against his throat. Vincent dug his fingers into lean muscle along her rib cage. He'd imagined this moment so many times before, to the point he hadn't been able to tell the difference between reality and his fantasies as he'd wrapped his arms around her back in the cave. The moment was real—she was real—but this couldn't happen between them. "We can't."

She swiped the tips of her fingers against his lips, a combination of salt and her sweetness flooding his system. An extra surge of desire exploded as she maneuvered off the bed and straddled powerful thighs on either side of him. Her frame fit against him perfectly as she explored the sensitive spot under his ear, and he couldn't hold back the quake of desire rocketing through him. "Don't say anything."

"This is just the stress of the situation." He'd said the words to convince himself more than anything else. They'd been through a lot over the past eighteen hours. The crash, nearly getting buried in the avalanche, surviving the night with only each other's body heat. Now the hit team tracking them through the wilderness. He couldn't blame her for giving in to the adrenaline. Hell, right now that seemed like the best damn idea to ignore reality, but he wouldn't take advantage of it. She'd made her feelings about him—about the way he worked— abundantly clear since they'd investigated their first case together. Even in the face of death, she didn't trust him. Gripping her arms, Vincent slowly settled her back onto the edge of the mattress. "We don't want to do anything we'll both regret."

When this happened between them—and it would— it wasn't going to be because of some chemical reaction brought on by fear or desperation. She'd want him as much as he'd wanted her these past few months, and there'd be no claiming it was a mistake in the morning.

Shea blinked at him, her lips parted, almost as though she didn't know what'd come over her. "You're right. I think I got caught up in the moment. That won't happen again." Brushing her curls back with one hand, she leveraged one hand against her knee, her attention on the lantern he'd lit. A quick laugh burst past the seam of her lips as she slid her gaze to him without turning to face him. "Are you going to be completely awkward around me now?"

He couldn't help but smile. The woman owned up to her impulse and tried to get him to laugh about it in the process. Damn that only made him want her more. If it weren't for the fact that their lives were at risk, Vincent wouldn't have stopped her. "Totally."

"Great. Glad we're in agreement on something." Pushing off the bed, she crossed the main room of the station. The same fingertips she'd brushed against his mouth slid across the desk against one wall, then the stone fireplace as she moved deeper into the shadows the lantern's light couldn't reach. All too easily, he imagined that fireplace alight, the flames reflected in her gaze as she whispered his name in pleasure. "These stations usually only have a minimal food and water supply, no firearms or ammunition, and too many sight lines for the two of us to cover. With all these windows, we're easy targets to whoever's tracking us, and we can't just hunker down until we contact your team. So what's our next move?"

His thoughts exactly, which only left them with one option. "We wait." Vincent hauled himself to his feet, his steps thundering across the old wooden floor as he closed the distance between them. "Let them come to us."

"You want to set a trap," she said.

It was the only way to keep her safe, to ensure the coming fight didn't affect her chances of getting her son back. "I recovered what I thought was a partial fingerprint before I escaped the fire that night. It'd been melted into the handle of a gasoline can nearby. I ran it in every database I could get access to after I relocated to Anchorage with no matches, but now I don't think it was a partial at all." Vincent scrubbed his hand down his beard, tugging on the hair toward the end. "I think whoever set that fire, whoever wanted to destroy all the evidence of that IAB officer's murder, I think the killer burned him or herself in the process bad enough to erase half of their print. I want to know who."

"You think the person who killed your vic is the one who hired the team waiting out there." Shea parted the curtains he'd drawn over the windows to lower the shooter's visibility, just enough for her to scan the area. Apparently satisfied, she turned back toward him. "Why send them now? You said you recovered that print a year ago, that you've been running searches in the databases all that time."

He'd been wondering about that, too, but Vincent already knew the answer. He'd known it the minute the plane's engine had failed. Maybe even before that, but the work he and his team did for Blackhawk brought all kinds of threats. Being followed came with the territory. Their clients came to them for one reason: protection. Stood to reason the operatives hired to do the protecting would be put at risk in the process. Hell, he'd be surprised if he wasn't being followed on a daily basis. "Because I got on a plane to New York."

"Someone was watching you." Shea clasped her hands over the back of the desk chair, dropping her head down as she widened her stance. "They were waiting to see if you'd keep the investigation going on your own, and when you got on the plane, they wanted to make sure you wouldn't have the chance." She straightened, hands on her hips. "No matter who else was on board."

A sickening swirl of nausea churned in his gut. "Shea, I never meant for you to get involved. If I'd known—"

"I am on the brink of losing my son because of you.

The custody hearing is in two days, and I'm not going to be there to fight for him. Everything I've done over the past year to prove I can be the mother he deserves was for nothing." Controlled rage raised the veins in her arms, the tendons between her neck and shoulders stark in the dim light. She pointed one long finger toward the floor. Disgust and fire contorted her expression before she turned away from him, shadows darkening the bruise on her face. Unshed tears reflected the small flame from the lantern. Facing him again, Shea stepped into him, every bit the officer he'd encountered during their investigations. "You could've gone to the police. You could've involved your former CO and gotten the case reopened, but instead of following the rules like everyone else, you put other people's lives in danger. Our pilot is dead out there with a gunshot in his chest because you and your team think you're above the law, that you're better than everyone else." She collected her gun and backpack from the desk where he'd set them earlier and headed toward the short hallway separating the front of the station from the rooms in the back. "I hope you can live with that when this is over."

Vincent only stared after her, curling his fingers into his palms. Because she was right. He could keep telling himself he'd pursued this investigation on his own to protect the people around him, but he knew the truth. Just as she did. It'd been his personal need for justice that'd kept him from reaching out to his old commanding officer, from trusting anyone else but himself with the evidence he'd recovered. He wanted to be the one to punish whoever'd killed his teammates that night, who'd tried to kill him. Just like the vigilante she'd accused him of being. But no matter how many times he'd convinced himself otherwise, he wasn't alone in this. Shea had been dragged into this nightmare the moment she'd stepped on that damn plane.

He traced her steps down the hall, following the sounds of rustling in one of the back rooms, then stilled as he studied her from the doorway of the communications-room-slash-pantry. Dark, curly hair fell in waves down her back as she riffled through the boxed food on the single shelf, and the blood drained from his upper body. No apology could possibly make up for what he'd done, especially if missing the custody hearing kept her from her son permanently, but he'd sure as hell try. "Shea—"

"We should use the station's radio to try to put the call out to Anchorage PD." Lean muscle flexed along her arms as she scooped extra food and supplies into the backpack, the gun at the hollow in her back. She wouldn't look at him, wouldn't even turn in his direction, her anger a physical presence between them. "Assuming the tactical team out there is listening, they'll know exactly where to find us. Then we can put this whole thing behind us and go our separate ways. Move on with our lives."

Move on. She'd already gone out of her way to avoid working with him on joint investigations with Blackhawk Security these past few months. How much more distance did she intend to wedge between them? Vincent stepped into the room, gripped her arms and compelled her to look up at him. Her muscles stiffened beneath his hands in warning. Or was that her body's natural defense kicking in? Either way, Shea Ramsey obviously saw him as a threat, which was the last thing he wanted. He released his hold on her. Gave her the space she needed. "You were right. I could've involved the police or my team, but I wanted to be the one to bring down the bastard who tried to kill me that night." Hearing the words coming from his own mouth made them real, confirmed what he'd felt deep inside since escaping to Anchorage over a year ago. The NYPD didn't want him anymore, but that wouldn't stop him from getting justice the victims of those unsolved cases deserved. That he deserved. "Say what you want about Blackhawk and the work we do, but my team and me? We will do whatever it takes to get the job done, even when that means we have to break a few rules along the way. We fight for our clients. No matter the cost." Vincent swiped his knuckles alongside her jaw, smooth skin catching against the rough patches on the back of his hand, and her green eyes widened slightly. "Because when it comes to protecting the people we care about, there are no rules."

He crushed his mouth to hers.

She couldn't think. Couldn't breathe. Couldn't believe she was kissing him back.

His mouth on hers seared her skin, through muscle and into bone, and Shea couldn't force herself to turn away. She'd dreamed of this moment so many times. Late at night, alone in that empty house after she'd gotten home from working a long shift. Most of the calls she and her partner responded to on the job included robbery or violent crime, but the ones when she'd been paired with Blackhawk Security—with Vincent—brought her back from the darkness piece by piece.

The cases they'd worked together challenged her, tested her mental and physical endurance, gave her something new to focus on, even if she didn't agree with the firm's methods. Working investigations with him had given her a strength she'd forgotten she'd had, to the point she'd finally asked for professional help from her obstetrician then the department's counselor a few months ago. Vincent had unknowingly given her hope, a reason to keep going when the postpartum depression had convinced her she couldn't help anyone. Not even herself.

He maneuvered her backward until the back of her thighs hit the small desk with the radio equipment with a jolt, not breaking the kiss once. His tongue penetrated the seam of her mouth and the world exploded around her. He skimmed his hands around her lower back, wrapping her in the protective circle of his arms. That single touch awakened a sense of safety, of warmth, she'd forgotten existed since her ex had served her with custody papers, and she never wanted it to end. The small gasp of satisfaction at the back of her throat was followed by a laugh, and she set her hand against his chest to push away.

Her skin felt too tight, the thud of her heart too fast in her chest. Damn, the man could kiss, but he was right. This was nothing more than a pressure release in a stress-induced situation. A biological reaction her body needed to get back that sense of adrenaline. Hardened muscle formed ridges and valleys under her fingertips.

Because when it comes to protecting the people we care about, there are no rules.

Had he meant her? Shea traced a piece of loose thread in his shirt, a distraction from the wave of desire washing over her from the inside. "Why did you request me as your partner on the joint investigations between the department and Blackhawk?"

After seeing for herself how Vincent worked—how many laws he and his team ignored in their search for justice—she'd asked her captain to remove her as one of the investigators from the small partnership their respective organizations had formed. Only to learn the truth in the process: Vincent had specifically asked to work with her on the threat that he'd shut down the task force if her captain partnered him with anyone else.

Seconds ticked by. A minute? Shea forced herself to raise her gaze to his, the beat of his heart spiking under her palm, and she was immediately captivated by the inferno in his eyes. The walls closed in. There was a team of killers outside those walls, but right in that moment, he made her feel as though they were the only two people in the world.

"I've never been able to ignore a good puzzle. You're driven but adaptable. You stick to your core values and uphold the law, even at your own personal risk, but you'll pull your weapon on me for the chance to get your son back. I think you truly care about the people you serve and protect in this city, but you won't align yourself with Blackhawk because you don't agree with our methods when we're trying to do the same thing." His hands slid along her lower back, fighting back the cold creeping in as the sun went down. The battle invoked a shiver she couldn't repress across her shoulders, and she hated the fact that her body reacted to it, to him. "You're out to prove yourself, and that makes you a good cop, one I'm proud to have at my side. But to tell you the truth, none of that matters to me. Not really."

"It doesn't?" she asked.

"No." Vincent tangled his fingers through the hair at the nape of her neck; his large palm settled under her ear. "I requested you because not only are you a top-notch pro, but also one look from you makes me forget the nightmare I live with every day since waking up in the middle of that fire." He stared down at her, his eyes glittering in the dim light of the lantern she'd brought in here with her, and her breath caught. "The only thing I can't figure out is what you're hiding."

The hairs on the back of her neck stood on end, and Shea dropped her hands away from his chest. Impossible. There was no way he could see through her defenses that easily. Not with all the hard work she'd put into keeping up appearances. Her partner hadn't known she and Logan had divorced until she'd told him a few months ago. Had Vincent seen more? "What makes you think I'm hiding something?"

"I'm good at my job." Vincent stepped back, taking his body heat with him, and the cold started creeping in again. Physical or mental, she had no idea, didn't want to know. "I don't need to know your secrets, Shea. I need you to trust me. I'll do everything I can to get us out of this alive, and I'm not going to give up until I do. I'll get you to your son."

She'd spent the past year in a fog, unable to focus, so mad at everyone and everything around her because her mind hadn't been able to handle the transition to motherhood. She'd isolated herself from her friends, her family, from the things that'd once made her happy. She'd lost everything that mattered to her in the span of a few months. First, her husband when he couldn't understand what was happening, then Wells when Logan had moved in with and married a woman he'd met only a few months before. The job became her entire life, and soon her parents had stopped calling; her friends had stopped asking her out. Her partner stopped trying to talk to her on patrol. They'd all given up on her. The only one who hadn't turned away from her had been Wells, with his beautiful green eyes and chubby hands reaching for her as her ex had walked out the door with their son in his arms for the last time. And she'd just stood there. Frozen. Incapable. Weak.

But Vincent had just promised not to give up on her.

"I'm sorry for what I said. You've saved my life, I don't know how many times now, and you deserve better. I *know* the plane crash wasn't your fault, and it's not your fault I lost my son, either. I should never have put that burden on you." She nodded, lowering her gaze to the floor as she rubbed the goose pimples from her arms. Forcing herself to take a deep breath, she attempted to clear the last remnants of emotion from her system—in vain. It'd been so long since she'd been able to feel anything, she wasn't sure how to control her emotions anymore. If she could at all. "The truth is I'm the reason my ex started seeing another woman during our marriage, why he filed for divorce. And why he took Wells from me."

The weight of his attention settled on her chest, a

physical presence she couldn't ignore. "He cheated on you?"

The anger in his voice rocketed her awareness into overdrive.

"Yes, but my point is… I wouldn't be here without you, and if trusting you gets me to my son, then that's what I'll do." Hell, did any of this make sense to him? She swiped her hand across her forehead. She shrugged despite the battle that'd been raging inside for so long. "Everything else…none of it matters."

"It matters to me." Vincent clasped his big hands around hers, invigorating her senses with a fresh wave of his wild, masculine scent. "Your ex-husband has to be the stupidest man on the planet to push an incredible, strong, determined woman like you out of his life. It doesn't matter what reason he had. You are worthy of a man who will treat you with the care and respect you deserve. Someone who will stand by your side, no matter what. Who will protect you until his last breath and risk his life to be with you."

All too easily, she imagined Vincent as that man, the one who would wake her and Wells with breakfast in the mornings before he headed into the office for his next assignment, the one who'd spoil her to the ends of the earth with attention and love, the one who'd place a flower over her left ear to announce to his family he'd claimed her body, mind and spirit. She swayed at the intensity of the fantasy, at how incredibly real it was. At how much she wanted it to be true, but this, being stranded out here with him, it was about survival. Nothing more. Because there couldn't be anything more with her. Not anymore.

"I'm not the person you think I am, Vincent." Shea tugged her hands out of his. She'd already hit rock bottom over the past few months. What more could she have to lose by telling him the truth, by telling him that despite that gut-wrenching kiss and explaining the way he made her feel, nothing could happen between them? It was sweet the way he'd stood up for her, called her strong when she'd convinced herself otherwise the past nine months. But in reality, he was only able to see what she'd wanted him to see. What she'd wanted everyone to see, including herself. That strength, the determination? None of it was real.

Vincent studied her with those incredibly dark, sexy eyes and her nerve endings fired in rapid succession, keeping her in the moment. Would he still look at her as though she were the only woman in the world after he learned the truth? That she was broken? That she wasn't worthy of all those things he'd described? "You have this picture of this immovable, dedicated public servant, mother and wife in your head, but it's all wrong. I'm not that woman." Shea dropped her gaze to the dimly lit floor, unable to stand another second of his worshipful attention. "You have no idea how much I wish I was her, but a woman like that doesn't cut herself off from everyone she loves. I'm not anything remotely close to that."

"You are to me." He tucked his knuckle under her chin, forcing her to look up at him, and every nerve ending she had responded. "Nothing you say is going to convince me otherwise."

Chapter 6

Cold worked its way under his heavy jacket as Vincent dropped the magazine out of their only weapon, checked the rounds and slammed it back into place. The sun had gone down, and his fingers numbed with temperatures dropping by the second. The trap was set, but he had yet to see any movement from the surrounding trees. Shea had drifted off to sleep in the only bed in the station about an hour ago, and he'd offered to take the first shift on patrol. He couldn't sleep. Not with their last conversation echoing through his head. He might've worked forensics for most of his career, but he'd read the truth easily enough: Shea didn't believe she was worthy of love. Not just from her ex-husband—the cheating bastard—but from her son, from her friends, family. Everyone in her life. She'd severed her connections to the people she was supposed to care about.

And he wanted to know why.

He'd gotten his hands on her case files before they'd started working together with permission of the Anchorage PD's chief of police, studied the way Shea worked, if she stayed within the lines of the law as she claimed. There'd been a few close calls on the job, mostly domestic disputes that hadn't ended when she and her partner had arrived on the scene. One armed robbery in which she'd intercepted the getaway driver at gunpoint. Nothing to make him think something had drastically altered her life or would dictate how close she got to those she cared about the most. There was no doubt she loved her son. He'd seen her desperation to get Wells back from her ex-husband, how missing the custody hearing was tearing her apart from the inside. So what could've possibly happened for her to believe she didn't deserve to be happy, to be loved?

A branch shifted off to his right, and Vincent homed in on the movement. Waited.

A wall of muscle slammed into him from the opposite side of the clearing, knocking the air from his lungs, and he landed face-first in two feet of snow. Twisting, he grabbed a handful and tossed it into the face of the man who'd tackled him and took aim. His attacker grabbed the weapon and slammed it into Vincent's face. Once. Twice. Vincent blocked the third attempt, but, faster than he thought possible, the gun disappeared into the trees. White stars flashed in the corners of his eyes as he raised his fists. It'd take a lot more than a couple hits to the face to bring him down. His heart threatened to pound straight out of his chest as Vincent lunged, slamming his opponent into a nearby tree. Flakes fell around them, blocking his view of his attacker, as he clamped his grip around the bastard's throat. A knee to his kidney sent pain ricocheting through his entire right side, and his hold loosened. The station blurred in his vision as the SOB landed a solid hook to his jaw.

Movement registered as he straightened, closing in on either side of the cabin. Damn it. The bastard hadn't come alone. Sliding his index fingers between his lips, he whistled as loud as he could to give his partner warning. Shea. He had to get to Shea. He pushed his hair out of his vision, facing off with the first attacker once again. He couldn't let them breach the station. Pulling the small blade at his ankle, Vincent swiped high. His opponent threw himself backward, thrown off-balance, and Vincent rushed forward to strike again. Pain exploded through his right shoulder as a bullet tore through muscle and tissue from behind, and his scream filled the clearing. He clung to the wound as he spun toward the newest threat, switching the blade to his other hand. He threw it end over end as hard as he could.

The knife penetrated the gunman's coat and brought the shooter to his knees. One down, three to go. Blood trickled beneath his jacket down his hand as he turned back in time for the original attacker to close the space between them. Vincent hiked his injured shoulder back, ignoring the pain shooting through his nerve endings as a guttural growl worked up his throat. No time to check the wound.

Smoke tainted the air a split second before the flames registered. The two operatives had made it into the station. He only hoped the trap he'd set combining gasoline and the lantern's flame when they'd barged through the front door had distracted them long enough to give Shea a way out. Vincent dodged the swipe of a much larger blade, then another. He blocked the third attempt and turned the knife back around on his attacker before sinking it deep into the man's side.

A gasp filled his ears as his opponent's legs failed him, but Vincent kept the man upright. He wasn't finished with him.

"You've got about twenty minutes before you bleed to death, and believe me, you don't want that to happen out here." Vincent strengthened his hold on the blade, both the wound in his thigh and the latest in his shoulder screaming for relief. "Tell me who sent you after me, and I'll make sure you aren't paralyzed for the rest of your life when I'm finished with you and your buddies."

"We're not only here for you, Kalani." The attacker sagged in Vincent's arms, his breath turning into shallow hisses from between his teeth. He spit a mouthful of blood into the snow, staring up at Vincent with agony contorting his expression. The man's jacket slid to one side and exposed the brass shield at his hip. "You should've left well enough alone."

"You're NYPD." Hell. The bastard confirmed his theory. The murder of the officer from the Internal Affairs Bureau had been connected to someone on the inside. Whether that meant IAB Officer Walter had been working for them was something Vincent would have to prove another day. Right now, he only had one priority: getting to Shea. He'd gotten her involved in this, and he'd get her out. Vincent pulled the knife from his attacker's side and pushed him off-balance. "You shouldn't have come after me."

His attacker hit the ground as flames inside the station broke through windows and consumed everything in its path. Two gunmen left. He swept the gun from the hole it'd made in the snow into his hand. Smoke billowed around him, and he covered his face in the crook of his elbow as he tracked a set of deep footprints around the north side of the ranger station. Heat seared his exposed skin, sweat building at the base of his spine as he maneuvered around the flames, but he'd push through the memories racing to the front of his mind. This wasn't New York City. He wasn't trapped by the fire here. Although the situations were more similar than he cared to admit.

The trap had done its job. First, to incapacitate the two remaining gunmen hunting them, and second, to signal fire and rescue. With their luck, emergency personnel was already on their way. Shea had been instructed to head west as soon as she escaped the station, to another ranger station they'd located on a map inside about three miles from here. Now he just had to find her and take down anyone still on her trail.

"Vincent." That voice. *Her* voice. "Don't come any closer."

He slowed, every muscle down his back tensing for battle as he took in the sight of her. Blood dripped down her nose and mouth, those impossibly green eyes even brighter in the flames. Gunmen flanked her on either side, weapons aimed at her midsection. Tendrils of her hair clung to her skin, the glow of the fire accentuating the freckles across her nose and cheeks. She hadn't gotten away. A soft buzzing filled his ears as he curled his hand around the gun. "She has nothing to do with this. You came for me. Let her go, and you can have me."

"What?" Shea tried to rip her arm from one man's grip, but he held on tight. "No."

"You brought her into this, Kalani. That makes her a loose end." The gunman at her right stepped forward, and a sense of recognition surfaced. Short brown hair, dark eyes, sharp features with a bristled jawline. Vincent had met this man before. But where? "You just couldn't stop yourself from looking into that IAB officer's death, even after we gave you a second chance." He jerked Shea into his chest and pressed a gun to her temple, and everything inside Vincent raged. "How many more people are you going to put in danger before you take a hint? First your teammates back in New York, now this one. She must not mean much if you were willing to risk her life to get what you wanted."

The opposite rang true. She was a motivating factor for him getting on that damn plane, the reason he didn't want to spend the rest of his life looking over his shoulder. She was…everything. His attention slid to Shea, to her almost imperceptible nod as the station burned behind him, and the pressure behind his sternum reached full capacity. "You have no idea who you're dealing with."

An evil smile stretched the gunman's mouth, and a flash of memory darted across his mind. His stomach dropped out as Vincent realized where he'd met this man before. The last homicide he'd worked… The gunman had been at the outer perimeter but inside the crime scene tape taking statements from witnesses.

"I've done my research on you, Kalani. I think I'll take my chances."

The bastard was a cop, same as his attacker bleeding out on the other side of the station. Vincent studied the second gunman, caught the briefest hint of the SIG SAUER similar to his old service weapon. They were all cops. NYPD, if he had to guess. Alaska was far outside the lines of their jurisdiction, which meant the squad wasn't here in an official capacity. He locked his gaze on Shea. The tactical team that'd been hunting them these past two days was made up of corrupt NYPD officers.

"I wasn't talking about me." Vincent lunged forward, targeting the attacker on her right as Shea threw her elbow back into the man at her left. In an instant, he'd closed the distance between him and the first gunman. A bullet ripped past his ear as he collided with the cop, taking them both down. He hauled back his injured shoulder and launched his fist into the officer's face to finish the job.

Shea's sharp groan pulled at his attention from behind. The second gunman stood over her, and a predatory growl was torn from Vincent's throat. Nobody put their hands on her. No one. He shoved to his feet, but he'd made it only one step before something hard slammed against his head. He collapsed into the snow, pitched into darkness.

Her face throbbed. Shea blinked against the sudden brightness around her as her body jerked to a stop. Hot. Why was it so hot? She'd spent the past two days chilled to the bone, but now sweat built beneath her heavy

clothing. She tugged at the zip ties around her wrists
and ankles. Ringing filled her ears as she twisted her
head to one side, to the trees within arm's reach. Her
last memories played across her mind in flashes and
tensed the muscles down her spine. She'd been knocked
unconscious. The tactical team had found them, and
she'd barely escaped the station before the old wood
floor had caught fire from Vincent's trap. She hiked her
head back over her shoulder, snow crunching beneath
the crown of her head. Now two members of that same
team were hefting something heavy closer to the flames
destroying the ranger station. The air rushed out of her
lungs, but she bit back the scream caught in her throat.
Not something. Vincent.

"Boss said destroy the evidence. Then we can get
the hell out of here," one of them said.

No. Shea rolled onto one side, feeling for something—anything—she could use to break the zip ties.
Her fingers sorted through loose rock, chunks of ice and
broken twigs from the trees above. Eyes on both men,
she slowly sat up and fisted a large piece of ice from
beneath the powder. If the edge was sharp enough, it'd
cut through the plastic. Unless the heat from her hands
melted it first. She placed the icy blade's edge between
her feet and started sawing at the ties around her ankles. Fire crackled and popped from less than ten feet
away, her skin burning hot to the point she had to turn
away to protect her face.

Pain pulsed across her cheek from where the second
gunman had struck her, but she pushed it to the back of
her mind as ice turned to water in her hands. Damn it.
The ice was melting too fast. She wouldn't be able to get

both her hands and her ankles free at this pace. Not before the gunmen dragged Vincent into the flames. She worked faster, harder. She strengthened her grip around the melting weapon as desperation clawed up her throat and clenched her back teeth against the numbness in her hand. "Come on."

The zip tie snapped from around her feet, but relief was short-lived. A shadow crossed over her, instantly cooling her exposed skin.

"Well, well, well. Looks like we've got ourselves a fighter here." The gunman, the one who'd knocked her unconscious, wrapped a strong grip around her arm and wrenched Shea to her feet. The sting of too much cologne burned her nostrils as he pulled her into his chest. Perfectly straight white teeth battled with the sneer stretching the man's cracked lips wide. His bruising hold on her arm increased as she maneuvered her bound wrists between their bodies. "I've always liked a challenge."

"Then you're going to love me." Shea brought up her hands, striking him right in the face as hard as she could. Her knuckles tingled with the hit, but she struck again. The gunman stumbled back, and she followed but didn't catch him drawing a blade in time before stinging pain exploded across her arm. She blocked the next swing and clamped both hands on to his forearm as she rammed her knee into his kidney. Once. Twice. He lost the knife, then she used his own fist to follow through with another punch to his face, knocking him unconscious. Shea dived for the blade as her attacker collapsed at her feet and cut through the ties at her wrists.

She unholstered the gun at his hip, catching sight of the NYPD badge on the other side of his belt.

The men who'd attacked them, brought down the plane, they were…cops.

Breathing heavy, vision blurred, she reached out to the nearest tree to keep her balance. She took aim at the first gunman near Vincent as he unholstered his weapon. "Drop the gun and get your hands up where I can see them."

"Gotta say I'm impressed, Officer Ramsey." His voice sent an uncontrollable quake down through her as he raised both arms above his head, gun still in hand. One shot. That was all it would take to rip the man who'd helped bring her back to life away, but she'd pull this trigger just as quickly. "Although we've gotten close over the past hour, so I feel like I should call you Shea."

Her stomach lurched. Whether from the possible concussion or the fact that the man pointing a gun at Vincent had done his research, she didn't know. Her attention dipped to Vincent, to the slight rise and fall of his chest. He was alive. She still had a chance to get them out of here. She caught sight of their supply bag where their attackers had thrown it after intercepting her dash into the trees. She hadn't been fast enough, but she wouldn't make that mistake again. "Is the fact that you know my name supposed to scare me?"

"I could've gotten your name off the plane's passenger manifest or threatened to shoot your pilot unless he gave me the names of his passengers, but I didn't have to do either of those things." The gunman shook his head, dark eyes glittering with help from the fire. A humorless laugh burst from his Kevlar-covered chest. "We found out you've been partnering with Vincent here for a few months when we stopped in to check up on him. I got the feeling he wasn't going to heed our warning to back off his…independent investigation into a case from back home, maybe even trusted someone here with the intel he thought he had. Turns out, I was right. Then I find out you're on the same plane he is heading to New York, and that gets me thinking. Vincent could've been trying to use Anchorage PD resources to find out who killed his IAB friend. And, well, we can't have that." He waved the gun toward her, and she slipped her finger over the trigger of her own weapon. "I know what kind of cop you are, Shea. I know there's nothing I can say to get you to walk away now. So instead of coming in here and trying to convince you to forget you ever saw us, I had my guys in New York pay a visit to your ex."

The blood drained from her face. Logan? Her heart pounded hard in her chest, threatening to burst through her rib cage. She swiped her tongue across her lips to counter the sudden dryness in her throat. It was a manipulation, a desperate measure to get her to believe he had leverage over her. These dirty cops had come for Vincent, and she had no doubt in her mind they'd say anything to get what they wanted. But they couldn't have him. Her arms shook with the weight of the gun in her hand, but she held strong. "I said drop the gun."

"I get it. Exes are exes for a reason, right? You probably don't feel the same way about him as you would about, say, that little boy of yours." That smile was back, and her gut knotted tight. "What was his name?" The gunman lowered his hands slowly, and Shea stepped forward in warning. A slight pull at one corner of his mouth accentuated the sharp angles of his face. "Wells, right? Cute kid. It'd be a shame if he got caught in the middle of what we have going on here." The gunman nudged Vincent with his boot. "It's too late for your partner here, but you can still walk away. You can go to New York and get your son back. That's what you want, right? I can make that happen. All you have to do is stand down, Officer Ramsey."

He was threatening her son. Threatening Vincent. Seconds slipped by. A minute. She had a chance to get to Wells, to fight for him as she should've done in the first place. Sweat fell from her temples, her hands damp against the gun's grip. All she had to do was walk away. The fire had destroyed the ranger station in a matter of minutes and had started spreading to the nearby tree line. A groan reached her ears from behind. The attacker she'd taken down was coming around. She was out of time.

"I swore an oath to protect and serve." Shea lowered her weapon, shortened her shooting stance. Made herself a smaller target. Her gaze dropped to Vincent as his hand splayed across the white snow, leaving a print of red behind. He'd been injured trying to protect her, and every cell in her body screamed in retaliation. The man giving her the chance to run was a cop. His entire squad was made of cops, but they weren't playing by the rules. She wasn't an officer out here. She didn't have the manpower to arrest these men. So maybe Vincent had been right. Maybe the rules didn't always apply, and he and his team weren't the vigilantes she'd believed. She lifted her gaze to the gunman. "And that's exactly what I'm going to do."

Shea raised the gun and fired.

Vincent's attacker pulled the trigger at the same time his shoulder ripped back from the impact of her shot, but his bullet went wide. He fell with a pain-filled scream, the sound echoing off the rock around them.

"Vincent!" She dashed toward him, gun still in hand, and tugged him to his feet. Taking the majority of his weight, Shea half dragged him to their discarded supply bag and then into the tree line just as the second gunman got to his feet. Her attacker ran for his superior, taking up a nearby weapon as she hauled Vincent to her side. "Come on, we've got to get out of here."

Three shots exploded from behind, but she kept them moving. Blood trickled down onto her hand from his shoulder as she fought to keep Vincent upright. The faster they ran, the faster he'd bleed, but they couldn't stop. Couldn't look back. No matter what happened next, they were in this together.

Chapter 7

Shea had chosen him.

His vision blurred as they stumbled through the trees, gunmen once again on their trail. Three miles of wilderness and bullets stood between them and the next ranger station, but Shea had taken her chances with him. Given up a shot at seeing her son again to save his life. Vincent pitched forward as another surge of pain crushed the air from his lungs. The bullet was still inside his shoulder, tearing through muscle and tissue. Every swing of his arm, every brush with the trees, was another lesson in pain tolerance, but he couldn't give away their position. Distraction. He needed a distraction. "You could've walked away."

"What kind of person do you think I am? I wasn't going to leave you with them to die." Her heavy breathing hitched as she checked back over her shoulder, the gun still in her free hand. The glow of the fire lit her eyes in an unnatural display of brightness, and Vincent couldn't look away. "I think you were right. The IAB officer's murder you were looking into in New York goes a lot deeper than the investigating officers reported. The men trying to kill us are cops."

"They're corrupt cops. Part of an organization inside the NYPD I've only heard rumors about until now. Back in New York, I collected evidence from four different homicide scenes that'd been cleaned a bit too well, like the perp knew how to hide evidence. I even found proof a detective had broken into a witness's home in order to intimidate her to drop a complaint against his partner. They're not just cops. They're hit men, but these guys won't answer to just anyone." He locked his jaw against the shooting pain all along the right side of his body as deep snow jerked him down. The shrapnel in his thigh, a bullet in his shoulder and the hit to his head from behind. He was lucky he was still standing. Lucky to be alive. Vincent tried to keep most of his weight off of Shea, but any extraneous shifting on his part only increased the discomfort. Hell, he wouldn't be here if it wasn't for her. "They've got to have a superior officer giving orders. Someone in the NYPD who needed to cover up IAB Officer Walter's murder and put out the hit on me and my team that night. I'm going to find out who."

"The NYPD is made up of over fifty thousand officers and civilian employees," she said. "It could be anyone."

"I didn't say it would be easy." Numbness spread from his toes up his calves. The sun had gone down hours ago; every exhale froze instantaneously on the air. If they couldn't make it to the next station, there was a chance they'd die out here. Vincent slowed. "Why did you do it?"

He didn't have to elaborate. They both knew he wanted to know why she'd given up the promise of seeing her son again in order to save his life.

"They've already killed our pilot, an innocent man who, as far as we know, had nothing to do with your case in New York. I don't care what they were promising. They weren't going to let me walk away. Not after I'd seen their faces." She redirected her attention to the darkness growing behind them. Her voice hardened, the muscles along her jawline flexing in the dim light from their flashlight. "But I pulled the trigger because he threatened my son. I wanted him to realize he'd made a mistake bringing Wells into this."

"I think he got the message." Vincent put more pressure on his injured leg but kept his arm around her shoulders for support. How the hell had she dragged him at least half a mile through the wilderness without showing a hint of exhaustion in her features? She was strong, stronger than he'd originally estimated, but small cracks had begun to surface back at that station. She blamed herself for her divorce, for losing custody of her son to her ex, but when it'd come down to the wire, she'd stepped in to protect a man she'd resented from day one from a group of corrupt cops. She'd been right before. She wasn't the woman he'd built up in his mind. She was better. "Whatever the reason, thank you."

The growl of a distant engine reached through the trees.

"That sounds like an ATV," she said.

And it was closing in.

They didn't have much time before the cops who'd shot him headed them off. It'd be easy to track his and Shea's path through the snow, but ATVs couldn't navigate through these trees. Hell only knew how many of them were out there now, on foot. "That would explain how they found the plane so quickly. We wouldn't have been able to hear the engines from the amount of snow blocking the entrance of the cave."

"I thought it'd take them longer to regroup." Shea rubbed her hands together, then swiped her hand across her face. She tucked the gun into the back of her jeans and covered it with her coat, all the while never taking her arm from around his lower back. "These guys are persistent. I'll give them that."

"Which means we can't go to the next ranger station. They'll be waiting for us there." If they weren't already. He couldn't take the chance. Not after Shea had risked her life to save his. He'd promised to get her to New York to fight for her son, and he had no intention of failing her again. "We have to go deeper into the woods. North. They won't be looking for us there."

"Every minute we spend out here is another chance we don't make it out of these mountains." Wide eyes searched his face. "If we head north, we'll just be saving the guys with the guns the trouble when we die out here from exposure."

"I know what I'm asking of you, Shea." He'd never wanted any of this, but it was the only way. "We have to take the risk. Otherwise, they'll shoot us on sight. I need you to trust me." They still had their supply pack with the extra food she'd packaged and plenty of fresh snow to keep hydrated. The problem would be heat. They'd used all of the kindling he'd had and lighting a fire would only give away their position, and any they found out here would be too wet to catch fire. If they were going to make it through the night, they'd have to rely on each other. Trust each other. Completely. Vincent lowered his voice. This was it. This was the moment that would either drive them apart or bring them together. There was no going back. "We survive together."

"Or we die alone." With a small nod, Shea adjusted her hold around his back and brought him into her side. Her body heat seeped through his coat down into muscle. Her rich scent gathered at the back of his throat as they moved north through the trees as one in some kind of demented three-legged race. Only this race was for their lives. "I hope you're right about this."

"Me, too." Vincent couldn't let his past ruin her future. He'd never forgive himself for tearing apart her life. Not when she'd risked everything to save him back there at the ranger station. But even before then, he'd known he'd do whatever it took to ensure she made it out of this alive. She had to. For the innocents she protected, for her family. For him.

A grouping of flashlight beams bounced in the distance.

Vincent instantly killed theirs to stay hidden but kept them moving. Damn it. How many of them were out there? A dozen? More? He spun them northeast and took a step forward. More flashlights. He turned back the way they'd come and froze. Shea's uneven breathing registered in the darkness as the lights danced around them.

"We're surrounded." She'd lowered her voice to avoid giving away their position, but it wouldn't do a damn bit of good. The corrupt officers he'd worked to expose back in New York had found them.

But he and Shea weren't dead. Not yet. He could still get her out of this mess. The flashlight beams steadied as the hit men carrying them slowed, closing the circle around them. His eyes had already adjusted to the darkness. He counted eleven hostiles, all heavily armed, and stepped away from Shea as every muscle along his spine contracted with battle-ready tension. A chance to escape. That was all he needed to give her. Vincent slipped his hand beneath the seam of her coat, over the gun at her back, but didn't draw. Any movement on their part could be his and Shea's last, but he wasn't finished with her yet. He studied the single officer stepping forward from the circle of cops, the one Shea had shot back at the station. The SOB's name had pierced through the haze as he'd watched her pull the trigger. Officer Charles Grillo.

"I gave you the chance to walk away, Officer Ramsey, and you shot me." Grillo raised his weapon, aimed directly at Shea. The flashlight beams highlighted the blood spreading across the officer's coat a split second before he pulled the trigger.

She wrenched back, her scream loud in his ears as Shea hit the ground.

"No!" Vincent crouched over her, applying pressure to the wound in her side. Her breathing shallow, her eyes shut tight as she fought against the pain of the bullet tearing through her. Rage—unlike anything he'd felt before—surfaced in a dark, overwhelming current. He focused on Grillo as he suffocated the agony from the shot to his shoulder. The cold had slowed the bleeding, numbed the area around the wound, but now he felt everything. "You're going to die for that, Officer Grillo."

"You got her involved in this. Not me. You could've walked away, started your life over, but instead you decided you wanted to play the hero." The officer swung the barrel of his weapon at Vincent. "We already know about Officer Ramsey here. Who else did you bring into your investigation?"

Containment. That was the only reason he and Shea were still alive. Whoever'd sent these bastards wanted to ensure nobody else had gotten hold of the evidence from Officer Ashton Walter's death scene. Otherwise, Vincent had the feeling Grillo and his team of corrupt cops would've already disposed of their bodies. Blood welled between his fingers as he increased the pressure on Shea's wound. She wasn't struggling anymore, her breathing slow. He'd run that print through the Integrated Automated Fingerprint Identification System—IAFIS—with the help of Blackhawk's network security analyst, which meant his entire Blackhawk team could be at risk now. Because of him. "Go to hell."

He wrapped his fingers around Shea's service weapon, drew and fired.

Gunshots exploded from all around.

Shea forced her eyes open, but the haze at the edges of her vision threatened to pull her into unconsciousness. More shots echoed through the night, shadows shifting around her. She couldn't make out anything distinctive. The ringing in her ears was too loud to discern the shouts, but the feel of her weapon at her back was gone. Vincent. He must've taken her gun. Curls slid into her vision as she turned on her side. Clamping her hand over the wound, she pushed upright. Lightning fired through her pain receptors, and she ducked her chin to her chest to keep the scream working up her throat at bay. Where was he?

Chaos pulled her attention to the broken ring of gunmen as another round of bullets pierced the night. Getting to her feet, Shea stumbled forward, free hand outstretched as her boot collided with something heavy and unmoving in the snow. Rocking back on her heels, she landed on her butt in the powder. She clawed for the flashlight discarded a few feet away and swept it over the body, her throat tight. Instant relief coursed through her. One of the gunmen. Not Vincent. She collected the officer's weapon and killed the flashlight beam. He was out there, taking on an entire ring of corrupt cops on his own. He needed help.

Shea straightened again, hugging her arm into her side, and took cover behind the nearest tree. There. Another gunshot exploded from nearby and a flashlight hit the ground. Several more closed in on the shooter's position, and she turned to approach the group from behind.

Stinging agony spread across her scalp as a fist clenched her hair, her back hitting solid muscle and a wall of Kevlar.

"Where do you think you're going?" The man Vincent had called Grillo shoved her forward, and she hit the ground face-first. "You're as much a part of this as your partner is now, and we're not done."

Ice worked beneath the collar of her coat and T-shirt, shocking her into action. Shea flipped over just as he lunged for her again and rolled out of his reach but lost her newly acquired gun in the snow. The wound in her side screamed in protest, but she forced herself to get back to her feet. He came at her, his fist aimed directly for her face. Dodging the first attempt to knock her out, she slammed her forearm into his as he tried again, but she wasn't fast enough to block his free hand. Bone met the flesh of her face. The momentum of his hit twisted her head to the side, her eyes watering from the hit, but she kept upright. Copper and salt filled her mouth. She spit the blood, the inside of her cheek stinging where her teeth had cut into the soft tissue.

"You shouldn't have sided with Kalani, Officer Ramsey," he said. "Because now I'm going to have to hurt you."

Dread curled at the base of her stomach. This man had access to her son. And no matter which way she looked at it, as a mother, as an officer, she couldn't let him leave this clearing. Not without risking him contacting the men he had watching Wells. Shea shot her fist forward, connecting with one temple, then landed a kick center mass to his chest before he could recover. "And you shouldn't have gone after my son."

Grillo stumbled back, but didn't go down, and she raised her fists for another attack. Unsheathing a knife in one hand, her attacker tried to circle around her position. He rushed forward, the knife leading the way, and the snow slowed her down. The tip of the knife cut through her thick coat and sliced across her upper arm. "You have no idea how much I'm going to enjoy this."

Another wave of pain helped her forget the bullet that had embedded in her midsection. She wrapped her numb fingers around his wrist as he lunged forward again, maneuvered behind him, and put as much pressure as she could manage against his injured arm. He let go of the knife as she forced him to double over, the weight on his elbow too much to do anything else. With enough pressure, she'd do irreparable damage. Her heart pounded hard in her chest. Blood pooled beneath her clothing, dripping into the waistband of her jeans. "Call off your men." Only his breathing registered, and she applied more pressure. His groan heightened the effects of the nausea swirling in her gut. She didn't like hurting people. She'd sworn to protect them, but she wouldn't let Vincent die out here while he fought to protect her. "Now."

A rumble of laughter vibrated through Grillo's chest and into her grip on his arm. "You going to kill me, Ramsey? Because that's the only way you're walking out of here. That's the only way you're going to save your son before my guys get to him."

She didn't get a chance to respond as Grillo swung his opposite hand up, grabbed on to her neck, and slammed her into the ground. The air crushed from her lungs, the darkness threatening to consume her all over again. Her head pounded in rhythm to her racing heartbeat as his shadow moved over her, but she wasn't going to die here. Shea kicked out, catching him in the stomach, and clawed for the gun she'd lost a few minutes ago. The metal chilled her hand as she brought it out in front of her and aimed. Her chest heaved as her lungs fought to catch up with the rest of her body. "Don't move."

"You already shot me once, Ramsey. You sure as hell better make sure you kill me this time." Grillo took a step forward, and she pulled the trigger.

Nothing happened.

She tried again, and again, but the gun wouldn't fire. Her lips parted. No. No, no, no, no. Silence descended. Ice worked through her veins, and it had nothing to do with the dropping temperatures. Raising her gaze to Grillo's, she caught the hint of a smile thinning his lips.

"Now it's my turn." He unholstered a hidden weapon from his lower back, centering her in his crosshairs, and her insides clenched.

She'd been on the wrong end of a gun before in the line of duty, but nothing like this. No one had ever wanted to kill her, to kill one of her partners, to hurt her son. Whoever these people were working for—whoever'd sent them to kill Vincent—they were going to get away with it if she didn't get up. But she'd already lost too much blood. The ringing in her ears was back, weblike patterns at the corners of her eyes. She tried sitting up, tried blocking the path of Grillo's bullet with one hand, but the very idea didn't even make sense. There was nothing she could do. She couldn't save Vincent. She couldn't save her son. She couldn't even save herself. Just as she hadn't been able to after giving birth to Wells.

Vincent. His name echoed in her mind, and the fear holding her in place evaporated. The gunfire had died down. Was he injured? Would she survive long enough to make it to him in time? The man she'd kept at a distance due to her own private battle with the way he'd made her feel these past few months had saved her life out here. More times than she could count. Vincent and his team had skirted the law when it came to their investigations time and time again, but Shea couldn't deny the fact that they'd saved so many lives in the process. Including hers. The thought of this team of corrupt cops burying the forensic investigator she'd come to rely on churned her stomach. Shea put everything she had into getting to her feet, but it wasn't enough. Her knees buckled as a wave of dizziness washed over her. Now it was time to save his.

"You don't know when to give up, do you, Officer Ramsey?" he asked. "Maybe you and I aren't so different after all."

"I took the same oath as you to protect the innocent. The only difference between us is I actually try to hold up my end." Shea rushed her attacker. She'd trained in active shooter situations. The best chance she had of surviving—of Vincent surviving—was to get control of that gun. Dark eyes widened a split second before a wall of muscle slammed into Grillo from the right, knocking all three of them to the ground. The trees surrounding them blurred in streaks of black and white as she rolled down an incline. A scream escaped up her throat as she slammed into a boulder mere feet from where Grillo and another man struggled to their feet. "Vincent."

She scanned the area, counted the bodies around the clearing. Ten. Not including Grillo. He'd taken them all down. Who the hell had she partnered with these past few months? Shea smothered the fear climbing up her throat. He was injured, favoring his right leg and the gunshot wound in his shoulder. Grillo shook his head as though trying to clear it and attacked. Vincent blocked the first hit, then the next, but took the third and fourth directly to the kidneys. Pressing her hand to her own wound, Shea hauled herself to her feet. Adrenaline narrowed her focus on the weapon Grillo had dropped as they'd rolled down the hill. Wrapping her hand around the grip, she brought the gun up.

"I told you I enjoyed a challenge." A hand clamped over her mouth, wrenching her back. Icy metal pressed against her temple, the scent of stale cigarettes and cologne overwhelming, and everything inside her went cold. The cop, the one who'd knocked her unconscious back at the ranger station, lowered his mouth to her ear. "I'd prefer not to put a bullet in you before I've had my chance to pay you back for the new scar to my face. Get rid of the gun."

Hesitation coursed through her, but she'd lost the upper hand. The breath rushed out of her. Tossing the weapon a few feet away, she fought back the nausea and pain swirling through her as Vincent took another hit. He collapsed to the ground, those mesmerizing brown eyes settling on her as Grillo launched his knee into Vincent's face. Her protector slumped to the ground. Out cold. Grillo gathered the discarded gun and shot Vincent two times to the chest. Center mass. Exactly as she'd been trained.

"No!" she screamed from behind the hand braced over her mouth, the sound distorted and desperate. Her legs threatened to give out as the last of her adrenaline drained. Tears burned in her eyes, and she wrenched herself out of her attacker's grasp and launched forward. Only she couldn't reach Vincent in time.

Grillo pushed her toward his partner, his grip bruising.

The officer at her back spun her around and pressed the gun's barrel to her temple once again. Those perfect white teeth flashed in a wide smile. Dried blood flaked from the laceration at his temple where she'd hit him as Grillo circled around to face her. "Let's talk about what's going to happen next, Officer Ramsey."

Chapter 8

Vincent sat up, gasping for air. His lungs protested the sharp bite of cold as pain radiated outward from the two slugs Grillo had buried dead center in his chest. He locked his jaw against the groan in his throat as he battled to stay upright. Hell, it was hard to breathe with this damn thing on. Not to mention the impact of two bullets to the chest. Leveraging his back against the nearest tree, he closed his eyes against the soreness as he unzipped his heavy coat to examine the damage. A combination of pink and orange filtered across the sky, giving him enough light to pick one crumpled bullet from the Kevlar vest. The metal was still warm to the touch. Patterns in the snow a few feet away demanded his attention. Divots cut a path around him, south through the trees. And blood. His gut clenched as he crawled the few feet between him and the drops. Shea.

They couldn't have gotten far. If he hurried, he still might be able to save her. He'd gotten Shea into this mess. He'd fight to get her out of it, but more than that, he couldn't stand the thought of working with a new partner on the department's joint investigations with Blackhawk. Couldn't stand the thought of losing her. Not when he was beginning to break past those icy barriers and see the vulnerable, fiery, secretive woman beneath. They'd survived this long as a team. He wasn't about to give that up.

Struggling to his feet, he ignored the slight drag of his right leg and the throbbing in his shoulder as he patted down one of the men he'd taken down. He unholstered an extra weapon, checked the magazine, and loaded a round into the chamber. Numbness had worked through his fingers and toes, but oddly, the rest of his body was slick with sweat. These bastards had taken her, and he was going to get her back. Then he'd hunt down the SOB who'd ordered Grillo and his team to take him out. "Hold on for me, Shea."

He followed the droplets of blood until the trees thinned, every cell in his body screaming in protest. The faster his heart pumped, the more blood he'd lose, but he wouldn't stop because his body was tired. Only when the job was done. The trail ended at the bank of a frozen lake nestled between two mountains, but there was nothing but open views and thick ice out here. Pops and cracks echoed in his ears. Grillo wouldn't have crossed the lake with a hostage in tow. Not with these open sight lines and the chance of falling through the ice. Too risky. Realization hit as strong as another shot to the chest as he turned to study the trail. "The bastard must've doubled back."

He'd been following a dummy trail, made to look as though the corrupt SOBs who'd taken Shea had come this way. Puffs of air crystalized in front of his mouth. Damn it. He had to stay dry. Any hint of moisture led to hypothermia, and Shea was already running out of time.

Movement caught his attention from behind, and Vincent swung around, gun at the ready. Grillo's partner—the one who'd taken Shea at gunpoint—latched onto his wrist and slammed Vincent into the nearest tree. The bastard went for the weapon, and Vincent let him as he swung a hard left directly into his attacker's face, followed by a kick to the gut. The partner stumbled back with a groan, but recovered fast, trying to deliver the same kick. Only he missed. One hit to the kidneys knocked the guy off-balance, but the next to the cop's collarbone resulted in a sickening crack of bone. The attacker's scream pierced the silence as snow fell from the sky. Threading his fingers between Grillo's partner's, he twisted the bastard's hand backward and brought the cop to his knees. "Where is she?"

Laughter mixed with a pain-filled moan. The dirty cop spit blood into the snow a few feet away. "Interrogate me all you want, Kalani. I'm not giving you a damn thing."

Light from the auroras above glinted off a hint of steel a moment before pain seared across Vincent's leg. He released his hold on the SOB but closed the space between them fast. Dodging the next swipe, he pushed the man's arm away with one hand and slammed his palm into the bastard's broken clavicle with the other.

Grillo's partner dropped to one knee. Swiping the gun from the snow, Vincent crouched, pressing the barrel to the cop's temple. Just as he'd done to Shea before Vincent had been knocked unconscious. He ripped the badge off the man's waistband, the nickel silver heavy in his hand. City of New York Police. Detective. A humorless laugh escaped Vincent's bruised chest, resurrecting the ache from the two rounds Grillo had shot into the vest. He'd had a shield almost exactly like this. Before he'd lost everything.

Vincent tossed the detective's badge into the snow. "You know, back in New York, my forensic team and I were called out on a handful of homicides that made us believe the perps had to have knowledge of crime scenes. Everything had been wiped down. The bodies had been moved from one location to the other, which made it nearly impossible to identify the original crime scene, or we couldn't even identify the victims because there was barely anything left to identify. Evidence connected to the cases even started going missing from lockup, which led me to believe the killer had to be law enforcement."

Vincent studied the deep laceration on the side of the cop's head, right where Shea had knocked the jerk out cold, and a rush of satisfaction washed over him. "Of course, I couldn't prove it. You and your buddies back there in that clearing had done too good a job, and nobody up the chain of command wanted to hear that their own officers were involved in the very homicides we were trying to solve." He crouched beside Grillo's partner. "So I took my theory to Internal Affairs. I'm guessing when Officer Walter got too close to identifying the cops involved, your boss had him killed, right? But not before someone tortured him to the point he gave up the source of his intel. Me. That's why you tried to have me killed, isn't it? Only there's something you and your buddies here are forgetting, Detective."

He lowered his voice as the rage he'd caged all these months started to break through the cracks. "I was one of the best forensic investigators in the country, and I know exactly how to dispose of your body without leaving any evidence behind. Your family won't ever know what happened to you when I'm done." A flash of fear contorted the detective's face as Vincent released the safety on the weapon. "So I'm only going to ask you one more time before I pull this trigger. Where is Shea Ramsey?"

"Grillo didn't tell me where he was taking her." Panic outlined the tendons between the cop's neck and shoulders as though he expected the bullet to come next. "He left me here to take care of you in case you came after us again, but I swear I don't know where she is now. Said the less I know, the less could be tied back to us in case Blackhawk Security or Anchorage PD started looking for her. We had orders…that's all. None of this was personal, Kalani. I swear." The guy closed his eyes as Vincent increased the pressure of the gun against his head, hands raised in surrender. The bastard had to know something—anything—that could get him to Shea. "Go on, do it. If you don't kill me, if they think I gave you anything, they'll go after my kid."

The inferno burning through him cooled in an instant, and the gun's barrel slipped down a few centimeters as he processed each word out of his attacker's mouth. "What'd you say?"

His expression smoothed as he opened one eye, then the other, to stare up at Vincent. "The people I work for, they'll go after my kid if you don't kill me."

The same way they'd go after Shea's son if she didn't walk away. Grillo had been in touch with the men watching Wells back in New York. Which meant his team had to have a satellite phone or radio that worked out here between the mountains. If he could get his hands on it, he and Shea had a chance to call in backup and send one of Blackhawk's operatives to intercept the men sitting on the boy. The scent of smoke clung to his coat and hair as he forced himself to breathe evenly. Vincent adjusted his grip around the gun, finger positioned alongside the trigger. "Which direction did Grillo take her?"

"Out there." He motioned with his chin out across the lake.

The pops and cracks he'd heard before... They hadn't been the lake naturally settling. They'd been initiated by the extra weight of two adults moving across the surface of the ice. Vincent lowered the weapon to his side. What exactly had been Grillo's plan? Kill her, then drop her body beneath the ice? Despite popular belief that water washed away evidence, the freezing temperatures would only preserve it out here. Only no one would know where to look for her. Not even the most aggressive district attorney would be able to charge Grillo with first-degree murder without a body. No. He couldn't think like that. Because if he lost her... If he didn't get the chance to tell her what he'd been afraid to admit over the past few months—how she'd been the source of his need to finally solve this case—he feared he'd never stop hunting the SOBs who'd started this war in the first place. He refocused on the detective at his feet. "You're going to want to take some pain medication when you wake up."

Confusion contorted the cop's expression. "What—"

Vincent slammed the butt of the gun into the base of his attacker's neck and let him collapse forward. The bastard would wake up with a hell of a headache, but he'd live long enough to get his kid to safety. He trusted the guy could find his way back to the city. Right now, he had to get to Shea. Holstering the weapon at the small of his back, he put his weight back into his heels as he descended toward the lake's shoreline and stepped onto the ice.

One more step.

The ice groaned and snapped under her weight, dendritic patterns spreading out from where her boots landed. An ache flared as Grillo pressed the gun into her back. They must've walked at least half a mile by now. How much farther did he expect her to go with a gunshot in her side? If he didn't kill her soon, the blood loss from her wound or hypothermia settling in would do the job for him. Maybe that was his plan. Other than the bullet lodged inside her, not even the best forensic investigator in the world would be able to tie her death back to him or his ring of dirty cops, but he could remove the slug easily enough. When she wasn't able to fight back. Shea blinked to clear the haze clouding her vision. One more step. She only had to make it one more step.

"How much farther?" She dared a glance over her shoulder, back toward her attacker as her boot skidded across the surface of the lake. Throwing her bloodied hands out for balance, she held her breath until the world righted. Her body ached, her head hurt, and her heart... she'd just watched it take two bullets to the chest in her defense. Vincent. She cleared the tears—the memories of blood and gunpowder and pain—and forced herself to keep moving forward. The hole she'd struggled to patch over the last nine months after losing her son had ripped wider and more violently than she'd expected when Grillo had pulled that trigger. And now... Now she was being led across a frozen lake threatening to engulf her at any moment with a gunman at her back.

"Until I say stop." Grillo knocked her forward, and her palms hit the ice hard.

She skidded to a stop, exhales ricocheting back into her face. Cold burned the exposed skin of her palms, but she didn't have the energy to move. In the past two days her plane had gone down, she'd barely survived an avalanche and she'd been knocked unconscious and shot. How much more was she expected to endure before her body shut down completely?

"Get up." His boot nudged at her injured side.

Shea bit her tongue against the agony tearing through her, fingertips melting through the thin layer of snow that'd built between her and mere inches of ice. If Grillo pulled that trigger again, would the bullet break through? Could she force him beneath the hardened layer in a last-ditch effort to make it out of here alive?

The thought penetrated through the cloudiness clinging to her brain. The effects of hypothermia had already started settling in. Confusion, slurred speech, lethargy, but the idea she could survive the organization that'd killed Vincent long enough to bring them down on her own brought clarity. In a sea of family and friends whose faces had drained of color in her fight against the postpartum depression, his had stood out in full hues. Working cases with Vincent had been a lifeline when she'd needed it the most, his challenging yet easygoing nature the only thing she'd been able to hold on to during her fight for mental health. Bringing her in on the joint investigations had saved her life in more ways than one. Physically. Mentally. Emotionally. She owed him this.

A gust of wind kicked up snow and dead foliage around her, and the hint of something clean, masculine even. She breathed it in a bit deeper, reminded of the way Vincent had so easily closed the distance between them back at the ranger station. How he'd grazed her jawline with his knuckles, resurrecting pulses of desire she'd never thought she'd feel again after her divorce. The memory of his kiss chased back the tremors racking her body now. Vincent had given his life to ensure she survived. She couldn't let it be for nothing.

"I said get up, Ramsey." Grillo fisted her hair, pulling her upper body off the ice, and her hands shot to relieve the pressure—to no avail. He was stronger than her, faster than her, but Shea wasn't going to give up. "Unless you're perfectly happy dying here. I was planning on burying you in a nice spot up here a ways, but—"

Launching her heel into his shin, she braced for impact as Grillo lost his balance and slammed down on top of her. The air crushed from her lungs, but she forced herself to her feet as his gun slid across the ice. She clawed for it, Grillo catching her ankle before she was able to reach the weapon and hit the ice again. Pain receded to the back of her mind as her fight-or-flight response focused her attention on getting free. She rocketed her heel into his nose, heard the sickening crunch, and he released his hold on her.

The ice underneath her dipped with a loud, echoing crack. Her heart rate spiked into dangerous territory as water flooded up through the crevices around her. Shea scrambled back, kicking at the ice for purchase, but it only broke apart faster.

"Shea!" Recognition flared.

In an instant, she locked on the figure running across the ice toward her. Vincent. He was alive. Fear and relief battled for supremacy as she flipped onto her stomach and dug her fingernails into the ice. A sob built in her throat, but she couldn't let the emotions tearing through her free. Not until she confirmed he was real and not some construct her mind had created in an effort for survival.

But with one more gut-wrenching crack, the surface of the lake broke. Both she and Grillo fell through, their screams cut off by ice-cold water. Every nerve ending in her body shrieked in shock as the subzero temperature paralyzed her limbs. She couldn't think. Couldn't move. Strands of her hair blocked the view of the dim light of the auroras filtering down through the hole above, and of her attacker.

Grillo tugged her into his body, squeezing what precious oxygen she'd held on to from her chest. The bubbles tickled her overexposed skin as they raced to the surface. She targeted the gunshot in his shoulder, digging her finger into the wound, and twisted as hard as she could. His muffled scream barely reached her ears, blood spreading around them fast. She wrestled for freedom, but he only held her tighter.

The brilliant dance of lights above the surface diminished. Without air, they were sinking in a violent battle for dominance to the bottom of the lake. There were no guarantees the hole they'd fallen through would still be there when she came back up. Grillo maneuvered behind her, locking her neck in the crease of his elbow. She jerked her knee toward his head as hard as she could, but the water only slowed her momentum. Her body was growing heavier by the second, her movements rigid. This man was a corrupt cop, following someone else's orders. Was he really willing to risk his life to ensure she lost hers? Blackness clouded the corners of her vision, the cold and lack of air leaching her strength faster now, but she wouldn't give up. Couldn't. Not when she'd just started to explore the possibility of getting her son back, of moving on with her life. Of seeing if the connection between her and Vincent was real.

A shadow passed above them.

Grillo jerked behind her. His grip loosened from her neck as the water in front of her face turned red with blood.

She was still sinking, limbs refusing to respond to her brain's commands. Muscled, tattooed arms surrounded her, and her head sank back into a wall of familiar ridges and valleys. Gravity warred with the lightness overtaking her as they shot toward the opening in the ice. Below, the dark outline of her attacker faded into the deep. Her head broke through the surface, lungs automatically gasping for oxygen.

"I've got you." His voice penetrated through the erratic pounding of her heartbeat in her ears, but she couldn't win the fight against the sinking sensation taking over. Her head fell back against one muscled shoulder as he struggled to get them onto solid ice. "You're safe now."

"Where…is your…coat?" Her words slurred, her tongue too heavy in her mouth. Shouldn't he be wearing more clothes out here in the open? He was going to freeze to death. A low thumping filled her ears. Shea fought the exhaustion, the pain, the heaviness, but it was all too much.

"Don't worry about me. Help is coming. Focus on staying awake, you hear me?" Vincent increased the pressure around her middle. Sounds of dripping water overwhelmed the thumping in the distance as he slid her onto the ice, but she didn't have the energy to do anything more than close her eyes. Her body was shutting down, she knew that, but at least she wasn't alone this time. A hint of warmth bled into her face as Vincent framed her chin with one hand. "Shea, look at me. Open your eyes."

She wanted to. With every fiber of her being, she wanted to commit his face to memory. Wanted to thank him for saving her life. Wanted to tell him how working with him had given her a reason to keep going when she had nothing left to lose over these last few months. Putting the remnants of her strength into following orders, Shea narrowed on dark brown eyes tinted with a hint of green in the middle. She'd never noticed that before, the green. She'd spent so long trying to tamp down the way he made her feel when they were in the field together, she hadn't taken the time to really appreciate the man above her. But right now, her body was making the choice for her. She had all the time in the world. Water clung to his beard and hair, the tips already crusted with ice. His normally smooth, tanned skin had lost a bit of color, but the fire in his gaze pierced straight through her.

The pounding grew louder, vibrating up through her legs and into her chest. They'd taken down Grillo and his team—together—but the job wasn't done. Her attacker had contacts back in New York, people he'd ordered to surveil her ex-husband and her son. The organization that'd sent him, it was bigger than she and Vincent could've imagined, but she couldn't protect them anymore. "Find... Wells."

Vincent engulfed her hand in his, pressing the backs of her fingers to his mouth. "We're going to find him, Shea. Together. Just hang on."

The steady thumping pulsed at the base of her neck as rotors and a chopper's frame moved into her vision, but she couldn't win this war anymore.

"Shea," he said. "Shea!"

Chapter 9

"You look like hell," a familiar voice said.

Vincent breathed through the relentless pain around two cracked ribs, a gunshot wound and the beginning of infection in his thigh, then focused on the woman beside the hospital bed. His stomach dropped. Not Shea. Although he wasn't disappointed to see Kate Monroe—the team's resident psychologist—hers wasn't the face he needed right now. Fluorescent lighting reflected off her blond-streaked hair pulled back in a low knot. She looked good, considering she and her thought-to-be-dead husband had barely survived a serial killer's hunt less than two months ago. Now here she was, her skin almost glowing, but maybe that was a side effect of the pregnancy. Vincent leveraged his weight into the mattress with his uninjured hand, careful of the new sling around his arm, and positioned himself higher in the bed. His head throbbed at the base of his skull, the lights too bright. "You say the nicest things, Doc." He couldn't stop the groan rumbling through his chest as he moved to throw off one of the hospital's heavy blankets. "Where's Shea?"

"Officer Ramsey is resting comfortably down the hall. The surgeon was able to retrieve the bullet in one piece without any complications. She'll make a full recovery as long as she gets the rest she needs. But knowing what I do about her, I don't see that happening anytime soon. That being the case, I'm having Braxton keep an eye on her." Kate crossed one leg over the other and sat back in the chair, that all-too-knowing gaze weighing on him. "You want to talk about what happened out there? About why you used Blackhawk resources to investigate a case, but didn't feel the need to involve the rest of your team?"

"Elizabeth." The network security analyst's name was torn from his mouth. He'd asked her to run the fingerprint he'd recovered from the warehouse fire that night through IAFIS. He should've known she'd push it up the ladder, but he couldn't blame her, either. Blackhawk's founder, Sullivan Bishop, required honesty from all his operatives. It wasn't fair of him to put that kind of pressure on one of his teammates. Or one of his closest friends.

"Give her credit." Kate crossed her arms and sat forward. "She didn't brief Sullivan about the fingerprint until after Search and Rescue recovered you and Shea on that lake. I think she was honestly more worried she'd missed something than anything else." Bright green eyes assessed him, as though she were trying to see inside his head. "We were all worried, Vincent. You've helped save every single one of your teammates' lives in the field. Did you really think we weren't going to do the same for you?"

Nausea replaced the focus of pain. "Everyone I've involved has paid the price, Kate. I've already lost two of my best investigators in New York, and I almost lost Shea out there." The thought spiked his blood pressure as acid climbed up his throat. This was on him. Everything—the plane crash, the bullet in her side, the fact that her son had been put in danger—it was all because of him. Her death would've been on his shoulders for the rest of his life. Just as IAB Officer Walter's would be. "I'm not going to risk the team."

"It's not over, is it? The people who shot you, whoever brought down your plane... They're still out there," Kate said. "They're not done with you or Officer Ramsey."

She was right. Shea had become as much a part of this as he had the moment he'd requested her as his partner on the joint investigations between Blackhawk and Anchorage PD. Had those bastards been watching her all this time? Watching her son and ex-husband in New York? If he'd known whoever'd killed IAB Officer Ashton Walter would come for her, Vincent would've stayed the hell away, kept her out of danger. "I can't tell you anything, Kate. Not without putting you and the baby, even Declan, at risk."

"We're a team, Vincent. You were there for me when the Hunter started closing in on Declan and me. You've been there for every single one of us. No matter the personal cost. Now it's time for us to be there for you."

Her shoulders sank away from her ears with a hard exhale. Kate produced a pale manila folder, those inquisitive green eyes centered on the name written on the tab. Even from this distance, he read the label easily: Shea Ramsey. "When Blackhawk and Anchorage PD partnered on investigations a few months ago, I was asked to vet the officers who'd be working with us and get permission for the department to share their psych evals with me. Including Shea Ramsey."

Vincent sat a bit higher in the bed, the pain in his shoulder and thigh forgotten. "Don't do this, Kate."

"I can hear the difference in your voice when you talk about her, Vincent. I've seen the way you study her when you're working together." Kate ran her fingers over the edge of the folder. "I was there when the EMTs pushed you two through the emergency room doors. You were asking for her, even when your body was shutting down from diving into that lake. You're already falling for her, but she owes you the truth—"

"No, she doesn't." He bit back the anger in his voice as her head snapped up, shock evident in her expression. His pulse pounded hard behind his ears in perfect rhythm to the machines tracking his vitals, creating a tingling sensation beneath the skin of his face and neck. He understood the firm's need to vet the officers involved in their joint cases, but nothing—not a damn thing—would change his feelings for Shea. Anything important enough he needed to know about, she had the right to tell him herself. Not some department shrink who'd spent less than sixty minutes with her and come to some half-baked conclusion. Tugging the IV from the inner crease of his elbow, Vincent swung his legs over the bed. Over two hundred stitches, a mild concussion from being knocked unconscious, beginning stages of hypothermia…none of it mattered. He needed to see her. "I understand you're trying to look out for me, but this isn't the way to do it, Kate. Not only would I be betraying her privacy, but you're also putting yourself at risk by even thinking about telling me what's in that eval. I know who Shea Ramsey is, and nothing in that file is going to convince me otherwise."

The profiler stood. Giving him room to maneuver to the end of the bed, she lowered her gaze to the floor, the file still clutched in her hand. "Even if it means she's not in a position to love you back?"

Vincent slowed. Cold worked up through his bare feet and deep into muscle. From the white tile floor or Kate's question, he had no idea and didn't care. Shea had stood by him when Grillo and his men had given her the chance to walk away. She'd prevented those bastards from throwing his body into the ranger station fire and given him something he'd lost a long time ago: hope. He wouldn't have made it this far without her, would've never discovered the truth about that night in the warehouse. She'd given him that, and so much more. Whether she realized it or not, he owed her his life. In more ways than one. Kate wasn't wrong. He'd started falling for Shea Ramsey a long time ago, and if she didn't feel the same way because of some deep-seated secret spelled out in that file… The pain in his ribs flared on a slow inhale. He wanted to hear it from her. "That's not your call to make."

"I don't want to see you get hurt," Kate said.

"You've seen the scars on my back, the stitches in

my shoulder and the bruises on my ribs, Doc. Seems all I've known lately is hurt." Stillness enveloped him as he thought back to that moment between him and Shea in the ranger station, before Grillo's men had burned the place to the ground. To the moment she'd blamed herself for her ex-husband cheating on her, for him filing for divorce and for the bastard taking her son from her. There were only a handful of reasons he could think of for a strong, determined woman like Shea not to fight back every step of the way, but for her to sever ties with her family and friends, for her to throw herself into her work more over the past few months than ever before, narrowed it considerably. Only one reason stood out from the rest, explained why she'd been able to show up for her city day after day as though nothing could break through that hardened exterior she was determined to hide behind despite the hardships going on in her personal life. And it'd all started after she'd given birth to Wells. Vincent met his teammate's gaze as understanding hit. He hadn't seen it until now, how much Shea had been suffering all this time. Afraid. Alone. How could he have been so blind? "Better than feeling nothing at all, right?"

"Right." Kate picked up a duffel from beside her chair he hadn't noticed until now and handed it to him. "Just be careful. With yourself, and with her."

He nodded. Vincent took the bag, waiting for the profiler to leave before he dressed in the fresh set of clothes she'd brought, but he'd have to leave his boot laces untied on account of the bullet wound in his shoulder. He couldn't wait any longer. Wrenching open the door with his free hand, he headed down the hall, to the door where Braxton Levitt—Elizabeth Dawson's chosen partner and father of her child—stood armed and ready to protect Shea. Vincent acknowledged the former intelligence analyst, then knocked as Braxton stepped away from the door before pushing his way inside.

The breath rushed out of him as he caught sight of her at the end of the hospital bed. Long damp hair rested across her shoulders, revealing smooth hills of lean muscle along her back. He studied her wound beneath the bandage in nothing but a black lace bra and an unbuttoned pair of dirty jeans. Muscle and bruising. So much bruising his gut tightened. In an instant, fierce green eyes locked on him, and every cell in his body forgot the haziness of morphine he'd been under for the past few hours. She'd just gotten out of surgery. They both had. Now it looked like she was ready to run. "Where the hell do you think you're going?"

"I'm going to New York." Dropping her hands from the gauze taped at her side, she notched her chin level with the floor. "I'm going to get my son back."

Tension drained from him. Vincent tried crossing his arms over his chest, only to be reminded one of them was in a damn sling. She wanted to go to New York? Fine. He couldn't stop her, but he wasn't letting her get away that easily. Not after everything they'd survived together. "All right. When do we leave?"

"Anthony and Bennett have already made contact." Vincent maneuvered into his seat beside her, his clean, masculine scent overriding stale circulated air and body odor. He was trying to distract her. They'd taken off from Ted Stevens International Airport a few minutes ago, along with a hundred other passengers, and right now, she didn't want to focus on anything else other than him. Not the plane crash. Not the fact an organization of corrupt cops had gone after her son and nearly killed her in the process. And not about what her ex-husband would have to say the minute she showed her face at the safe house after he'd told her she'd never see Wells again unless she got herself help. "We'll be meeting your ex-husband, his wife and Wells in a secure location in two days to avoid tipping off Grillo's men. Until then, we'll hole up at one of Blackhawk's safe houses in Brooklyn."

"Two days." Anthony Harris, Blackhawk's weapons expert, and Bennett Spencer, the firm's newest investigator Shea had never met, had both volunteered for the job to protect her son. If Vincent trusted them to protect Wells until she could reach him, then so did she, but her nerves still hadn't settled. Had nothing to do with the chance the plane would go down, or that she'd nearly died in the exact same mountains they were flying over right now. It was Vincent. No matter how many times she'd tried, she couldn't reconcile the vigilante operative she'd known with the man who'd risked his own life to dive into that lake and save her. The man who'd fought off almost a dozen armed corrupt cops to keep her safe. It'd been in those last few moments, with Grillo's arm around her throat as freezing lake water had seeped past her lips, that'd she'd realized the truth. Vincent wasn't who she'd believed. Not the secretive, infuriating know-it-all keen on breaking the rules whenever he got the chance, but more. He'd detached himself from everyone around him in order to protect them, kept them all in the dark about his personal investigation, including his team, but he'd trusted her. Why?

The plane jerked downward, and she couldn't stop the flood of memories crashing through the barrier she'd built as a distraction. The uncertainty, the fear, the terrifying thought she'd never see her son again. She closed her eyes against the incessant shriek of the plane's engines, forced herself to breathe evenly as her heart threatened to beat out of her chest. It was just turbulence. She knew that, but—

Warmth enveloped her hand clutched around the shared armrest, and everything inside her stilled. The thudding at the back of her skull faded, nothing but her own breathing filling her ears as she opened her eyes. Her wet hair had dampened the back of her T-shirt after she'd showered back at the hospital, but that had nothing to with the sensations running down her spine now.

It was Vincent.

He'd pulled his hair back, exposing the fresh bruises along his jaw where Grillo had left his mark—bruises similar to hers—but none of it took away from the gut-wrenching intensity in his expression. Sensations simmered low in her abdominals the longer he studied her, and she suddenly found herself incapable of pretending he hadn't gotten to her these past few months. That he hadn't broken through the haze she'd been hiding behind for so long. The edges of where his tattoos met the scars on his back peeked out from beneath his T-shirt, and in that moment, she wanted nothing more than to trace the flesh with her fingertips. Just as she'd wanted to do back in that cave, buried under all that snow. His exhale tickled the oversensitized skin of her neck, and she couldn't fight back the shiver spreading across her shoulders.

"Careful, Freckles." His words practically vibrated through her, he was so close. "You keep looking at me like that and I might start to get ideas of finishing what we started back at the ranger station."

Heat surged through her. That kiss…it'd been everything she'd imagined and more between them. The desire, the rush of adrenaline, the familiarity despite the fact that they'd practically been strangers before getting on that plane. The backs of her knees tingled at the memory of his mountainous body pressed against hers, the feel of his heart beating hard beneath her palm. She'd done that to him. She'd spiked his pulse higher with desire, but with one kiss, he'd ripped her apart. Helped her remember who'd she'd been, and she never wanted to go back. Never wanted to be trapped in that lonely shell again. If anything, she wanted more. Because of him. What that meant for the future—if they had one—she didn't know, but the idea didn't seem impossible anymore. Not after everything they'd been through. His eyes glittered with brightness as though he could see the battle wreaking havoc inside her. "Thank you for what you did. For…getting me out of the plane, for sharing the food your mom packed, even when it meant you'd starve if I didn't make it."

"Oh, don't worry, she packed more." Vincent released her hand and hauled his bag from between his feet, showing her the row of food containers inside.

"I'll be sure to thank her." A laugh burst from her chest, resurrecting the agony in her side. She couldn't remember the last time she'd let go like this, but the hollowness in her chest still hurt, and her laugh died in a renewed drone from the plane's engines. She set the crown of her head back against the headrest. Flittering her fingers over his forearm, Shea noted the rise of goose bumps across his skin where she touched him.

"I haven't felt like myself for a long time now, but you…" She forced a smile, the pressure of unshed tears building. The swirl of brown in his eyes warmed her straight to her core, drowning the uncertainty clawing through her. He deserved to know the truth after what he'd done for her, deserved to know that her path to healing wasn't over, that anything that happened between them might not end the way they imagined. Not right now. But she would always be grateful for him demanding to be her partner, even if he and his team believed they were above the law. She breathed in his light hint of soap, held on to it as long as she could. Would he still view her as that strong, determined, independent woman he'd described back at the ranger station when he learned the truth? Would he still want to partner with her when all of this was over? Dread pooled in her stomach. Would he still trust her?

"Shea?" he asked.

Shea removed her hand from his arm. Her ex-husband hadn't understood why there were days when she hadn't been able to get out of bed, hadn't been able to make love to him or to take care of Wells. Why she'd thrown herself into her work to the point she couldn't keep the details of her cases straight from working double and triple shifts straight through. Tears prickled at her lower lash line, but she held on to them. The answer was clear. Nobody could understand the mental war she fought to stay present every day. Not even Vincent. "Working with you these past few months saved me. Thank you."

"You would've saved yourself sooner or later." He maneuvered the duffel back onto the floor between his feet, the pain in his ribs evident as his expression contorted. He'd taken two bullets to the chest for her. If it weren't for the Kevlar vest he'd retrieved from one of Grillo's men, she wouldn't have made it back to the surface of the lake. She owed him her life, and she'd do whatever it took to pay him back. "I was just there to get the crap kicked out of me."

"Oh, *that's* why you were following me down the mountain. It all makes sense now." Stinging shot through her mouth as she forced another smile, and she set her hand against her lips. They'd fought off the men sent to kill them two days ago, but the pain of her injuries hadn't lessened. "For what it's worth, I wouldn't be here if it weren't for you."

"Guess that makes us even." He leaned back in his seat, closing his eyes. Couldn't blame him. He hadn't gotten a whole lot of rest before she'd checked herself out of the hospital to get on the next flight to New York. Neither of them had, but she wasn't going to sit around and wait for whoever'd sent Grillo and his men to take another run at her son. She'd already failed Wells once. She wouldn't fail him again. "Blackhawk would be looking for my toasty remains if you hadn't shot that bastard."

"Right." A minute passed, maybe two. The flight attendant's voice from the front of the plane fought to keep her in the present, but Shea only had attention for him. The way his dark lashes rested on his cheeks, how a set of stitches from his fight with Grillo slashed down through one naturally arched eyebrow. She couldn't help but memorize every detail, every imperfection, every ridge and valley of muscle exposed in the light of the plane's dim lighting. All too easily, she envisioned the woman lucky enough to have him all to herself. He was a warrior and a hell of an investigator. He'd protect his life partner until his last breath, just as he'd protected her after the crash, and a knot of jealousy formed behind her sternum. What would it be like to be his? She followed the curve of his neck to the point where his tattoos climbed to the base of his skull.

"You still want to touch them, don't you?" he asked.

How had he known? The pressure of his attention gave her pause, and a prickling sensation spread into her face. She didn't know what to say, didn't know how to explain the compulsion to touch him. Not the Blackhawk Security investigator he presented to the world but the man he'd been before that, the one he kept hidden under sarcastic remarks, secrets and banter. She wanted to touch the cop who'd almost died in a fire in the middle of a crime scene so he could find the truth.

His seat protested over the high-pitched drone of the engines as he shifted forward, close, so close. Dark brown eyes steadied on her, and the hairs on the back of her neck stood on end. "All right, Freckles, as soon as we're safe, I'm all yours."

Chapter 10

He'd meant every word on the plane.

Shouldering his duffel up the eight stairs off Herkimer Street, Vincent hit the four-digit code into the keypad beside the large black double doors leading into the safe house and motioned Shea inside. Instincts on alert, he scanned down both ends of the street. Her fresh scent chased back the smell of recycled air, diesel and humidity as she maneuvered past him, but he couldn't pay it much attention now that they'd finally made it to New York. Grillo was dead, but that didn't mean he and Shea hadn't been flagged by the rest of his organization when they'd landed. The brownstone Blackhawk's founder and CEO had secured them for the next two days had to have cost the firm well over Vincent's yearly salary, but in this situation, no amount of money was too much to keep his partner safe.

Windows positioned only at the front and the back of the property, military-grade security system installed by Blackhawk specialists, closed-circuit surveillance at the front and back doors recording every car that passed, every face that came within ten feet of the door. The place was located less than ten blocks from the safe house Anthony Harris and Bennett Spencer had secured for Shea's son. He'd made her a promise, and Vincent didn't intend to back down. He'd get her to Wells.

She slid her backpack—the same one that'd saved their lives in the wilderness—from her shoulder, but still clutched the worn strap as she studied the house. The front entryway led into a massive living room with pale hardwood floors and an extravagant old fireplace repainted white, with the entire upper half of the wall made of worn red brick. Gold-and-white art had been hung on either side of the fireplace, attempting to bring the hundred-year-old building into this decade, but there was a physical history to these houses. Vincent heard it in the way the floor creaked as Shea moved toward the turquoise couch positioned at one end of the living room, saw the dust that'd built up on the higher rows of bricks along the wall. Sunlight pierced the floor-to-ceiling glass doors at the back of the house, just beyond the modern white kitchen, making the green of her eyes somehow brighter. In that moment, the bruises faded, the color in her cheeks returned, and shadows under her eyes disappeared. She made broken look beautiful, and he couldn't look away. "This is a safe house?"

He nodded toward the alarm panel set behind him off one side of the entry doors. "We did the security work for the owner a few months ago. When I briefed the team about the case, Sullivan reached out to see if he'd be willing to let us rent the house for a couple days. Guess they came to an arrangement."

"It's beautiful." She skimmed long fingers over the railing of the banister leading up to the second floor. Notching her chin over one shoulder, she refused to meet his gaze. "And the security system—"

"We'll be safe here." He'd make sure of it. Vincent closed the small space between them, his boots echoing from the combination of hardwood flooring and the open concept architecture of the home. He dropped the duffel at his feet. Sliding his hand to her hips, he tugged her into his chest. Stress corded the tendons between her neck and shoulder as he traced his mouth along the outside of her ear, and she relaxed back into him. Ebbing pain spread from the bruises where he'd taken two to the chest, but he'd choose the discomfort over ending up six feet under. Pain had become his friend after the fire, his ally. It told him he wasn't dead yet. "I gave you my word, Shea. I'm not going to let anything happen to you or your son. I'm going to end this."

"No." She turned in his arms, her tired gaze locked on his. Dark hair fell in curls around her face, and he ached to run his hands through the strands to confirm they were as soft as he remembered. "We're in this together, remember? A team. Survive together or die alone."

"This isn't your fight." Grillo and his men had nearly killed her. He couldn't stand the thought of putting her life—her son's life—at risk again because he hadn't been careful enough, but letting her walk away, move on with her life… Vincent breathed in her sultry scent, held on to it, made it part of him, then let it go. He'd walk away to keep her safe, to help her get her life back. No matter what'd happened in the past or what that damn psych evaluation said, she deserved to be happy. With or without him. He spread his free hand over her arm, locking down the flood of desire rushing through him. "Elizabeth can get you and your son new identities. You could go anywhere you wanted, get as far away from this nightmare as possible. You'd be safe. They'd never be able to find you."

For her protection, neither would he.

Shea lowered her chin, and his heart jerked in his chest. Would she take him up on his offer? Would she disappear from his life? Reaching out, she intertwined her fingers with his, then looked up at him through long dark lashes. She pulled him toward the stairs leading to the second floor, her hair falling in waves over her back. Nervous energy pulsed down his spine as they climbed each stair, then exploded as she led them into the first bedroom on the second floor. The same pale hardwood ran along the length of the room with another wall of deep red brick wrapping one wall. The fireplace, similarly painted as the one downstairs, demanded attention near the queen-size bed, but Vincent only had awareness for her, for the hesitation in her expression as she faced him in the center of the big room. Her lips parted, her tongue swiping between them, and his insides jumped. "I'm safe with you."

Angling her head up, she stepped into him, fingers fisted into his T-shirt as she rose on her toes to reach him. Her soft mouth smoothed over his slowly, unsure, but after a few moments worked to claim every part of him. Faster, deeper, desperate. Her fingernails bit into the back of his neck, searing his skin, as though she intended to make them one, but he didn't pull away. Hints of mint toothpaste teased his senses, and goose bumps rose on the back of his neck. Hell, he couldn't get enough of her. She tasted of strength, stubbornness and vulnerability, and she was hiking his blood pressure higher with each stroke of her tongue against his. The bullet wound in his shoulder protested as he leveraged his free hand under her rib cage and lifted her against him.

She wrapped those powerful legs around his waist, easing the pressure in his arms, but he didn't give a damn about the pain. There was only her. Threading her fingers through his hair, she broke the kiss as he pressed her back against the brick wall surrounding the ornate fireplace. Her unsteady exhale skidded across his neck as she framed his jaw with one hand. Desire swirled in the jade-green depths of her eyes. "I'm glad you're here."

"Me, too." He toed off his boots, still holding on to her as best he could. Because there was no way in hell he was letting her go. Not now. Not ever. Stitches pulled tight in his right thigh, but there wasn't a damn thing that was going to stop him from memorizing every inch of her body. "Otherwise I might not be able to get this sling off myself."

"I can help with that." The sensual promise in her voice hit him square in the gut. With a brilliant smile, she straightened her legs, sliding along the length of him until she hit the floor.

She worked her fingers under the straps of his sling,

and within seconds, he was hauling the material and his T-shirt over his head. Her eyes widened as she took in the damage from the two bullets he'd caught in the vest, the bloodied gauze taped to his shoulder. But before he had the chance to tell her it was okay, that they didn't have to do this, her hands were on him. Heat tunneled down through his skin, into muscle, as she traced the patterns across his chest. "I don't want to hurt you."

Even if it means she's not in a position to love you back? Kate's words echoed through his mind. The truth was, Shea could hurt him. Worse than any fire, any bullet and any piece of shrapnel, but for the first time since Sullivan Bishop had found him in that warehouse with second-and third-degree burns over 30 percent of his back, Vincent was willing to take the risk. He didn't give a damn what some department shrink had written in her psych eval. They didn't know Shea like he did. He caught her hand in his, brought the tips of her fingers to his mouth. The lie came easily enough. "You couldn't ever hurt me, Freckles."

"What makes you so sure?" she asked.

He slid his hand into the waterfall of hair above her ear. Hell, it was just as soft as before, maybe even more so, but he saw past that beauty to the steel underneath, to the woman who'd risked her life for a chance to save his, the woman who'd suffered so much, yet kept putting others' needs ahead of her own. "Because you protect people. I know you'd never hurt anyone if you could help it. Not even me."

He offered her his hand, as she had downstairs, and maneuvered her through the bathroom door to their left. He hit the light, out of patience to notice anything other than the wall of glass housing a large open shower. In seconds, he twisted the rain shower head on and stripped them both bare as steam filled the space, being careful of her wound. Leading her beneath the spray, Vincent reveled in the feel of her skin against his. Hot water seared his skull and seeped into his wounds, but it was nothing compared to the sensations her hands generated as she traced the pattern of scars on his back. He claimed her mouth again, sweeping his tongue past the seam of her lips, memorizing her, making her part of him. Making them one.

She hadn't been intimate with anyone since her divorce. Not until Vincent.

She could still smell him on her, the hint of soap and man that somehow had been driven deep into her pores. Shea shifted in the passenger seat of the rental SUV as the memories of those delirium-inducing hours played across her mind. After their shower, they'd managed to make it to the bed, and she'd lost herself in him, in pleasure, in escape, to the point she hadn't been able to tell her fantasies from reality. There'd only been him. He'd been all male, full of power he barely contained as he'd pushed her entire body into overdrive. His touch had awakened feelings and sensations she'd lost to the darkness of her depression. Within just a few hours, everything had returned to full color.

They'd talked, laughed, learned about each other. She'd listened as he recounted the night of the fire, how Blackhawk's founder had found him barely breathing and gotten him the help he'd needed. How Sullivan Bishop had recruited him to the firm and promised to help Vincent find the people who'd lit the match. She'd opened up about her brother's death, how she'd become a cop to keep the blood running blue in her family. How she'd crossed oceans for people her entire life who hadn't ever considered crossing a bridge for her, people like her ex. She'd drifted off to sleep sometime in the afternoon, wrapped in his arms. Wrapped in safety. Shea cut her gaze to him in the driver's seat, her breathing steady despite the pain in her side. She hadn't felt that kind of peace in a long time.

Now they were parked outside the warehouse where it'd all begun. The murder scene of IAB Officer Ashton Walter and the two technicians Vincent had lost the night of the fire remained eerily quiet, nothing but her rhythmic pulse soft at the base of her throat. Dim street lighting revealed graffiti painted across boarded windows and doors. A strip of yellow crime scene tape lifted from the pavement in front of one of the rolltop doors with the breeze. Burn patterns darkened the perimeter of the second-floor windows at one end of the warehouse, and her insides clenched. All too easily, she imagined Vincent at the center of an entire building threatening to come down on him at any moment, the flames closing in, the pain. All because he'd been doing his job. If it hadn't been for the man who'd become his boss, would Vincent have made it out alive? She didn't want to think about the answer.

"No movement." Nothing to suggest they were walking into an ambush, but they weren't going to move into position until they were absolutely sure Grillo's organization hadn't been doing their own surveillance. Sliding her hand over his, she studied his hardened expression. "Are you sure you want to do this?"

"I have to. It's the only way to uncover the truth." In her next breath, he reached into the back seat for the pair of bolt cutters and a borrowed forensic case and shouldered out of the SUV. He hit the pavement, and she followed close on his heels.

Shea scanned both ends of the street lined with warehouses, parked cars and strobing fluorescent lighting from worn signage. The district played host to a variety of industries, mostly industrial with lots stretching as far back as the East River like this one. Easier access for deliveries from the docks. Jogging across the street, she followed him to the east side of the building and pressed her back against the cinder blocks while he cut through a padlock located beneath the warning sticker NYPD had sealed against the door. Her instincts told her they should've looped in local authorities, but then again, the men who'd attacked her and Vincent in the mountains had been local authorities. They couldn't trust the police. And if she couldn't trust the very people who were supposed to protect innocent lives, she didn't know who to trust anymore. Except Vincent.

"Got it." The door hinged inward, nothing but darkness and the scent of burnt toast and gasoline on the other side. With a glance toward her, he nodded once before his mountainous outline disappeared inside.

Shea retrieved the flashlight from her jacket and brought the beam to life before unholstering the weapon Vincent had given her back at the safe house. The hairs on the back of her neck stood on end as she shuffled through debris, broken glass and puddles of rain water that'd come through the leaking roof. The small amount of research she'd done on that night reported it'd taken NYFD close to six hours to extinguish the fire. An accelerant had been used, officials narrowing it down to gasoline, which explained the slight burn in her nostrils. She tried breathing through her mouth, focusing on Vincent's outline, and pushed ahead to a cleared section of ashes. Dread collected in the pit of her stomach. Every inch of the floor had been covered in debris, except for the two body-sized areas here. Was this where EMTs had found Vincent's team?

"Over here." His voice echoed off what was left of the aluminum roofing, intense, isolated, and warning slid up her spine.

She found him crouched over a similar cleared section of ash, her beam highlighting the tension in the muscles down his back. Winter in New York City wasn't quite as frigid as Anchorage, but the cold still worked through her clothing and into her bones. Her breath solidified into crystalized puffs in front of her mouth as she redirected the flashlight beam to the floor—and froze. "That's a bullet casing." Warped from the looks of it. At least old enough to blend into the landscape of ash, dried blood and dirt. She wouldn't have recognized the casing for what it was unless she'd been looking in that exact spot for evidence. She scanned the area around the casing but couldn't see more than a few feet in circumference. "Hard to believe the techs or the fire department managed to miss something like that after the fire. They would've had investigators all over this place."

"Without having access to my lab, my guess is the

casing is about the same age as the fire. This one is nearly melted into the floor." The sound of plastic over gravel shot her heart into her throat as he slid his forensic case closer and popped the lock. He snapped latex gloves over his hands and peeled an evidence bag from the roll in his kit. Carefully, he collected the casing from the floor and dropped it into the bag, and she couldn't help but watch every move he made. This was what he'd been trained for. He was in his element here, intense, focused, alert, and she couldn't help but admire his attention to detail. "But the casing over there is newer." Vincent redirected his flashlight a few feet from where he crouched, highlighting the metallic shell. "Both were shot from a .38 Smith & Wesson. Same caliber the medical examiner recovered from Ashton Walter's body."

Two casings. Two different time lines. "You think the people who killed that IAB officer might've kept using this location to carry out their executions?" On one hand, that theory made sense. FDNY and NYPD had condemned the building after the fire, making it impossible for another business to occupy the space, which gave an organization of corrupt cops the exact opportunity they needed to carry on with business as usual. On the other hand, using the same location where they'd committed their previous crimes could be considered careless. "I don't see a man like Grillo leaving evidence behind for us to find."

"No." He studied the first casing in the glow of his flashlight. "In my experience, cops make the best criminals." Shifting his gaze to her, he straightened and pocketed the evidence bag. He directed his flashlight to the second piece of evidence. "They know how to clean up after themselves, which means someone could've left this beauty behind on purpose, or the shooter has gotten too comfortable with their overloaded sense of power and figured no one would be able to connect the evidence to them if it was recovered."

Warning screamed through her.

"But Grillo knew you hadn't dropped the case. He knew you'd come back to this scene if he didn't stop you." Shea spun on her heel and swung her weapon high as movement registered from the door they'd broken through. She backed up a few steps, instinctively maneuvering herself in front of Vincent. Her shoulder brushed against his arm, and she lowered her voice. "The casing could be a distraction to keep us here."

"It's a trap." Vincent wrapped his uninjured hand around her arm and tugged her back. Her foot collided with a metal bracket, the scrape of steel and concrete loud in her ears. Exactly what the people who'd followed them would need to locate them. Staticed voices echoed through the shadows. "Follow me. Stay low and use me as a shield if you have to."

"We can't leave the other casing here. It's evidence." She reached for the shell.

Vincent pulled her into his chest and shoved her forward before she had a chance to collect the evidence. "We don't have time."

She switched off her flashlight to conceal their position, gripping the gun in her hand tighter. Before her eyes had a chance to adjust, Vincent was pulling her deeper into the warehouse, her hand enveloped in his. Shouts pierced the sound of her shallow breathing, then a gunshot overhead. She ducked low while trying to keep pace with Vincent, heart in her throat as they ran through the maze of debris and structural damage. How could've Grillo's organization known they were here?

Glass shattered to her right a split second before a bright burst of light and an ear-piercing boom threw her off her balance, but Vincent fought to keep her upright and moving. "I've got you. Just keep going."

Smoke filled her lungs as they raced to the back of the property. There were more flashes, more explosions from behind. The muscles in her legs burned. They couldn't go back to the SUV. If the same people who'd sent Grillo had been surveilling the building all this time, there was a chance they'd already flagged the plates and were waiting to follow her and Vincent back to the safe house. They couldn't risk it. They'd have to escape on foot.

Vincent released her hand, then lowered his uninjured shoulder as he rammed into the only door at the back of the warehouse. But it wouldn't budge. He tried again. Nothing.

The door had to have been padlocked, like the one they'd come through at the front. The voices were getting closer, the smoke from the stun grenades thinning. Shea raised her weapon, bracing one leg slightly behind her as she'd been trained, her weight on the balls of her feet. The windows back here were boarded, nothing but burnt cinder blocks surrounding them. There was nowhere else to go, and she wasn't sure she had enough rounds to take on another team of corrupt cops. Her breath rushed out of her. "Vincent…"

The door swung open, and Shea twisted around to follow him out. Only someone was blocking the door.

Two shots. Three. The bullets ripped past her left arm almost in slow motion before embedding into two gunmen who'd broken through the layer of smoke. They both went down, and Shea turned to confront the woman with the gun.

"Hello, Vincent." Long blonde hair draped over the woman's shoulder as she lowered her weapon to reveal a stark face and bright blue eyes. "I told you this case would get you killed."

Chapter 11

"Officer Shea Ramsey, Anchorage PD, meet Lieutenant Lara Richards, my former commanding officer." The last person he'd ever expected to see. Vincent pressed his back against the cold countertop in the kitchen of their safe house. They'd barely made it out of the warehouse alive. Wouldn't have if it weren't for Lara, but he didn't believe in coincidence. Grillo's people hadn't been the only ones watching that location.

"Nice to meet you." Shea stretched out her hand with a nod, shook Lara's hand and stepped back. "Not sure we would've gotten out of the building if it weren't for you."

Lara's bright blue gaze studied Shea. At well over five foot ten, with lengthy, model-like features, perfectly straight teeth and lithe movements, Lara Richards had done their forensics unit proud for the nine years she'd been his commanding officer. With her help, his team had an 85 percent closure rate. They'd closed so many cases—new and cold—she was being considered for a captain's position at the Eleventh at the time he'd left the squad. Vincent had even considered taking her job once she made the move. Until she'd shut down his theory IAB Officer Ashton Walter's murderer had come from law enforcement. She'd warned him to drop the case, said his personal investigation into who shot Officer Walter would get him killed. She hadn't been wrong. After the fire, Sullivan Bishop had gotten him out of town so fast, he didn't have the chance to prove his theory to her. Now here she stood. "Can't say I was there by coincidence. I've been watching one of the officers who was at the warehouse tonight for the past few months. Ever since I heard about what happened to Vincent here the night of the fire." Lara turned her attention back to him. "You're lucky to be alive."

Wasn't the first time someone had said those words to him. "What are you doing here, Lara?"

"For starters, I wanted to apologize. I should've listened when you originally came to me about the four unsolved homicides over a year ago. If I had, maybe I wouldn't have lost three of my best investigators that night." She pulled her shoulders back, the lighting from overhead shifting across her leather jacket. She lowered her chin toward her chest, eyes downcast to the purse she'd set on the counter. Pulling a tablet from within, she swiped her fingers across the screen, then handed it to him. "But maybe I can make up for that now."

"What's this?" He scanned the documents on the screen. Case files. The four files he'd been assigned to investigate. Shea stepped into his side, her light scent in his lungs, and just like that, he fell into the memories of her body wrapped around his between the sheets. She'd trusted him for those short few hours, given him a part of herself she hadn't given to anyone since her divorce. He'd never forget that, never forget the glimpse of unfiltered happiness he'd witnessed as they memorized every inch of each other's bodies. He'd never seen anything more beautiful than when she'd smiled at him afterward. His back tingled in remembrance, the feel of her nails tracing patterns across his scars fresh. Unlike the other women he'd been with, she hadn't turned away from him in disgust or refused to look at the damage. If anything, she'd been drawn to it, as though she understood the physical and mental pain he carried.

"After you disappeared, I went back through your files and dug these out of cold cases. In your notes, you'd reported all four scenes had been cleaned by a professional, maybe someone in law enforcement or with forensic training." Lara crossed her arms over her chest, sinking in on herself as she leaned against the countertop. "You couldn't find any connection between the victims other than the first two, an investigative reporter for a local paper and her assistant." Her heels clicked on the tile as she rounded the island, and she swiped her finger across the tablet's screen in his hand. "The third victim was a public defender, and the last a rookie barely out of the academy more than two months. All four victims were shot with a .38 caliber, matching most of the NYPD's service weapons, and I think they were all killed for trying to uncover the truth."

"That's the same caliber of the casing we recovered

from the warehouse," Shea said. "So you know there's a group of corrupt cops growing within the NYPD?"

"Yes." The weight of Lara's gaze pinned him in place, and she swiped her finger across the screen once more. "And I have proof. Like I said, I've been following one of the men from the warehouse for a few months now. I was able to clone his phone to see who he's been contacting, surveil his email, access his photos, everything. It seems the NYPD is aware of the group's existence and what they've been doing, but it's impossible to identify members of the organization or bring charges against them without raising suspicion. Any threat to the organization, like these four victims, is dealt with in-house. And they're good at what they do."

Vincent understood that better than most. "Brass has to be involved then. There's no way an entity like this could cover their asses so thoroughly unless they had upper management running the show."

"You might be right," Lara said.

"What have you been able to recover from the officer you're following?" Shea took the tablet, long fingers scrolling through the evidence his former commanding officer had gathered. "Anything we can use to expose the organization and what they've been doing?"

Lara straightened. "As far as I can tell, he's low on the totem pole, more like an errand boy. He and a partner hit up small-business owners for protection money, deliver and collect shipments, surveil and photograph targets. Guys like this follow orders, even the ones that involve executions like your four victims here." She stopped Shea from swiping to the next screen. "And those orders? They're all coming from one source. Officer Charlie Grillo."

Shea's soft exhale filled his ears, and it took everything in him not to bring her into his arms. Looking at the face of the man who'd threatened to kill her son, who'd almost killed her, was bound to cause a reaction, but now wasn't the time to forget why they'd come to New York in the first place. "Grillo came after us in Alaska. He brought down our plane, tried to kill us because Vincent ran the fingerprint he recovered from the death scene of that IAB officer through IAFIS. Ashton Walter."

"You think Walter was another victim who got too close?" Lara asked.

"I went to IAB after you refused to run my theory up the chain of command, and Grillo's people killed him for it. Then the bastards tried to kill me." Dread pooled at the bottom of his stomach as he studied the SOB's service record. Vincent had seen the original homicide crime scene photos before, but now, knowing who might be behind the killings, his blood pressure spiked higher. He could've stopped this, could've done something to keep these dirty cops from endangering innocent lives sooner. Like their pilot, like Shea and her family, his team. Vincent tried to keep the emotion out of his voice. It'd be easy to pin everything that'd happened up until now on Officer Charlie Grillo. There was just one problem. "Grillo was a beat cop. Hard to believe he had the power to keep an entire organization in line on his own, let alone convince his superiors to look the other way. Someone else—someone with a lot more authority—has to be pulling the strings now that Grillo's dead."

"If there is, I haven't been able to prove it." Lara shifted her weight between both feet, her expression never changing. "The two men who came after you tonight have been sitting on that building for a while. My guess is they were waiting for you. There's a chance they don't know their boss is dead yet. Could've just been following orders."

Or the real head of the organization was waiting to finish the job Grillo had started.

"You said you recovered a casing from the warehouse where I found you?" Lara asked.

"Haven't gotten the chance to run testing on it yet, but it could be exactly what we need to bring these bastards down." Vincent wrapped his hand around the warped bullet casing recovered from the warehouse inside his jacket pocket. He'd left his forensic kit back at the scene once the bullets started flying, along with the second piece of evidence, but his instincts said this casing was more important than being simply used as a distraction. He needed to get it analyzed. "But without access to the NYPD's labs, I'll need my team to run the tests, and that's only going to put the rest of them in danger."

"I can get you access," Lara said.

Shea's sharp gasp hiked his pulse higher, and she closed the distance between herself and the counter, shoving the tablet at Lara, and every cell in his body woke with battle-ready tension. "This photo… Where did you get this photo?"

"I don't…" His former commanding officer's mouth

parted slightly, obviously taken aback by Shea's panic. "I don't know. Maybe from the officer's phone I've been surveilling. I didn't see how it was relevant to the case, so I... I buried it in the back of the file until I had more time to identify the subjects."

Vincent spun the tablet toward him. The photo had been taken with a phone, nothing fancy, but clear enough for him to recognize Anthony Harris, Bennett Spencer, Logan Ramsey, Logan's new wife and Shea's son. Wells. "We can identify them." He shifted his attention to Shea, watched the color drain from her face. She stumbled back a few steps, but he caught her in time before she hit the opposite counter. Bringing her into his side for stability, he leveled his attention on Lara. "The location, too."

Damn it. The second safe house had been compromised. Shea's family was still in danger. He tapped the information button on the screen to check the time the surveillance photo had been taken, but it didn't look like the image had originated from the officer's phone. It'd been sent to him. Three hours ago. Right as he and Shea had arrived on scene at the warehouse. Gravity pulled at him. Shea had been right. Grillo's people had been counting on him to return to the warehouse, left the fresh bullet casing as a distraction to keep them occupied. So the bastards could follow through with their threat.

"Call them." Shea's voice shook as she stared up at him. "Now."

"What's going on?" Lara studied the photo, confusion evident in her expression. "Who are these people?"

Vincent didn't answer, punching in Anthony's cell

number, and brought the phone to his ear. One ring. Two. Before voice mail. Desperation climbed across his chest, into his wound. He dialed Bennett's phone next.

No answer.

The fog was back.

Her pulse thudded loud behind her ears, the floor pulling at every muscle she owned. Everything seemed to move in slow motion. Three hours. Three hours since they'd gotten confirmation the safe house where Wells had been secured had been raided. Three hours her son had been out there, alone, in the hands of killers.

Blackhawk operatives moved around the house, re-laying orders, taking both Logan's and his new wife's statements as they patched head lacerations and checked their cognitive reflexes, more men and women trying to get a location for her son. Light from a laptop screen illuminated Elizabeth Dawson's face as she reviewed hours upon hours of traffic camera footage. Elliot Dunham, Blackhawk's private investigator, had never looked more serious than he did right then huddled over Elizabeth's shoulder. Sullivan Bishop checked and inventoried weapons as he barked orders at the rest of his team. Even Kate Monroe, the psychologist, had caught the next plane to New York, her green gaze steady on Shea, but she wasn't in the mood to talk about her feelings, about what was going through her head. She wanted her son back. Anthony Harris, the operative assigned to protect Wells, was still missing, along with Bennett Spencer. The entire Blackhawk Security team had rallied with a single call from Vincent.

Shea didn't recognize the other agents. Didn't care.

The safe house had been secure. How had Grillo's organization found her son? Her ears rang, and she pressed the tips of her fingers to her temples in an attempt to drown out the horde of bees buzzing in her head. Wells was supposed to be safe.

"Shea." Vincent crouched in front of her. His warm hands slid up her thighs for balance, but she couldn't focus on him. Not even with him this close. "I need to know what's going through your head right now."

"I should've been there." The words left her mouth without any inflection, a mere ghost of the numbness clawing through her insides, and she winced against the effect. Sliding her gaze to his, she felt as though she were standing on the edge of the cliff. All it would take was one tug, one slip, and she'd lose everything all over again. "I should've protected him."

He shook his head as though to tell her there was nothing she could've done. "We had two of our best operatives assigned to protect him—"

"Then how the hell did this happen?" Anger exploded through her, sharp, hot and unfiltered. Shea pushed to her feet, forcing him to back up a few steps, and slammed her hands against his chest. Then again. Heat seared from her scalp down to her toes, and she gave in to it because it was better than feeling nothing at all. "How did they get to my son, Vincent? I want to know!"

He didn't answer. Only took everything she had to give and more, absorbing each hit as tears burned in her eyes. Wrapping his arms around her, he fought to contain her, to comfort her, but it wasn't any use. She'd failed her son. Again. Vincent tugged her into his chest as the sobs tore through her until she stilled, her ear pressed against his heart. He tangled his hands down through her hair, his cheek pressing against the crown of her head. "Whoever's behind this—whoever sent Grillo—they're trained just as well as we are, they're armed, and they've already proven the law doesn't apply to them." Silence descended in the house, but she didn't dare open her eyes, didn't want to see how many people were watching them. "But I told you Blackhawk protects their own, no matter what it takes, and we're going to get your son back."

She forced her eyes open, nails biting into his chest.

Every single operative in the room stood around them, frozen. Then the ice she'd felt for the team she'd resented for so long started to melt. Elizabeth stood up from her laptop and nodded. Elliot Dunham half saluted with that sarcastic grin she'd come to hate over the course of the past two years. Vincent's former commanding officer took position beside Elizabeth, and Kate Monroe smiled as Sullivan Bishop approached with a gun in his hand. Sea-blue eyes steadied on her. "When someone attacks one of us, they attack all of us, Officer Ramsey. And we're not going to let them get away with it. You're not alone in this fight." He studied the team behind him, then turned back to her. "You never will be again."

A fresh wave of tears threatened to fall, but Shea forced herself to straighten, to wipe the back of her hand across her face. To do what it'd taken her so long to do the first time: accept help. With the entire Blackhawk Security team on her side, the last people she ever would've asked for help, her confidence grew. They were going to get her son back. "Thank you."

"I want a location on Anthony and Bennett in the next minute, Liz, or I'm going to partner you with Elliot to hunt them down on foot." Another nod from Sullivan ended the conversation, and his agents got back to work. He shifted his attention to Vincent. "Get this woman a gun."

The buzz in her head died as Vincent pulled a weapon from his lower back and offered it to her, but she didn't dare meet his gaze when her fingers brushed his. He'd always viewed her as a strong, driven, independent woman, but her weakness had just rushed front and center for everyone to see. She cleared her throat as she checked the weapon. "Did Logan and his wife say anything that will give us a lead on who took Wells? Or how Grillo's organization found him in the first place?"

"Last thing Anthony reported back was his intention to move your family to another location because he'd spotted the same man walking past the safe house three times within a couple hours. From what Logan and his wife stated, Anthony left the safe house after telling them to lock the doors behind him, and that's when the explosion happened. A car bomb right outside the building. It happened so fast, Bennett hadn't been able to enable the security system before they breached the safe house." His hand remained on her lower back, steadying, comforting, but nothing could chase back the fear boiling under her skin. "With Anthony out of the way, he wasn't able to hold off the four-man team as they went for Wells. They were outnumbered and outgunned."

She couldn't breathe. Couldn't think. Shea closed her eyes against the images in her head, her fingernails biting into the center of her palms. Setting her forehead against his chest, she listened to the beat of his heart in an attempt to escape the desperation spreading through her. Fire and police were on scene at the safe house, but without the location of her son, there was nothing they could do. "And there hasn't been any contact from the team that took him."

"No, but…" Vincent's hesitation took on physical form when he didn't elaborate.

The tension only increased as she looked up at him. Living through the numbness over the past year had been the worst experience of her life. She didn't want to fall back into that cloud of darkness. She wanted to be there for her son, to be the mother he deserved, to feel like the woman Vincent believed her to be. But if she lost Wells… "But what?"

"I need you to understand something, Shea. Anthony and Bennett are two of the best-trained operatives we have. Both served in the military and never would've given up Wells easily, even under torture. Anthony's got a kid of his own and one on the way, and Bennett risked everything to find his sister when she went missing." Pressure built in her chest the longer he stared down at her. "The only way they would've backed down was if the gunmen threatened to hurt your son."

She pulled back as the truth hit. "They're using Wells to draw me out."

"You're not just a loose end anymore, Shea." His uninjured hand slid along her forearms, eliciting goose bumps along the way. "Whoever's behind this is targeting you because they know how I feel about you, and they will use any means necessary to take me out."

The breath rushed out of her, heat flaring in her face. "How you feel about me?"

He closed the small distance between them.

"I lost everything that night. After I recovered from the burns, I couldn't trust anyone with what I knew for fear it'd put their lives in danger, which only isolated me more from the people around me, including my team. I was at the point of giving up on this investigation, of living with this guilt for the rest of my life because there was nothing else I could do. Not without risking more innocent lives." Vincent wrapped her hand in his. "Until I met you. You're the reason I want to solve this case, Shea. Working with you these past few months, getting to know the woman who wouldn't back down from any challenge in her way, gave me the push I needed to see this through. Because if I don't solve this case, I don't have a future. And I want a future, Shea. With you."

He did? Her mouth parted, her response on the tip of her tongue. "I—"

"Vincent." Elizabeth's voice penetrated above the buzz of voices and chaos around them. "I've got something."

The world sped up, throwing her back into the present, back into the safe house filled with Blackhawk operatives and Vincent's former commanding officer doing everything in their power to recover her son. Had Elizabeth found a location? Shea pulled out of his grip, heading straight for the network analyst, but couldn't ignore the rush of pleasure rolling through her. He wanted a future with her. "What do you have?"

"Since Lieutenant Richards has been tracking these guys for a few months, she's helped me narrow down a list of possible locations the organization might be using as stash houses." Elizabeth spun the laptop toward Shea as Vincent stepped in beside her. The picture zoomed out to show a map of the city with five circles pinned across the screen.

"Each of these locations has been used as a drop point for the cash and drugs Grillo's runners collect off the streets. Runners go in with the goods, come out empty-handed." Lara tapped each one on the screen. "There's a chance your son is being held in one of these sites."

They had a lead. Her heart threatened to beat out of her chest, pent-up energy telling her she had to go after him now.

"Then we split up." Vincent took the weapon his former commanding officer offered over the table. "And we don't stop searching until we find him."

Chapter 12

Shea's strength didn't come from how much she could handle. It came from how she'd survived after she'd already been broken.

Hell, he'd watched her crumble right in front of his eyes, and there hadn't been a damn thing he could do about it but hold her, but she'd held her head high. Only now the cracks had started to show through. She stared out the back passenger-side window as he studied her from the SUV's rearview mirror, a line of tears in her eyes. She hadn't spoken a word since they'd left the safe house, her expression neutral. She'd thrown those invisible walls he'd worked so hard to tear down back into place the minute they'd gotten into the vehicle.

"This is it." Lara Richards pointed to the dominating shadow of the abandoned power plant on the shore of the Hudson River as the sun rose to the east. Two massive smokestacks demanded attention as his former CO shouldered out of the vehicle. Abandoned since 1963, the Glenwood power plant would make the perfect location for Grillo's organization to operate from, but every window from this vantage point remained dark. No sign of fresh tire tracks as he hit the dirt. Nothing to suggest they had the right location, but Vincent wasn't about to give up. Not with Wells's life at stake. Graffiti covered the original red bricks of the building and boards nailed against the windows. "I followed one of Grillo's men here about two weeks ago. He went inside with a fresh stack of cash for a few minutes then came back out empty-handed."

"He didn't notice you were tailing him?" Hard to believe, seeing as how there was nothing but open water, hills of dirt and rock, and few places she could take cover, but it was possible her suspect had only been focused on making the drop. Shipping containers cut off sight lines to one side of the structure. They'd have to go around to access the main entrance. The odor of river algae and something toxic burned his nostrils as he rounded the front of the SUV. His pulse hiked higher as Shea did the same, and he slowed. She hadn't given him an answer—hadn't said anything—since he'd laid it all on the line back at the safe house. They'd risked their lives for each other out there in the wilderness, trusted each other. In a matter of days, she'd become the single most important connection he had to the world, and she'd deserved to know. If she didn't feel the same—if she couldn't because of her past... His stomach jerked. No. He couldn't think about that right now. Getting to Wells. That was all that mattered.

"Must've been in a hurry." Lara hiked her hands to her hips, showing off the Smith & Wesson holstered under her jacket. "Guy never even looked my way before he fishtailed out of here like a bat out of hell."

Dirt kicked up around Shea as she bolted around the sand hill straight ahead of them and disappeared behind a grass-green shipping container.

"Shea, wait!" Vincent ran after her, the wound in his thigh protesting with every step. Dust dived deep into his lungs as he raced to catch up with her, but it was too late. She'd already gained a substantial distance on him, not even looking back toward him as she ripped open the door to the plant. Footsteps pounded behind him as he pumped his legs harder. Lara. They hadn't had time to do a proper perimeter search, to evaluate the risk, to clear the area. Shea could be walking into the middle of a—

The explosion knocked him back with the force of a brick wall headed straight for him at seventy miles an hour. Air crushed from his lungs as the fire and debris engulfed the door where she'd gone inside in an instant. He slammed into the dirt, rolling head over heels, as the all-too-familiar feeling of fire lanced across his exposed skin. A high-pitch ringing filled his ears. He fought to cough up the dirt stuck in his throat and locked his jaw against the pain as he rolled onto his back. Black smoke filled his vision, and the ringing grew louder. Twisting his head back over his shoulder, he searched for her. No. Not her. Vincent put every last bit of strength he had left into getting to his feet. He stumbled forward and hit the dirt again. "Shea!"

Her name growled from his mouth.

The bastards must've known they were coming,

must've rigged the explosion to trigger once the door was opened. "Shea!"

"Vincent!" His name barely made it through the ringing in his ears. Lara Richards covered her mouth with one hand as she stumbled toward him coughing. Caked with dirt, her normally blonde hair had darkened considerably, the blood from the laceration across her forehead staining the strands red. She clutched him, nearly tugging him to the ground. He had to get her back to the car. His former CO was alive because she'd been far enough back from the epicenter of the explosion. But Shea... He searched the massive hole blown into the side of the building. Had she been lucky enough?

He fisted Lara's leather jacket, dragging her to safety. The bullet hole in his shoulder screamed for relief, but he couldn't focus on that right now. Shea. He had to get to Shea. He deposited Lara near their vehicle. Turning back toward the plant, he forced one foot in front of the other. Fire climbed the boarded windows, scarring the bricks of the plant. He raised his uninjured hand to block the heat of the flames from his face. Images of that night—memories—lanced across his brain. The pain, the smell of gasoline, the screams of his team echoing around him. He physically shook his head to shove them into the box he'd kept stored at the back of his mind for so long, but there were too many similarities. The people responsible, the abandoned building. Only this time it wasn't his team in danger. It was his partner, and he wasn't going to lose her. He couldn't. Her son couldn't. "Shea!"

Still no answer.

The high-pitched keening in his ears subsided with

every step gained. Ornate brick fell in chunks at the edges of the hole the device had ripped into the side of the building where the door used to be. Humidity hit him in a wave as he hiked through the opening, loose rubble threatening to trip him up. Pools of water and garbage lined the vast atrium that used to hold the plant's turbines. Windows above created a cathedral-like feeling, trapping smoke against the glass. A steel girder fell from the second floor, and Vincent flinched as the combination of metal on cement vibrated through him. She had to be here. There were no other options. Not for him. "Answer me, Freckles."

Another sound broke over the crackling of fire, and he spun around to narrow it to the source. Had it been her? Brick and remnants of the large wooden door she'd gone through piled against the southern wall after the blast, and he vaulted over the mass in order to sift through the rubble. His heart launched into his throat as he spotted a single ash-covered hand among the debris. There. "Shea." Tearing his sling from his injured shoulder, Vincent groaned against the pain as he worked to clear the debris from on top of her. He didn't care how much damage he caused to the muscles and tissues in his arm. He'd take a hundred more bullets if it meant getting to her in time. "Almost there, baby. Hang on."

"Vincent." Her voice came from behind, and every cell in his body awoke with awareness. He twisted around to find her standing at the opposite side of the atrium. Ash clung to her pale skin, eyes shadowed, but there she stood. Unharmed. Alive. But if she'd gotten enough distance between her and the explosion, who had he been trying to unbury from beneath the rubble?

She stepped forward, reaching for him as he maneuvered around the piles of rock and steel to get to her. Relief coursed through him as she buried her head against his chest, his fingers threaded into her hair. She shook her head. "He's not here."

"It's going to be okay. We're going to find him. I promise." He'd already deduced that fact after the effects of the explosion had cleared from his head. Whoever'd taken Wells wouldn't risk harming him until they got what they wanted. Her. In order to hurt him. Pushing her back, he searched her for fresh blood, injuries, anything that contradicted the fact she was standing here, unharmed, after the blast. "How did you get clear from the explosion so fast?"

"It doesn't matter." Her watery green gaze, brighter when surrounded by dark ash and dirt, shifted to the body beneath the rubble. In an instant, she slid her attention back to him, her hand pressed flat over his heart. "Wells is still out there somewhere, and I need to find him." She leaned her cheek into his palm, closing her eyes. "But after what just happened, after everything that's happened over the past few days, you should know I…" His beard bristled as she opened her eyes and trailed a path down toward his chin with one hand, his nerve endings burning. "I want a future with you, too."

His heart skipped a beat. "Really?"

"Yeah." Her nod was all the confirmation he needed. Shea pushed her hair from her face, that brilliant smile tunneling through the nightmare of the last four days and straight into his core. His wounds, the organization they were up against, the case he hadn't been able to solve for over a year, none of it mattered. This, right here. She mattered. There wasn't anything he wouldn't give for her. "I was lost, for a really long time, but working with you on the joint cases these past few months has been the most frustrating and exciting time in my life." Nervous energy played across her expression. "There's something I need to tell you before we decide to give whatever this is between us a chance."

"Shea." He smoothed the pad of his thumb beneath her eyes, ash and dirt smearing across her soft skin. "I don't care what's in your psych eval. I told you before. There's nothing you can do or say to convince me you're not the woman I've gotten to know over these last few months."

Surprise contorted her expression, and she stepped out of his hold. Her mouth parted, eyes narrowing at the edges, and Vincent realized his mistake. Too late. "What did you just say?"

Vincent had access to her department psych eval? No. Not possible. That information was privileged. In order for him to get his hands on it…

"Blackhawk Security got a copy of my eval." The words left her mouth no louder than a whisper, her voice hollow. "They wanted insurance the officers you'd be working with during the joint investigations were trustworthy or mentally stable, right? Even though all that information falls under doctor-patient confidentiality." The blood drained from her face, gravity pulling her body toward the ash-covered floor. She'd managed to avoid getting blown up after charging through the front door. She'd spotted the explosives around the doorframe

and pulled Grillo's man in front of her as a shield before
the blast, but right now she felt as though the organization that'd kidnapped her son—that'd tried to kill her—
had succeeded. Her stomach soured, bile working up her
throat. She shook her head to dislodge the truth. "But
this is the kind of thing Blackhawk does, isn't it? You
and your team skirt the law when it suits you. Anything
to solve the case. Everyone else be damned."

Including her. What had Sullivan Bishop said back
at the safe house? That she was one of them, that they
protected one another? Rage burned hot and fast in her
veins. They protected one another, all right, but she'd
never been part of their team. She'd been a resource, an
access point in which to collaborate with Anchorage PD
and evaluate sensitive information for investigations.
Nothing more. But what hurt more? Vincent had been
an integral part the entire time.

"Everything you said is true. Our psychologist vetted
the officers we recruited for the task force with the department's permission in case one of our investigations
went sideways." He tried to close the distance between
them, but she countered his every step. A combination
of hurt and surprise contorted his expression, but she
didn't have the energy or the motivation to let it affect
her. Not anymore. He dropped his shoulders away from
his ears, almost as though in defeat. "Yours was one of
the evaluations, but Shea, I swear I never read your file."

"I don't believe you. I know exactly the kind of lengths
you and your team will go to to get what you want, Vincent. Why should this be any different?" If he hadn't read
that file, he wouldn't have known about the one thing
that'd kept her from giving herself over to him fully,

that'd resurrected her fear of him walking away every time she'd wanted to tell him the truth. Smoke burned her nostrils, sweat building at the base of her spine as the embers continued to consume the plant. Everything inside her ached, head pounding in rhythm to her pulse. She'd trusted him, had started to imagine a future with him, believed him when he'd said he'd never turn his back on her. He'd taken that trust and used it against her. Same as her ex-husband had when she'd found him in bed with his assistant, just before he'd walked away with her son. Same as her family and friends had before deciding she wasn't worthy of their help or love. "Was that why you requested me as your partner all those months ago? Because you thought you could use my mental health in order to leverage me to cooperate?"

He took another step toward her, but this time she held her ground. "What? No. I would never—"

"Don't lie to me." She wouldn't let him see how much it hurt. Instead, Shea gave in to the familiar explosion of rage she'd tried to keep locked away. Anything to help her sever the connection they'd forged over the last few days, to keep herself from admitting how hard she'd fallen for him. The muscles in her jaw ached as she steadied her gaze on his. "How long have you known?"

"I had an idea of what you'd been struggling with that night in the ranger station. You kept trying to convince me you weren't the woman I thought you were, and I didn't want to believe you. Nothing you said lined up with what I saw during our joint investigations." Vincent's voice deepened, his throat working to swallow. "But Kate confirmed it in the hospital when she confronted me about how I feel about you. She said you might not ever be in a position to love me back."

Shock of his admission rolled through her, but she did everything she could to make sure her expression didn't change. He loved her. But that wouldn't alter the fact that she couldn't trust him—or his team—ever again. Her fingernails bit into her palms as loss tore her apart from the inside, a distraction to keep the tears at bay. She'd wasted enough time. Wells was still out there. Alone. Afraid. Clearing her throat, Shea kept her head high when all she wanted to do was sink onto the floor as the power plant collapsed around her. She stepped into him, ignoring the rush of heat his body elicited inside, and drove her hand into his jacket pocket to extract the SUV's keys. She clutched them harder than necessary, forcing herself to stay in the moment, then looked up at him. "Kate was right. I won't ever be in a position to love you, Vincent. Not as long as I can't trust you."

"Shea, don't do this." He locked his hand around her arm. "If you go after Wells alone, they're going to kill you, and I won't be there to stop them. Please. Let us help you find him."

"I've always been alone." That'd been a truth she'd accepted until she'd crash-landed in the middle of the Alaskan wilderness with a forensic technician who'd given her a glimpse of real happiness. But as she'd come to realize too late, it'd been a fantasy all along. She ripped her arm out of his grip, her skin burning where he'd touched her. "Grillo gave me the chance to walk away, and as soon as I recover my son, I'm taking it. I'm sure your team can give you a ride back and help you bring down his organization without me."

Shea maneuvered around him and headed for the hole blasted into the side of the power plant. Tendrils of fire climbed around the edges but not hot enough or dangerous enough to stop her from escaping. The weight of his attention on her back crushed the air from her lungs. The tears fell then, but she wouldn't turn back. There was nothing to go back to. Wrenching the SUV's door open, she caught sight of him positioned where the door she'd gone through used to stand. Heat waves distorted his features, his intensity burning hotter than the flames around him. It must've been difficult for him to charge into that fiery building for her after what'd he'd already been through, but right now, she couldn't let herself care. She climbed inside the vehicle and hit the button to start the engine. Dirt kicked up behind the SUV as she sped from the scene, entirely focused on the road. Elizabeth had messaged them a list of all of the stash houses the network analyst and Lieutenant Lara Richards had narrowed in on as part of Grillo's operation. She'd hit every single location until she found her son.

Lieutenant Richards… Shea hadn't seen Vincent's former CO since she'd breached the power plant. Lifting her foot from the accelerator, she let the SUV slow to a crawl before turning onto the main road that'd take her to the next location. Had there been another operative stationed at the power plant, one who could've gotten to Lara while Vincent had torn Shea's heart from her chest? She hesitated at the thought of turning back around, of facing the man who'd betrayed her after what'd just happened, but Lara deserved better. The lieutenant had helped them every step of the way with the investigation, handed them leads Blackhawk Security wouldn't have been able to find, offered to run testing on the casing she and Vincent had recovered from the warehouse...

Shea stepped on the brakes, her weight shifting forward as the SUV skidded to a stop. Leather protested under her hands as she tightened her grip on the steering wheel. Lara Richards had been at the warehouse last night, arriving within moments of Grillo's men closing in, and shot two corrupt officers with a .38 Smith & Wesson without hesitation. So why hadn't NYPD dispatched homicide detectives or IAB investigators to get her and Vincent's statements about what'd happened? Why hadn't Lara called it in?

Lara's weapon was standard issue for the NYPD, and the lieutenant had admitted to taking a keen interest in the organization's movements over the last few months. To the point she seemed to know more about Grillo's crew than the NYPD did. What if her involvement in the case was more than an attempt to make up for turning her back on Vincent before the fire? He'd theorized the killer who'd shot the four original victims and the IAB officer must've had forensic experience. As a lieutenant, Lara Richards would have authority over Grillo. She could've ordered him and his team to bring down her and Vincent's plane, to take care of loose ends.

Shea swallowed around the tightness in her throat. Only problem was everything running through her head right now would be viewed as circumstantial evidence, but if she was right, Lara Richards had means, opportunity and motive to take out both her and Vincent.

She had to go back. She had to at least explain the possibility to Vincent. Slamming the SUV into Reverse,

Shea hooked her arm around the passenger-side head-rest. And gasped.

"Hello, Officer Ramsey." Cold metal pressed against her temple as Lieutenant Lara Richards straightened from the second row of seats. Dirt was caked to her leather jacket and jeans, the collar of her white T-shirt underneath crusted with blood from the wound across her forehead. Blonde hair slid over her shoulder as she leaned in closer, close enough for Shea to catch hints of smoke and perfume. "Hand over your sidearm, please."

Her breath sawed in and out of her chest. She shifted her attention to the weapon Vincent had given her back at the safe house, fingers tingling. Could she get to it fast enough? "I should've seen it sooner. You're not investigating Grillo's organization. You *are* Grillo's organization."

"This isn't how or when I wanted to reveal myself, but you and Vincent just wouldn't leave well enough alone. Not even after I tried to have you killed." Lara reached over Shea's shoulder, unholstering the weapon herself, before setting it on the back seat beside her. "No one has gotten as close as you and Vincent. I'd normally take care of the problem myself, as I did with all the others, including IAB Officer Walter, but you have something I want."

The casing. Lara was trying to clean up her own mess. "And you have my son."

"I'll make you a deal." Lieutenant Richards pushed the barrel into Shea's temple, breaking skin. "You tell me where Vincent is keeping the casing he recovered from the warehouse last night, and I'll let you see your son again."

Chapter 13

He didn't know how he was going to win her back, but he sure as hell was wasn't going to lose her. Vincent stepped away from the nearest explosive device, gun in his uninjured hand. Blocks of C-4 had been wired to detonate when triggered above every door and window of the plant. But as far as he could tell, this location had never been used as a stash house or a place Grillo's organization would use to hold a nine-month-old boy hostage. Warning settled between his shoulder blades. One signal. That was all it would take to make it so the best medical examiner in the state couldn't identify his remains, but rigging one of their own places to blow didn't make sense.

Unless it'd been a setup from the beginning.

He bit back the curse on the tip of his tongue. Shea was out there on her own trying to track down her son.

He'd screwed up. Even if he hadn't read her department psych eval directly, he'd given her mistrust weight by not telling her his employer had access to it in the first place. She'd trusted him, and all he'd done was prove she was right about him, about his team. Sullivan Bishop had founded Blackhawk to take cases the police couldn't or wouldn't prioritize, asking his operatives to do whatever it took to protect the client. Including skirting the law as Shea had accused. Vincent had solved dozens of cases over the past year by living up to that standard. He'd made a difference he hadn't been able to as an NYPD officer, but in the end, the same principle that'd given him purpose—that had saved so many lives—had driven her away.

She deserved better. Better than him.

She'd survived the worst kind of mental torture he could imagine for a new mother to suffer through, but now, looking back, he understood it wasn't the fact that Blackhawk had access to her psych eval at all. Her desperation to fight for custody of her son, her determination to lose herself in her work, the walls she'd built to keep everyone out. It was all part of the fear that everyone would know—that he would know—how weak, worthless, she'd convinced herself she'd become. But Vincent knew the truth.

Underneath that fear of failure, past her invisible defenses and the guarded expressions, there was a woman who'd never backed down from a challenge, even when she'd lost everything that mattered to her. She was charming, intelligent, authentic and gracious and had more ambition than anyone he'd come across. She wasn't weak. She wasn't worthless. She was everything he'd ever wanted, everything he'd needed to keep him going these past few months. She was…the woman he needed in his life.

She'd brought out the best in him, kept him from isolating himself even further, from losing all contact with the people he cared about in the name of protection. By working at his side, she'd kept him in reality when all he'd focused on the past year was the case that'd almost gotten him killed. He loved her. And it didn't matter if she couldn't love him back. He owed her his life. That would be enough for him.

Vincent moved farther along the atrium floor, kicking rubble and garbage out of his way. Scaffolding lined the walls, an impressive collection of cogs courtesy of the Philadelphia Alfred Box & Co. The crane demanded attention from above, rust and buildup clear from thirty feet below. Grillo's organization might not be holding Wells here, but the officers involved had been here. They'd rigged every entrance and exit with explosives and left a man behind to detonate. It was Locard's principle. Everyone left a piece of themselves behind and took something with them from a crime scene. Fingerprints, fibers, DNA evidence. Which meant there had to be something here.

This was what he'd been trained to do. Search for the evidence, analyze the scene, find the suspect. He cleared a set of stairs leading up to the second level but slowed. "Evidence."

Holstering his weapon, he pulled the warped casing he'd collected from the warehouse from his jacket pocket. Sunlight reflected off the bronze, even through the plastic evidence bag. He'd left his forensic kit back at the warehouse, but there were other ways to lift prints from evidence in the field. Vincent wound his way back into the atrium and out through a side door facing the Hudson. Collecting a handful of fine dirt, he settled on the edge of an old set of stairs that protested under his weight. A light breeze pushed his hair into his face, his throat burning from the instant drop in temperature. Perfect conditions.

He ripped the adhesive section from the evidence bag, keeping it close, but froze. The second he touched the casing without gloves, it'd be inadmissible in court. Whatever defense attorney would go to bat for these bastards could argue the evidence had been tampered with, and in a case like this, where a large part of the NYPD could possibly be linked to Grillo's organization and charged with a slew of felonies, he'd land behind bars right beside them.

Then again, he wasn't part of the NYPD anymore, and there was nothing he wouldn't do to protect Shea and her son.

He extracted the casing with his index finger and thumb, keeping contact with the metal to a minimum. His shoulder protested as he tried to grip the evidence, but this was the only way to prove what his instincts had been telling him since he and Shea had barely escaped with their lives from the warehouse last night. He picked up the dirt with his free hand and held it above the casing. Then let it go. The wind did exactly as he'd hoped, redirecting most of the sand away from the casing, but the few grains that'd made contact with the bronze clung tight to the oils that whoever'd handled the evidence had left behind. Fingerprint ridges formed in arcs, whorls and loops, but abruptly stopped at one edge as though the print was only a partial.

Just like the fingerprint he'd recovered from the gas can the night of the fire.

Whoever'd loaded this casing into their weapon's magazine and been at that scene the night he'd lost two teammates to the fire. Maybe had even lit the match. The smooth surface of the print on that side meant one thing: whoever'd started the fire that night in the warehouse had burned themselves badly enough they'd lost half of their fingerprint.

His own scars tingled as though remembering what that kind of pain had felt like, which was impossible. He'd lost feeling in almost all the nerve endings in over 30 percent of his injury site. Except when Shea had run her hands over his skin. Hell, he'd never meant to betray her trust. He had to get her back, had to prove he was the one person in this world she'd be able to count on.

But first, he had to bring down the organization Grillo worked for. Dropping the casing inside the evidence bag, he shoved it back into his pocket and retrieved his phone. Every rotation he forced his shoulder to make shot pins and needles down to his fingers, but nothing—not even a gunshot wound—would stop him from getting to Shea. He brought the phone to his ear, and the line connected. "Elizabeth, I need you to send me the location of my SUV and a replacement vehicle to the Glenwood power plant."

Making his way around the side of the building, toward where he'd parked their rental SUV, Vincent scanned the landscape. Where was Lara? He'd left her right here. He dropped the phone away from his ear and spun full circle. No movement. No body.

"Vincent?" Elizabeth's voice barely reached his ears over the rush of wind coming across the river, and he brought the phone back to his ear.

"Yeah, I'm here." Two sets of footprints led away from the plant, but he only recognized one of them belonging to Shea. Dark drops of blood peppered the second set. Had to be Lara. She'd suffered a laceration across her forehead after the explosion. From where the SUV's treads indented the ground, he traced her to the back passenger seat of the vehicle. Confusion rushed through him. Lara wouldn't climb into the back seat in order to catch a ride with Shea. She'd take the front. He gripped the bullet casing in his pocket, the muscles in his jaw ticking with his heartbeat. Something wasn't right. Shea had every reason to get the hell away from him, but Lara? She wouldn't have left him out here without a good reason. "Have you heard anything from Lieutenant Richards or Shea Ramsey?"

"Let me get this straight. You need a replacement SUV because yours suddenly went missing, and you lost both of the officers you took with you?" Keyboard strikes filtered through the line. "I think this is going to put a strain on the relationship Blackhawk has with law enforcement."

He searched the area again to make sure he hadn't missed anything, but there was no sign of either of them. "It's a long story."

"Only Sullivan has checked in. He recovered Bennett at one of the addresses Lieutenant Richards gave us for possible stash house locations," Elizabeth said.

"They did a number on him before leaving him to die, but he'll pull through. Autumn is flying in from Anchorage as we speak. Still waiting for Kate and Elliot to call with what they've found at the other two addresses I gave them."

Damn it. Which meant Anthony Harris was still out there. Without him, they might not be able to ID the bastards who'd taken Shea's son. He unclenched his hold from around the evidence bag. Unless... Vincent had already come into contact with the suspect. "I'm going to have to call you back."

He ended the call, studying the footprints in the dirt. Lara's wound hadn't been bad enough that she should've climbed into the back seat of the SUV. Pocketing his phone, he dropped to one knee, his shrapnel wound screaming in protest. He'd recovered the same print from both the gasoline can the night of the fire and the evidence from the warehouse. The suspect had been at both locations, but unless Grillo's organization had been surveilling the murder scene of that IAB officer, which was possible, no one in the NYPD had known Vincent and his teammates were investigating the case on their own. No one except their commanding officer. He scanned the property again. The lack of tire tracks, the explosives... They'd been lured to this location.

His stomach shot into his throat, and he unholstered his weapon with as little contact with the metal as possible. He'd gone to Lara with his theories over a year ago, but she'd shut him down despite the evidence he'd handed over. Solid evidence. Was it possible she hadn't been at the warehouse last night by chance? That'd she'd been waiting for him and Shea all along? That she'd been the one to send Grillo and his team to sabotage their plane? Vincent ran the same test on the barrel of his weapon as he had with the casing, the gun Lara had handed him back at the safe house. Once the dust had settled, the pieces of this murderous puzzle slammed into place. The second print, her middle finger. It was an exact visual match to the others he'd lifted.

Lieutenant Lara Richards was part of the organization bent on killing him.

"Damn it." She'd inserted herself in the investigation to stay a step ahead of them. Now she had Shea in the vehicle with her. He extracted his phone once again and hit redial. The line connected instantly. He didn't bother with small talk. He was running out of time to save the woman he loved and her son. "I know who kidnapped Shea's son, and I know where she's headed."

A groan slipped past her lips, waking her from a dreamless unconsciousness. How many times were people going to hit her over the head before her brain decided it'd had enough? Rolling onto her hands at the small of her back, Shea blinked up at the pattern of lights dancing over a white ceiling as the crevices in the floor rubbed against the newest addition to cuts on the back of her head. She'd been restrained in cuffs. Lara... The lieutenant had knocked her unconscious with the butt of her weapon. The floor jerked beneath her, and her entire body slid across the slick surface. Not a floor. The cargo space of a van. The pattern of lights on the ceiling was headlights from oncoming cars.

She struggled against gravity in order to sit up. Keeping out of sight of the rearview mirror in case the driver spotted her through the thick metal mesh separating the driver's cab from the cargo area, she leveraged her boots against one side of the van. She pressed her back against the other and positioned herself behind the driver's seat. She'd always kept a spare handcuff key in her back pocket. If she could reach it, she—

"I know you're awake, Officer Ramsey. I can hear the change in your breathing." That voice. No. It wasn't possible. She'd watched him sink to the bottom of that lake. "Looking for something?" Officer Charlie Grillo held up a set of handcuff keys for her to see. "As long as you're in those cuffs, I have the chance to pay you back for the damage you and your partner inflicted to my men."

"You couldn't kill me back in Alaska." Every instinct she owned screamed warning for her to get out of the van right then, but when she drove her hands into her back pockets, she only met denim. Shea searched for something—anything—she could use to pry her hands out of the cuffs or as a weapon, but the van had been emptied, presumably to keep her right where Grillo wanted her. She bit back the panic rising, forced herself to keep her voice even. "What makes you think this time will be any different?"

"Because no one is coming to save you this time, Shea." His use of her name—almost intimate—raised the hairs on the back of her neck. "I gave you the chance to walk away back in those woods. You should've taken it."

Those same words echoed in her mind as she thought back to her last moments with Vincent. He'd hurt her far more than Logan had when he'd left, almost as much as it'd hurt when she'd been served with custody papers for Wells. Blackhawk Security had knowingly gotten her psych eval without her knowledge and proven her assumptions about the way Vincent and his team worked. But the worst part? If she was being honest with herself, it wasn't the fact that they'd skirted the law. Vincent alone brought down almost a dozen corrupt cops in those woods to save her life without hesitation and promised to do whatever it took to bring her son home. She hadn't questioned the lengths he'd go to protect her for a single moment.

No. The worst part was he no longer saw her as the woman he'd convinced himself existed, the one she'd desperately wanted to be for him. Strong, full of passion, valuable to their joint investigations, determined, worthy of a man like him. Happy. He'd made her feel as though she had become the center of his entire world, but now that he knew the truth, that she couldn't measure up to the woman he may have built her up to be in his head, it'd be impossible to get that feeling back. No matter how many times he tried to convince himself otherwise, he couldn't love her. He didn't even know her. Not the real her.

The van slowed before taking the next turn, bringing her back into the moment. No windows. Nothing that could tell her where they were without exposing herself to the driver. She closed her eyes against the sudden nausea churning in her stomach. Grillo was supposed to be dead. She had to get out of here. She had to get to Wells. Setting the crown of her head back against the side of the van, she caught sight of wiring framed along the back doors leading into a junction box a few feet away. She forced herself to take a deep breath, then slowly pressed her hands into the floor behind her to scoot toward it. The wires most likely led to the van's brake lights and blinkers. If she could signal the drivers behind them, she might have a chance. She twisted her head toward the driver's cabin as she moved. "Where is my son?"

The moment she got free of these cuffs and escaped, she was going after him.

"Don't worry, Shea. Lieutenant Richards will take good care of your boy." Grillo took a sharp right, pressing her into the frame. "Little guys like that sell for a lot of money nowadays. Plenty of needy couples willing to pay top dollar for a chance at being parents. Think of it this way. We're doing you a favor. He'll have a good life, never knowing you weren't strong enough to take care of him yourself."

"What?" The floor felt as though it'd disappeared out from under her, and even after a few seconds, she couldn't regain her footing. They were going to put her son up for illegal adoption, and she'd never see him again. Blinking against the fog threatening to consume her, Shea pulled at the cuffs around her wrists until she drew blood. It trailed down the back of her hands, dripping from her fingertips. The pain forced her to focus. No. They weren't going to sell her son to the highest bidder. She'd fight for him until she couldn't stand. She'd sacrifice everything to get him back. Because she was strong enough, damn it.

Shea worked her palms beneath her glutes, ignoring the strain in her wrists until she was able to maneuver them to the backs of her thighs. In seconds, she threaded her feet through the hole her arms made and brought her hands to the front of her body. She slid to the breaker box beside the doors and pried it open. "You read my department psych eval."

She had to keep him talking, distracted.

"Part of the job. I've seen what depression has done to a few guys on the force. Most of them ate their guns at the end, leaving their families with nothing but debt and anger, but you didn't. That says something," he said. "You're a good cop, Ramsey. I think you would've done the NYPD proud given the chance. Unfortunately, we'll never find out if that's true."

The van slowed. Grillo was going to finish the job he'd started back in those woods. Tie up the loose end. Her.

Adrenaline dumped into her veins. Diving her hand into the mechanical box, she gripped a white metal lever that would cut power to the vehicle and pressed her feet against the doors as she pulled it back as hard as she could. The metal groaned loud in her ears, then snapped, and she fell back. She didn't have time to pick the lock on the cuffs. The best chance she had in getting to Wells in time was survival. And she'd do whatever it took. Her breathing shallowed as her nerves hiked into overdrive with awareness.

"What the hell?" Grillo hit the brakes.

Momentum threw her deeper into the van, and she slammed against the mesh separating the cargo area from the driver's cabin. He shouldered out of the driver's-side door. The handle. Where had she dropped the handle? She felt along the cold surface of the van's floor but couldn't find it anywhere. The back door was wrenched open, Grillo's dark outline taking up her only escape.

She didn't have time to think—only act.

Shea lunged, tackling her abductor head-on. She hit the dirt and forced him to roll with her but ended on her back with him hovering above. Thrusting her palms into the base of his throat, she knocked him off-balance, then swept the bastard off his feet with both legs, but he recovered faster than she thought possible as she struggled to her feet, still in cuffs. He aimed a fist directly at her face. She dodged the attempt to knock her out, and he launched forward. Hurtling her elbow into his spinal column, she shoved him with her entire body, and Grillo went down. She stood over him, ready to end this once and for all. "You're not taking my son from me."

"We already have, Officer Ramsey," a familiar voice said from behind.

Something hard struck the tendon between her neck and shoulder. She hit the ground, the sound of footsteps loud in her ears as she struggled to get her bearings. A pair of black heels moved into her vision.

"You weren't supposed to be part of this, Shea. So I'm going to give you one last chance before I have Grillo get rid of your body where not even the best forensic investigator in the country could find it." Lieutenant Lara Richards crouched beside her, her rich perfume surrounding her. Clean blonde hair skimmed Shea's face, no sign of blood from the cut on the lieutenant's head. No sign of the cut at all. Had it really been there or had Shea imagined it? Had anything been real? "Where is the casing Vincent recovered from the warehouse?"

Shea twisted her wrists inside the cuffs, halfway sitting up, but the wound in her side wouldn't let her do much more than that. "Go to hell."

A light laugh rolled off Lara's lips, her forearms crossing in front of her body as Grillo got to his feet behind her. "I can see why he likes you so much. You must've been one hell of an investigator to get Vincent's attention. I know how little he lets get to him when he's focused on solving a case." The lieutenant gripped Shea's chin between long fingers, and it took everything inside Shea not to pull away. "Pity for all that talent to go to waste. I could've used someone like you on my side." Lara straightened. "Get her inside. It's time to put an end to this."

Chapter 14

There was only one place this could end.

Vincent pressed his foot down on the accelerator, the momentum pinning him back into the seat. If he was right, Lieutenant Lara Richards wasn't just part of Grillo's organization. She *was* the organization. She'd turned cops into criminals, all while taking a cut along the way, and he hadn't seen it until it was too late. Now she had both Shea and Wells. If his former CO hurt either one of them… Vincent tightened his grip around the steering wheel until his knuckles turned white.

He redialed Shea's number for the tenth—or was it the eleventh?—time. She wasn't going to answer. Not if Lara had gotten to her, but he couldn't stop himself from trying again and again. The SUV's interior filled with her voice as the ringing cut to voice mail, and the tension in his hands drained. Streetlights blurred out the side windows as he sped through the city. "I'm not giving up on you, Freckles. Ever. If you don't believe anything I've said this far, I need you to believe that. I'll be seeing you soon."

He ended the call from the steering wheel and took the next left toward the waterfront. Rain peppered the windshield, the hint of humidity clarifying.

"Five minutes out. Everyone check comms." Sullivan Bishop's orders came through loud and clear from the device in Vincent's ear. The founder and CEO of Blackhawk Security hadn't spent much time in on assignment since proposing to his army prosecutor, Captain Jane Reise, but when it came to the safety of his own people, the former SEAL preferred the field over his massive oak desk.

"Monroe and… Monroe checking in," Kate said over the line, her husband's laugh reaching through the comms.

"Dunham's got your back." An engine growled in the background of Elliot Dunham's earpiece. As much as Vincent hated to admit it, he needed the private investigator's help to recover Shea. He needed all their help. He'd tried solving this case on his own for so long and gotten nowhere. Now he needed his team. "But I'd like to point out, Waylynn is making a bigger sacrifice than all of us by babysitting your demon spawn for this event."

"And there you go ruining the moment." Elizabeth laughed, parent to one of those demon spawn. "Dawson and Levitt checking in."

"Chase in position. I've got eyes on at least two dozen hostile NYPD officers positioned at the west and south sides of the warehouse." The echo of a rifle loading crackled over the channel. Former Criminal Investigation Command special agent Glennon Chase, Anthony Harris's pregnant wife, had jumped at the opportunity to bring down the organization responsible for taking her husband. And if there was one thing Vincent could be certain of tonight when it came to Glennon, she wouldn't fail. Her former partner, newest Blackhawk Security investigator Bennett Spencer, had already been left for dead. She wasn't going to lose anyone else. The woman had fought too long and too hard to keep her small family together.

They all had.

Vincent tapped the earpiece. "Kalani on location." One breath. Two. The weight of the situation settled under his rib cage. He pulled up beside another Blackhawk SUV on the north side of the warehouse and got out, gun in hand. Streetlights highlighted the dozens of officers and squad cars positioned between him and the woman he wanted to spend the rest of his life with. "I owe you guys one."

"I might just be speaking for myself, but we wouldn't mind some of your mom's cooking in exchange for our services," Elliot said.

"Elliot, one more word out of your mouth, and I'll revoke your firearms permit." Sullivan's warning ended the conversation as he climbed from his SUV and stepped to Vincent's side. The former SEAL had seen battle plenty of times and fought a war with his own brother to save his woman. Vincent wouldn't do any less. "You ready for this?"

Within thirty seconds, the rest of his team pulled

into the parking lot and took position, each armed and ready for the coming fight on either side of him. Eight Blackhawk operatives up against an entire organization of corrupt NYPD officers. At least two dozen cops studied them from across the street, in addition to the snipers Vincent had no doubt had centered his team in their crosshairs. No one was going to get out of this fight unharmed, but he wouldn't back down. Not this time, and not when it came to Shea and her son. Squaring his shoulders, he strengthened the hold on his weapon. "I am now."

"This is the NYPD," a staticky voice said over a megaphone from one of the patrol vehicles nearby. "Drop your weapons, get on your knees and put your hands behind your heads or we will be forced to take lethal action."

"I don't have a clear visual inside the warehouse. The windows have been boarded," Glennon said from one of the buildings east of their location into their earpieces. "No confirmation on the target's location or if the hostages are inside, but I do have a great view of the two snipers aiming their rifles directly at your heads."

Vincent tapped his earpiece. "No matter what happens, Glennon, I need you to get me inside that building."

"You got it," she said.

Stepping forward, he holstered his weapon. There still might be a way out of this that didn't include bloodshed. He shouted loud enough for his voice to carry across the street and dug the evidence bag from his pocket to put it on display. "I know you're in there, Lara, and I know what you want. Send out Shea and her son, and we can both walk away from this. Nobody else has to die."

"You expect me to believe you're willing to walk away from your little investigation once I hand them over?" The grouping of officers under her control cleared a path as Lieutenant Lara Richards stepped into view. Her laugh hiked his warning instincts into overdrive. She'd been a good cop once, a good commanding officer. What the hell had gone wrong? Or had he even really known her at all? Her wide smile vanished, that cold gaze steadying on his as she unholstered her service weapon and brought it to her side. "I know you, Vincent. I know what you're capable of, and that even if I let Officer Ramsey and her son go free, you'll never stop coming for me." She brought the gun up and aimed. "You're too good a cop."

"You set the fire that night." He tightened his grip on the evidence bag. "You killed two of your own men to try to cover up your operation."

"I warned you before you went to the warehouse that night this case was going to get you killed." She cocked her head to one side. "You should've listened to your CO."

"And the others? The journalist and her assistant, the rookie, the defense attorney and IAB Officer Walter. They were getting too close, right? They suspected your organization was turning the NYPD into nothing more than a hit squad for hire, and you couldn't let them find out the truth." Everything was starting to make sense. "You were willing to risk everything to keep yourself in power, but you made a mistake." He held up the casing discarded after Lara shooting Officer Walters center mass, and lines deepened around the edges of her eyes. He'd questioned the motive behind the shooter leaving evidence at the warehouse scene, but now it made perfect sense. It hadn't been used to keep him and Shea in that building longer after all. "You did the dirty work yourself, but you handed off the cleanup to someone else. And now it's going to cost you."

Lara lowered her weapon, closed her stance as she straightened. "Kill them and pry that casing from his cold, dead hand if you have to."

Gunfire exploded from inside the warehouse, the crack of thunder loud in his ears. Blood pooled in his lower body, cementing him in place. "Shea."

The first bullet sliced across the skin of Vincent's injured arm as Lara's men closed ranks around her. He took cover behind the driver's-side door of his SUV and pulled the trigger. The officer who'd shot at him hit the ground as the rest of the Blackhawk Security team took position and returned fire. Adrenaline coursed through him and sharpened his senses. He tapped his earpiece. "Glennon, get me inside that warehouse. Now."

"Snipers neutralized." The former CID special agent fired again. "I'll clear you a path between the first and second cruisers straight ahead of your position." The sound of rifle shots ricocheted off the surrounding buildings, and Glennon's targets collapsed. Lieutenant Richards's men shouted, crouching behind their vehicles as they searched the rooftops. One called into the radio strapped to his shoulder, but Vincent doubted the bastards would get an answer. "That's your cue, Kalani. I'll cover you until you're in the building. After that, you're on your own."

"Give 'em hell," Sullivan said. "We've got it handled out here."

"Copy that." Vincent pumped his legs as fast as he could as Glennon kept the path through the two head squad cars positioned in front of the main warehouse door clear. He jumped over an officer who'd collapsed to the pavement, then ducked to avoid the fist of another keen on keeping him from breaching the line. Swinging his elbow back, he slugged the SOB and kept running. Pain in his shoulder and thigh clawed for his attention, but the sound of those gunshots from inside pushed him harder. Fifteen feet. Ten. Another officer closing in hit the ground as Glennon kept her word to get him inside the warehouse. He slammed into the door, the rusted hinges detaching as the wood hit the wall behind it. Every nerve ending in his body caught fire as the scent of charred wood and ash filled his senses.

Gun raised, he hugged the east wall as he heel-toed it toward the area where he and Shea had recovered the bullet casing the night before. Muted gunfire from outside punched through the sound of his own breathing. His heart pounded hard at the base of his skull as he took cover behind a blackened stack of pallets. Craning his head around, he spotted his former CO. "Give it up, Lara. There's nowhere to run."

"Run?" Lara fired at him, splinters of wood exploding over his right shoulder. The growl of an engine filled the warehouse, and he chanced another look around the pallets. Brake lights darkened Lara's outline behind her. "I built this organization from the ground up, Vincent. I'm not going anywhere, but I can't say the same for Shea and her son."

* * *

"It's okay, baby. I've got you." Shea leaned against Wells as much as she could as she tugged at the cuffs around her wrists. His soft hair tickled the underside of her throat. She set her cheek against his head as his screams filled the back of the van. She couldn't hold him. Not with her hands cuffed to the anchor above her head, and everything inside her screamed that if she could get him into her arms, he'd be okay. They'd both be okay. The sound of gunfire was giving him anxiety, and the fact that he'd been ripped away from her ex-husband wasn't helping. Who Lara's men were fighting off, she had no idea. The police who hadn't bought into the lieutenant's ideals? Blackhawk Security? Vincent?

The cuffs cut deeper into her skin as she used her feet to reach for the diaper bag Grillo had thrown into the back of the van before slamming the door in her face, but she had to push the pain to the back of her mind. The canvas slid across the van's floor easily but fell to one side and spilled its contents. His pacifier tumbled from the bag. She pinched it between both boots and brought her knees into her chest to drop it beside him. He clutched it in his tiny hand and brought it to his mouth, but his tears hadn't dried. "I'm going to get us out of here. I promise."

The driver's-side door slammed shut, and Grillo started the van's engine.

No. Sitting up, she tried twisting around to see out the windshield, but the angle only made the cuffs cut into her deeper. The gunfire outside had thinned. No more than a few shots here and there. Had Lara's organization succeeded? Shea kissed the top of Wells's head as the van lurched forward. She caught sight of the white metal handle she'd pried loose before Grillo had brought her to the warehouse. He hadn't seen it when he'd thrown the diaper bag in, and she straightened. "Where are we going?"

No answer.

A bullet dented a section of the van's back door. Wells's cries pierced the ringing in her ears again, and she tried to bring him in closer but couldn't reach him. She had to get out of these cuffs. Someone was still out there, and she found herself wishing it was Vincent. He'd risked his own life for hers. He'd given her a glimpse of real happiness, their cases taking so many layers of hurt and fear away that'd built over the last year. He'd shown her what real strength looked like, and that she could be the woman he'd imagined her being if she only believed it was possible. She wasn't ready to give that up. She wasn't ready to give him up. "Grillo, where are we going?"

"I've got my orders, Ramsey." Darkness fell over the inside of the van as they passed through the warehouse's rolltop door at the north side of the property. The side that faced the water. "And no one is coming to save you or the boy this time."

"What do you mean?" Panic rose in a hot rush. She kicked at the van floor, but her heels only slipped along the surface. "You said you were going to have him adopted. That he'd get to live out the rest of his life with a new family."

"Change of plans," he said, the weight of his responsibility in his words. "Boss doesn't want any evidence left to come back to haunt her."

"No." She pulled at the cuffs as hard as she could, biting back her scream as the metal ripped across her skin. She turned around toward him. "Please, don't do this. Please. You can have me but let him go. He doesn't deserve any of this. He's just a baby—"

The driver's-side door flew open, a rush of salt-tinted air filling the van. Her hair flew in chaos around her face a split second before a hand reached in and pulled Grillo from the driver's seat. His scream was silenced as the van's back tires rolled over something solid. The officer's body? Vincent climbed behind the wheel and slammed his foot on the brakes. Her heart was full enough to burst.

"Vincent!" His tangled mass of hair penetrated through the mesh as he tried the brakes again, but the van didn't slow. Something was wrong, and her stomach sank. Realization hit. Oh, no. "Vincent…"

"Bastard cut the brake lines and disabled the button to take the van out of cruise control. Looks like he was going to ditch the vehicle on the way to the water." He hit the brakes again, a sea of blackness growing closer over his shoulder out through the windshield. They couldn't swerve surrounded by rows and rows of steel girders, couldn't stop without putting everyone in the van at risk. Vincent half spun toward her. "Shea, I'm going to need you and Wells to brace for impact."

"No! I can't protect him with my hands in the cuffs." Her heart launched into her throat as reality set in. Closing her eyes, she accepted the truth of the situation. He wouldn't have enough time to save them both. Shea set her head back against the metal mesh, then turned her attention to her son. She committed everything about him to memory in the matter of seconds, the way his hair smelled, his big green eyes that matched hers, how his thumbs never properly straightened. Logan would have to make sure the doctor took a look at them when he was older. "I love you. No matter what your dad tells you or what you find out on your own when you get older, please remember that. You're everything, and I will always watch over you."

Calm settled over her then, not the numbness she'd become accustomed to, but something lighter, warmer. These past few days with Vincent had done that. Because of him and the word they'd done together, she knew her son would grow up happy and healthy. The man she loved would keep Wells safe.

Leaning down, she kissed Wells one last time and raised her voice loud enough for Vincent to hear. "When we started working those cases together, it was like I'd been pulled out from beneath a crushing wave. Our investigations were the only thing that got me out of bed most days, but if I'm being honest with myself, part of it was you, too. I wanted to see you, to be around you. When you requested me to work on the task force, you helped get me through the worst year of my life, Vincent. I don't know how, but I know I'll never be able to thank you for that. And it seems unfair for me to ask anything more of you, but, please. You have to get him out of here. Save my son."

Wells's cries filled the inside of the van once again, and she couldn't fight back the tears as the weight of what she was asking drilled straight through her. She was asking him to make the choice to save Wells's life over hers.

"I'm not leaving you. We're all going to walk away from this." Shadowed brown eyes lifted to the rearview mirror. "I give you my word."

"You're good at keeping your word. That's why I know you'll do this for me." The tears fell then, and the pressure that'd been building for so long released. She'd fought like hell to gain some semblance of the woman she'd been before giving birth to her son, but because of Vincent, because of the work they did, she realized she wasn't that woman anymore. She was more self-assured and stronger than ever. And she'd give anything to have her son grow up knowing his mother loved him as much as she did. "I know you'll protect him."

Vincent's voice overwhelmed the drone of the van's engine. They were running out of time. The dock was coming up so fast. "Shea, what are you—"

She braced herself against the oncoming pain before breaking her right thumb. Her scream filled the cabin, scaring Wells into another round of tears, but she pushed past her urge to comfort him to do the same to her other hand. This time, she bit back the groan and slipped her hands free of the cuffs. Sweeping the metal handle she'd detached from the van's breaker box in to her hand, she wedged it down into the small space between the mesh and the driver's seat and pushed as much of her weight into it as she could. The metal gave way, but not enough to get her son to Vincent. She inserted her uninjured fingers into the slots and pulled with everything she had left. The bolts around the edges of the mesh held tightly to the van's frame, but she'd created a hole big enough to get Wells through. Scooping her son into her arms, she kissed him one last time then handed him off, his small fingers sliding against her palm. "Get him out of here."

The van jerked up over the beginning of the dock. "Shea—"

"Go," she said. "Now!"

"I'm coming back for you." Vincent wedged the driver's-side door open with his foot, those brown eyes she'd loved so much steady on her. In her next breath, he jumped from the vehicle with her son in his arms.

She clutched the metal mesh as she watched her partner and Wells disappear beneath the surface of the water in the van's side mirror. Then she was flying. A sea of black consumed the windshield as the vehicle launched itself over the end of the dock. The impact slammed her against the divider, her fingers automatically tightening in the slots as the cabin slowly filled with water. Her head ached where her face had met metal, slowing her reaction time. She'd saved her son and told Vincent the truth. He'd changed her life, helped her heal in more ways than she could imagine. Wells would know she fought for him and become the mother he'd deserved from the beginning. That was all that mattered.

Murky water seeped through the mesh, and Shea forced herself to stand. She had maybe another two—three—minutes before her remaining oxygen escaped the cargo area, but she wasn't ready to die. Not yet. The van hadn't sunk entirely yet. There was still a chance she could escape. She stared straight up at the back doors of the van. The slick surface and her broken thumbs would make it hard to climb, but as Vincent had made abundantly clear, she'd never backed down from a challenge. Least of all given up. "You can do this."

Wiping her wet hands down her jeans, she used the wheel wells of the back tires for leverage. The water soaked her ankles now and was only filling the van faster. Her boot slipped off the wheel well, threatening to pull her back into the water, but she held on to a bracket that made up the frame of the vehicle with everything she had. Her feet dangled below her, the water climbing higher now. She just had to get to the back doors.

A hard thud reverberated down through the frame, and she forced her head up as one back door of the van swung open. Strong, familiar hands wrapped around her wrists, and she couldn't help but trust he'd carry her weight. Just as he always had. "I told you. We survive together."

Chapter 15

Vincent pulled her from the water after their short swim to shore, careful of her broken thumbs, and into his chest. Red and blue patrol lights swept across her features as she steadied herself on the end of the dock. Long hair trailed over her shoulders as she studied the scene behind him. Sullivan, Kate, Elizabeth, Elliot and Glennon watched her and Vincent's backs as a fresh wave of NYPD officers closed in on the scene, Wells safely held in Elizabeth's arms. In an instant, she stepped out of his hold and reached for her son. The boy was all too eager to see his mother again, a giant four-toothed smile crinkling the edges of his eyes as he reached right back for her. Vincent had protected him as best he could when they'd hit the water, determined to keep his promise to Shea, but that was when his team had arrived. With their help, he'd gotten to her before the van submerged. He could've lost her forever if it hadn't been for the support of the men and women around them.

"Thank you," she said to the team.

Sullivan nodded. "Like I said, we protect our own, Officer Ramsey, and Vincent has made it clear that list includes you."

"Damn right it does." Wrapping one arm around her waist, he reveled in the feel of her body pressed against his, in the strong beat of her heart in her chest. Wells tugged on his beard with another gut-wrenching smile—his mother's smile—and laughed. Not even fazed from their short dive into the river. Vincent couldn't resist the wrap of the little guy's fingers around his thumb. "It's over, Shea. We don't have to run anymore."

"I wouldn't be here without you, without any of you." She turned toward Glennon with Wells wiggling in her arms. Smoothing her hand over his nearly bald head, she readjusted her hold on him with a wince, and Vincent couldn't help but smile at the idea of her being so affectionate with their own babies. If that was what she wanted. After everything she'd been through the past year, hell, even the past five days, he'd understand her hesitation to have another kid…or six. But there were more ways to have children than getting pregnant, and he couldn't wait to see her in action. "But what about Anthony? Were you able to find him?"

Glennon's smile broke through the tension of possibly losing one of the best, most-trusted members of the Blackhawk Security team. "Why don't you see for yourself?"

They piled into Vincent's SUV, Shea and Wells beside him in the back seat. Because there was no way he was going to let either of them go. Not now. Not ever. She'd admitted she'd loved him seconds before the worst moment of his life—watching the van launch off the end of the dock into the river. And he loved her. If Shea gave them the chance, he'd spend the rest of his life ensuring they were happy, and that no one would take them from him again. He slipped his arm around her, bringing both her and Wells into his protective hold. Jade-green eyes raised to his as she relaxed her head back against him, and everything inside him heated.

"Did Grillo…survive?" She stared up at him, the slightest quake in her voice.

"Paramedics didn't get to him in time." But Vincent couldn't gather any sympathy for the bastard. Officer Charlie Grillo had tried to kill the woman he wanted to spend the rest of his life with, along with her son and his team. The NYPD would be better off without a man like him in their ranks. "He'll never touch you again. No one will."

Sullivan maneuvered the SUV back toward the warehouse where spotlights and a perimeter had been set up by NYPD. The low vibration of the engine through his body urged him to give in to the exhaustion of the past few days, to fall asleep with Shea in his arms, but he knew she'd spend the rest of her life looking over her shoulder if she couldn't confirm the nightmare had really ended. That was just the kind of woman and cop she was. The vehicle stopped beyond the officer rolling out crime-scene tape across the rolltop door where he'd watched Grillo escape with Shea and Wells in the van, and Vincent intertwined his fingers in hers. Tugging her from the vehicle, with Wells on her hip, he held the tape up for her to pass beneath, and they stepped back inside the warehouse where his entire life had changed course.

Orders echoed off the cinder block walls as Shea slowed, her attention focused on the woman in the middle of the room. Cuffed and on her knees, Lieutenant Lara Richards and a dozen surviving officers she'd recruited into her organization waited to be hauled back to the precinct. With Anthony Harris, aviator sunglasses and all, standing watch. "You found him."

"Lara had me pinned down behind those pallets over there while Grillo took off with you and Wells in the van." Vincent motioned to the stack, the memories of those few agonizing seconds where he'd given in to the fear of never seeing her again still so clear. He turned to her, fingers tracing a path over her wet clothing. Hell, he still couldn't believe she was here, standing in front of him as though he hadn't almost lost everything that'd mattered to him. "I didn't think I was going to make it to you in time. I was willing to do anything—and kill anyone—to get you back, but before I pulled the trigger, Anthony caught her by surprise. Without him…" Vincent steeled himself against the emotions rushing through him. "I don't know what I would've done if I'd lost you again, Freckles. I love you. I want to be with you, make babies with you, wake up beside you every morning, even if I have to compete with this guy. I will do anything it takes to keep you two safe." He framed her jaw with one hand. "I should've told you I had access to your department psych eval, but I promise you,

I will never keep anything from you again. If you'll just give us a chance. Please."

They were in the middle of a damn crime scene, officers collecting evidence and making arrests around them, but seeing as how that was exactly how he and Shea had met, the location for this conversation couldn't be more perfect.

"Vincent, I don't care about you or your team having access to that damn report. I was surprised, angry, and yeah, I felt betrayed you'd kept the truth from me, but…" Shea closed her eyes, spotlights deepened the shadows under her eyes, and his gut clenched. She shook her head, then lifted that beautiful green gaze to his. "I just… I wanted you to keep believing that I was the woman you admired back in that ranger station, the one you'd requested as your partner all those months ago, and I was worried once you discovered the truth, you wouldn't feel that way about me anymore. So many people have walked out of my life because they didn't understand what was wrong with me. I didn't want to lose you, too."

His heart pounded loud behind his ears. He tried to process her words, over and over in the span of a few short seconds, but shock still coursed through him. The pain in his leg and shoulder, the controlled chaos going on around them, it all disappeared. Until there was only her. Vincent threaded his fingers through her hair. "You're never going to lose me, Shea. I might not understand what you're going through, but I'll do whatever it takes to find out. I'm going to be there for you. I'll go to doctors' appointments, I'll watch Wells when you need a break, I'll cook for you and talk you through your cases. However you need me, I'll be there." He trailed a path down her forearm and slipped his hand into hers. "And if that means Kate was right, that you're not in a position to love me back, I'll respect that. I just want you to be happy."

"Really?" Tears welled in her lower lash line as he nodded. She swiped her tongue across her lips, and she dropped her attention to his T-shirt. A distraction. "You said you wanted to make babies with me, but I don't know if I can do that, Vincent. I don't think I can go through what happened to me after I had Wells again."

"I know," he said. "So we'll adopt if we decide we want those babies. We'll babysit Katrina and Hunter and Kate and Glennon's babies when they get here. We'll have Wells when he's not with Logan, and I will still be the happiest man on this planet because I'll be doing it all with you."

The shadows in her eyes dissipated, and his heart jerked in his chest. "Partners?"

"For the rest of our lives." He pushed wet hair behind her ear.

"That would make me happy." Stepping into him, she set her ear over his heart. Right where she belonged.

"Wells?" Logan Ramsey's voice penetrated through the bubble he and Shea had created in the middle of the crime scene, bringing them back to reality. Shea's ex-husband and his new wife pushed past the perimeter, but Anthony Harris cut them off before they got anywhere close. "Wells!"

"The court date." Her eyes widened, and she fisted his shirt with her unbroken fingers with one hand as she clutched her son with the other. "Vincent, I missed the custody hearing. Logan is going to make sure I never see Wells after this. He's going to take my son away. Maybe for good." Closing her eyes, she smoothed her lips against Wells's forehead, and a sudden calmness unlike anything he'd experienced came over her. She opened her eyes. "But I can't keep him from his father, either. I've lived through that, and I wouldn't wish it on anyone. Not even Logan." Shea maneuvered around him, but Vincent wasn't far behind. "It's okay, Anthony. I've got this."

Vincent nodded at the weapons expert in appreciation as arresting officers hauled Lieutenant Lara Richards to her feet. Blazing blue eyes locked on him before his former commanding officer—and what was left of her crew—was forced into the back of NYPD squad cars. Corruption of justice, murder, attempted murder. The district attorney was going to make himself a hell of a career out of this one. Reaching into his pocket, Vincent pulled the bullet casing he'd recovered and handed it off to one of the officers searching the scene. They were going to need it, and in a few months, Vincent would have to come back to New York City to testify. She'd gone after Shea, after her son, and nearly killed him. He'd make sure the lieutenant got everything coming her way. With Shea, his partner, at his side.

Vincent smoothed his hand across her lower back, but nothing would help her process her ex-husband's words any better. Not even him.

"What do you mean? I came all the way to New York for the hearing." The hollowness she'd fought back for so long threatened to consume her, and she could only hold on to Wells tighter. If this was another way for her ex-husband to get back at her, to punish her even more... "Now you're telling me you've already talked to the judge? Logan, please, I know things haven't been easy between us. I wasn't there when you both needed me, but we can work this out—"

"A team of armed men showed up at the house claiming they worked for some security company, told us we were in danger and whisked us away to a safe house, Shea. Then a bomb exploded in front of us, and a bunch of cops took our son out of my arms. They kidnapped him because of something you got him involved in." Logan Ramsey reached for Wells, and it took everything in her power to hold back. She'd meant what she'd said to Vincent. She wouldn't keep Wells from his father. Her son deserved better than that. He deserved to be happy, and if that meant she couldn't be involved in his life, she'd have to live with that. Logan's new wife slid her hand across his shoulders, and the tension seemed to drain out of the man she'd once planned on spending the rest of her life with. "But the men you sent to protect us, Bennett and Anthony, they told us what you did. They told us you were taking on an entire organization of corrupt police officers to make sure we would be safe. So yes, I talked to the judge about custody. Since I'm his legal guardian, I had him approve a new custody agreement while you were searching for our son." Logan pulled a white envelope from his inner jacket pocket and handed it to her. "It goes into effect immediately."

Her hand shook as she took the thick envelope. Vincent pulled her into his side, the only thing keeping her on her feet. She unfolded the documents, tried to read the small print, but it took a few tries before everything became clear. A flood of surprise rocketed through her, her knees threatening to collapse right out from under her. "You…" She looked up at her ex-husband for confirmation. "You're giving me equal custody?"

"After everything you've done for Wells, after hearing how far you went to protect him, I realized you're not the same woman you were when we left Anchorage. You've changed. You seem…better. Stronger than before." With a glance toward Vincent, Logan switched their son to his other arm and pulled his wife to his side. "I want Wells to grow up knowing both his parents love him. Even if they're not together. We want you to see him as much as you can. Here in New York or in Anchorage. We can work out the details later. I just needed you to know."

She couldn't think, couldn't breathe. Vincent's hand at her back warmed her straight to the core, and for the first time in so long she was…happy. She'd found love with the man who'd saved her life and had a strong future in line for her son. "Thank you."

With a final nod, Logan Ramsey, Wells and his wife were escorted toward a police cruiser that would most likely take them straight home. After living through the chaos of the last few days, she couldn't blame them for not sticking around. Every cell in her entire body wanted to collapse into bed and try to forget the feeling of almost losing her son, the panic. Of almost losing her partner.

"Let's get those thumbs looked at." Vincent led her toward one of the many ambulances parked outside the perimeter of the scene as police worked to clean up Lieutenant Richards's mess. Dozens of bodies littered the ground from an apparent shoot-out, but the Black-hawk Security team—Sullivan, Elizabeth, Kate, Elliot, Glennon, Anthony—looked as though they'd pulled through. Leaning against their vehicles, they watched as NYPD processed the scene.

Whatever they'd done, however many laws they'd broken in the process, she owed them her gratitude. She let EMTs examine her thumbs and the back of her head where Lara had struck her, all the while trying to keep Vincent from lunging when she groaned from them resetting the bones. As the investigating officers took their statements, Shea couldn't keep herself from touching him as he settled beside her on the back of the ambulance. Just as she'd done in that cave after their plane had gone down. She'd known then she'd fall for him, this intense, protective and thoughtful man. It was inevitable, but she had the feeling it wouldn't end here. It'd be the forever kind of fall. The investigating officer returned to processing his scene, and Shea rested her head against Vincent's shoulder.

"Well, we managed to bring down an entire organization of corrupt cops and solve five cold cases, Officer Ramsey. I'd say we make a pretty great team when we get along." His mouth pressed against the top of her head, his warm breath fighting to chase back the bone-deep cold of the river. He slid his hand up her throat and tipped her head back. He closed the distance between them and pressed his mouth to hers, and everything around them disappeared. The red and blue patrol lights, the fact that his team stood nearby, the crime scene techs. None of it mattered right then. He pulled back enough to speak against her lips. "So does this mean we get to keep working joint investigations together when we get back to Anchorage?"

She couldn't help but smile at the idea. He was right. They did make a great team, and she couldn't wait to see what kinds of investigations they'd be partnered on next. Over the course of the last few days he'd become more than her partner. He'd become her protector, her everything. "Not if it means spending nights in caves, outrunning avalanches or nearly drowning in the back of a van."

"I think we'll survive." Vincent's laugh rumbled through her before he kissed her again. "Somehow we always do."

* * * * *

Amazon bestselling author **Melinda Di Lorenzo** writes in her spare time—at soccer practices, when she should be doing laundry and in place of sleep. She lives on the beautiful West Coast of British Columbia, Canada, with her handsome husband and her noisy kids. When she's not writing, she can be found curled up with someone else's good book.

Books by Melinda Di Lorenzo

Harlequin Romantic Suspense

Worth the Risk
Last Chance Hero
Silent Rescue
First Responder on Call
Serial Escape
High-Stakes Bounty Hunter
The Negotiator
Cold Case Witness

Harlequin Intrigue

Trusting a Stranger

Harlequin Intrigue Noir

Deceptions and Desires
Pinups and Possibilities

Visit the Author Profile page
at Harlequin.com for more titles.

TRUSTING A STRANGER

Melinda Di Lorenzo

As always, I owe the deepest gratitude to my family. Without them, I would never have been able to add the title of "writer" to my list.

Prologue

Mike Ferguson crossed and uncrossed his legs, then crossed them again.

Even though the swanky hotel room was loaded with testosterone-fueled tension, the movement was the only indication that any of it affected him.

So far anyway.

Unflappable. It was a characteristic he valued above most others. A characteristic each of the two men in front of him lacked utterly.

The one with his meaty fingers around the other's neck…he was on edge. On *the* edge, maybe. He should've been calm. Self-assured. Those were the things that would make a man good at a job like his. Instead, he used ego and coercion tactics to get his way.

The one on his knees was just as bad. A blubbering mess. Or he would've been blubbering, if he'd been able

to do more than gurgle. Had he shown a little more fortitude, the first man would've released him long ago and
traded violence for a reasonable conversation.

Ferguson sighed.

Either way, both men were weak, as far as he was
concerned. An embarrassment to work with.

Ferguson cared so little about them that he couldn't
even be bothered with their names. Unfortunately, they
were a necessity for this particular issue. Because they
were also the only two men on the planet who knew
as much as Mike did about his activities. The only two
men who could implicate him for the one time in twenty
years that he'd lost his cool while trying to protect everything he'd worked so hard to achieve.

"You think you found Mike Ferguson," the first man
growled at the second. "What were you going to do
about it? Turn me in?"

Gurgle, gurgle.

"Or were you going to tell our mutual friend and
let *him* turn Mike in? Or maybe just skip the preamble
and kill me?"

Gurgle, gurgle, gurgle.

"Fat chance you'd get to that badly disguised weapon
of yours before my palm crushed your trachea."

Gurgle.

Ferguson was tired of the theatrics.

"Drop him." The command came out as if he was
talking to a dog about a bone and, truthfully, it was kind
of the way he saw them.

Beta dog. And even *more* beta dog.

The presently dominant one flexed his hand once
more, then released the submissive one to the ground.

"You know I'd never turn him in," the second man croaked.

"We *all* know that," the first replied. "Takes a hell of a lot more guts than you've got to do the job that I do. You've been looking for Mike Ferguson for how long? And nothing. You couldn't find him until *I* let you."

"You think that's what happened?" The other man finally sounded a little gutsier. "I've suspected all along that he was under my nose. What I was looking for was *proof.* Because that's how *I* do things."

Ferguson rolled his eyes, came to his feet and stepped between them. "Your pissing contest is starting to get to me, boys."

"Waiting is starting to get to *me*," the first man snapped. "I want the other half of my money."

"Relax," said Ferguson. "Both of us want to be paid. And I agree. Enough time has passed, and we've all exercised enough patience for one lifetime. Your *friend* has stewed long enough. He needs to be smoked out."

"He'll never leave," said the second man. "And he's stupidly stubborn. Bad enough that if we go to him, he'll probably die before he tells you where he's hidden what you're looking for."

"So motivate him."

"Motivate him? It's been four years," pointed out the first man. "I'm tired of hanging around, waiting for him to show his face, hoping he'll turn up and lead me to the painting. I think *I* could motivate him just fine."

Ferguson gritted his teeth. "This doesn't need muscle. It needs finesse."

He reached into his pocket and pulled out his preferred weapon of choice. Photographic evidence. He held it out, knowing it was far more menacing than any gun.

"You recognize the kid?"

"Yes!"

"His life is in your hands."

The man on the ground was immediately blubbering all over again. "Please don't!"

"Motivation," Ferguson stated coldly. "Just enough to get the man to his own house. Then we can decide whether we move on to muscle. Two days, no more. Understood?"

"Yes."

The reply was barely more than a whisper. It didn't have to be. Ferguson knew the beta dog had been motivated enough.

Chapter 1

Keira Niles stepped on the gas, checked her rearview mirror and smiled.

Admittedly, it was kind of a forced smile.

But it was a smile nonetheless.

Because today was going to be the day.

The one where she said yes.

The one where she gave in to Drew Bryant, the handsome, friendly neighborhood businessman whom she'd been flirting with for four years.

Today, she would tell herself—and believe it—that his business-minded attitude was a complement to her socially conscious one instead of a sharp contrast to it.

Yes, she was finally ready to dismiss the doubts in her mind that had never seemed all that reasonable to start out with.

Drew was as close to a perfect man as she'd ever met.

Calm and predictable, financially stable and kind. Tall enough that when they kissed for the first time, she'd probably have to tip her head up at least a little, and good-looking enough that he'd probably stay that way until both of them were too old to care anyway.

It was a good list. A good cross section of pleasant characteristics that were totally at odds with the nervous butterflies in her stomach.

Go away, Keira grumbled at them.

But no. She was nervous, and the butterflies were prevailing. So she did the only thing she could—she beat them down as forcibly as she knew how.

No more excuses, no more waiting for this, that or the other thing.

She straightened her dress over her thighs and glanced at her bare ring finger on the steering wheel one more time. Maybe soon it wouldn't look so naked and exposed. So free.

Don't be silly, Keira, she chastised herself.

But it wasn't that silly, if she thought about it.

Her parents would be happy if she settled down. They weren't getting younger, and neither was she. Or Drew. He was nearly forty, and he'd hinted enough times that he was just waiting for the right girl. He'd also hinted enough times that maybe *Keira* was that girl. Jokingly called her his girlfriend on repeat since he moved in beside her parents just a few years earlier.

He was a good, stable man. Handsome. Friendly. A catch.

Just this morning, when she'd come by to water her mom's rhododendrons, he'd paused to say goodbye before he left for his business trip. He'd given her a peck on the cheek—and while it hadn't lit her up with fireworks, it hadn't felt bad, either. It wasn't until he drove away that Keira saw that he'd left his briefcase behind.

And a man on a business trip needs his briefcase.

It was a sign. A subtle push that she ought to take a spontaneous, romantic leap.

After only the briefest hesitation, she'd decided to do it. No call, no warning. Just a seizing of the moment. So she grabbed the overnight bag she kept at her parents' house and set out on the four-hour trip to the Rocky Mountains and the aptly named Rocky Mountain Chalet.

It was a chilly oasis right in the middle of the mountains—a hot spot for honeymooners who preferred ski hills to sandy beaches and hot toddies to margaritas. The surrounding resort town had year-round residences, too, but the chalet was really the hub of activity.

It would've surprised Keira if her parents' soft-spoken neighbor had chosen a place like this for a weekend of business, but she doubted he'd picked it himself. His clients, who often stopped by his house, and whom she'd had only a few occasions to meet over the past few years, seemed like the kind of men who liked nice things. Bespoke suits and menus that didn't have any prices.

Not that Drew was any less classy. He was just a little more understated than overpriced. A little more golf shirt and chinos, and little less glossy necktie and cufflinks. A square-cut diamond versus a marquise.

You're stalling.

Keira realized that she *had* stopped, her hands on the wheel at exactly ten and two, her eyes so glazed over that they almost didn't see the forbidding sign that pointed out cheerily how solidly she was about to seal her fate.

No Turnaround, Twenty-Two Miles, it read.

The drive time had passed far more quickly than she thought. The hours had felt like minutes, and the resort was close now.

Was what she was doing crazy and impetuous? Maybe. But it was also the perfect story to tell their friends. Their kids, if they had them. Plus, she got the feeling that settling into a life with Drew wouldn't allow a whole lot of wildness.

Which is a good thing, she reminded herself.

She was mild mannered and easygoing, too. So they were kind of perfect for each other.

And she was almost there. That final turn up the mountain was all it would take.

"Well," she said to the air. "This is it."

Somehow, the second she clicked on her turn signal, the air got colder.

And when she depressed the gas pedal and actually followed through on the turn itself, Keira swore she had to turn the heat up.

Graham woke from the nightmare far too slowly.

It was the kind of dream that he deserved to be ripped away from quickly, not dragged from reluctantly.

In it, he'd been chasing Holly through their home. She'd started out laughing, but her laughter had quickly turned to screams, and when Graham caught up with her at the bottom of the curved staircase, he saw why. Sam's small body was at the bottom. Graham had opened his mouth to ask what Holly had done, but she beat him to it.

"What did you do?"

The words were full of knowing accusation, and try as he might, he couldn't deny responsibility for the boy's death.

The image—and the question—hung in Graham's mind as he eased into consciousness.

In reality, he'd never seen Sam's body—just the aftermath and the blood.

In the dream, though, it was always the same. Holly alive and Sam dead, and Graham left broken and unable to shake the false memories. He wished desperately that they would disappear completely, or at least fade as he opened his eyes. Instead, they tightened and sharpened like a noose around his psyche.

Survivor's guilt.

Graham was sure that was a large part of what he felt. The problem was he was increasingly sure he *wasn't* surviving.

The leads had dried up long ago, his investigation into who had pulled the trigger growing frustratingly colder with each year.

Even the name—Michael Ferguson—the one thing he'd had to go on, had never panned out.

Graham had always believed the truth would come out and, with it, justice. It had never been a part of his plan to live out his days—to *survive* them—in the middle of the woods in a cabin no one knew existed. He sure as hell never thought he'd wake some mornings wondering if he was as guilty as everyone thought he was.

What kind of man admitted publicly that he didn't love his wife just days after being accused of her murder?

Did an innocent man escape police custody and promptly disappear?

In the early days, those questions seemed easy to answer.

An innocent man ran only so he could give the authorities enough time to *prove* his innocence.

Four years had gone by, though, and instead of gaining traction and credibility, Graham's story had at first exploded in hatred and bitterness. Then faded to obscure infamy.

Dreams like the one he'd just had made him question every choice he'd made since the second he picked up his cell phone on that morning.

What if he hadn't answered it at all?

What if he'd called 9-1-1 himself instead of giving that nosy neighbor the time to do it?

What if—

The squawk of Graham's one and only electronic device cut off his dark thoughts. The bleep of the two-way radio was so unexpected that he almost didn't recognize it.

The mountain range that held the cabin hostage also insulated the location from uninvited transmissions. The two-way mounted to the underside of Graham's bed could only be reached one of two ways. Either the message sender had to be less than a hundred feet away, or he had to be right beside the tower at the top of the mountain, tuned to exactly the correct frequency.

The first would mean initiating lockdown mode. Which Graham wasn't in the mood for.

The second meant someone was trying to reach him on purpose.

And only one person knew where he was.

"G.C., do you read me?"

Dave Stark. A friend. A confidant. The only person who'd stuck by him over the years. He was the man who'd placed the call to Graham on *that* morning. Whose voice threw Graham back every time he heard it.

"You there?" Dave asked.

Graham swung his legs from the bed and reached down to flip the switch.

"I should be asking if *you're* there. And why you're calling me sixteen days ahead of schedule. We're regimented for a reason."

"G.C., stop being your bullheaded self for one second... I have good news."

Graham went still. *Good* news? He wasn't sure what to do with the statement.

"Come again?"

"I found the man we've been looking for."

The world spun under Graham's feet. His mouth worked silently. Four years of waiting to hear those words, and now that he had, he couldn't think of a single damned thing to say.

"You still there, G.C.?"

Graham cleared his throat. "Where is he?"

"A place you know well."

"Stop being cagey, Dave. It doesn't suit you. Or the situation."

"Home."

Home. Forty-nine miles of nearly inaccessible terrain and two hundred more of straight highway driving

*is all that stands between you and the man who very
likely killed your wife and son, and robbed you of your
life. Michael damned Ferguson.*

Hmm. Graham was far from stupid. What were the
odds? And why had he surfaced now?

"He's there on business. Must've thought enough
time had gone by that no one would be looking," Dave
added as if in answer to Graham's silent question.
"Booked in a hotel under another name, but I swear to
God, G.C., I'd recognize the man in my sleep."

"You've got the snowmobile ready to go?" Graham
asked.

There was the slightest pause. "Yeah. But there's a
weather advisory out. They're expecting a blizzard and
the whole town is shut down already. No one can get in
or out. Blockades up and everything."

"You can't get around them?"

Another pause. "Of course I can. But I won't. Had
to flash my ID just to get away long enough to come
up to the tower."

"So flash it again."

"It's taken me this long to find him, I don't want to
get caught because of a stupid decision. The blockades
will be up all night, and probably into tomorrow. If
it's clear enough by morning, I'll find a way out. One
that won't arouse the suspicion of every rent-a-cop in
the area."

"If he gets away—"

"He won't. His hotel reservation in Derby Reach is
good until Wednesday morning, G.C., and I paid the
clerk a hundred bucks to watch him. Two full days is
plenty of time."

Graham stifled his frustration. "Fine."

"Over and out."

By the time the radio screeched, then went silent, Graham was already pulling clothes from his freestanding closet. No way was he waiting another twenty-four hours to get to Dave.

And Ferguson.

Chapter 2

Keira stepped on the gas and squinted into the snowy onslaught, then glanced in the rearview mirror, trying desperately to see...anything. It was a hopeless endeavor. Someone could be right on her bumper, and she wouldn't know the difference.

Just minutes after she pulled her car onto the road that led up to the resort, the big, friendly flakes had turned into tiny, angry ones that threatened her vision.

Then she'd heard the announcement. They were closing the roads down. Emergency access only. She couldn't turn around, even if she wanted to. She just prayed that she'd get there in one piece.

In fact, if her calculations were right, she was kind of sure she should *already* have gotten there.

She gripped the wheel tightly.

The terrain underneath her car seemed to be growing

steadily more uneven and the front-wheel drive hybrid was starting to protest.

But she pushed on.

"So much for signs," she muttered, and shot Drew's briefcase a dirty look.

Keira looked at the rearview again.

If someone was behind her, would they be able to see her, even with the lights on?

Unconsciously, she pushed down on the gas again, and her car heaved underneath her.

"C'mon, you stupid thing," she muttered. "Any second we'll reach the turnoff for the resort and you can go back to being your eco-obsessed self again."

After another few minutes of driving, the trees on the other side of the road still hadn't thinned out, and there was no break in the blizzard.

It really did seem to be a blizzard now. Even though it was technically daylight, the whiteness of the snow somehow darkened everything in Keira's line of vision.

So that's what a whiteout *means.*

She flicked on her high beams. They made no difference.

At last, Keira turned to the logical voice in her head for guidance.

Its reply was an unexpected shout.

Moose!

The huge, hairy beast stood out against the blank whiteness. It stared down the car. And it wasn't moving.

It's not moving!

"I know, dammit!" Keira yelled back at the voice.

She swung the steering wheel as hard as she could. In reply, the tires on the hybrid screeched their general disapproval of the maneuver. As the speedometer dropped down to ten miles an hour, the car skidded past the moose and, for just a moment, relief flooded through Keira's body. But when she tore her eyes away from the animal, she saw that she'd simply traded in one disaster for another. A yawning chasm beckoned to her hybrid.

And all she could do as she sailed over the edge was close her eyes and pray.

As Graham stomped through the ever-thickening storm, his feet grew heavier. Even his snowshoes seemed to protest the slow trek. The route was steep and a lot of it bordered on treacherous. The bonus was that vertical climb turned a forty-mile hike into a ten-mile one instead.

Sweat built up on Graham's skin, dripping down his face and freezing in his beard. He flicked away the ice and paused to take a breath. The air was cold enough to burn. But neither the snow nor the wind were enough to block out the raging of his thoughts.

You knew the storm was coming but you picked this path anyway and you don't have a damned thing to complain about. You're sure as hell not giving up.

He slammed down his snowshoes with even more force and moved on. His internal monologue was right in so many more ways than he'd meant it to be. He hadn't just picked this particular path at this particular moment. He'd picked all the paths that led up to the metaphorical storm—perfectly matched to the actual one—which was his life.

The king of bad decisions.

With a crown of regret.

He almost laughed. Today of all days was not the day to turn into a poet.

Been alone far too long, he thought.

Then he *did* laugh. Solitude was so much more than a choice. It was an absolute necessity.

So, no. He didn't need poetry or cynicism or even hope. Cold, hard facts. That was where this was leading. A long-awaited resolution.

He laughed again, and the rumble of his baritone chuckle punctuated the cold air for just a second before the wind cut through and carried it away. As the laugh faded, another rumble followed it, this one far deeper, and so loud it echoed over the sound of the storm.

Graham froze.

An avalanche?

This thought was quickly overridden as he realized the noise was actually a human one.

A car engine and tires on the icy pavement.

It had been years since he'd been close enough to any kind of traffic to hear the sound. Graham's eyes lifted in search of the road above. With the snow as heavy as it was, he couldn't see anything more than a few feet ahead.

The rumble continued, growing even louder.

What kind of maniac is out in these conditions? Graham wondered, then shook his head.

Clearly someone who had even less regard for their own safety than he did.

Graham took another few steps, expecting the noise to fade away. It didn't. In fact, it seemed to be building. And then it stopped abruptly.

Something wasn't right.

Graham's ears strained against the muted broil of the storm and caught a high-pitched shriek, almost indiscernible from the wind. Then his eyes widened. The horizon was blank no more.

A purple streak shot off the cliff above, crashed through the trees, dropping first a dozen angled feet, then another ten. Then—incredibly, unbelievably—it slammed to the forest floor somewhere ahead.

Move!

He didn't stop to think about the consequences, but tore across the snow, beating branches out of his way as he ran. He was too determined to reach the site of the crash to let his awkward, snowshoed gait slow him, and in only a few minutes, he reached the car.

A girl.

He went very still for a very long second.

The driver was a young woman. With a flaming crown of auburn hair and her head pressed into the steering wheel, arms limp at her side.

The smell of gasoline was all around him, and the threat of explosion was very real.

And Graham felt something shift inside him.

Every part of him that had gone numb with shock now went wild with a need to save her.

Chapter 3

Keira couldn't open her eyes. She had no idea if minutes had passed or if had been hours. She only knew that she was cold. Frozen right through her secondhand, designer sweater and her teeny-tiny dress to the bare skin beneath. A little pseudodrunkenly, she wondered why she hadn't dressed for the weather.

She should probably move. Try to get warm. But the chill was the bone-freezing kind that makes it impossible to move anything but chattering teeth.

Sleep threatened to take her, and though she knew instinctively that she should fight it, she was really struggling to find a good reason to stay awake.

The click of a seat belt drew her attention.

A car.

Her car. She was driving. Then falling.

Now she was being lifted.

Good.

But her relief was short-lived.

Next came the ripping, and the tearing off, of her clothes.

I'm being attacked.

The assumption slammed home fear and brought with it a burst of furious energy. Keira's arms came up defensively while her feet lashed out with as much aggression as she could muster. She wasn't going down without a fight.

Her knee connected with something solid, and for a moment she was triumphant.

Her eyes flew open, and this time when she froze, it was from something other than cold.

A pair of dark-lashed eyes, so gray they were almost see-through, stared back at her. They were set in a fully bearded face, partially obscured by a knitted hat, and they were pained. And angry. Furious, even.

Keira tried to shy back from their icy rage, but she was positioned in a deep dip in the frozen ground, and the hard-packed snow all around her was as unyielding as the man above her.

Roll over! Roll away!

Except she couldn't. Because the man had one hand over her collarbone. His palm was just shy of the base of her throat.

"Please," she gasped around the pressure he was exerting just below her trachea. "Please don't hurt me."

His eyes widened in surprise. Then very, very slowly, he shook his head. Then he let go of her neck. Cold air whipped across the exposed skin, making her shiver uncontrollably.

The man pulled away and disappeared from view. And the *r-r-r-rip* of fabric started up again immediately.

Oh, God.

In spite of the way Keira's body was shaking, she attempted to sit up. But in less than the time it took to draw in one ice-tinged breath, the man's hand shot out once more, closing over the same spot he'd released just moments earlier. He pursed his lips, and in spite of the cover of the beard, Keira could see the frustrated set of his jaw. He shook his head again.

What did he mean? Did he want her to just lie there while he stripped her down?

Keira didn't realize she'd spoken aloud until he nodded.

She tried to tell him she wouldn't do it—that she *couldn't* do it—but when she opened her mouth, the wind swept in and cut the words away.

She thought he must've taken her silence as acquiescence, because he disappeared again, and suddenly Keira was stripped almost completely bare. Her dress had been so skimpy that she hadn't even bothered with a bra. And without the dress, all she had left were her lacy boy-cut undies, and if she remembered correctly, they didn't leave much to the imagination.

Very abruptly, Keira didn't feel cold anymore. She had a bizarre urge to look down and check if her panties were as revealing as she believed them to be.

Not a good sign.

She tried to lift her arms, and when she found them to be too leaden to move, frustration shot through her.

"I need to see my panties!"

The words came out in an almost shout, and they struck Keira as hilarious. A giggle burst from her lips.

The bearded man was at her side in an instant, concern evident on his face. Keira thought *that* was funny, too. One second he had her by the throat, the next he was worried about her.

"What are you staring at, hmm, Mountain Man?" she asked.

Her laughter carried on, and even though it sounded a little hysterical, she still couldn't stop it.

The man stood up abruptly. From her position on the ground, Keira could see he was huge. Strikingly tall. Wide like a tree trunk.

And he was dressed in clothes that her mind couldn't make sense of. His enormous shoulders were draped in white fur, but underneath that was a Gore-Tex jacket. The hat—which she'd noted before—was incredibly lopsided and almost laughable. His pants were leather, but not the kind you'd find on a biker or on badly dressed club rat. Tucked into boots crafted of the same suede and held together with wide, sinewy stitches, they looked like something out of a seventh-grade social studies textbook.

Keira's giggles finally subsided, but only because her jaw had dropped to her chest.

In a move that made Keira concerned for his safety, the man began to undress.

What the heck?

He tossed the weird ensemble off without finesse.

For several long, inappropriate seconds, Keira had an opportunity to admire his naked form. Her gaze traveled the breadth of his muscled torso, taking in the cut of perfectly formed muscle. He had well-defined pecs and biceps, and a puckered scar just above his left collarbone.

Unclothed, he looked less like a mountain man and more like…well, more like a mountain itself.

Keira's eyes moved south, even though she knew she should stop them. Just as her gaze reached his belly button, though, he tossed the long underwear–style T-shirt he'd had under his jacket in her direction. It ballooned up, then settled about four inches above her head, suspended there by the walls of the dip where she was lying.

Before Keira could ask what he was doing, the man dove in beside her.

Very quickly, he slipped his boots onto her feet, then used the rest of his clothes to build a cocoon around them. His pants hung over their chests. The white fur that had been on his shoulders covered their legs and feet.

When he was done, he rolled Keira over forcefully. He wrapped the jacket around them and pulled her back into his chest. The world seemed to be vibrating, and it took her a long moment to realize it was because she was still shivering.

Without her permission, Keira's body wriggled into the stranger's, trying to absorb all the heat he was emitting. She attempted to fight it. She told her hips they shouldn't fit against his legs so perfectly. She mentally commanded her head not to tuck into the crook of his arm.

But it was a losing battle.

He inhaled deeply. And with his exhale, he flung his

free arm over her waist and dragged her even closer. His bare leg slipped between Keira's newly booted feet and she couldn't even pretend to fight the need to be right there, exactly like that.

At long last, her shaking subsided.

Don't fall asleep.

But that, too, was an inevitability.

Great. Crash your car, then get stripped down and forcibly cuddled by an equally crazy man. Only you, Keira.

His heat lulled her. His solidity comforted her. His presence made her feel unreasonably safe.

And as she drifted off, she finally clued in to the Mountain Man's intentions. He wasn't trying to hurt her at all. He was just trying to keep her warm.

And he was very likely saving her life.

Naked flesh pressed to naked flesh. The oldest trick in the Boy Scout handbook for staving off hypothermia. It was effective, too, judging from the amount of heat in the snowy alcove.

The girl beside Graham adjusted a little, and one of her hands grazed his thigh.

Okay maybe Boy Scout *is the wrong choice of words,* Graham amended.

Every bit of movement reminded Graham that he was the furthest thing from a do-gooder kid in a uniform. Especially now that the panic that she was going to die on his hands had worn off.

The girl shifted beside him once again, wriggling ever closer and heightening his awareness of her petite form all the more. Her mess of auburn hair tickled his chest, and its light scent wafted to his nose. Her silky skin caressed him.

I'm in hell, Graham decided. *The worst kind of hell.*

She murmured something soft and breathy in her sleep, and Graham groaned.

Saving her might have been a mistake. An impetuous decision fueled by the man he used to be.

That...and her pretty face.

Her still, lifeless body behind the wheel had been almost too much for him to bear.

Bend. Lift. Drag.

She was easy to carry. So small. Almost fragile looking. Fair in that way that redheads often are, but with no smattering of freckles. In fact, the paleness of her skin rivaled the snow, and Graham wasn't sure whether it was a natural pallor, or something brought on by the accident and the cold. It didn't matter; she was entrancing.

Then he'd pulled her into the clearing, shaking and shivering and seemingly so needful.

Graham grimaced. She *was* beautiful, no doubt, but she definitely wasn't frail. An accident like that should have killed her. Coming out alive was a feat. But the fight in her when she'd woken up...that was a whole other story. It had impressed him as much as it had ticked him off.

Under the fine bones of her face, she was a firecracker, no doubt about it.

Graham slipped his hand to hers, touching the soft pad of her open palm, just because he could.

And because you want *to*, scolded an internal voice that sounded a little too much like his late grandmother.

It was true, though. He did want to. It had been a long

time since his fingers last found residence in someone else's hand.

The girl's hand closed reflexively, and Graham jerked away.

Nice work, he thought. *Save a girl, then get creepy. You could at least wait until she tells you her name.*

Her name.

He felt an impatient compulsion to know what it was and, after just a second of considering it, he decided to see if he could find out. Maybe check for her ID in the car. She was warm enough now that she wasn't at risk of dying, and he could safely give her—both of them—some space.

He pushed aside his clothes-turned-blanket and tucked them around the girl's body. Then he slipped from the dip in the ground, stood silently and surveyed the area. The cold air buffeted against his skin, but he was accustomed to the weather, and as he came to his feet, the strong breeze in his eyes bothered him more than the temperature did. The storm had slowed quite a bit. The snow was light, mostly blowing around from the residual wind.

He glanced down at the girl and adjusted the overhanging shirt so she wasn't bared to the elements. She'd be fine alone for a few minutes while Graham had a closer look at her car and attempted to figure out who she was. Then he'd have to decide whether it was better to keep her close, or try to get her back into town.

Into town.

In the heated excitement of saving her, meeting up with Dave had gone out of his head. In fact, *everything* had gone out of his head, and he wasn't sure how that was possible.

Graham turned back to the girl.

In the past four years, his pursuit of justice had been relentless. Single-minded to the point of mania. He'd thought of nothing but finding the man who took Holly and Sam from his life. Now, very suddenly, he was distracted from his purpose.

By this girl.

He took another step closer to the car. The front end dipped down from the pressure exerted by Graham's body as he'd clambered across it on his insane rescue mission. The purple paint had been slashed to hell by the branches surrounding it, and the rear wheels were completely flat. Remarkably, the rest of the car was intact.

Graham stood underneath the vehicle, frowning. Damned lucky. The vehicle could have smashed to pieces, taking the girl with it. Or she could've gone off the road just a few miles up, and Graham would never have found her. She had to have some incredible karma stored up.

What if someone's waiting for her?

Graham's gut roiled. He had to assume that time wasn't a luxury he had. The second they—whether it was an emergency crew or someone else—found that car in its weirdly whole state, with its empty driver's seat, the relatively far distance to his place in the woods grew that much smaller.

Get control, man, he commanded himself.

He needed a plan.

His gaze sought the car and the spot where the girl

lay hidden. A small, greasy puddle—presumably the source of the gasoline smell—had formed under the driver's side door and it gave him an idea.

They can't find the car in one piece.

He would make it harder for anyone to locate her. Harder to locate him.

Graham squinted up at the sky. Clouds obscured the waning sun.

Graham didn't own a watch. It had been years since the batteries in his old one wore out, and it had never seemed like much of necessity. Right that moment, though, he wished he had one so he could pinpoint the hour, predict the sunset and time it just right.

But you don't *have one*, he said to himself. *And you don't have time to wait, either.*

All he needed was a spark. One that could easily be generated with some of the electrical wires in the car engine.

Once he got started, it took less than an hour for Graham to render Keira's car satisfactorily unidentifiable. The dark, sour-smelling smoke was already dissipating, though he was sure he still reeked of fuel himself.

He took a step back to survey his handiwork once more. He thought it looked as natural as any burning car could. A branch puncturing the fuel line, the angle of the car conveniently leaking accelerant from the line to the engine, and the rest had gone up in smoke.

So to speak.

Graham was actually a little surprised at how efficiently the fire took hold. Not to mention how well the whole thing cooperated. Several minutes of blistering, blue-green flames, an enormous puff of black smoke, then a fade-to-gray cloud that blended in nicely with the fog that had rolled in from above.

Not that Graham was complaining—it sure as hell made his task a lot easier. The husk of the car continued to smolder, but with the fuel burned up and the decidedly frozen state of the surrounding area, he wasn't even worried about it spreading any farther.

Not bad for my first arson attempt.

The thought only made him smile for a second. The last thing he needed was to add another felony to the list that already followed his name around.

"Is that my car?"

At the soft, tired-sounding question, Graham whipped around. For a second, he just stared down at her, mesmerized by the way her long, dark eyelashes brushed against her porcelain skin, and entranced by the enticing plumpness of her lips.

He'd never seen a more beautiful girl, or felt an attraction so strong.

"Is it?" she said again.

Reality hit Graham.

Saving her had been a hell of a lot more than just a *bad* idea. If Graham's instincts were right—and they usually were—then this walk in the storm turned impromptu rescue mission...would be his undoing.

Chapter 4

Keira met the stranger's wary gaze with one of her own. For a moment she saw something heated and intriguing in his eyes that cut through the cold air and sizzled between them. Then it was gone, replaced by the guarded look he wore now, and Keira was left wondering if she'd imagined it.

Maybe it was a hallucination brought on by a head injury, she thought.

Her brain did feel fuzzy, and when she blinked, the snowy world swam in front of her. Even the big man—who was as solid a thing as she'd ever seen—seemed to wobble. Then a wicked, head-to-toe shiver racked Keira's body, and the Mountain Man's face softened with worry. Very quickly, he undid his own big red jacket and stepped closer to offer it to her.

Keira only hesitated for a second before she took it

gratefully. She vowed silently to give it back as soon as she was thawed. But right then, it was warm *and* it offered her a decent amount of cover, and with it wrapped around her body, she felt a little more in control. Still woozy. But better.

"My car…" Her voice sounded hoarse, and her throat burned a little as she spoke.

When the Mountain Man didn't answer her third inquiry, she tipped her head toward the smoking mess of metal, then looked back at him again. He just stared back at her, a little crease marking his forehead.

Keira let out a rasping sigh. "Do you speak English?"

He nodded curtly.

"So…what? You're just testing me out? Deciding if I'm *worthy* of speaking to?"

Her question earned a crooked smile. An expression that said, *Yeah, that's about right.*

Keira sighed again. A few silent hours with this stranger, and she could understand him perfectly. She doubted she could read Drew that easily, and she'd known him for years.

Drew.

Damn. A kicked-in-the-gut feeling made her shiver once more, and the Mountain Man reached out a hand, but she waved him off.

"I'm fine," she lied.

He raised an eyebrow. *Liar.*

"I don't care if you believe me or not," Keira stated. Her eyes narrowed with an irritation to cover her embarrassment, and then she muttered, "I'm just not used to sitting nearly naked in the snow."

He chuckled—a low, attractive sound that warmed

her inexplicably—sat back on his heels and waited. Those piercing gray eyes of his demanded answers, and Keira found herself wanting to tell him the truth.

Her job as a child and youth counselor had given her the ability to form good, quick judgments. And something in this man's handsome face made her think she could trust him.

Handsome?

The descriptor surprised Keira, and if her blood had been pumping through her body properly, she might've blushed.

Because yes, he *was* handsome.

He had full lips, an even brow and in spite of his facial hair, he had strong features. Keira was close enough to him that as she realized just how attractive he was, her heart fluttered nervously in her chest.

She was alone with him. In the middle of nowhere. She was injured. Maybe badly. And now she was remembering that glimpse she'd caught of his muscular torso when he'd stripped off his clothes so he could warm her up. Keira had been too out of it to think about it before. She was wishing she could see it again so she could memorize it.

What's the matter with you? she chastised herself.

She couldn't remember the last time she'd looked at a man like this. At least not long enough to notice how prettily translucent his eyes were, or how their wintry appeal so sharply contrasted with his burly frame. She certainly hadn't come close enough to one to know how well his body fit beside her, or how comfortable it was to be in his arms.

No way could Drew come close to this kind of magnetism.

Mountain magnetism.

And he was watching her again, that same not-so-muted heat in his eyes.

Maybe he's remembering the way you *felt cuddled up beside* him.

That thought was finally enough to draw the color to her cheeks, and Keira could feel the heat spread from her face down her throat and across her chest. She was sure she must be the same shade of red as the borrowed coat.

In an attempt to ease the increasingly palpable tension between them, Keira shifted her gaze back to her smoldering car.

Midway between the vehicle and spot where she was sitting a black flash caught her eyes.

My phone.

She knew that's what it was, and that she had to get it. And for some reason, she also knew that her benefactor—if his intentions were even good enough to call him that—wouldn't let her just go grab it. Not willingly.

Butterflies beat against Keira's stomach as she offered him a weak smile.

"Can you excuse me for a second?" Her voice was weak, even to her own ears. "I think I need to…uh… use the ladies' room."

Graham narrowed his eyes and considered calling her bluff. He was sure whatever reason she had for suddenly getting up, it had little to do with the most basic of physical needs.

Graham had to admit that he was surprised she could

stand at all. What surprised him more, though, was that she took off into the dark. The borrowed boots flew off, and she moved at a hobbling, barefoot run.

What the hell?

Graham was so startled that he almost forgot he should chase her down. He stared after her, a puzzled frown on his face. Her creamy legs poke out from under the big coat, as sexy as they were ridiculous.

She really should tuck those away before she ruined them with frostbite, he thought absently.

She glanced over her shoulder at him and stumbled forward a little farther.

Where the hell did she think she was going? Her ridiculous flight was going to run her straight into the thickest part of the forest. It was going to tear up those pretty little feet of hers. And was going to create unnecessary work for Graham.

First World, fugitive-about-to-turn-kidnapper problems.

Still, Graham might've been tempted to let her go a little longer if he hadn't spied the wound on her thigh.

Dammit, he growled mentally.

How had he not noticed the slash before?

Her movement across the snow opened up the cut, and even from a few dozen feet away, Graham could see the blood ooze out of it.

Belatedly, he jumped to his feet and strode after her, his long legs closing the gap between them.

In seconds, he was on her, and without preamble he reached down, wrapped his arms around her knees and threw her unceremoniously over his shoulder. She beat weakly at his back, but he ignored it.

"Let me *go*!" Her order was almost a squeal, and Graham ignored that, too.

He carried her across the ground like a sack of potatoes, and when he had her right back at the spot she'd run from moments earlier, he dumped her to the ground—not quite hard enough to hurt, but just hard enough for her to squeak.

He shot her a look that commanded her to keep still and, although her eyes flashed, she didn't try to get up again. From the shallowness of her breathing and the deep flush in her cheeks, Graham doubted she *could* get up.

But as soon as he leaned back, she was off at a crawl.

If we were at the hospital, Graham thought, *I'd insist that an orderly strap her down.*

For a moment, he considered calling after her.

No. Speaking to her will only create more issues. Make you slip up and give something away. Too much risk.

He watched her shimmy helplessly over the snow for another second—she barely got more than a few inches—then stretched out, closed a hand over one of her ankles and dragged her back.

He righted her, set her between his thighs and held her there.

Using his teeth, Graham tore his T-shirt into strips—one to bind her hands together, another to bind her feet together, and a third to stop the flow of blood from her thigh. She fought him on the first two things—and he couldn't blame her for that—but when she finally spotted the wound, she stopped struggling.

Graham could feel her eyes following the quick, sure movements of his hands as he fashioned the stretchy cotton into a tourniquet. He was disappointed that the blood soaked through almost immediately. He tore off another strip from his T-shirt, bundling the wrapping as thick as he could and as tight as he dared.

The flow of blood ebbed, but she was going to need stitches, and Graham had nothing on hand that would do the job.

"Mountain Man?" Her voice was soft. "I'm really hurt, aren't I?"

Graham nodded curtly.

She was silent for a minute, leaning her back into his chest. Then she shifted a little, tipping her head just enough that he could see her tempting, pink lips.

"I should warn you," she murmured. "I'm not going to make this easy."

Graham rolled his eyes. As if *that* surprised him.

In spite of her words, though, she turned sideways and settled her face against him. Then her eyelids fluttered shut, and her knees curled up as if she *belonged* in his lap.

With a frustrated groan, Graham tried to ease away, but the sleeping girl wriggled closer and then she murmured something else, and instead of trying to disentangle himself from her, Graham found himself straining to hear what it was. He tucked the coat over her legs and leaned down, pressing his face close to hers.

She shifted in his lap, and her lips brushed his ear.

Graham's body reacted immediately. Desire shot through him, and his grip on her tightened.

Slowly, he untied her wrists. He breathed out, waiting for her to wake up, realize she was free and level a punch at his face. Instead, she flexed one free hand, then slipped it up to his shoulder, her thumb grazing his collarbone.

Graham groaned and crushed down the ridiculous longing coursing through him.

A lock of auburn hair slipped to her cheek. Graham reached to brush it away reflexively. When his hand slid against her cheek, he realized the heat he felt could be blamed on more than just desire. Her skin was hot to the touch, and though her face was still pale, two spots of pink had bloomed in her cheeks.

Graham frowned and placed the back of his hand on her forehead, then trailed a finger down her face. Yeah, she was definitely far warmer than she ought to be.

He needed to get her somewhere safer, cleaner and functional enough for treatment. The clinic in the resort town was out of the question. Anywhere public was.

Home.

It was the best option.

Graham glanced up at the sky. The sun had completely set, and the sky was pitch-black. Travel now would be dangerous.

More dangerous, he corrected silently.

The climb down was steep, and he would have to carry her. Graham had no idea how long he'd be able to do that.

He looked back to the girl.

He didn't have any other choice.

Whatever circumstance had brought her to him, she was still in need of medical care, and however long ago it had been, Graham still held fast to his oath.

First do no harm.

Chapter 5

The ground beneath Keira was moving. It thumped along rhythmically like a conveyor belt made of nearly smooth terrain. It was soothing. Almost.

A sudden bump jarred her and sent her head reeling. Her eyes flew open, and the world was upside down. She realized it wasn't the ground that was moving. It was *her*. Them.

The big man had her cradled in his arms, and he was traveling across the snowy ground at an alarming speed. She could see the bottom of his bearded chin. His neck was exposed and a sheen of sweat covered it. His breathing was a little heavy, but he seemed oblivious to her added weight.

"Excuse me?" Keira's voice was far weaker than she wanted it to be, and if he heard her, he didn't acknowledge it.

She struggled to right herself, the quick pace making it difficult for her to do more than lift her head. All she could see was sky.

She blinked, and the sky stayed. The expanse of it was so big above her that it was almost dizzying. No moon. No stars. Just a solid spread of grayness. Keira closed her eyes to block it out as she tried to orient herself.

The big, red jacket was still wrapped around her, cinched at the waist and tied at the throat. A scarf was wound tightly around her head, insulating her face as well as her skull. The Mountain Man had used the white fur to cover both her feet and her legs. She wasn't in danger of freezing anymore, though the terrible cold she'd felt right before slipping into oblivion wasn't completely gone.

She felt weak. Really weak. She sought something tangible to grasp at in her sea of straw-like thoughts.

Wrists tied together. Not that. *Blood.* No. *The smoky, woodsy scent of the Mountain Man's skin.* Definitely not.

And at last she found something.

My phone. Yes.

She'd managed to grab it in her stumble across the snow. She'd shoved it into the coat pocket just seconds before the Mountain Man caught her and hoisted her over his shoulder, caveman-style.

Was it still there?

She desperately wanted to reach into the coat to find out.

But right that second, her hands—which were no longer bound together, she noted—were actually *under* his shirt, pressed into his nearly rock-hard chest. And there was no hope of drawing away with any chance of subtly. Her fingers fluttered nervously, and even though he didn't react, Keira was sure the stranger's pulse jumped with the movement.

Curiosity fueled her to see if she was correct.

She uncurled her fingers slowly and moved her palm up, just an inch. The big man's heart was already working hard with exertion, but there was no mistaking the double beat as her hand came to rest on his sternum.

Oh.

Keira moved again, and this time she couldn't tell what was more noticeable—*his* heartbeat, or *hers*. Because she was definitely reacting to the way his skin felt under her hand, and the tightening of his arms didn't help, either. A lick of heat swept through her, and her light-headedness increased, too.

Focus on something else, she told herself. *Think of Mom and Dad. Think of work and the kids who need you. Think of Drew.*

But right that second, she couldn't even quite recall what Drew looked like. When she tried, his features blurred away, and the rugged looks of the unnamed Mountain Man overtook her mind instead.

Ugh.

Keira was *not* the kind of girl who rebounded from the idea of a marriage-potential relationship into the arms of a grunting, hulking man straight out of a hunting magazine.

Well. Not figuratively anyway.

Because she *was* quite literally wrapped in his firm grip, her head pressed into the crook of his arm.

Just how long had the Mountain Man been carrying her? And to where?

"Hey," she called, happy that her voice was a little louder.

But she still got no response. She tried again.

"Mountain Man?"

He didn't slow.

"Hey!" This time, she said it as loudly as she could manage, and from the way his grip tightened on her, Keira was sure he'd heard her.

But he still didn't acknowledge her directly.

Stubborn.

With a great deal of effort, she wiggled an arm free from inside the jacket, snaked it out and yanked on his beard.

He drew in a sharp breath, snarled and released her. Keira tumbled to the ground. Hard. Her back hit the snow, nearly knocking the wind out of her.

He looked down at her, regret in his gray eyes made visible by the moonlight behind him. Except then she opened her big fat mouth.

"You jerk! You dropped me!"

His expression tightened and he rolled his eyes.

Yeah, you think this is my *fault, don't you?* Keira thought. *Well, I didn't ask for the car accident. Or for the damned moose.*

"And I especially didn't ask for you and the stupid beard," she muttered.

He reached for her, concern evident on his face, and she shuffled backward along the snow.

"What?" Keira said with a head shake that made the world wobble. "You're worried about me because I don't want to be manhandled? I've got news for you. Non-forest-dwelling women have high expectations nowadays. No way are you getting those Sasquatch hands on me again. Not unless I ask you to."

She colored as she realized how that sounded. And she strongly suspected that underneath that beard, he was trying to cover a sudden smile.

"Jerk," she muttered again.

He crossed his arms over his wide chest and gave her an expectant, eyes-narrowed glare. Silently daring her to stand up on her own.

"Yeah, I will," Keira snapped.

She pushed both hands to the ground and came to her feet. Rocks dug into her skin. Ice bit at her toes. And worse than that, her head was spinning again.

There was no way she was going to be able to walk more than a few feet. But there was also no way she was going to admit it to the smug Mountain Man.

And sure enough, his expression definitely said, *You need me*.

No way was she giving in to *that*. No matter how true it might be.

Keira straightened her body, grimacing as pain shot through her pretty much everywhere. In particular, her thigh burned, and she had to resist an urge to lift the jacket and have a closer look. Instead, she made herself meet the Mountain Man's stare.

"Where to?" she asked through gritted teeth.

He shrugged, then pointed to the black horizon.

"Great!" Keira said cheerily.

She had no idea what she was looking at. Or for. Vaguely, she thought again that she should probably ask him what he intended to do with her. But she was feeling rather stubborn, and the longer she was on her feet, the foggier her head was getting.

The Mountain Man stood still, watching her as she took two agonizing steps. He probably would've watched her take even more, except he didn't get a chance to. Because the world swayed, and Keira was unexpectedly on her rear end, staring up at the sky, transfixed by the few stars that managed to shine through the snowy sky.

Apparently, her little nap in the Mountain Man's arm hadn't done much of anything to renew her energy.

And now he was standing in front of her with that frown growing deeper with each heartbeat.

As he stared, Keira *did* begin to feel warm. But it had nothing to do with the weather or the accident, or anything at all that she could pinpoint.

Except maybe just…*him*.

Keira swallowed a sudden thickness in her throat and forced herself to look away.

Immediately she wished she hadn't, because the first thing that her eyes found was the fabric that had been wrapped around her thigh. When she'd struggled futilely to escape, it had slipped off and fallen into the snow. Keira frowned at it. It *had* been a light color, grayish or tan, it was hard to say which. But now it was dark.

Blood.

Instinctively, she knew that's what it was. And not just any blood. *Her* blood. Lots of it.

She brought her slightly floppy arm up so she could feel her leg.

Yep. It was damp and sticky. No wonder she was so

woozy. And no wonder the Mountain Man had been in such a hurry.

She sat there for a long second, then sighed in defeat.

"Hey, um, Mountain Man?"

He raised an eyebrow and looked down at her.

"So, yeah," she said. "I've decided we're not going to get very much farther if you stop carrying me."

His brow furrowed for one moment, then a wry chuckle escaped from his lips, and he plucked her from the ground as if she weighed nothing. But he only carried her for another minute. She looked at the run-down cabin that appeared before them. It screamed "horror movie."

They'd reached their destination.

Chapter 6

Graham could read Keira's expression perfectly as she looked from him to the wooden house.

Seriously? it said. *You're taking me in* there, *and you expect me to go without a fuss?*

If he'd felt inclined to speak, he would've replied, "Actually, I don't expect you to do anything without a fuss."

Instead he just shrugged, which made her emerald eyes narrow suspiciously. She went back to assessing the single-story structure with its rough shingle roof and its wide porch hung with ancient wind chimes. And likely found it lacking.

For the first time since he'd moved in semipermanently, he wished it was a more impressive abode.

The outside was purposefully left in disrepair, meant to deter anyone who saw it from wanting to enter.

He moved up the stairs, but as he reached the threshold, Keira's hand shot out, and Graham was too startled to realize what she was reaching for before it was too late. Her fingers closed on the well-worn sign. It was handcrafted by Graham's great-grandfather almost a century earlier when he'd built the cabin as a hunting outpost. Graham had meant to remove the handmade plate a long time ago.

"Calloway?" she said as she ran her fingers over the barely discernible lettering, then wriggled a bit so she could look at him. "That's you?"

She eyed him with patient curiosity, and a battle waged inside Graham's head. The last name wasn't an entirely common one, but it clearly hadn't sparked any recognition in her.

Given time, would she make the connection between him and the crime attached to the surname? If she did, would she simply chalk it up to coincidence, or would she investigate further?

In the end, Graham took a leap of faith and nodded tightly.

"Calloway," she repeated thoughtfully and added, "Is that a first name or last name?"

Graham tensed, but after a second, she smiled—the first genuine one Graham had seen since he found her—and he relaxed again. Her teeth were even, but not perfect, and the grin transformed her face. She went from porcelain perfection to devilish beauty.

"Or are you one of those people who just has the one name?" she teased. "Like the Cher of the survivalist world?"

Graham rolled his eyes, loosened one of his arms,

tore the sign from its chain and tossed it with perfect aim into a wood bin on the porch. Then he carried her up to the door, turned the knob and let them into the cabin.

The heavy curtains ensured that it was almost dark inside, but Graham kept his modified woodstove on low, even when he wasn't in the cabin. As a result, the air was an ambient temperature. The only light—not much more than a dim glow—came from the same stove. At that moment, it highlighted the Spartan decor.

The furniture was limited to a set of rough-hewn chairs and a matching table, and Graham's own lumpy bed. He carted the girl across the room and deposited her on the latter. She tried to stand, but Graham pushed her back down and shot her a warning glare before he slipped to the other side of the room.

He wasn't doing anything else until he'd given her a more thorough look-over and tended to the mess of a wound on her leg.

Whether she likes it or not.

He dampened a clean cloth, then set some water to boil. He refused to think about anything but the immediate tasks at hand, and once he had the pot on the stove, he moved back to the bed.

As he seated himself beside her, she crossed her arms over her chest, and her mouth set in a frown. Graham ignored her expression, raising the cloth to her face. She snatched it from his hand.

"I can do it," she told him, but there was no bite in her words—just exhaustion.

Graham watched as she wiped away the grime left behind from sleeping in a hole and several hours of being carried through the woods. He was unreasonably pleased when she handed the cloth back and he saw that she only had the tiniest of abrasions on her otherwise perfect face.

Perfect face? Calm your raging manhood, Graham, he growled at himself. *It's clearly been far too long since you've seen a woman. And her prettiness is not your focus anyway. Her health is what's important. She needs to heal so you can get on with meeting up with Dave.*

He stood up stiffly, filled a tin mug with spices and pressed juice, topped it with the now-boiling water, then added a generous helping of his homemade booze. It wasn't as good as a painkiller or a sedative, but even if either had been available, he doubted she'd take one from him.

In moments, Graham was back at her side, offering her the steaming liquid. She eyed it suspiciously and didn't reach for it.

"I don't think so," she said.

Graham rolled his eyes, then grabbed the mug and took a pointed swig. Even the small mouthful warmed his throat as he swallowed.

He offered it to her again.

She still sniffed the drink, and Graham had to cover a smile.

"Fine," she muttered. "I guess you're not trying to poison me."

At last, she relented and took first one cautious sip, then another.

Satisfied that she was going to drink it, Graham slipped away again. He banged through the cupboards until he found each item he thought he might need and placed them on a tray. None of it was ideal—he didn't even seem to own a Band-Aid—but it would have to do.

Once he had everything ready, he opted to get changed. His clothes were dirty, and in some places soaked with the girl's blood. All of it risked contamination, and the last thing he wanted was to give her an infection.

Graham shot a quick glance in her direction. She was still engrossed in sipping the spiked drink, so Graham dropped his pants and stepped into a fresh pair of jeans instead. Then he stripped off his damp shirt and doused his hands and forearms with soap and some of the boiled water, then rinsed the suds off into a metal pot.

When he turned back to the girl again, the tin mug was at her side, and her eyes were fixed on him. They were wide, their striking shade of green dancing against the fairness of her skin. The orange firelight glinted off her hair, adding otherwise invisible hints of gold to the red.

Another bolt of electric attraction shot through Graham's blood.

Damn.

She really was beautiful.

Without meaning to, he let his gaze travel the length of her body. The white fur that had been covering her legs had slipped to the floor, leaving her calves bare. She still wore Graham's big, red jacket, but it didn't cover anything past midthigh. She tried to tug it down, but when one side lowered, the other rose, and after a second she gave up. It didn't help at all that he knew she had nothing but panties on underneath the coat.

Even from where Graham stood, he could see two spots of pink bloom in her cheeks. The added color in her fair skin did nothing to dampen his desire.

Double damn.

He forced himself to turn away and take a breath, rearranging the items on his tray until he was sure he could trust himself to get closer to her. He had to count to twenty to normalize his breathing, and even when he was done, he wasn't sure he was completely in control.

As he turned back, she looked as if she was bracing herself for an attack, and Graham couldn't say he blamed her. He felt unusually animalistic as he took careful, measured steps toward her. When he sat down, he made sure to leave a few inches between their knees.

Graham balanced the tray of makeshift first aid supplies between them and took her horrified expression in stride.

He met her eyes and raised a questioning eyebrow.

"What? You're going to start requesting my permission *now*?" she asked.

Graham didn't cover his eye roll at all. He let her have it full force. Then he tipped the tray in her direction and waited as she inventoried the items there.

A white square of fabric he was going to use as a bandage. A mini airplane-serving size of vodka that would double as a disinfectant. A homemade, gelatinous salve Graham had created for treating the occasional burn. A punch-out package of antibiotics labelled Penicillin in bold letters and, finally, a hooked needle, threaded with fishing line.

Graham had to admit that the last thing glinted ominously in the dim light, but the rest was pretty innocuous.

Though clearly the girl didn't think so.

"Hell. No," she said.

She pushed the tray away and took a long pull of cider. Then she moved to set the mug down, but Graham closed his hand around hers, and he forced her fingers to stay wrapped around the handle. He tipped the mug to her lips. She swallowed the last of the cider, and he gave her an approving nod.

For one second, she looked offended.

But her eyes were already growing glassy and unfocused. Graham took the cup from her hands and placed it on the tray, opened the vodka, dabbed it onto the square of fabric and reached for the wound on her leg.

Keira batted at his hand, and when Graham frowned irritably, she just giggled and threaded her fingers through his. Startled, Graham didn't pull away immediately. Instead, he stared down, admiring the way her hand looked in his. Small and delicate. Soft and comfortable. In fact, it fit there. Just the way she'd fit in his lap.

"Hey… Mountain Man?"

Graham dragged his gaze up to hers. Her eyes were far too serious.

"You're not exactly my type," she said. "But if— *if*—I went for the angry, brooding hero kinda thing. I'd pick you." She paused, frowned a little, then added, "I don't think I meant to say that out loud. Am I *drunk*?"

She wobbled a little, almost slipping from the bed. Graham caught her. He eased her back onto the bed, smoothed back the mop of hair from her face and waited for her eyes to close.

Chapter 7

Keira woke slowly, feeling slightly unwell.

Which should have alerted her to the fact that something was wrong even before she remembered where she was and how she got there.

She'd always been a morning person, awake and ready to go before the coffeepot finished brewing. When she'd lived at home with her parents, she and her dad got up at the crack of dawn. The two of them often watched the sun rise together. Then he would read the paper while she made breakfast for her mom, who would get up a solid hour after they did.

Keira valued those early hours, and when she'd finished her degree three years earlier and taken a job in social work, moving into her own place, she continued with the rise-before-dawn ritual.

So if she felt sluggish, as she did right at that moment, she was either hungover or seriously sick.

Which is it now? Keira wondered, somehow unable to recall quite what she'd been up to.

Then she pried her eyes open, and the sight of the cabin sent a surge of recollection and panic through her. A half a dozen thoughts accompanied the memory.

Calloway and his cider. Calloway, holding her hand, easing her back onto the bed.

And worse... Keira telling Calloway he wasn't her type.

Keira blushed furiously as she recalled the last few moments before she passed out. She'd been distracted by the way his palm felt over top of her hand. It was warm. Warmer even than the mug. And rough in a way she'd never experienced before. If she took the time to think about—which she now realized she hadn't—she supposed that Drew's hands were probably soft from the hours he spent sitting in an office and the occasional indulgence of a MANicure.

But not Calloway's. He had calluses on top of calluses, and Keira had had a sudden vision of him *actually* wielding an ax. Chopping wood for this very toasty fire. Topless. Because even in the snowy woods, that kind of manual labor worked up a serious sweat.

And there was no denying the potentially romantic ambience.

Secluded location. Check.

Tall, dark and handsome stranger. Check.

The gentle crackle of a fire. Check.

So maybe it wasn't that she *couldn't* recall what she'd

been up to. Maybe it was that she hadn't *wanted* to re-member it.

Clearly, what she needed was a minute to collect her thoughts and assess her surroundings. So she held very still and took stock of everything she could.

She was on her side, lying with her back pushed to the wall and her hands tucked under a pillow. She had a blanket wrapped around her, but there was an empty space beside her. The last bit made Keira swallow nervously. There was no denying that the spot was just the right size to hold a big, burly man.

Had he slept beside her?

Keira's face warmed again—both with embarrassment and irritation—at the thought.

Somehow, lying in the bed beside him seemed much more taboo than curling up beside him in a desperate attempt to keep warm postaccident in a snowstorm.

Still without moving, she scanned the limited area that she could see, hoping to find proof that she hadn't actually spent the whole night cuddled up next to Calloway. But it was a one-room deal—not huge, not small—with a table and chairs in one corner, and the still-burning woodstove in another. She supposed the bed where she lay was in a third corner. So, unless the fourth and final corner was home to a recliner or a second lumpy mattress, her fears were true.

She'd officially slept with the Mountain Man.

An inappropriate giggle almost escaped her lips as she pictured telling her best friend that she had no problem getting past the failed, so-called sign that was supposed to lead her to Drew. At all. She'd simply climbed into bed with the next man she met instead.

Keira knew her cheeks were still red, and she was glad Calloway wasn't there to see her reaction. If just the *idea* of sharing a bed with him made her feel so squirmy, actually confronting him about it would be a nightmare.

Where was he anyway?

"Calloway?" she called.

Keira wasn't expecting a spoken reply from the thus far mute man, but she did half anticipate his looming presence to step from some hidden alcove so he could stare down at her with that smirk on his face. But right that second, the cabin was completely silent. Which wasn't too terrible, considering the dull ache in her temple. The rest of her hurt, too, and she wondered if she needed medical attention beyond that of a serving of liquored-up cider, a questionable dose of penicillin and the makeshift care of a bona fide mountain man.

She pushed herself to a sitting position, and was pleased that her head didn't spin and that the ache eased off a little. But when she stood, her legs shook, and she realized she was still far weaker than she was used to. With a dejected sigh, she glanced around the room in search of something that would approximate a crutch. She spied a fire iron beside the stove, decided it would do and hobbled toward it.

Maybe there was something in the cabin itself that would answer her questions. She took another slow look around the single-room cabin.

Most of what she saw appeared to be pretty basic. The kitchen contained a wraparound cupboard, an ancient icebox and a rubber bin full of cast-iron pots.

She walked over and opened the icebox. It held the

required slab of ice, several flat, wrapped packages that looked like steaks and—

"Beer?" Keira said out loud, surprised.

Calloway seemed more like the moonshine type than Bud Light. But there it was anyway. She closed the ice-box and moved on to the cupboards. She didn't know what she thought she'd find, but it definitely wasn't instant hot chocolate and packaged macaroni and cheese. A bag of oatmeal cookies peeked out from behind a stack of canned soup.

So he wasn't that much of a survivalist after all.

As Keira let her gaze peruse the cabin a third time, she took note of some of the more modern accoutrements.

Sure, there was no television or microwave, but there was a dartboard and a current calendar and a digital alarm clock. A stainless-steel coffee mug sat on one windowsill, and a signed and mounted baseball adorned another.

For all intents and purposes, it was a middle-of-nowhere man cave. Minus the requisite electronics, of course.

Her curiosity grew.

Keira took a few more steps and banged straight into a dusty cardboard box, knocking it and its contents to the ground.

Dammit.

She reached down to clean it up. And paused.

A notebook—no, a scrapbook—lay open on the floor. An ominous headline popped up from one of the newspaper clippings glued to its page.

Heiress and Son Gunned Down in Ruthless Slaying.

A gruesome crime scene was depicted in black-and-white below the caption, and Keira's fingers trembled as she reached for the book. She flipped backward a few pages.

Home Invasion Turns Deadly. And a photo of a tidy house on a wide lot.

She flipped forward.

Debt and Divorce. Police Close in on Suspect in Henderson Double Murder. A grainy shot of a short-haired man covering his face with the lapel of his suit jacket.

Something about the last headline struck Keira as familiar, and she frowned down at the page, trying to figure out if it was a case she'd heard about. She scanned the article. It was enticingly vague, just the kind of sensationalist journalism that baited the reader into buying the next edition. The suspect was listed as someone close to the victims and the words *unexpected twist* were used three times that she could see with just her quick perusal, making her think the "twist" was probably not "unexpected" at all, but that the reporter wanted to play it up anyway.

Then she clued in.

Derby Reach.

A chill rocked Keira's body. It wasn't just a familiar case. It was *the* case. The affluent community where she'd grown up, home to doctors, lawyers and judges—like her father—had been blown away by the double murder.

Keira remembered the day it occurred, but embarrassingly, not because of the tragedy itself. She'd met Drew that day. While the neighbors stood on their porches, gawking and gossiping, Drew had been walk-

ing through the street, totally clueless, as he searched
for an open house he'd been booked in to view. She'd
been the one to explain to him why no one was thinking about real estate at that moment. And his casual romantic pursuit of Keira started the moment he knocked
on her parents' door by accident.

Now Keira wished she'd paid more attention to what
was happening in her own backyard.

But why did Calloway have the scrapbook in his
house? What connection could a man like him have
with a wealthy socialite's death?

With the book still in her hands, Keira took a cautious, wobbly step back to the window.

Across the snowy yard stood Calloway. In spite of
the subzero temperature, he hadn't bothered zipping
up his coat. The wind kicked up for a second, tossing
his thick hair and ruffling his beard. Calloway didn't
seem to notice at all.

As Keira squinted through the glass, she frowned. A
narrow figure in full protective gear—helmet, fur-lined
hood, thick Gore-Tex pants and knee-high boots—stood
facing Calloway, his hand resting on a parked snowmobile. Something about the way the two men faced each
other made Keira nervous. And as she tried to puzzle
out the source of her distinct but unspecific unease, the
wind changed and a loud voice carried in her direction.

"I've had a change of plans."

The breath Keira had been holding came out with a
wheeze, and she stumbled back in surprise.

Calloway.

It was he who'd spoken.

Even though he'd turned so that his back was to her

and he was blocking her view of the other man, Keira knew it was him. The deep, gravelly nature of the voice couldn't have suited him more perfectly.

Keira pressed her face almost right against the glass, and gasped again, this time not at Calloway. The other man had a gun, hooked menacingly to his side.

Keira took a step back. Her head spun. She needed to get away. From Calloway *and* his armed friend.

"My phone," she murmured, then looked toward the window again as she remembered.

It was in the pocket of the coat Calloway wore right that second.

Chapter 8

The silence of the woods, combined with his habitual alertness, usually gave Graham plenty of notice whenever someone got even close to near to the cabin. More often than not, he could hear them for miles out.

This afternoon had been an exception.

A stupid exception, considering you knew *he was coming.*

But Graham had spent the whole night lying awake beside the girl, worrying about every pause in her inhales and exhales, overthinking every shift of her body, and second-guessing both his stitching job and his decision to ply her with the booze.

Was the fishing line too coarse to be effective? Were the stitches evenly spaced? Would the alcohol worsen the side effects of her concussion?

Graham had been so distracted by his concern that

he didn't hear the approaching snowmobile until it was so close he could actually look outside and see it. He'd barely had time to close the door behind him before the man in front of him—who was currently struggling to unfasten his helmet—parked his vehicle at the edge of the house.

Graham worked at fixing something like a smile on his face.

As much as he trusted and relied on Dave Stark, he had a feeling that the girl's presence might jar the man's loyalty. It was one thing for the two of them to keep Graham's hideout a secret—adding an innocent unknown would be a whole different story.

So Graham stood with his hands in his jeans' pockets and waited with as much patience as he could muster for the familiar man to unclip and remove his helmet, and was careful to keep his gaze forward. He didn't let his eyes flick worriedly toward the cabin. Toward *her*.

The other man finally got his helmet free, and when he whipped it off, Graham frowned. A deep purple bruise darkened one of Stark's eyes, and a long abrasion led from his left eyebrow to the corner of his lip. He seemed indifferent to the damage.

Graham gave the other man's appearance a second, more scrutinizing once-over. Even aside from his injuries, he did look unusually worse for wear. His jacket was dirty and torn in a few places. When he turned slightly, the cold sun glinted off a metallic object at his waist.

A pistol.

Graham's eyes skimmed over it, then went back to Dave's face. Never before had his friend seen a need to bring a gun to the cabin. He wasn't brandishing the weapon, but he wasn't trying to disguise its presence, either. There was something about the way he wore it that Graham didn't like.

"What the hell's going on?"

"I was about to ask you the same thing," Stark countered.

"Me? I'm not the one who looks like he just rolled out of a bar fight."

Dave shrugged. "Occupational hazard. You wanna tell me what you meant by 'change of plans'?"

"I meant that I'll make my own way into town."

Dave couldn't hide his surprise. Or the hint of fear in his eyes.

"Why would you do that?" he wanted to know.

"Few loose ends to tie up."

"Four years, we've been waiting for this. You've sunk every available penny into finding the man. What loose ends could possibly—" The other man cut himself off and narrowed his eyes shrewdly. "What's this about?"

Graham held his gaze steady. "I can't just walk away from this setup, Dave. If things go south with Mike Ferguson, I need to know that my space isn't in danger of being compromised."

Dave sighed. "It's *already* compromised."

"What do you mean?"

"Been an accident up on the road that comes in from the resort town," Dave replied. "Happened to catch it on the radio right before I left town. Car went over a cliff yesterday. Burned to a crisp. Couldn't even get a discernable VIN."

A dark chill crept up Graham's spine. "Not sure what a car accident's got to do with me. Or you, for that matter."

Dave's eyes strayed to the cabin. "You wanna rethink that?"

Graham refused to follow the other man's gaze. "Why? I've been up here four years and nothing has ever turned the radar my way."

"Is this how you want to play? Because if you can't trust *me*…"

It was Graham's turn to let out a breath. He trusted Dave about as much as he trusted anyone.

Which isn't much at all.

But there was no way he was admitting that. The man had been his best friend for two decades, and the only person he could count on for the past few of those.

"Explain it to me, then," Graham said instead. "Tell me how the accident affects me."

"I know cops, my friend. That radio chatter—it's suspicious. They think the burn was a little too perfect."

"So?"

"So, the only thing I know better than cops is *you*. And I know exactly what was going through your head yesterday when we talked on the radio. You were champing at the bit to get to Ferguson. I spent the whole day assuming you'd show up at the resort and that I'd have to hold you back. So I think maybe you *did* leave the cabin yesterday. And I think maybe something stopped you. Something that started out as a vehicle and ended up as a burned-up piece of trash."

"The road is forty miles from here. You think I could've trekked through that and made it back here already?"

Dave shook his head. "I don't think you took the traditional route. The back way is only ten miles. Really rough terrain. But again...this is you we're talking about, isn't it? You've never done things the easy way."

Graham refused to take the bait. "The road is the last place I want to be. So I'm still not seeing what the accident has to do with me."

"It wasn't just a little crash. They're going to be looking for answers. And this isn't all that far to look. Come with me now. Unless you have some other reason for staying..."

As Dave trailed off, all the hair on the back of Graham's neck stood up.

"Get on your snowmobile, Dave," he replied, just short of a growl. "I'll come to you when I'm ready."

"C'mon, Graham—"

"*Now*, Dave."

"All right. This is your deal."

The other man slipped on his helmet, swung one leg over his snowmobile, then flipped up his protective visor and met Graham's cool stare.

"One other thing," he said. "She's a neighbor."

A neighbor? What the hell did that mean?

"She?"

"The driver."

"How could you even know the driver was a she?" Graham scoffed. "You said the car was burned to a crisp."

"It was. But I found *this* right alongside those snowshoe tracks."

Dave reached to the side of the snowmobile, unsnapped a storage compartment and pulled out a black purse, then tossed it through the air. Graham caught it easily. He didn't have to open it to know it was hers.

"Best guess, it'll take them two days to expand their search out this way," Dave added. "Tops. But that won't matter, right? Because you'll be on your way back home."

"Right," Graham agreed, hoping the word didn't sound as forced as it felt.

As Dave's vehicle disappeared into the snow, Graham's hand squeezed into a tight, angry fist, crushing the purse for a moment before he regained control.

Very slowly, he peeled his fingers from the purse. Even more slowly, he unsnapped it and opened the zipper. He reached straight for the wallet and slid out the driver's license. And there it was in black and white.

Keira London Niles. Resident of Derby Reach. The city where Graham had found Holly's broken body. What were the odds?

Slim to none.

Graham took three determined steps toward the cabin, then paused.

The front door creaked open, just a crack.

What the hell?

Graham took another cautious step. No way had he forgotten to close the door properly. He spun around just in time to see the girl—dressed in a pair of his boots and too-long sweatshirt—lift a metallic object behind her shoulder as if she was wielding a baseball bat. Her legs were more than a little shaky, but her face was set in a determined glare as she swung the fire iron straight at his chest.

Chapter 9

The big man was too slick. As Keira swung with all her might, he leaned back like an action-movie hero, easily dodging the blow.

You might have overestimated your own abilities, too, she thought as she lost her footing and stumbled forward.

Keira shoved down the nagging voice. She preferred to blame it on him. Especially since he had his arms outstretched as if he was going to *catch* her of all things.

Ignoring him, she drew back the weapon again. And Calloway took a half a step back.

Good.

"Give me the coat," Keira commanded.

He frowned wordlessly, and Keira rolled her eyes.

"You can drop the silent, brooding stare," she said,

just the slightest hint of a tremor in her voice. "I heard you talking to that other man. Who is he?"

Calloway gave her a long considering look before replying gruffly. "Drop the weapon and I'll drop the stare. Tell me what you heard."

For a moment, Keira went still as her brain caught up to her ears.

Calloway's voice had that same gravelly tinge she'd noted when it had carried on the wind into the cabin, only this close, it was amplified all the more. It was a good voice.

"I heard just enough to know you're a liar," she snapped. "Give me the coat and tell me who that man was."

He stared at her again, then shrugged and slipped the Gore-Tex from his shoulders.

"I don't know why you care," he told her. "And it's funny that you think *I'm* the deceptive one."

"What does *that* mean?" The defensive question slipped out before Keira could stop it, making her blush.

He held the jacket out. "It means I don't believe in coincidence."

"That makes two of us. Throw it."

Calloway tossed the jacket, and Keira caught it in the air, careful to keep one hand on the fire iron as she did it.

"I played all-star baseball in high school," she warned as she started to dig through the pockets in search of her phone. "And I once hit a home run with a broken arm. So don't assume that my injuries will make me any less willing to swing with everything I've got."

"I wouldn't dare."

Keira narrowed her eyes. She strongly suspected he was trying not to smile.

If he laughs, I'll hit him anyway, she decided.

But he stayed silent.

Keira stuck her hand into another pocket. One she was sure she'd already explored. Where the hell was her phone?

"Are you looking for something in particular?" Calloway asked, his voice just a little too innocent.

She glared at him. "Listen. You might have saved my life—"

"Might have?" Graham interrupted. "You were unconscious. In a blizzard. I'm not sure *might* is the right word."

Keira's cheeks heated up. "I didn't mean it like that."

"So how did you mean it? The way *I* mean it when I say I might be standing outside, freezing, while a woman who I carried for ten miles, who I took into my house, who I gave my own *bed* to, aims a weapon at my head?"

The pink in Keira's face deepened to a cherry red, and he noticed her hand wavered. "I—"

Graham shook his head and cut her off again. "Or did you mean it like how I mean it when I say I might just be considering tossing you over my shoulder—again—carrying you *back* to the crash site and leaving you there?"

"You wouldn't!"

"I *might*."

His voice was dark, and Keira's eyes widened in surprise. She took a step back, her gaze no longer fixed on his face, but on his hand.

"That's my purse." She heard the tinge of fear in her statement.

"Keira London Niles of Derby Reach. There has to be a story in that name. Active member of Triple A. Twenty-four years old, just last month," he reeled off. "Happy birthday, by the way. Did you know your license was expired?"

"Give it back!"

He held it out, but there was no way for her to take it without losing her already tenuous hold on the fire iron in her hands.

"You don't want it anymore?" he asked.

"I'm not stupid," she grumbled.

"Far from it," Calloway agreed.

He set the purse down on the railing, reached into his pocket and pulled out a familiar black object. Keira felt the color drain from her cheeks, and the jacket slipped to the ground.

Well. That explains why I couldn't find it, she thought.

"Who were you going to call?" Calloway wondered out loud.

It was a good question. One Keira wasn't even sure of how to answer. Calling Drew seemed out of the question. Her parents were away on their annual European cruise. And her best friend would probably just laugh her butt off.

"The police," she whispered, not certain why she sounded so unsure.

Calloway tipped his head to one side, as if curious, and tapped the phone on his chin. "Not someone from *Derby Reach*?"

Why had he said it like that, with the tiny bit of emphasis on the name of her hometown? She recalled the scrapbook full of newspaper clippings about the murder in her hometown, and a little chill crept up her spine.

Graham examined the little crease between her brows, then the probing look in her emerald gaze. His gaze traveled down her face to her pursed lips. He almost believed the puzzled look to be genuine. And as a result, he also almost missed the subtle adjustment in her stance as she pulled an elbow back and prepared to strike.

I'm a sucker, he realized. *One pair of big green eyes, one bossy mouth, and I'm a mess.*

She swung and Graham ducked backward. He charged at her, and she lost her balance, stumbling toward the stairs. Automatically, Graham switched from an attack mode to defense mode. He reached out to stabilize her, and realized a moment too late her clumsiness had been an act, her near fall a feint.

Rookie mistake, he growled at himself.

She was already off at a run.

"What the hell!" Graham yelled after her.

She had to know she didn't stand a chance of getting away from him. Even if she hadn't been weakened by her injuries, Graham was at an advantage. His legs were longer, he was far more accustomed to the terrain than she was and he wasn't wearing boots five sizes too big.

Apparently, she wasn't going to let that stop her from trying.

Graham caught up with her just inside the tree line on the edge of the clearing. His arms closed around her shoulders and the fire iron dropped to the ground. With a mutual grunt, the two of them fell straight into the snow.

She wriggled away, kicking viciously. Keira's foot met his chest, and when she drew it back for another round, Graham flung himself backward.

"Dammit!" he cursed as he landed hard on his rear end.

"Damn *you*!" Keira countered angrily.

She crawled along the snow, found a tree trunk and pulled herself up. But Graham was there in a flash.

"You can't win," he cajoled.

With desperation clear in her eyes, she charged at him. The surprise of the attack—more than the force of her body weight hitting him—knocked him to the ground once more. Graham let out another annoyed growl and sprung to his feet. By the time he was up-right, Keira had the tire iron in her hands again, this time raised over her head.

"Stay back!" she yelled, and waved it around a little wildly.

Graham eyed the weapon dismissively, then focused on Keira instead. "Put it down."

"Fat chance."

"Put it down, or I'm going to *make* you put it down."

"I don't think so."

"Fine. Let's do things the hard way."

He stalked toward her, and with a cry, she tossed the fire iron at him, then turned and attempted to flee once more. She didn't make it more than four steps. Graham counted them. Then he slipped his arms around her slim waist and he lifted her easily from the ground.

Keira screamed, probably as loud and as long as she could, but her voice just echoed through the forest, bouncing back at her uselessly. She flung an elbow in the direction of Graham's stomach, but the attack didn't elicit more than a grunt. In a slick move, he flipped her around and pinned her to a large evergreen, then fixed his eyes on hers.

Keira continued to struggle, but Graham wasn't even pretending to let her get away. She finally seemed to give in, and she stopped fighting. She slid to the ground, but he continued to hold her arms as he glared down at her. Her breath was coming in short gasps and her limbs were shaking.

On the ground, she looked small and fragile once more.

For a second, Graham felt guilty. He'd made himself responsible for her well-being. Taken her in to care for her. Yeah, she'd lashed out at him for some reason he couldn't understand. But she was probably scared as hell and still shaken up. And maybe her hometown *was* just a coincidence after all.

Graham loosened his hold, just slightly. Then she attempted to twist away, and guilt evaporated. He squeezed her wrists together over her head, pressed a foot—as gently as he could while still being firm—into *her* feet and immobilized her.

"I'm done playing games," he told her in a low voice.

She lifted her chin defiantly. "What are you going to do? Kill me?"

Her question hit him hard, square in the chest. She *did* know him. Or thought she did.

No coincidences.

"I'm not a murderer," Graham replied coldly, and dropped her wrists. "And what I'm going to *do* is take you back inside. Where we're going to eat breakfast like two normal adults. And where you're going to tell me exactly what the hell you were doing up this mountain in the first place. Understood?"

She nodded meekly, and Graham had to shove down the reflexive regret at dampening the fire in her eyes.

You need answers, he reminded himself.

He pulled back, and as he did, Keira tipped up her head. The new angle gave him a perfect view of her eyes, and Graham saw with relieved satisfaction that the fire—quite clearly—wasn't extinguished. Just banked.

Chapter 10

As Calloway's seemingly enormous body eased away from Keira's own petite one, she realized how ridiculous it was to think she could have overpowered him in the first place. The self-defense training she received at work was no match for his brute strength. No makeshift weapon would outdo him.

"Let's go," he said.

Even if his voice hadn't demanded obedience, he didn't release her, and that gave her little choice but to go where he propelled her. They moved toward the cabin, Graham's hands pressed firmly into Keira's shoulders, her feet dragging a little in the oversize boots.

Stupid, stupid, she cursed herself as they moved along. *I would've been better off taking my chances by*

*running into the woods instead of thinking he owed me
some kind of explanation.*

Because he really *didn't* owe her one. And if Keira
thought about it, she was probably the one who owed
him something. Had she even thanked him for saving
her? She couldn't remember. She opened her mouth to
do it now, then paused as she second-guessed the impulse. Should she still thank him now that she suspected
he had something to do with the four-year-old homicide
in her hometown?

I'm not a murderer, he'd said.

Did that make it true? Keira desperately wanted to
believe him. And not just because she was trapped on
the mountainside with him, and her only way out—so
far—was a man with a snowmobile and a gun. Something about Calloway felt intoxicatingly *right*. Especially when he was standing as close to her as he was
now, his hand on her body, guiding her where he wanted
to go.

When they moved up the stairs, and he reached
around her to push open door, his clean, woodsy scent
assaulted her senses, rendering her brain temporarily
nonfunctional. Her booted toe caught on the transition
board at the bottom on the door frame, and before she
could stop herself, she was falling forward. She braced
herself to hit the ground. But the impact didn't come.

She still fell, but not the way she'd been thinking
she would. One of Calloway's arms slipped under her
legs, and the other closed around her shoulders. As she
went down, he took the full force of the ground to his
own elbows and knees. He had one hand on the back

of her neck, the other on her thigh, and his gray eyes held her where she was.

They were both breathing heavily, and Keira refused to acknowledge the treacherous parts of her body that demanded to know why it felt so good to be looking into one another's eyes, chests rising and falling in near unison.

A drop of water fell from his face to hers, and he eased his hand out from behind her hair to wipe it away gently. His fingers burned pleasantly against her skin, and it didn't help at all when he looked her straight in the eyes and gave her the clearest understanding of the term *white-hot* that she'd ever had. It was the perfect way to describe the way ice gray met fierce need in Calloway's eyes. They were burning so bright, she almost had to look away. But couldn't.

Lying above her, looking at her like that, Calloway wasn't just handsome. He was gorgeous. The perfectly rustic look had basically turned him into the supermodel version of his Mountain Man self.

And, oh, he smelled good, too. Even better than he had when he was carrying her up the mountainside. Raw and woodsy and tinged with smoke.

He was unpredictable and dangerous, and it was totally unreasonable to be this attracted to him. The smart part of her brain knew it. But the smart part didn't seem to be attached to the rest of her. In fact, there were a few distinct bits that seemed *remarkably* detached from her brain altogether.

Keira's whole body was alight.

Kiss me, she begged silently.

And as her heavy gaze continued to hold Calloway's, she knew he was going to.

Thank God.

Then, so slowly she was sure he was very carefully gauging her reaction, he slid his hand from her cheek to her chin and tipped it toward him. He inched forward. Keira fought an urge to speed it up, to drive her lips into his, to close the miniscule gap between them and take what she was dying to have. What she suddenly realized she'd been dying to have since the second he put his arms around her in the snowstorm.

Don't rush this, whispered a small voice in her head.

And Kiera suspected that the voice was right. This kiss—this first kiss with such an intense, unusual and mysterious man—was something to be savored.

His mouth touched hers, his eyes still wide-open.

It was the softest kiss. The gentlest one. But it ignited more passion in Keira than she'd felt in her entire quarter-of-a-century-long life. She gasped because she couldn't help it. She closed her eyes because she had to. And when Calloway's palm skidded to the back of her neck again, her arms came up, all on their own, to encircle his waist. She pulled him close, and he let her. The aches in her body eased away as she let the rest of the kiss take her, as his lips became hungry, and everything but Calloway faded to the background.

But it was painfully short.

He pulled away, ending the embrace with an abruptness that contrasted sharply with its slow beginnings.

It left Keira full of longing.

"Calloway," she whispered.

He leaned in once more, grazing her mouth, and

then—without warning—he abandoned his pursuit of her lips to swoop in and lift her up instead. He carried her straight to the bed, and for a dizzying moment Keira thought he was going to skip the preamble and go straight for the main attraction.

Quicker than she could decide whether or not she should protest, he reached beneath the frame, grabbed a rope, wrapped it around her wrists tightly and secured her to the bed.

Dammit.

Complications were low on Graham's list of priorities. Liking Keira Niles was *very* complicated.

And he did like her. Even before they'd shared the most intense kiss he'd ever experienced.

He liked that she was wearing his clothes. He liked the way the lithe muscles in her thighs disappeared under his shirt, hinting at what lay farther up. He even liked the way she was glaring at him right that second, mad instead of scared, a hint of residual passion evident in the way her lips stayed slightly parted and the way her gaze kept flicking between his eyes and his own mouth.

Beautiful, resilient, strong and smart.

His *like* was making it hard to see her as a threat, and he really needed to overcome that. Somehow.

"What do you think you're doing?" she snapped.

"Did you know I was here?" he replied softly, ignoring her angry question. "Or did you just get lucky?"

"I wouldn't call this lucky."

Keira pulled emphatically on the rope around her arms, and Graham winced. Coercion didn't suit him, and in spite of what people thought, he wasn't a violent man. Not habitually anyway. He just did what he had to do, when he had to do it.

"If you're not going to answer my questions," Graham said, "then I'm going to go back to our previous arrangement."

"What previous arrangement was that?" she replied, just shy of sarcastic.

"The one where I don't speak at all."

He started to turn away, but she snorted, and he stopped, midturn, to face her again.

"More of the silent treatment? What are you?" she asked. "A ten-year-old boy?"

For some reason, the question annoyed him far more than her lack of candor. Graham strode toward her, and once again she didn't cower. She raised her eyes and opened her mouth, but whatever snarky comment had been about to roll off her tongue was cut off as Graham mashed lips into hers. Uncontrollably. He kept going until he'd possessed her mouth completely, and when it ended, Keira was left gasping for air—gasping for *more*. For good measure, he dug his hands into the hair at the back of her neck and trailed his lips from her chin to her collarbone before he stopped.

"When you're ready to talk—with some honesty— I'll be just over there, waiting," Graham growled against Keira's throat.

Then he stood and moved across the room to dig out the things he needed to prepare breakfast.

Just a morning like any other, he told himself.

Except that he needed two plates and two forks instead of the usual one of each. And twice the amount of pancake batter and extra coffee. Oh, and there was also the faint feminine perfume that somehow managed to override the scent of fire that usually dominated the air in the cabin. Those things, coupled with the way her heated gaze followed each of his movements while he stoically ignored her presence, left no doubt that the morning wasn't *any*thing like any other.

Why couldn't he have rescued a hideous beast of woman with no spark in her whatsoever? Why did it have to be a girl who so thoroughly piqued his interest and so easily distracted him from finding Mike Ferguson? He should be trying to think of a way to get her out of his house as quickly as possible so he could get back to his mission. Not standing there daydreaming about her. He could barely blink without seeing her enticing form on the back of his eyelids.

"If I answer your questions, will you answer mine?"

Keira's voice startled Graham, and he spun toward her. The pan went slack in his grip, and the golden breakfast item flew right past both it and him, and landed on the floor at his feet. They both stared at it for a moment before Graham bent to snatch it up.

"Well?" Keira prodded.

Graham shrugged. "Depends."

She blinked, looking surprised. Had she just expected him to agree with no further terms? Not a chance in hell was he giving her the freedom to ask anything she felt like.

"It depends on what?" she asked.

Graham took a breath, popped the floor pancake into his mouth, then chewed it slowly and deliberately before swallowing it and answering her puzzled question. "On whether or not I think you're telling the truth. And whether or not I think giving *you* an honest answer will put you in danger."

"Shouldn't I be the one who decides if I'm in danger?" she countered.

Damn, he liked her stubbornness. He ran his fingers over his beard to cover his smile.

"Not today," he told her.

"Listen to me, Mountain Man. You might have saved my life—" Keira paused when Graham raised an eyebrow, and quickly amended, "You *did* save my life. But you also lulled me into a drunken stupor with your liquored-up cider, then crawled into bed with me, and now you've tied me up, and—"

He cut her off. "I also stripped you down, searched your body for signs of any other deep cuts or contusions, or internal bleeding. Then I stitched you up as best I could."

With each word, Keira's face grew redder, and by the end of Graham's speech, she was nearly purple.

"You *stripped* me?" she asked, her voice a squeak. "Why would you *strip* me? And then *tell* me about it?"

Graham shrugged. "I thought it best that I get that out of the way now. And it would've been hard to be thorough if you'd been clothed. That's two questions you owe me now, by the way."

"I don't owe you anything," she almost yelled. "You cannot touch me or kiss me, just because you feel like it. You cannot carry me around, just because it's easier than asking me nicely."

"You think I did all that for *me*?" Graham argued.

"I'm sure it was horribly inconvenient for you to get me naked."

Graham bit back an admission that it *had* actually been damned inconvenient. He'd covered her body carefully while searching for anything more serious than the slice in her thigh. For the first time in his life, he'd been barely able to keep his professional detachment in place, and the guilt of it had made him want to perform the careful examination of her body with his eyes closed. Except the thought of a hands-only exploration brought with it a whole host of other, far from clinical, ideas to mind. He had never been so happy to finish an exam.

Now he was sorry he'd brought it up.

"You were asleep," he growled.

"And sleep made me what? Unwomanly? Unattractive?"

Hell. No.

"High on yourself, aren't you?" Graham asked, his voice just a little too dark to be called teasing.

"What does that mean?"

"You clearly think your nudity is enough to turn a man into nothing more than a slobbering sex-crazed maniac," he stated.

"That's not what I said!"

"That's what I heard."

Keira's face was still pink. "It's just that that stuff makes it a little hard to trust that you've got my best interests at heart."

He *had* done all of those things she'd mentioned. He'd also covered her each time she kicked off her blankets in the night, panicked each time her breathing changed and had his own night thoroughly ruined.

Ruined? he thought. *Or made more worthwhile.*

He growled at the voice in his head and pushed it away.

"You're welcome," Graham said.

"You're—I'm—what?"

Ignoring her incomprehensible, sputtering reply, Graham walked over to Keira and unfastened the rope. Then, in a quick move that made her squeak, he scooped her from the bed, carried her over to the little table and secured her to one of the chairs.

"I'll let those first two questions go, and even let you ask another. In the name of chivalry," he said, and raised an eyebrow expectantly.

Chapter 11

If her hands hadn't been tied together, Keira would've crossed her arms over her chest in indignant frustration.

"You think you're chivalrous?" she demanded.

The big man grinned smugly. "Yes."

"You may want to buy a dictionary."

"Either way...it's my turn. You've asked three questions, and I've asked none."

"I haven't even asked my *first* question yet!" Keira protested. "And you said you were going to let the first two go."

"Changed my mind. My house, my rules," he replied.

"You are an infuriating man."

He nodded. "I'm also loyal, thorough, a tad controlling and a damned fine cook. Are you hungry?"

"Is that *your* question?"

"As a matter of fact...it is."

Keira rolled her eyes. "No, I'm not hungry."

"First question and already you're telling me a lie," Calloway said and he pushed a plate of pancakes toward her.

She shoved it back. "It's not a lie."

Calloway gripped his fingers on the edge of the plate and pushed it across the table. When it reached Keira, she tried to send it back again, but he didn't let it go.

"I'm not going to eat just because you tell me to," she informed him.

In reply, he dragged the pancake away.

Ha, Keira thought triumphantly. *Take that.*

But he wasn't letting her win. He was just upping his game. He smiled and began to cut the pancake into bite-size pieces. Then he scraped his chair over the floor so that he was right beside her. He jabbed a fork into one of the pieces and held it up to Keira's mouth.

It smelled damned good.

She turned her head away anyway.

Calloway exhaled, clearly frustrated.

Keira tipped her face back in his direction, prepared to snap something mean and clever at him. But the second she opened her mouth, his fingers were there. A piece of pancake slipped into her mouth, and it was syrupy and sweet and so soft it practically melted away when it hit her tongue.

Oh, my God.

It was the best pancake Keira had ever tasted. Maybe the best *food* she'd ever tasted. All thoughts of ropes versus chivalry went out of her head. When Calloway lifted another piece from the plate, there was no hope in hell she was turning it down. She opened her mouth eagerly, and he popped it in. Keira couldn't even act embarrassed as her mouth closed quickly and she nipped his fingers. It really was that good.

A little noise—just barely shy of a *yum*—escaped from her lips as she swallowed.

Calloway raised an eyebrow.

"Fine," Keira relented. "I take back the breakfast thing. But on the other one, I stand firm. No touching."

He smiled as if he didn't believe her, lifted another piece of pancake from the plate, raised an eyebrow and held it out. After the briefest hesitation, Keira opened her mouth, and Calloway popped it in. He let out a deep laugh, and the fourth piece he offered to her a little more slowly. When Keira parted her lips eagerly, he drew the pancake away.

"Hey!" she protested.

Graham leaned his elbows on the table. "You ready to answer another question? Truthfully, this time?"

"I wasn't *lying*," Keira argued. "I just didn't know I was hungry."

"Uh-huh."

"Besides which. I'm pretty sure it's *my* turn to ask a question."

"We both know that's not true," Calloway said, and grinned again.

He held the pancake positioned between his thumb and forefinger, just out of biting distance. Keira bent forward to grab it. This time, when he tried to tease her, she jerked her bound hands up, and just barely managed to get enough slack that she could close them on his forearm.

Calloway chuckled, but he let her take the pancake.

She made an exaggerated *mmm* noise as she sucked it back, not realizing that she wasn't nibbling on just the pancake. Calloway's fingers were still sandwiched between her lips, pleasantly smooth and soft on his calloused skin. Heat shot through her, and when she relaxed her jaw to release his fingers, he didn't pull away. Instead, he swiped his thumb over the corner of her mouth, collecting a drop of syrup. Then he pushed it back to the tip of her tongue, and Keira gave his thumb a little lick, relieving it of the wayward syrup.

"Thank you," she said softly. "For helping me and fixing me up."

"Anytime."

There was a weight behind his tone that didn't match the typically dismissive expression. As if he meant it literally.

Anytime.

Keira's pulse raced, and her heart swelled pleasantly at the thought that Calloway would drop everything just to help her. That maybe he had *already* dropped everything to help her.

In the soft, wintry sunlight filtering through the cabin, there was no mistaking the want in his eyes. A matching one flowed through Keira.

Slowly, he loosened the rope on her wrists. And when she was free, she didn't make a run for it. Instead, she let him twine their fingers together, then lift their joined hands to her cheekbone. He ran them across her skin. She leaned closer. Her mouth was so near to his that she could already almost taste him.

At every turn, she wanted him more and cared less about what had brought her there in the first place. Two more seconds of his knee pressed between hers under the table, and she was going to be insisting that he take her back to that lumpy bed in the corner.

"You okay?" he asked.

The question threw her a little.

"Am I okay?"

His shoulders went up and down. "Give me a sliding scale? One through ten."

He really did sound serious.

"My head aches. So three out of ten for that. You untied me, so five out of ten for that. And I'm not dead. So I'll concede a ten out of ten for that."

"So…an overall of about six out of ten. Sixty percent isn't too bad."

"It's not exactly A material."

"Maybe you could bump it up to a C+ if I lent you some pants?"

The burn of desire, just under Keira's skin, came back, full force. Her legs *were* bare. And they were wrapped around one of Calloway's denim-clad ones. Put that together with the way his beard was close enough to tickle, the deep rumble of his voice making her chest vibrate, and Keira knew she was in a completely different kind of trouble. One that had nothing to do with Calloway's secrets or the armed man with whom he was acquainted. That stuff—that dangerous stuff—seemed ridiculously far away at the moment.

But she needed to remember it. And to do *that*, she needed space. Reluctantly, she pulled away.

Forcing a measured tone, Keira whispered, "Pants don't outweigh the left-me-tied-to-a-bed, rifled-through-my-purse creep factor. Can I ask my question now?"

"Can you..." Calloway trailed off, looking at her as though he couldn't quite understand the request.

Then he cleared his throat and shoved back his chair, irritation making his eyes flash as he stood up and yanked away the nearly empty pancake plate.

Guilt tickled at Keira's mind, but she pushed it down.

"Can I ask my question?" she repeated.

With a coolness that didn't match the burn of his gaze, Calloway replied, "I think you're still in the red, as far as questions are concerned."

He crossed his arms and glared down at her.

Refusing to be intimidated, Keira jumped to her own feet and opened her mouth to argue, but an abrupt wave of dizziness made her head spin.

Immediately, Calloway seemed to sense the change. His eyes filled with concern. And then his hands were on her, easing her close with a gentleness that contrasted dramatically with his bulky form. He lifted her from the ground and cradled her to his wide chest.

Right away, Keira felt better. Sleepy, but better. Almost content.

He brushed her hair back from her forehead, letting his palm rest there for an extra second.

"Overdid it," he murmured.

His apologetic tone made Keira want to absolve him of responsibility. It had been her careless disregard for that weather that had led to the accident. Her attempt to come after Calloway with the fire iron that made her arms ache.

But she couldn't form the words.

After a moment, she gave up trying and pushed her face into the soothing firmness of his body instead. She could hear his heart. It was beating loudly, and she liked its steadiness. Appreciated its strength. Appreciated *his* strength.

A little sigh escaped Keira's lips as she let both him and his heartbeat surround her.

As Calloway moved across the floor, she noted that his pace matched the thumps. And in a light-headed way, she wondered if the blood rushing through her was going to match it soon, too.

But in a few steps, he reached the bed, drew back the blankets and laid her down, and Keira realized she wasn't going to get a chance to find out.

Regret made her heart ache.

Why was I arguing with him?

Keira couldn't remember.

Using the last bit of her strength, she reached for him. "Stay," she managed to whisper.

Keira knew the muddled way her head felt was what made her say it. Or what *let* her say it.

But she didn't care.

He met her eyes, and some undefinable emotion brimmed over in their silvery stare, and he peeled back the blanket and slid into the bed, and Keira didn't just not *care* that reason had slipped away…she was glad.

Graham woke abruptly, inhaled deeply, then froze as Keira's scent filled him.

What the…

Then he remembered. She'd looked up at him with those half-closed eyes, issued the one-word plea, and he'd been unable to do anything but indulge her, crawling in beside her and cradling her close until she was sound asleep.

She wasn't the only one being indulged. You could've at least tried to resist. Would have, if you really wanted to.

That was the truth.

He could use whatever excuse came to mind—checking her breathing, making sure she was just exhausted and not injured further or feverish—but when it came down to it, Graham simply wanted her close.

Not just close...in your bed.

He couldn't even remember the last time he'd even *thought* about taking a girl to bed.

Somewhere between four years and never again.

Or longer.

Because even before your life fell apart, things on that front were less than satisfying.

Graham ran his fingers through a loose strand of Keira's hair and watched her eyelids flutter. He sure as hell didn't lack desire right that second. Or any second since she'd appeared out of thin air. In fact, his desire for this girl seemed more central to his life than any other thing.

Keira shifted a little beside him, and her slim fingers found his shirt. She tightened her grip on the fabric for a moment, and then she stilled again. As if she'd just been making sure he was still there. Graham's heart squeezed a little in his chest before he could stop it.

Stupid.

Very carefully, he put his hand over hers and loosened her hold on his clothes, then eased out of bed.

As silently as he could, he slipped on his favorite plaid jacket, then let himself out onto the porch.

Graham was startled to see that the sun had dipped down behind the mountain and that dusk was already settling in. He'd done none of his usual chores, performed none of the ritualistic tasks that had occupied him for the past four years. No perimeter scan, no check to make sure everything was ready to go should he have to leave suddenly, nothing. He'd somehow slept the day away. With Keira London Niles.

Graham took a deep breath, trying to clear the thoughts in his head and her delicate aroma out of his nostrils. The inhale of cool air helped with the second, but did nothing at all in regard to the first.

He fought to keep from heading straight back inside, then tightened his jacket and shoved aside a pile of snow so that he could slump down onto the rarely used porch rocker. The wood underneath him was icy enough to creep through his jeans, but Graham continued to sit there anyway. It seemed like a suitable punishment for the heat that stirred in him each time his mind drifted toward Keira.

Dammit.

He couldn't afford to be feeling like this about a girl he barely knew.

Hell. He couldn't allow himself to have feelings at all. His soft side was what got him into this mess in the first place.

What *was* she doing there? Was she telling the truth about not knowing Graham was on the mountain?

The second she was well enough, he was going to demand answers. Not because he wanted to, but because he had to. To protect himself, and more important, to protect her.

Graham's chest constricted again as he thought of how dangerous it was for Keira to be there with him. She couldn't have picked a worse savior. Even just knowing his name was enough to pull unnecessary, unwanted attention her way. If she repeated it, the authorities would descend on her.

Or worse.

Mike Ferguson might come looking.

Graham needed to ensure that didn't happen. More than he needed anything else. And sitting around thinking about that didn't help any more than lying in bed beside her did.

He started to stand, but only got as far as putting one hand on the arm of the rocker.

Keira was up. Awake. Standing in the doorway. Even though she'd draped a blanket around her shoulders, Graham could see that she'd taken the time to get dressed in one of his T-shirts and a pair of his sweats— cinched tight, but still hanging off her hips. She looked sleepy and sexy and about as perfect as one person could.

Graham stared for a long second, mesmerized by the way the waning light brought out the creamy tone of her skin and deepened the auburn in her hair.

He took a breath, then wished he hadn't because her sweetness was in his nose once again. He did his best to ignore it and forced himself to speak.

"You shouldn't be up," he greeted gruffly.

"Morning to you, too, Mountain Man," she replied.

Graham's eyes flicked to the moonlit sky.

"Evening," he corrected.

"Always have to have the upper hand, don't you?"

He gave her a considering look, wondering how she could possibly believe he had the upper hand. Just looking at her made him feel…not exactly helpless. Not exactly powerless.

Spellbound, maybe.

"You should go back inside," Graham said, deflecting her question so that he wouldn't have to admit just how out of his element he felt right then.

In reply, she narrowed her eyes in the already-familiar way that told him she wasn't interested in doing what he thought she ought to do.

With the same stubborn look on her face, Keira moved toward him instead of away from him.

Graham opened his mouth to point out that she might not like the way things turned out if she did as she wanted instead of as she should, but he didn't have to say a word. Right before she reached the porch swing, the slippery ground did it on his behalf.

Keira's feet, which were dwarfed inside a pair of his socks, skidded along the ice and with an "Oomph," she landed in his lap.

She made as if she was going to get up, but Graham wasn't going to let her go so easily; she felt far too good, right there in his lap.

"Stay."

He realized immediately that he'd echoed her earlier request—the one he hadn't been able to deny—wondered if she noticed it, too. If she did, she didn't say.

But after a minute, she leaned against him and tucked her feet up. Automatically, Graham's arms came up to pull her even closer. It was strange, how natural it felt to hold her like that.

"At least this way, I know you're not freezing your rear end off," he said into the top of her head.

There was a tiny pause before she asked, "Is that why you want me to stay?"

"No," Graham admitted.

"But you're still not going to tell me anything, are you?" she replied.

He ran his hands over her shoulders, then down her arms and rested his palms on her wrists.

"No," he said again. "Not because I don't want to."

"What's stopping you?"

"My gut."

"Your gut tells you not to trust me?"

Graham chuckled. "Actually, my gut tells me that I *should* trust you."

Graham moved his hands from her wrists to her hands and threaded his fingers through hers.

He suddenly found himself wondering if *she* trusted *him*. What *her* gut had to say.

Maybe she hadn't even considered it.

Did he want her to?

She really shouldn't trust him. His past was too troublesome, his heart too marred. He might hurt her in his attempt to keep her safe. Hell, he had nothing to even offer. Not until he'd taken care of Mike Ferguson and all that went along with finding the man.

But he wanted her faith, and not blindly. He wanted to know that he hadn't lost the quality that made a girl like Keira believe in him.

"So…" she prodded after his long moment of silence.

Graham jerked back to the present moment. "My gut tells me to trust you. But it's warning me even louder that if I tell you my story, it'll put your life at risk."

"Isn't that my risk to take?"

"It should be, yes," he agreed.

"But not now?"

"I didn't save your life just to let you get killed, Keira."

Her hands tightened on Graham's. "Are you sorry?"

"Sorry about what?"

"That you saved me."

The quiet, trying-not-to-sound-hurt voice cut into Graham's chest. He couldn't stand the thought of her believing that.

He released her hands so he could reposition her, so he could see her face and she could see his.

"No matter what happens, Keira," he stated softly, "I'll never be sorry that I saved you."

A little smile turned up the corners of her so-kissable lips, and Graham wanted to make it even wider.

"I'll tell you what," he said. "If you come inside and let me feed you dinner *and* you manage to stay awake for more than five minutes after, I'll answer one question. Your way."

"Carte blanche?"

That smile of hers reached her eyes.

In spite of his head screaming at him *not* to say yes, Graham couldn't help but give in.

"If you promise not to ask me anything too terrible during dinner, then yes."

"What do you want? Small talk?"

Graham nodded. "Small talk. In exchange for carte blanche."

And her full lips widened into a grin, and that spellbound feeling slammed into Graham's heart once more.

Chapter 12

True to his word, Calloway kept the conversation light. He fed the woodstove and heated up some thick soup and told her he hadn't seen so much snow in the mountains in a long time. With a head shake, he deflected her question about precisely how long.

And in spite of her resolve to stay awake, and her nearly daylong nap, the second she finished her soup Keira could feel her eyes wanting to close and sense her mind wandering. She tried to keep it focused. But when she pushed her bowl away, a yawn came out instead of a question.

If she did manage to stay awake...what would she ask?

Just a few hours ago, she swore that she had a dozen all-important, totally articulate things she *had* to know about who Calloway was and what he was doing there on the mountain. About his interaction with the man outside. About the box of newspaper clippings.

Now all the specifics were muddled.

"Keira?"

His voice, rumbling with amusement, made her jerk her head up from its unintentional resting place on her hand.

Calloway had cracked one of the beers from the fridge and looked far more relaxed than Keira expected.

He looks so...normal.

Which was somehow comforting. A beer and a fire and cozy evening. Keira wished wistfully that it could be that simple.

"You awake?" he asked.

"Yes," she lied.

Clearly, she'd drifted off enough to give him time to get the beer from the fridge. Funny that she was already so comfortable with this man—complete with all his dangerous edges—after such a short time. And not a single alarm bell was going off, either.

Calloway took a swig of his beer and gave her a considering look that matched her own. "So. Does this mean you have something to ask me?"

Keira tried again to recall what, specifically. She'd had something in mind. It eluded her now.

"Did you feed me soup to make me sleepy?" She wanted to know.

A grin broke out on Calloway's face. "I give you carte blanche and that's the question you choose?"

"You know perfectly well that wasn't it at all." Another yawn took away from the emphatic way she meant to make the statement.

"Why don't you lie down while you think about it?" he suggested.

"Nice try."

Calloway's smile widened. "I could carry you over to the bed again."

"You'd like that, wouldn't you?"

"Maybe I would."

His eyes did a slow head-to-toe inventory of Keira's body. They rested on each part of her just long enough to make the object of his attention warm, then moved on to the next.

Feet and ankles. Knees and thighs. Hips and waist. The swell of her breasts.

He paused at her lips and lingered there before he raised his gaze up again, and then he came to his feet and began to clear their table.

And even though Calloway had broken the stare and his eyes were otherwise occupied, Keira knew there was no *maybe* about it.

He would enjoy taking her to bed.

And if Keira was being honest, she craved the closeness, too. She wanted the feel of his arms around her and she wanted to taste his lips again.

Maybe the heated desire she felt was amplified by her surroundings, maybe it was made more intense by how close she'd come to death just yesterday.

Probably.

It made sense psychologically—reasonably. Her training in the social work field had taught enough about transference.

But underneath that, Keira felt a stronger pull.

He'd rescued her, at the risk of his own safety. And he was still putting her life ahead of his own.

A man like that…he deserved appreciation.

Appreciation. Yeah, that's *what you feel.*

She shoved aside the snarky thought and watched Calloway rinse their bowls, then dry them.

His body moved smoothly and confidently, undaunted by the stereotypically feminine activity. Keira liked the glimpse of domesticity. A lot.

"Keira?"

She jumped in her seat. "Yes?"

"Nothing. Just checking."

"Checking what?"

"Whether you'd fallen asleep or whether you were staring at my rear end."

"Very funny."

Calloway chuckled. "It was the only reason I could think of for you *not* offering to dry while I washed."

Keira's face warmed, and she stood up quickly. But the big man was at her side in a second, his hand on her elbow.

"Hey," he said. "I was kidding. You need to rest, not do dishes."

"I've rested an awful lot already."

"Not enough."

Warmth crept from his palm into her arm and through her chest, and she couldn't argue as he led her across the room to the bed. And she felt a little lost as he released her.

Definitely more than transference.

She looked up at his face, wondering how she'd ever questioned whether or not he was handsome. He was near perfect.

"In my other life," he told her, his voice low, "it was

my job to take care of people. I want you to get better, Keira. Soon. So all I need right now is to make sure you're all right."

He pulled up the blanket from the bed, tucked it around her face, then cupped her cheek. And that second, Keira remembered what he'd said about his gut and trust, and something clicked home for her.

"I work for child protective services," she said slowly, "and I have to form snap judgments sometimes. I need to know if I'm leaving a child in a potentially unsafe environment, or decide if someone is trying to deceive me into thinking it's safer than it is. And I know this is different, but I'm used to listening to my gut, too, Calloway. And it's telling me that even if you're not sharing everything... I should trust you, too."

For a brief second, a mix of emotions waged a war in the Mountain Man's stormy eyes. Relief. Worry. Fierce want. Frustration.

Then he kissed her forehead and strode across the cabin.

Keira considered going after him, but something told her she didn't have to. Calloway wasn't holding his secrets as tightly as he had been, just hours earlier, and she could be patient.

She leaned her head down on the pillow and squished up against the wall, making room for him. Whenever he was ready.

Graham busied himself with tasks around the little house. None of them really needed doing, but none of them took him very far from Keira, either.

He wasn't so bogged down in denial that he didn't

recognize the burgeoning feelings he had for the injured girl. Nor was he naive enough to believe that a relationship between them was possible.

Which was a good enough reason for not climbing in beside Keira.

The bigger problem was: it wasn't a good enough reason to stop him from *wanting* to do it. From wanting *her*.

He paused in his counting of his emergency candles to look over at her. She was pushed to the far end of the single-size bed, leaving just enough room for Graham's body. More than enough room if he wrapped his arms around her and held her close.

Her position on the bed wasn't an accident. It was an invitation. One that made an uncomfortable ache spread out from his chest and threaten to take over the rest of him.

You owe her an explanation.

Yes, she deserved some honesty about who he was and what he was doing there.

He just wasn't sure how he was going to go about telling her.

He leaned forward and put his head in his hands.

There just didn't seem to be an easy way of letting someone know you'd been accused of murder.

His eyes slid over Keira, then away from her.

And abruptly, he went still.

Maybe he wouldn't have to tell her after all. Maybe she knew already.

A box—one he'd shoved aside and forgotten about and hadn't touched in long enough to let it get covered in dust—sat across the room, its lid askew.

* * *

Keira woke to find the bed empty and she couldn't quite deny her disappointment that Calloway's warm body wasn't beside her. And her heart dropped even further when she sat up and spied him slumped over a cup of coffee. He was still dressed in the previous evening's clothes, his hair wild.

Did he sleep at all?

"Calloway?"

He turned her way, and she saw that his face was as ragged as his appearance.

"I need to ask you something, Keira."

"Carte blanche?" she replied, managing to keep her voice on the lighter side.

He nodded, but instead of asking a question, he made a statement. "Holly Henderson."

The murdered woman from Derby Reach. Keira felt the blood drain from her cheeks. Why was he bringing her up now?

"You know the name." Calloway said that like a statement, too, but Keira seized on it.

"Yes. I know her name. But so does every person in a hundred-mile radius of Derby Reach. And you saw my driver's license, so you know that's where I'm from."

"True enough. Holly Henderson was killed four years ago," Calloway said. "Big news in Derby Reach. And you're right, everyone did hear about it. But for some reason, I think it's a little fresher in your mind. When was the last time you heard the name, Keira?"

Without meaning to, she flicked her eyes toward the corner of the room. Toward the box full of incriminating news articles. Immediately, she regretted the slip.

Calloway's gaze followed hers. And when he looked back in her direction, his face was dark.

Not with guilt, Keira noted. Regret, yes. Sorrow, absolutely. And hurt. Yes, there was that, too.

And it managed to cut through her apprehension and froze her tongue to the roof of her mouth. Before she could regain the ability to speak, Calloway was on his feet, moving toward her. He reached down, grabbed the rope she'd all but forgotten about and looped it around her wrists. He cinched it just shy of too-tight and fastened her there. Lastly, he snapped up the box, gave Keira a furious, achingly heartbreaking glare and stormed out of the cabin.

Damn, damn, damn.

For several long minutes, she stared at the door. Her heart was still beating at double time, and she was sure he was going to come running back any second and offer an explanation.

What *was* his connection to Holly? For some reason, she was sure—so sure—that he wasn't responsible for her death.

But the door stayed shut, and the cabin stayed distinctly quiet, and she had to resign herself to the fact that he wasn't returning anytime soon. And she wanted to get free.

Keira followed the length of rope with her eyes.

It disappeared at the edge of the bed, so she shimmied toward the end. She still couldn't see where it was tied, but sliding to the edge of the mattress gave her enough slack to move a little more. She inched forward so that her whole head hung off the bed.

Aha!

There it was. The rope went from her wrists to the woven metal frame underneath the mattress. As Keira leaned down a little farther in search of a possible way to free herself, she lost her balance and toppled to the wood floor.

She decided to take advantage of her new position.

She worked her way under the bed, ignoring both the few slivers that found their way into her back and the fact that the frame was low enough to the ground that it dug into her chest.

She brought her fingers to the knot on the bed frame. It was as solid as the one on her hands. But a warped piece on the metal bed frame caught Keira's eye.

If she could twist it, even just a little bit, she might be able to create a gap wide enough to slip the rope through.

She began to work the metal. It hurt a bit. The fibers of the robe rubbed unpleasantly against her skin, and she jabbed herself twice on the metal, hard enough the second time to draw blood.

C'mon, c'mon.

When she finally saw some progress—a tiny space between the bits of metal—tears of relief pricked at her eyes.

With an unladylike grunt, she twisted the already bent piece of metal frame as hard as she could while shoving the rope forward at the same time. It sprung free.

"Yes!" she crowed, and propelled herself out from under the bed.

She crossed the room quickly, but paused at the spot that had housed the cardboard box.

Knowing it probably wasn't the best idea, but unable to resist an urge to do it anyway, Keira made her way to the front door. She cracked it open and a blast of chilly air slammed into her.

Too cold.

She snapped up the Gore-Tex jacket from its hook just inside, put Calloway's too-big boots back on and stepped onto the patio.

She limped down the stairs and into the yard, holding her arms tightly against her chest to fend off the cold.

How Calloway was able to stand it with no coat was beyond her.

Where had the man gone to anyway?

There were plenty of footprints at the base of the stairs and along the edge of the cabin, but no distinct ones that led away from the cabin.

She scanned the tree line. It was so thick that, had it not been for the tracks in the snow, Keira wouldn't have been able to tell where Dave, Calloway's not-so-friendly friend, had come in on his snowmobile. There was no evidence of a footpath in, either. But there had to be a way out. Didn't there?

She had the uneasy suspicion that if she climbed up one of the very tall trees surrounding her and looked out, she would see nothing but even more trees for miles on end.

Keira shivered, a renewed niggling of doubt brought in by the yawning forest before her. Her stomach churned nervously, too, and she had to look away from the suddenly oppressive view of the woods.

Trying to distract herself, she turned back to the cabin and planted her feet in the snow at the bottom of the stairs so she could give the wooden structure a thorough once-over. It *was* old. She'd noted it in the dark the night before. The logs were all worn smooth, and the roof sagged in some places.

But it wasn't falling down at all.

In fact, it looked like someone had made an effort to keep it looking rough while in fact reinforcing it. Near the top of a particularly high snowdrift, several strips of fresh wood had been nailed over top of one area, presumably to fix a hole. Even though the porch was covered in leaves and debris, it was actually quite new, with no sign of rot. The window from which Keira had watched Calloway argue with the armed man had a new frame, too. The front door was marked with pitting and the hinges looked rusty. But Keira knew that it was solid on the inside. The whole interior was airtight.

To the casual observer, the cabin appeared run-down. Not worth a second glance. But examining it closely, knowing what was on the inside…

"He's not just hiding something," Keira murmured. "He's hiding *himself*."

She took one more step back. And bumped right into Calloway.

Chapter 13

When Keira stumbled, Graham's hand came up automatically to steady her, then stayed on her elbow.

"For almost four years," he said, his voice full of poorly disguised emotion.

She twisted a little in his grip, but not to get away. Just to face him.

"Since just around when Holly Henderson and her son were killed," Keira stated softly.

He met her gaze. What *had* she seen inside that box? What had she read and then believed? And why the hell did what she thought matter so much more to him than the fact that she'd had a peek into his darkest secrets?

"Calloway?" she prodded.

Graham's heart burned a little inside his chest as he replied. "Yes. You're right. Since they were killed."

"She was your wife, wasn't she?" Keira asked gently.

Graham closed his eyes. "Yes."

"I'm sorry."

"Me, too."

There was a brief pause, and Graham wondered if his agreement had seemed like a confession. An apology. It wouldn't be the first time. But her next words, spoken in a devastated voice, refuted the idea.

"And the little boy..."

"Not my biological son." He opened his eyes again and saw that the pain on her face was genuine. "But I loved him like one. Every day for the last four years, I've ask myself if I could've done something differently. Something to save him."

"Four years..." Keira said. "And you've been on the run ever since."

"Not on the run," Graham corrected bitterly. "Running implies forward movement. I've been hiding, just like you said."

More than hiding.

Graham was stagnant. Stuck in the woods, surrounded by nothing but his own haunted thoughts.

When had he gone from using the cabin as a headquarters to using it as a home? He'd never meant for it to be permanent. Just a place to stay while he hung back as the details sorted themselves out. As Dave Stark did the legwork and searched for the man responsible for Holly's and Sam's deaths.

Graham had wanted to feel useful. He'd started collecting the newspaper articles, brought in by Dave, and made the scrapbook to keep things linear. He was so sure something in those stories would spark something in *him*, and set off a chain of events that would lead to proving he had nothing to gain from his wife's death.

A motive.

That's what he'd been looking for, hidden under the piles of half-truths.

Instead, the perpetual hounding, the mudslinging, all of the ignorant hatred directed Graham's way, laid out in black and white—and sometimes color, too— left him with the feeling that he would never become a free man. Not truly. How could he, with the details of every mistake he'd ever made on display for the whole world to see?

The collection of articles had the opposite effect that it should have anyway. The finger pointers seemed right instead of wrong. Graham understood why they hounded him, why the accusations came hurling his way. His and Holly's unhappiness was well documented. Hell, sometimes it was on public display. Some of it was on paper. If Graham had been on their end, he would be giving himself the exact same scrutiny.

Insurmountable.

That word was tossed around a lot and it stood out to Graham particularly. It's what the evidence had become. It's what his circumstances had become. The reason he felt it was better to stay here, locked behind his cabin door, rather than face a jury and tell a story that seemed unlikely, even to him.

When Graham realized just how desperate—how insurmountable—his situation had become, he'd tossed everything into that damned box and pushed it into a corner.

Before long, the media attention died off, and with

the waning interest in the murder, the clippings became few and far between. There was a little resurgence on the anniversary date each year, but aside from that, Graham had nothing to add to his collection.

Ignoring the box had become easy.

Except he couldn't ignore it anymore. Keira had opened it. Now she was staring at him, worry and curiosity plain on her face.

"Just ask me," Graham commanded gruffly.

"Ask you what?"

"The same question that every person who ever heard the story, who ever saw the news, who ever read an article in that box has asked me."

Graham braced himself for her version of it.

Did you kill them? Were you angry? In a fight? Was it an accident, maybe?

Instead, she looked him square in the face and said, "I don't think it's my turn, actually."

Graham couldn't keep the surprise from his reply. "Your turn?"

Was she kidding? Deliberately misleading him?

"I wasn't really counting anymore," she told him, her voice serious. "But I think I owe you at least one."

He thought for just a minute. She wasn't the only one who could throw a curveball.

"Are you still a six out of ten?"

"Is that what you really want to know?"

"Right this second...yes."

Keira pursed her lips as if she was really considering it. "Still a six."

Graham frowned. "I don't know if it's better than a six or worse than a six, but I know you're lying again."

"You sound awfully sure of that."

"I *am* awfully sure of it," he countered and took a step closer to her so he could run a thumb over her cheekbone. "When you lie, you get a little spot of red right *here*."

"I do *not*."

"You do."

The color bloomed further, covering the rest of her cheeks. He didn't release her face, and she didn't pull away. Graham stroked the curve of crimson. His palm cupped her cheek, the tips of his long fingers reaching just above her delicate brow and his wrist at her chin.

A perfect fit.

"Ask me something *real*, Calloway," she said. "Something you really want to know."

"Did you know I was up here, when you came?" Graham replied. "Did someone tell you where to find me?"

Keira's eyes widened. "No! Why would I... No."

The blush drained from her face, and Graham knew she was telling the truth. He released her face with a sigh. The realization disappointed him—no, not disappointed. That wasn't the right description. It sent a swarm of angry wasps beating through his chest, and he couldn't pinpoint the reason.

"Let me show you something," he said.

Graham didn't give her a chance to respond. He slid his hand down her shoulder, then her arm, then threaded his fingers through hers. He guided her gently to the back of the house, following an unnamed compulsion.

The box of newspaper clippings sat just where he'd tossed it, right between his wood bin and the rear of the cabin. Graham ignored it.

"Right there," he stated.

He let go of Keira's hand and pointed at a snow-free, almost perfectly circular patch in the snow at the bottom of the cabin. It wasn't huge and only seemed out of place when looking directly at it. Anyone walking by wouldn't even notice the anomaly.

Graham watched as Keira's stare traveled upward and landed on a narrow spigot, sticking out from between two of the log beams. A nearly indiscernible puff of steam floated from the metal cylinder, then dissipated into nothing.

"You could put your hand right into that and it wouldn't even burn," Graham told her.

"What is it?"

"It's what you don't see up on the roof," Graham replied.

Her eyes widened with immediate understanding. "That little bit of steam comes from that big fire in the stove?"

"That. Or from out here."

Graham bent down and lifted up a large, flat stone, revealing a hidden, in-ground fire pit.

"Oh!" Keira exclaimed.

Still not 100 percent certain why he was doing any of it, Graham snapped up the cardboard box and moved it a little closer to the pit.

It was high time he got rid of them. They'd never done him any good anyway. Only served as a reminder of how very little had been done in solving the case.

He slipped the lid off and reached inside for a stack of newspaper. Then he tossed it into the pit.

"I modified the woodstove into a rocket stove with a

heating component. So I feed the fire—from inside or from outside—and the fire exhausts into a specialized section of wall, where it then helps to heat the house. It cools significantly before it's finally filtered out, and by the time it gets *here*, it's not much more than vapor," he explained as he grabbed some more paper. "It took a year to do it, and it was worth the time."

Graham reached into the box once more, and as he did, his hand hit something cool and metal. He shoved his hand into the mess a little farther and yanked out a familiar container.

The flask was silver. Real silver, trimmed with real gold.

A little shake told Graham it was still full.

He disregarded the nagging voice in his head that pointed out that it was barely even noon, twisted off the cap and downed a healthy gulp of the amber liquid inside.

The Macallan.

It was a Scotch Graham would never choose for himself. Just like the flask, the drink inside was a gift from his wealthy father-in-law, a man who had never tired of putting Graham into his lower place on the evolutionary scale. A man who perpetuated the witch hunt that drove him underground.

Even the smooth flavor couldn't quite drive away the bitterness that came with it. Which was the very reason he'd dumped it into the box in the first place. To stash away the memories.

He took another swig, then offered it to Keira.

"If that's what you gave me the night before last,"

she said, "count me out. I don't want to wind up drunk and tied to another bed."

Graham managed to smile through his beard. "I'm afraid I only have the one bed. My alternatives are a wooden chair and a closet full of flannel."

He meant it as a joke, but Keira shot him a serious, searching look. "Or not tying me up at all."

"That would require a certain level of trust."

She didn't avert her gaze. "Does it look like I'm going anywhere?"

And Graham suddenly realized what he was showing her. What he was telling her. Why it made him wish she hadn't found him by accident.

Because it means I really am the one putting her in danger.

"Does it look like I'm offering to let you leave?"

Her eyes went a little wider as she caught the underlying darkness in his voice. He held out the flask again.

"This is plain old whiskey. Liquid courage." He sloshed it around.

"Do I need to be courageous?" Her question made her sound anything but.

"Always," Graham told her firmly.

Keira took the whiskey. Graham waited until she took a sip before he spoke again.

"My great-grandfather built the cabin here for its inaccessibility. He told no one but his son—who told my dad, who told me—it was here. And as close as the resort is, to get to this spot, you need an ATV in the summer or a snowmobile in the winter. Or you need to *crash* in, I guess, like you did. And who wants to make that kind of effort? So no one knows it's here. No one knows *I'm* here."

"No one except for the man with the gun," Keira pointed out.

He met her eyes. "Him. And now you. Which is a bad combination, I think."

"A bad combination?" Keira parroted.

Graham nodded. "They found what was left of your car."

Fear crossed her face, and he knew she was thinking about the consequences of being found. But she covered it quickly. "Who did?"

"The police found it. The man with the gun—Dave Stark—told me."

"The police? They'll come looking for me and—" She stopped abruptly, relief replaced by worry. "That's not good for you, is it?"

"No, it's not."

"Which is what makes it bad for me, too."

Graham nodded slowly. "I can't let them find me up here. And I can't let Dave get to you, either. As much as I rely on him, I'm not sure he'd make the right decision."

That same bit of fleeting fright passed through her features. "Who is he?"

"A friend. And a business associate, I guess. I pay him well to do the things he does for me. Food. Supplies. Information. Someone I trust." Graham paused, wondering if the last was still true. He heaved a sigh, then went on. "He suspects you're here, Keira. If he finds out he's right, I think it will upset the balance between us."

"Just tell him he's wrong."

"It's not that simple. Dave came up here because he was expecting *me* to come to him."

"Why?"

"He found the man we've been looking for—the one who actually killed Holly and Sam. He's come back to Derby Reach." Graham shook his head. "I'm going after him."

Keira stared back at him and swallowed nervously. Damn, how he hated being the source of her fear.

"What are you going to do to him?" she asked.

Graham had a list of what he'd *like* to do, and none of it was pleasant. But he wasn't that man.

"I'm going to get a confession," he said. "I'm going to find irrevocable proof. And I'm going to let Dave take him in."

"That's where you were going when you found me," Keira stated.

"Yes."

"I'm sorry."

"No. I'm sorry, Keira," he said softly.

She took a small step away. "You are? Why? This means what? That you're holding me hostage?"

"Not because I want to."

"You could just let me go," Keira suggested.

"And then what?"

"And then I walk away."

"Keira, just the accident by itself left too much of a chance that the wrong someone will poke their nose around and find my place. Which is what Dave pointed out. And I can't keep you *here*, either."

"I won't tell anyone about the cabin. You could always take me back to the crash site and I'll find my way out from there."

"And you'll do this wearing what? *My* clothes? Or that tiny dress you had on that's barely more than a rag now? And how will you explain these stitches on your leg?"

He knew his words had an edge again, and he tried to soften them by reaching for her. But she jerked away, and that cut to the quick.

"I could tell them I don't remember," she offered, the worry in her tone growing stronger.

"Selective amnesia?"

"Yes."

"Even if that wasn't as ridiculous as it sounds…could you make it believable?" Graham asked. "Could you make them think you'd forgotten me? I sure as hell couldn't forget you, Keira." He didn't give her time to respond to the admission. "Besides that…even if they bought the story, it would spike their curiosity, don't you think? A young woman miraculously survives when her car goes over a cliff. She not only lives, but receives medical attention. You think the cops will just walk away from that?"

"But if you don't let me go…they'll think I'm dead," she whispered.

"I'm aware of that possibility."

"So why *did* you even bother to save me, Calloway, if you're just going to hold me prisoner forever?"

Graham heard the desperation in her voice and when he answered, he heard it in his own, too. "Redemption."

The word hung between them, meaning so much, but saying so little.

Chapter 14

In spite of what she'd said just minutes earlier, Keira found her feet moving away from Graham. She wasn't running. Not really. She just needed to clear her head. But she still ignored him as he called after her.

She knew with absolute certainty that Graham hadn't killed his wife and son. She'd felt no need to ask when prompted.

But she also had a job and a life. Kids in the system who counted on her. And she sure as heck didn't want her family to assume she was dead. Just the thought of her mom hearing about the accident made her heart squeeze.

But she also knew she wouldn't expose his secret location. She couldn't risk his life just to go back to her own. Not if she could avoid it.

Not that Calloway was about to let her go anyway.

And suddenly she *was* running again. Not away, but as a release of emotion. Back around the house and toward the woods.

It only took seconds for Calloway to catch up to her. His arms closed around her waist, and he spun her to face him. She railed against his hold, her small fists driving into his wide chest. He let her do it. His hands ran over her head and through her hair, and he whispered soothing things as she let all the emotion, all the stress of the past few days fly from her body into his.

At last her energy waned, and she stopped fighting him off. It wasn't what she wanted to be doing anyway. She realized that at the same second she realized she was crying. Soft sobs that shook her shoulders.

She inhaled deeply, trying to stop the tears, and Calloway adjusted, sliding his hands to the small of her back. As if she belonged in his arms. As if they belonged together. As she looked up at him, his expression was soft.

"Have you noticed that every time you try to hurt me, you wind up in my arms?" Calloway asked, somehow teasing and serious at the same time.

"Have *you* ever noticed that I keep trying to get away?" Keira breathed, and now she could *feel* the telltale spots of color in her cheeks that went along with the lie.

"You sure about that?"

Keira shook her head, not sure if she was answering his question, or if she was just expressing her frustration with the whole situation.

"I've been meaning to ask you…were you really

going to club me to death with that fire iron yester-day?" Calloway asked.

Keira managed a smile. "I was going to aim for your legs. I just wanted to knock you down."

"A peg?" This time, there was no mistaking the teas-ing tone.

"That, too," Keira confirmed.

He touched her face, cupping her cheek with a fa-miliarity that warmed her insides.

"I just want to keep you safe," he said.

His sincerity almost made her break down again.

"Two days ago," she said, sounding as choked up as she felt, "I woke up thinking I knew where my life was going. *Exactly* where it was going. But today, it's like I woke in someone *else's* life."

"Every day," Calloway murmured, his voice heavy with understanding. "That's the exact feeling I've had every day for four years. It's been a living hell for me. Waking up thinking it will be the one when the truth comes out. Wanting justice. Or, if I'm being honest, craving revenge. I can't even remember if it started that way, or if time somehow changed it. Changed *me*. It's been so long since I even thought about anything else that I'm not sure. Yesterday, I could've had it. Revenge. But I saw you in that car. Pretty and fragile and so still. I pulled you out before I could even think about whether it was the right thing to do, considering my situation. It was instinct, I guess. I wasn't even sure you were still alive until I saw the blood seeping from that wound on your leg. Saving you reminded me that there are other things out there for me. You gave me purpose, Keira."

He said her name like he owned it, and her pulse skittered nervously through her veins.

Had any man ever looked as good as Calloway did right that second, with his brooding eyes and his half-apologetic frown? Had anyone else ever put themselves in danger to save her life? Had she ever been someone's *purpose*?

Even though he wasn't holding her tightly anymore, his eyes still held her pinned in place. And she felt a tether form between them. An inexplicable, inescapable bond from her heart to his.

Keira tilted her head in his direction. His lips were less than an inch from hers. She could feel his warm breath on her cheek. She could see the longing in his eyes. His whole body was tense with need. But he didn't make a move.

Keira was sure it should be her, not him, who was offering the most resistance. After all, it had only been two days since she decided she might date Drew. Might marry him. Though it felt like a lifetime now. And Calloway had been alone for a long time. Four years since his wife died, and who knew how many of those he'd spent in isolation?

But in the end, it was Keira who reached for him.

She threaded her fingers into his thick hair, stifling a little moan at how warm and soft it was, and how the longer bits curled against the back of her hand. She made herself caress it only lightly, afraid he was going to pull away. But he didn't. He leaned into the attention for a moment, pressing the back of his head into her palm. Then he let her explore the contours of his lips in slow motion, her mouth tasting his and igniting something in her that was so hot she was surprised the snow underneath them wasn't melting.

Calloway's hands slid over her shoulders, gently kneading her sore muscles, mindful of her most damaged areas. For the first time, Keira was glad he'd stripped her down without asking. He knew where her bruises and scrapes were, and his fingers were adept at avoiding them. But his hands never stopped moving.

They traversed over Keira's face and smoothed her hair back from her face. They tripped softly over her shoulders and down to her hips, not quite tickling, then slipped between the enormous jacket and the borrowed T-shirt to rest on her hips before sliding out again to creep up to her throat.

It was an incredible feeling, to be touched like that. His palms and the strong pads of his fingers and thumbs laid claim to Keira. They worshipped her. She wanted it to go on forever, and when Calloway finally pulled away, a regretful sigh escaped her lips.

Graham stared down at Keira, committing her features to his memory. He wanted to keep that worshipful expression—the one that believed in him, that trusted him—in his mind forever.

Kissable lips.

Curved cheeks.

Elegant nose with just the slightest bump, making it interesting.

And her eyes. God, they were stunning.

Green, so vibrant and dark, they looked like the Caribbean Sea after sunset, and in the cold sun, her hair was like a crown of fire.

This time, Graham was perfectly content to let himself have the poetic moment.

In mere days, her fiery temper and moments of vulnerability and misleadingly fragile appearance had gotten under his skin. He could barely wrap his head around how badly he felt the need to protect this girl he still knew so little about. He needed more of her story.

"Tell me what you were running from in that little purple car of yours," he commanded softly. "What was so bad that you were willing to risk your life by going out in that storm?"

She looked away. "Lately the only thing I've been running from is you."

Graham knew she was trying to deflect his question. "Do I need to bring out the list of checks and balances to see whose turn it is to ask a question?"

"No." Her chest rose and fell as she took a breath and went on. "His name is Drew. And I wasn't running *from* him, I was running *to* him."

Graham couldn't keep a hint of jealousy out of his voice. "Boyfriend?"

"Potential."

"Does he appreciate your very recent total and complete disregard for your own life?"

"No."

Jealousy morphed into irritation, which was ridiculous. He couldn't dampen it, though.

"Drew must be a complete idiot," he grumbled.

Keira smiled a small smile. "No. That's not it. He just didn't know I was coming."

Graham touched each upturned corner of her mouth

before asking, "So you drove all the way up here, unbeknownst to Drew, based on potential?"

"Kind of."

"Kind of yes, or kind of no?" Graham teased.

"It seems silly now," Keira replied.

"Tell me anyway."

"I thought maybe I was meant to be with him," she admitted. "I thought I saw a sign."

"Fate?"

She blushed. "Something like that. It was dumb, though. I took a chance, and instead of it being a sign, I wound up here."

"You don't think it could *still* be fate?"

The blush worked its way from her cheeks down to her throat. "You think my near-death experience was fate?"

"You know that's not what I meant, Keira. And to tell you the truth… I just straight up don't believe in coincidence, Keira. Fate, though, I'm onboard with, one hundred percent."

The pink of her blush extended from her throat to the top of her chest. Graham had an urge to reach up and unzip the rest of the jacket just to see how far down the pretty color went. He closed his hands into fists to stop himself from doing it.

"So what's fate got lined up for me next, then?" she asked softly.

"Getting you somewhere safe," Graham replied. "Somewhere that the man who killed Holly and Sam wouldn't be able to get anywhere near you."

"I'm sorry, Calloway."

"*You* are?"

She nodded. "If I hadn't been so reckless, taking off in the snowstorm when I did—"

Graham cut her off. "Listen. It was stupid of me to save you, Keira. Risky as hell. But it was *my* risk to take." He paused, released her to run both hands through his hair, then spoke again. "I'm glad I did it. In four years, nothing has seemed as real as the moment you opened your eyes and I realized you were alive."

Keira reached up and put a hand on his face, that same look of awe and appreciation on her, and forget unzipping her coat—it took all of Graham's willpower to stop himself from lifting her up and carrying her straight to his too-lumpy bed.

"In fact," he added gruffly, "you're the realest damned thing I've been around for as long as I can remember. So I don't ever want you to be sorry on my behalf."

She opened her mouth, but Graham didn't get to hear whatever she'd been about to say.

A boom echoed around them, and without taking the time to think, he threw himself into her, knocking her to the ground and shielding her with his much larger body. There was a long moment of silence, and Graham wondered if he was being paranoid. There were minor avalanches in the area all the time.

But as he jumped into a defensive crouch, a second bang—possibly closer than the first—shook the air.

It was a gun, no doubt about it. Not the first time he'd heard one out here, but the first time it had seemed so close.

And it's nowhere near *hunting season.*

Was someone firing *at* them?

It seemed unlikely, but...

A third shot rang through the air, and Graham was certain this one was closer again. Keira moved, then let out a muffled shriek as Calloway slammed into her and knocked her to the ground again.

"Can you do something for me?" he asked in a low voice.

"But—"

"Please."

After a breath, her head bobbed against his chest in assent.

"Stay down until I say otherwise."

He felt her nod again and he eased off her body. He was reluctant to let her go, even a little bit, but he needed to assess where the shots were coming from and figure out if they were targeted.

He scanned what little he could see. It wasn't much. The trees provided a perfect hiding place for a shooter. But Graham could use them, too. He and Keira could move quickly between them, using them for cover. If he could figure out which direction the shots came from, they could duck from tree to tree until they reached the cabin. Then Graham would shield Keira again. He'd grab his rifle and—

The rest of his thought was lost as a fourth shot rang out.

Bloody hell.

Graham yanked Keira to her feet, shoved her to the other side of the wide evergreen, then positioned himself in front of her, shielding her from whatever was about to come next.

Chapter 15

As much as Keira preferred to think of herself as strong, she was indescribably grateful to have Calloway between her and whoever was shooting at them. She was shaking so hard, her teeth were chattering, and Calloway was reassuringly solid.

Solid, yes. But not bulletproof, pointed out a small voice in her head.

Her hand slid up to his back, and she opened her mouth to remind him of that fact. But without looking, his hand closed on her wrist, stopping her midway. As if he could sense her movement before she even followed through.

The air was eerily silent now, and they stood like that for what felt like an eternity.

Is it over? Keira wondered.

Calloway spoke in a hushed voice, his eyes still scanning the forest. "You all right back there?"

Keira took a measured breath. "If it wasn't for someone potentially shooting at me in the middle of a forest… Nine out of ten on the sliding scale."

There was a pause, then, in spite of the situation, Calloway let a wry chuckle. "Are you going to tell me what gets me that all-important tenth point? Or am I going to die not knowing?"

"One small thing," Keira breathed.

"Which is?"

"Just keep us alive."

"Nothing would make me happier."

There was another long silence, then Keira asked, "Do you think someone found you?"

He spoke right beside her ear. "I don't know. If they did… Keira. Did you mean what you said about trusting me?"

She managed a nod.

"Good. Because I need you to do something for me."

"What?"

"Run."

Keira blinked. "What?"

"If someone *is* firing at us, it's me they're after," Calloway stated. "I'm going to go in one direction, into the woods. You're going to count to ten and go in the other, toward the cabin."

"I'm not going to do that!"

"Yes, Keira. You are."

He didn't wait for her to argue anymore. He took off across the snow, leaving Keira counting to ten silently, a little more dread filling her with each number.

* * *

Graham loped over the terrain, waiting for another shot to come his way and cursing his own stupidity. He'd left them exposed. He'd put Keira's life in danger even though he'd been trying to do the opposite.

He didn't bother to hide as he dodged from tree to tree. If the shooter was looking for him, he wanted his undivided attention. And to put some distance between Keira and the bad end of the gun.

"C'mon," he growled. "Follow *me*. Shoot at *me*."

The woods were silent except for the sound of his own feet hitting the ground. He finally slowed, acknowledging that maybe—a big maybe—he'd been overreacting. That possibly some off-season hunter had taken advantage of the aftermath of the snowstorm and was on his side of the mountain in search of some big game.

But what if he wasn't?

What if, somehow, the man who'd taken Holly and Sam from him found him? Found *them*?

Graham moved faster, getting angrier at himself by the second. Which is why he didn't notice the armed man in front of him until they were just a foot apart.

When he did spot him, Graham didn't stop to think. He just reacted, determined to use his strength to overpower the assailant, gun or no gun. It wasn't until he'd already pounced on the other man and smacked the weapon away that he recognized him.

Dave.

"What the *hell* is going on?" Graham demanded.

His friend was sucking wind, and when he opened his mouth, all that came out was a groan.

Graham eased off. "Explain yourself."

"Talk. To. You," Dave wheezed.

"And you were getting my attention by shooting at me?"

"Not. Me."

"Who?"

"Don't. Know."

Graham resisted an urge to shake a proper answer from him friend.

"Heard shots," Dave offered, still inhaling rapidly.

"Did you see the shooter?"

He finally seemed to have caught his breath, shaking his head. "Maybe it was a hunter. But it doesn't matter. You have to admit that it's too risky to stay here now. I can tell from your face that you know it."

Graham exhaled. Keira was safe. At least for the moment.

He opened his mouth to ask what Dave was doing back so soon—what he wanted to talk about—but before Graham could get an explanation, an engine sputtered to life in the distance, and both men turned toward the sound.

Keira tightened her already strained grip on the handlebars of the snowmobile. The seat was icy under her bare legs, but she ignored the discomfort. She needed to get the vehicle moving, to get it to Calloway. She'd run blindly, obeying this command even though so many parts of her mind—of her heart—protested against it. But halfway back to the cabin, she'd spotted the big machine. It was not quite hidden behind a low bush, and it seemed like a godsend. A way to get both of them to safety. Quickly.

"How hard can it be?" she muttered aloud to herself as she looked over the components another time. "Throttle. Choke. Kill switch if I need it."

She squeezed the gas, just a little, and the machine bucked as the skis snuck to the snow.

"Easy," she cautioned, not sure if she was still speaking to herself or if she was talking to the snowmobile.

She supposed either would work.

Keira climbed off, moved to the front of the vehicle and kicked away some of the snow blocking the way, then climbed back on.

She put a little more pressure on the throttle, and the machine jerked forward hard enough to send her flying against the handlebars. She held on for dear life as it rode forward a few feet, then stalled.

Damn.

Tears threatened to form in her eyes, and Keira forced them back. She didn't have time to waste being upset. Angrily, she pulled out the choke, yanked on the pull starter as hard as she could and willed the stupid thing to cooperate.

It roared to life, and this time when she closed her fingers over the throttle, she did it softly. The snowmobile slid over the snow at a crawl. It growled a little as she held it steady.

Apparently her options were very slow or very fast. No in between.

So, fast it was.

Keira gritted her teeth and squeezed.

Graham watched in awed horror—and with more than a little bit of admiration, too—as the enormous piece of machinery came tearing around the corner. Keira sat atop it, her stance awkward, her eyes almost closed and her hair flying out behind like a blazing red cape.

Her beautiful determination was clear, even through her obvious fear.

Then she spied him, and her eyes were no longer half-shut. They were so wide that their green hue was visible even from where Graham sat.

She seemed to clue in at the same second that Graham did that she was on a crash course, headed straight for him and Dave.

Sure enough, she tipped the handlebars, trying to angle away from them. Her motions became frantic, her arms flailing. Then the snowmobile bucked, and Keira was suddenly barely hanging on, her legs tossed to the side and her hands gripping the bars. The machine bounced along wildly as if it had a mind of its own.

Almost too late, Graham realized that the snarling vehicle was still aimed in his direction. At the last second, he dove toward Dave and shoved the other man out of the line of fire.

He wasn't swift enough to save himself.

The last thing Graham saw before the snowmobile clipped him, and his head exploded in pain, was the terrified look on Keira's face as she flew up and sailed through the air.

I'm sorry, he thought weakly.

But there was nothing he could do as the world blurred and he collapsed to the ground.

Chapter 16

Keira landed hard against a raised snowbank, taking the brunt of the hit straight in the stomach. All of the air left her lungs in one gust, and abruptly she couldn't breathe. She couldn't inhale or exhale or force the oxygen into her body no matter how badly she wanted.

I'm going to die. Calloway's going to die. And it's going to be my fault.

How cruel was *that* for fate?

For a second, the world stayed dark.

Then it was full of spotted pinpricks of light.

And at last, Keira felt her chest rise and fall, and the white-covered ground evened out in her vision.

She pulled herself across the snow until she reached Calloway's still body.

Please let him be okay, she prayed, her heart banging against her ribs so hard it hurt.

She dropped her head to Calloway's chest. It rose and fell evenly, and when Keira put her fingers to his throat, his pulse was strong.

Thank God.

And then a hand landed on her shoulder and Keira remembered they weren't alone.

She brought her eyes up nervously and, through her tears, stared at the man above her.

He looked rough and dangerous, with a cut in the corner of one lip, and one of his eyes looked almost black. Like the kind of man who would be firing a weapon in the woods.

"Ms. Niles," he said.

He knows your name.

And for a second, he looked vaguely familiar.

No. Impossible. She knew no one who matched his description.

"Ms. Niles," he repeated, this time a little more urgently. "Stay calm."

His words had the opposite effect that they should have, and panic set in.

She had to get away.

Keira's eyes flicked around the clearing in search of safety. Of protection.

The snowmobile.

Too complicated.

The cabin.

Too far.

A glint of silver in the snow.

Yes. The gun.

Keira sprang up and hurled herself past the worse-for-wear man in front of her and dove for the weapon.

She caught sight of the expression on his face—first full of surprise, then understanding—and he moved, too.

But Keira was faster.

Her hands closed on the gun and for a second she was thoroughly triumphant.

Thank God.

Then the blond man was on her, one hand wrapped around her ankle and the other clawing to get the weapon away from her.

"Don't do something you'll regret," he said through clenched teeth.

"I won't," she promised, then drew back her free foot and slammed it into his chest.

He flew back and Keira leaped up once more. With a sharp stab of remorse about leaving Calloway where he was, she took off at a limping run.

The thump of feet on snow told her that the man was following her. And gaining ground.

C'mon, c'mon, she urged herself.

She was close enough to the cabin that it was a viable option now.

Come! On!

Pushing through the throbbing pain in her thigh, Keira forced herself to keep going. And at last she reached the wooden patio. But as her hand found the doorknob, her head swiveled and she saw that her pursuer had caught up to her.

She spun, cocked the gun and pointed it at the blond man just as one of his feet met the bottom step.

"You're making a mistake," he told her, looking far less frightened than she thought he should.

"I do know how to fire this thing," Keira warned.

"You might want to rethink actually doing it, Ms. Niles."

"People love a good self-defense story," she retorted.

"Maybe. But the law rarely favors people who fire on those working with the police. Especially when they're shooting while in the home of a known criminal."

The police? A criminal?

Keira eyed the other man disbelievingly. Maybe the last part made sense.

Calloway *was* on the run from the police, after all. But nothing about the man standing in front of her screamed law enforcement. No uniform. No readily proffered ID.

No. He has to be lying.

"You expect me to believe that you're a cop?" she asked. "And Calloway is what, then…the robber?"

"This is hardly a game, Ms. Niles. My name is David Stark and—"

The rest of his statement was lost as Keira finally clued in to who this man was.

Dave Stark.

Calloway's friend. His business associate. Whom he'd known for years. And trusted.

A cop?

"I know who you are," Keira said.

"Then you know Graham and I are friends."

"Calloway told me about your business arrangement."

"But he didn't happen to mention that I work for the Derby Reach PD?"

"If you're a cop, and you knew he was here, why haven't you just arrested him?" Keira countered.

"Because I've been his friend for far longer than I've been a policeman. And because I've been helping him for as many years as he's been on the run."

"Prove it," Keira challenged.

"Fine. I have three things in my pocket," he said. "My badge, my driver's license and a pay stub to prove the ID is real. I'd like to reach in and get them. Do you mind if I do that?"

"Go for it," Keira conceded.

Slowly—as if *she* was the unpredictable one—he unzipped his jacket, pulled it open to give Keira a view of what he was doing, and stuck his hand into a side pocket. Just as slowly, he dragged out a little leather case and held it up. The front flapped open, revealing a gold badge.

He closed it up again, then traded it for a wallet, which he held out to Keira.

"*You* take the stuff out," she ordered.

He complied, first flipping out the plastic-covered license, then unfolding a piece of paper.

Without letting the gun go, Keira moved just close enough that she could read each of them. And as much as she wanted them to be fake, she was sure they were legitimate. "David Rodney Stark. Employee number 102 of the Derby Reach PD." Even Keira's desperate brain couldn't come up with a reasonable explanation for carrying around a phony pay stub.

Her body sagged.

Dammit.

Calloway had been paying a cop to…do what exactly? Bring him mushroom soup and information? Why was the other man even agreeing to it?

Then a low groan came from behind the man in question, and Keira traded in her concern about the cop for concern about Calloway, who was half standing, half slumping on the snow.

Graham let Dave slide an arm across his back and guide him into the cabin.

His attention, though, was on Keira.

Her hair was still wild from the crazy ride on the snowmobile. Even though she held a gun in her hand, she'd sucked her bottom lip between her teeth and looked like she was trying not to cry.

Because of you.

If he'd had the energy and the time, he would've cursed himself out for somehow managing to twist the situation so that instead of him worrying about her, she was worrying about him.

But you don't *have time*, he reminded himself. *And you can't protect her, get the cabin ready in case you don't make it back and keep your own body breathing at the same time.*

Which somehow seemed important now. Guns-out revenge wasn't an option. Not if he wanted a chance at something he hadn't thought about in a long time. A future.

So he spoke, and he wasn't sure if it was because of his recent brush with unconsciousness or if it was because he was saying something he really wished he didn't *have* to say, but his words sounded hollow and far away.

"Dave, you need to take Keira off the mountain. Now."

Keira stiffened and her mouth dropped open as if she was going to argue, but Dave beat her to it.

"The crash is all over the news, Graham. Which is what I came here to talk to you about. They're looking for a body, trying to identify the driver. What do you think they're going to do when they find out she's not so dead, after all?"

"You're not going to let them find out. You're going to take her to your hotel and stay there."

His friend ran a frustrated hand through his hair. "I came here to convince *you* to come with me. To remind you again that everything we've been working for is about to slip through our fingers. Not to transport some girl you just met, keep her hidden for you and *still* not accomplish what we've been trying to accomplish for the last four years."

Graham met his friend's eyes. "I'm asking for two days, Dave."

"This has nothing to do with her. You said it yourself just two days ago."

"What other choice is there?"

"Let the cops find her."

"And if they find out who she's been with? If that info gets back to the wrong person before I catch up to him?"

"Graham, something's gotta give. I'm tired of chasing down bad leads and using resources I have no right to be using. I'm sick of making excuses to my wife and not seeing my kids and worrying all the time that I'm going to get caught helping you. Four years is a long time to live like this. I thought we were done. Now I feel like we're starting up all over again."

Graham's temper flared. "I *lost* my wife, Dave. I *lost* my kid. And you come up here and expect me to lose someone else because you think things have been too hard on *you*? I won't take the risk that Ferguson might get ahold of Keira, too, and use her as leverage. The only way to ensure her safety is to take her away from here."

"You could turn yourself in instead."

Graham's gut clenched. "Turn myself in?"

"You'd rather have me help you with a kidnapping?"

"Stop!"

The emphatic protest came from Keira, who was shaking her head and fixing Graham with an achingly sweet glare. "Calloway isn't turning himself in to save me. He sure as hell didn't kidnap me. And you guys need to quit talking about me like I'm not here and not capable of making my own decisions."

"I can't let you stay here," Graham told her.

"And you can't make me leave," she replied.

He moved closer and lifted a hand to Keira's cheek. "You *have* to do this. It's the only thing that's going to keep you out of danger. Let Dave take you somewhere safe. I promise you, I won't be far behind. I'll take care of what needs to be taken care of and I'll come for you."

"And if you get killed in the process?" Her voice shook. "Calloway, I—"

Graham leaned down and cut her off with a kiss, not caring if Dave was watching. She brought her hands up and buried them in his hair, and he didn't let her go until her could feel her heart thumping through both layers of their clothes.

He leaned away. "I have a damned good reason to stay alive, Keira."

"Two days?" she asked breathlessly.

Graham exhaled and made a promise he hoped he could keep. "Forty-eight hours, no more."

Get in, get Mike Ferguson and get back to Keira. Then he'd figure out his next move.

Minutes later, he bundled her up—thoroughly if not comfortably—and was leading her to the snowmobile. There he kissed her again, this time tenderly, then helped her straddle the vehicle.

Dave looked unhappy, but Graham didn't care. His eyes were stuck on Keira's slim form, and they stayed there as the snowmobile roared to life and the two of them sped off into the thick woods.

Chapter 17

Keira quickly gave up trying to keep a reasonable amount of physical space between herself and Officer David Stark. Her helmeted face was pressed between his shoulder blades, and her legs squeezed his hips. She rode that way not because she was any more comfortable with him than she had been since the first second she'd laid eyes on him, but because he navigated the mountain with reckless abandon.

Trees whipped by in a blur. Snow kicked up and into Keira's shirt, then melted there. It made the wind hit her that much harder and made it that much more necessary to crush herself into Dave's back.

She was holding on to him out of necessity. And she wasn't happy about it.

The only good thing about it was that it helped to keep her mind from everything else. She deliberately blocked out her thoughts and focused on the scenery instead. It was nothing more than a blur of white, and they rode for so long that Keira was sure they were going to run out of gas.

Parts of her were frozen. Parts of her ached. And *all* of her wished she could go back in time to before her accident so she could just go back to being herself. No gunshots, no makeshift stitches, no crazy ache in her chest over a man she just met.

But her concern for Calloway's well-being overrode her efforts. And try as she might, Keira couldn't shake the fact that the most pressing of her worries was that he might never be able to keep his promise and come to her.

So maybe it wasn't that the accident skewed her view. Maybe she'd known all along that Drew wasn't right for her. Maybe she hadn't really been leading a full life at all. It just took crashing into the Mountain Man's life to reveal it.

Somehow, she was sure she could pick any moment from the past few days and attach more meaning to it than she could to any other part of her life.

So, no. She *wouldn't* erase the accident. Because without it—without Drew and her stupid trip to the chalet to make her move—she wouldn't have almost died and she wouldn't have had the best kisses in the world with the most interesting man she'd ever met.

And yes. She'd take those little glimpses of heart-pounding excitement over another twenty-four years of never realizing what she was missing.

As she came to that conclusion, a final blast of snow

flew from underneath the snowmobile, and she and Dave ground to a halt.

The seed of doubt in Keira's mind grew as she leaned away from him and took in her surroundings. The trees were well behind them, and there was nothing but a snow-covered hill in front of them.

Keira swung her legs off the snowmobile uncertainly, and Dave did the same, but with far more self-assurance. Then he tipped his goggles to his head and helped her pull off the borrowed helmet.

"Here's the deal, Ms. Niles," he said, his voice sounding extraloud now that the roar of the engine had cut off. "On the other side of that crest is the side road that leads into Mountain View Village. If we head into town, we might be walking straight into a sea of press. But what *I* want is to avoid them—and everyone else—if at all possible."

Keira stared at him. "You're not taking me to the hotel?"

"I want the same thing you do—to protect Graham. And to do that, I think we should steer clear of the resort town altogether. Get you somewhere safe and sound and far away from here," Dave told her.

"But Graham—"

"Hasn't thought this all the way through. Up here, I can't keep you hidden. Not effectively. Too many people are looking for you. If I take you off the mountain completely, I at least stand a chance of keeping you out of the limelight."

Keira waited for him to add something else about Calloway, something hopeful. But he just handed her the helmet again.

"We all set, then?" he asked.

So Keira nodded. She didn't see that she had much of a choice.

As much as Graham wanted to toss aside everything and throw on his snowshoes and start moving, he knew better.

Four years of waiting had taught him the value of patience, and as desperate as he was to get to Keira, his experience told him that he needed to be prepared. There was no way for him to avoid going back to the place where it all started. But if he had to do it, he could do it right.

He started with his hair, hacking it to nearly respectable length, revealing far more gray than he'd had when he went underground. Then he moved on to his face, shearing it so that the formerly bristly beard was gone completely. When he was done, the skin underneath it was almost raw with the effort.

He bathed head to toe, and though he kept himself fairly well-groomed anyway, he made an extra effort this time to scrub away every ounce of dirt. There was no sign of grime under his nails, no campfire scent lingering on his skin.

Toss on a white coat, Graham thought humorlessly as he gave himself a final once-over, *and I might be able to go straight back to the office.*

Right then, though, he laid out something far more practical. Snow-proof, waterproof pants. Lined, but not so thick that they would impede movement. On top, he'd wear a matching coat with good breathability and a removable interior. Both items were unused—Gra-

ham would have to rip the tags off before putting them
on—bought long ago with the assumption that one day,
he would have to abandon his home. Underneath those,
he'd put on running gear, completely practical and also
in new condition.

He had sharp jeans, a still-in-the-plastic T-shirt, and
just in case, a dress shirt and tie, ready to go into his
bag.

The cabin itself had been transformed, too. Graham boarded up the windows, careful to use well-worn
pieces of wood and nails that had seen better days. He
tore apart the bottom step in a way that made it appear
to be natural rot, and punched a hole through the front
part of the deck, too. He used a shovel to throw up
several mounds of snow in front of the house, as well,
and another snowstorm or two later, they'd look completely natural.

When Graham glanced up at the sky, he thought he
probably wouldn't have to wait long for Mother Nature
to help him out with that.

Finally, he stood back to survey the house once more,
looking for any other signs that would give away its
most recent use. He was satisfied that there were none,
and anyone who thought it was worth getting past the
snow and the broken patio would be sorely disappointed
when they got inside. Everything that *could* be burned,
had been burned. From the mattress to the curtains
to—regretfully—the food, it had all been incinerated.

Only the most necessary items had been saved, and
they fit neatly into Graham's backpack beside his extra
clothes.

Be Prepared. Back to the Boy Scout analogy.

* * *

From the moment Graham drafted his to-do list, to the second he completed it all, took less than four hours.

The sky was dark, the stars a speckled tableau above his head, and he was ready.

Traveling at night wasn't for everyone.

But to quote Dave, this is me *we're talking about.*

Graham turned away from his home, not even bothering with a second look. He'd once walked away from a thirty-year-long life. This was nothing.

The grueling hike brought Graham all the way to the edge of the resort town. He was covered in sweat, aching and no less determined.

He kicked out a shallow hole in the snow, then stripped off his travel gear in favor of his jeans and T-shirt. He stuffed his cash and falsified ID into his jacket pockets, and filled the hole with his discarded items and marked the spot with a distinctly shaped rock as big as his head. Graham was sure he could locate it again, but there was nothing personal left in the pack, so if found, it wouldn't arouse suspicion in the finder.

It wasn't ideal, but it would do. It had to.

From his spot, the lights were too close and bright enough to make his head hurt.

No time for self-pity, he growled silently and stepped back into the trees.

Graham traipsed up the road, mentally recalling the name of the hotel Dave used each month.

I'm not going to go in, he told himself.

He just wanted to make sure they got there before he found a way down to the city.

He paused at a large overblown map at the top of Main Street. He found the place—Rocky Side Hotel—quickly. As he scanned the location, he realized that even if he skirted the perimeter streets all the way in, he'd still have to pass through a very busy area in order to reach the hotel itself. He cursed the fact that Dave had chosen somewhere so public as his monthly stopping point. Mountain View had plenty of more out-of-the-way places to stay. Romantic bungalows. Three-star hotels. The only place more attention-drawing would've been the chalet itself.

Graham forced himself to keep going.

It was well past any reasonable hour to be out on foot anywhere else, but in Mountain View the second the sun went down, the skiers became partiers and they stayed out until it rose again. As a result, even keeping to the edge of town didn't stop Graham from running into people.

After so many years in isolation, it was overwhelming.

So he was nervous. Far more on edge than he should have been.

Maybe he *would* go in. Maybe he'd just check on Keira, then see if Dave had a reasonable line on a vehicle.

And to breathe.

He knew it was ridiculous to assume that someone would know him, but that didn't make the feeling go away. When he finally had no choice but to head into the busy square in front of Dave's hotel, and a grinning club rat caught and held his eye, he expected to see some flicker of recognition. Some frightened spark that said, *Oh, that's him. That's the man accused of killing his wife.*

When he tried to cross a street a little too soon and a stranger grabbed his shoulder to stop him from falling in front of a party bus, he just about punched the Good Samaritan in the face. Even after Graham stumbled through an apology, the wary look didn't disappear from the man's eyes.

Graham didn't breathe easily until he reached the building with the large hand-painted sign that declared it as the correct hotel. His hand closed on the metal door and he pulled. It didn't budge, and when Graham took a step back he saw why.

The Rocky Side Hotel was closed for renovations.
What the hell?

Graham squinted at the sign giving the closure dates. Dave hadn't been there at all. Not in the past thirty days anyway.

So where had he taken Keira? Another hotel?
No.

A sinking feeling hit Graham straight in the gut.

He must have taken her home.

What for? To give her up, like he'd wanted to? For a misguided sense of right and wrong?

Graham reached up to yank on his hair, but came away empty-handed. It was too short for the habit to be satisfying.

His friend *knew* how much danger Keira would be in if Ferguson learned about her. To bring her that much closer, even if he thought it was because he was doing the right thing...

Graham shook his head and took another few steps

away from the closed hotel and smacked into an unsuspecting passerby. The guy stammered an apology, but Graham cut him off by grabbing his arm.

"What's the easiest way to get out of town?" he demanded harshly.

The stranger's eyes widened. "Now?"

"Yes, now."

"It's two in the morning."

"I'm aware."

The man scratched his head, looking drunkenly puzzled, then grinned brightly. "Truck stop!"

"Truck stop?"

"Yeah. The delivery guys come and go all night so they don't mess with the tourist mojo during the day. Six blocks of back alley will get you there."

Graham released his arm. "Thanks."

"No problem."

The partier stumbled away, and Graham moved quickly.

Chapter 18

Keira stared out the window of Dave's car, blurry-eyed. The hours it took to drive from the mountain to Derby Reach had passed quickly, mostly because she'd spent them sleeping. Or *pretending* to be asleep so she wouldn't have to make small talk with the man in the driver's seat.

Now they'd stopped.

But they weren't anywhere near her apartment. It only took Keira a single second of peering into the dim predawn to clue in that they *were* somewhere familiar, though.

"This is my parents' house," she said, sounding as puzzled as she felt.

"I know," Dave replied.

"Why are we here? How did you even know where it was?"

"I looked up a few details about you. One of the perks of being a cop. And as much as I hate the idea, Ms. Niles, I need to leave you alone for a bit to take care of a few details. I figured it was safer to bring you here than it was to drop you at your own place. I hope you don't mind."

Keira's head buzzed with worry. And actually, she *did* mind. It felt like an intrusion of privacy. But she could hardly complain about the policeman doing his job. Assuming that's what he *was* doing. And when had he had time to look up the details of her life? He'd barely left her alone for longer than a bathroom break.

"My own apartment would've been fine," she said a little stiffly.

But Dave shook his head. "And take the chance that some well-meaning neighbor spots you and sees the news and reports it?"

"Right," Keira replied uncertainly.

"Besides. Your parents' house is empty, and this neighborhood is known for its privacy."

A sliver of worry crept up Keira's spine. Had she mentioned her parents' monthlong vacation? Or was that another detail he'd uncovered in his miniature investigation into her life?

And if he can find out those things in a few hours, how come he couldn't prove Calloway's innocence in four full years?

Dave put his hand on her arm, and she flinched.

"If you're worried about Graham finding you…don't. He's as resourceful as he is single-minded. And if things go wrong, having you here instead of at home will give me the extra time I need to get you out safely."

The sliver became a spike. "Wrong?"

"I'm not trying to scare you, Ms. Niles. I want you to feel safe and secure. But I'd be lying if I didn't admit that in the past, Graham has lashed out on the people he thought wronged him. There was a time when I would've called him dangerous. It's been years since he's done anything truly violent, but it's also been years since he had any reason to. He won't give up until either he's taken care of the threat, or until taking care of the threat becomes more dangerous than the threat itself. I don't want you in the middle of that."

Keira opened her mouth, then closed it again. She wasn't sure she agreed with Dave's analysis. Calloway might very well be single-minded, but it was only out of necessity. Who wouldn't want to prove their innocence in a case like this one? And as far as self-preservation was concerned…she was living proof that he was capable of caring more about others' safety than he did about his own.

She had a funny feeling that in spite of what Dave claimed to the contrary, he *was* trying to scare her. She just wasn't sure why.

"Can I trust you, Ms. Niles?" the policeman asked abruptly.

"Trust me?" she replied.

"To lie low until I've done what needs to be done to ensure that there's no danger to you. Or to the people close to you."

His words had an ominous undertone to them, and Keira bit back an urge to point out that leaving her alone seemed counterproductive to keeping her safe. And to be honest, she was just plain eager to be rid of the man.

"I can do that," she agreed.

Dave seemed satisfied. He opened the glove box and pulled out a business card, which he handed to her.

"This is my direct number," he said. "If you have any problems at all, call me first. Do *not* contact anyone else. Do *not* reach out. And most importantly, do *not* tell anyone where you are."

He squeezed her hand. She let him hold it just long enough to not seem unappreciative.

"Thank you," she murmured.

"Another thing," Dave said. "If you doubt what I've said, keep this in mind. Your car might've crashed, but the fire that consumed it was man-made. The cops have ruled it arson. And we both know there was only one man up there."

Keira almost laughed. But then she caught sight of the serious look on Dave's face. Yes, he was still definitely trying to scare her.

Except for the first time, she was also sure he was telling the truth.

"Like I said, just keep in mind that he's the type of man who will cover up evidence at someone else's expense."

She gave him a level stare. "I'll do that."

Then she pulled away, and as she did, Dave reached for his own seat belt. Keira realized he was probably planning on accompanying her up the driveway. It was the last thing she wanted.

"It's all right," she said quickly. "I'm fine by myself."

"I'd feel better if you let me walk you to the door."

She shook her head and forced what she hoped looked like a genuine smile. "I'm lying low, remember? The last thing we want is my parents' neighbors talking because a strange man is dropping me off. If you come up, they'll have a fit."

Dave frowned, but Keira swung open the door before he could argue. Then she slammed it shut and ran up the driveway. Without looking back, she retrieved the key hidden under her mom's near-dead potted plant and let herself into the house. She counted to sixty, peeked out the curtains and finally let out a breath when she saw that Dave's car was completely out of sight.

Graham jerked his head up from the condensation-laden window, his hands closing tensely on the jacket between his thighs. He wasn't sure how long he'd been in the restless, close-to-sleep state, but the city lights were visible on the horizon.

"You all right?"

The question—asked in a voice that sounded full of genuine concern—came from the senior-aged trucker who'd agreed to bring Graham down the mountain.

Graham cleared his throat and did his best to answer like a normal person would.

"Fine. Just tired."

"Might wanna ease up on the death grip of the coat, then," said the trucker.

"Thanks for the tip." Graham's reply was dry, but he did let go and force his hands to his knees instead.

The driver was silent for a long moment, staring out the windshield.

Maybe you really are *incapable of normal*, Graham thought.

Seconds later, the trucker confirmed his suspicions.

"I don't know what you're running from—or to—and I don't want to. But if you act that suspicious everywhere you go, you can bet the cops'll be on you before you can demand to have your rights read."

"Trust me. I'm so far past the reading-the-right part of things that it's not even funny."

The trucker laughed anyway. "Makes me glad that this is the end of the line, my friend."

He nodded out the front window. A brightly lit truck stop beckoned just a mile or so ahead. Graham knew the spot. It was just outside Derby Reach.

For the first time since his flight from the cabin, he hesitated. It was there that his original escape started. Five hundred and fifty dollars slipped to another trucker—one far less friendly than the one who sat beside him now—to take him 482 miles.

He'd worked hard to put the town behind him.

Graham had been smart about his movements. Careful. He'd created a trail. Money here and there. Verifiable appearances at gas stations and hotels and grocery stores. One overblown fight in a bowling alley and a faked slipup of credit card use in a city on the other side of the country. Until he deliberately tapered off in his endeavors to be seen. It only took four months to create the perfect wild-goose chase. Two months after that, he was well settled at the cabin. Dave knew where he was, but no one else was looking in the right place. No one was even *thinking* about the right place.

Now I know how they felt, he thought grimly. *Clueless.*
Where would the other man have taken Keira?
Not to her home. Too obviously risky.
Even Dave would know that.

Graham stared down at his hands, considering all the options.

But not to his own home, either. Keira would never agree to that.

Dave would want her to feel safe. Comfortable. Familiar.

Family.

Had Keira mentioned any? Graham couldn't remember, but his gut told him Dave would've found out. Then what?

"Too many damned possibilities," Graham muttered.

"Buddy?"

Graham's gaze flicked back to the trucker. "Sorry."

"Don't apologize for being scared. We all got stuff to worry us."

Scared?

Graham opened his mouth to deny it, but when he met the trucker's eyes, and the other man gave him a knowing nod, he realized it was true. He *was* scared. For himself, a little. For Keira, a lot.

He held in a growl.

Twenty years, he'd known Dave. Twenty damned years. More than two-thirds of his life. He knew—more than most—that Dave's priorities could get a little skewed at times, but Graham would never have thought he'd do something like this.

Whatever this *is.*

It didn't really matter anyway. Graham was responsible for what had happened to Keira. What might happen to her still. Damn, how he hated this helpless feeling.

I have to save her.

But first he had to find her.

"You sure you're all right?" the trucker asked.

Graham managed a forced smile. "Six out of ten."

The big rig came to a rumbling halt then, and the diner loomed in front of them, and Graham couldn't decide if it felt like a starting point, or the end. He just knew he *needed* it to be the former. Would force it that way if he had to.

"Have they got public internet in there?" Graham asked.

The trucker shrugged, reached into his pocket and handed over a smartphone.

"Not in there. But I've got it out here," he said. "Probably less traceable anyway. You can feel free to clear the browser history after, too."

Graham punched a button on the screen, then paused. One of the last things he wanted was to make this man culpable for his mistakes. The phone became a lead weight in Graham's hand.

"If I told you that you were aiding a fugitive, would you still hand this over?" he asked.

The driver met his eyes evenly. "Been working the routes for forty-two years. Picked up a lot of hitchhikers. Means I'm pretty damned good at two things—navigating the roads and navigating people. If you're one of the bad guys, I'll hand over my license right this second."

"Thanks," Graham replied gruffly.

He fumbled with the phone for a second, but in a couple of taps, he had a home address for H. Gerald and Karen Niles.

And it gave him another chill. Their house was just a block from the home where he'd lived with Holly and Sam.

He shoved aside the increasing concern and, as suggested, he swiped away the browser history before handing the phone back. If nothing else, it gave the man plausible deniability.

The trucker gave him one more long stare. "You sure you don't want to walk away from whatever this is? As soon as I'm done my pie, I'm turning left and going straight for a hundred more miles."

An image of Keira—worried eyes, fiery eyes, soft, caring eyes—flashed through Graham's mind, and any doubt fled once again.

"Thanks," he said. "But some things are more than worth the risk."

The trucker smiled smugly, as if he was expecting the answer and knew just what Graham was talking about. "She must be one hell of a girl."

"Damn right," Graham agreed and hopped from the truck.

A hell of a girl in a hell of a situation. And only another five miles away.

Chapter 19

Keira paced the length of her parents' living room, wishing she could shake the restless feeling that kept her moving.

Everything she normally found comforting about the house was putting her on edge.

The food she'd taken from the freezer, heated according to the note taped to the lid, then eaten, sat heavily in her stomach. It was shepherd's pie. One of her favorites and it had never given her such bad heartburn.

She'd bathed. But the light lavender-scented body wash she'd used reminded her of her mother and made Keira lonely for her. Why had she promised Dave Stark that she wouldn't call anyone? Just hearing her mom's voice, listening to her complain about the heat or the way the humidity made her hair puff out, would've helped. Even if she didn't tell her mom anything, even if she just sat quietly while her mom spoke…it would've gone a long way to ease her mind. But she didn't want to endanger her parents. She didn't even want to risk it.

And now that she was clean and fed, Keira didn't know what to do with herself.

The quiet—so different from the perpetual noise of her thin-walled, one-bedroom apartment—was stifling. And each time an unexpected sound cut into the silence, whether it was the rumble of the furnace or the bark of a neighbor's job, Keira jumped.

Even the twelve snow globes—one for each Christmas they'd spent in Disneyland when she was a kid— that lined the fireplace mantel offered little comfort.

And the policeman's actions and decision had done nothing to ease her worry. He'd created even more questions for her than she'd had before.

Keira sighed, overwhelmed by frustration. For a second, she considered whether or not she should go against her word and sneak over to her apartment. Even if it was just to grab some of her own clothes.

She plucked at the pajamas borrowed from her mom's drawer, wondering if they were part of what kept her from feeling comfortable. From feeling like herself.

She picked up the first snow globe from the mantel and shook the little white flakes over Mickey's head. It was a mistake. The snowy display sent her mind immediately to Calloway.

Was he okay?

Keira set the snow globe down, and her gaze found her parents' antiquated computer in the corner of the living room.

Trusting a Stranger

Dave had asked her not to contact anyone. But he hadn't asked her not to research anything on her own.

A little guiltily, she slid out her dad's office chair from its dusty spot under the mahogany desk, sat her still-aching rear end in the cool leather and booted up the old machine. It took several minutes for the thing to chug to life—just enough time to chew one pink nail to a ridiculously short length and to assess whether or not she was being a little crazy.

A police officer had just all but warned her outright how dangerous Calloway was. And really, just the fact that Calloway had a hideout should've been enough to set off a hundred warning bells. Or at least make her question her attraction to him. Instead, every self-preserving instinct she had reared its head when she thought of David Stark. And every bit of intuition she had encouraged her to seek answers.

At last, the computer beeped, announcing its some-what reluctant readiness to oblige Keira's amateur sleuthing.

Calloway, crime, she plugged in.

And right away, a series of news articles popped up. Keira scrolled through the list. Some were the same as the ones she'd found in Calloway's scrapbook. Some were different.

Home Invasion Gone Wrong? Or Cover-Up Done Right?

Police Seek Husband for Questioning in Gruesome Double Homicide.

Graham Calloway. Doctor. Husband. Stepfather. Killer?

Keira's hand pressed into the stitched-up wound on her leg. A doctor. Well, that explained that.

She sighed, clicked on the last article and began to read.

For Holly Henderson, a fairy-tale romance has ended in tragedy. The twenty-five-year-old (heiress to the Henderson fortune) and her young son were killed in their home nearly one year ago today. It was Dr. Graham Calloway, her estranged husband and the primary beneficiary of the young woman's will, who discovered the murder. Now the police have issued a countrywide manhunt in search of Calloway, who will officially be charged with his wife's and stepson's murders.

Keira read through article after article, piecing together both the murdered woman's life and her death.

From her teenage years on, Holly was a favorite of the local media. Her late mother was old money, her father on the rise politically. Holly herself lived wildly, partying hard and often, until a surprise pregnancy brought her craziness to a grinding halt. While quite a bit of scandal accompanied the announcement, by all reports, it was the best thing to happen to the young heiress. After the birth of her son, Holly's name faded to obscurity, with the only notable events in the papers being her mother's passing and her father's election to city councilman. She met and married her son's pediatrician, Graham Calloway.

Then came the murder.

Keira's heart hammered as she read the details.

The call came in to the 9-1-1 center at two in the afternoon, and in minutes the police were on the scene. When the officers got there, they found Calloway holding his wife's body tightly in one arm, a gun in the other hand.

In spite of the circumstances, Calloway was initially taken at his word. They accepted that he'd found the house and his wife and hadn't called 9-1-1 immediately, but instead tried to revive her. Property damage, missing items, forced entry—all of it pointed to a home invasion gone wrong. But as quickly as the theory was accepted, it began to be discredited. A grieving husband became an angry husband.

And that's when things grew scandalous again.

Calloway became a target, his squeaky-clean reputation dragged through the mud. Troubled, precollege years surfaced. Several articles noted an assault charge at eighteen, and a weapons charge at seventeen. Although the former was pardoned and the latter sealed, somehow each became public knowledge.

The whole marriage was called into question. Calloway reportedly accused Holly of having an affair. A restraining order was said to be in the works. Domestic disturbance calls from the neighbors were rumored. And there were hints at a custody battle over the young boy.

A neighbor came forward, stating she'd heard a noisy argument just minutes before the gunshots. Finally, it was leaked to the press that Holly, who had long ago made Calloway the beneficiary in trust to her massive family fortune, had been about to divert the funds away from her soon-to-be ex-husband.

More and more rumors abounded.

Formal charges were pending.

And then Dr. Graham Calloway disappeared, making every reporter scream about the surety of his guilt.

Keira paused in her reading, wondering why the revelations from the online news sources didn't fill her full of doubt. All she felt was sadness for Calloway. It hurt her heart that he'd lost his family to that kind of violence.

And she was sure that it was something done *to* him, not something done *by* him.

Maybe she could chalk up her conviction to an inability to accept the truth rather than a gut feeling, but she didn't think so.

Keira looked back to the computer, flipping through the last few articles about the investigation.

The police chased down dozens of leads, followed every rumor. Nothing. They'd chased him countrywide. Assets were frozen, the property and her mother's family's fortune tied up in red tape. Even her politician father couldn't get ahold of a cent.

Eventually, the case was put aside for newer, fresher, solvable ones.

Henry Henderson, Holly's father, catapulted to political stardom.

And Calloway remained at large.

Except he's not at large at all, Keira thought as she leaned away from the computer.

A perfectly capable policeman knew exactly where he was hiding. Where he'd been hiding for years. So why hadn't Officer David Stark turned him in? Somehow, friendship didn't seem to cut it.

Puzzled, Keira punched in Dave's name to the search

screen. Unlike Calloway, he had very little digital presence. The usual social media, security settings on high,
a mention of community service in the local newspaper
and nothing more.

But there *had* to be something more. Some really
good reason for not just handing Calloway over to the
higher-ups and being done with it.

Keira stared at the screen for a long time, willing
herself to see something she'd missed.

Nothing.

She blinked at the computer screen, the words blur-
ring in front of her, and she wondered if it was time to
give up, at least for now.

Her finger hovered over the Close Window button.

Keira immediately felt guilty. This wasn't some internet search for cute cat videos. It was a man's innocence. Or guilt. It was his life.

And then an article at the bottom of the screen caught
her eye. It didn't have Dave's name in the highlighted
link, but the fact that it had popped up in her search
struck her as odd.

Paternity Suit Dropped.

Keira brought the pointer down to the article and
clicked.

Link not found.

She tried again.

Link not found.

Keira sighed. She rested her chin on her palm, trying to decide if the dead link was even relevant. Irritably, she typed in its title, added a plus sign, then typed Dave's name.

The moment she hit Enter, the computer chose to stall, an evil little circle spinning around on the screen as it took its sweet time thinking about what she'd asked it to look for. It held Keira's sleepy gaze for a good three minutes before her eyes drooped again. Her lids got heavier and heavier, and her shoulders slumped tiredly, and she had to force herself to keep from putting her head down on the keyboard. She could barely make her eyes focus on the information anymore.

She rested her head on the crook of her elbow.

Just for a second, she thought. *While I wait.*

But minutes later, she was sound asleep.

Chapter 20

The neighborhood was eerily the same as it had been four years earlier. Though Graham didn't know why he'd expected it to change at all. A lifetime might've passed for him, but it was little more than a blip in the lives of people who lived in these houses with the well-manicured lawns, and the carefully pruned trees and the six-foot-on-the-nose fences. Graham knew, because he'd been one of them not that long ago.

It had seemed ideal. The perfect, ready-made life. So much better than his overpriced bachelor pad in the heart of downtown.

It was Holly—fun, and sassy and a little bit wild—who had brought the neighborhood into Graham's life. She'd thrown a first birthday party for her son at her in-herited house, and even though he didn't usually make

social visits to his patients' homes, Graham had felt
compelled to go.

In retrospect, it was Holly's cherubic son who drew
him in.

And probably who held me there, Graham admitted.

At the party, the little boy had been toddling straight
for the in-ground pool in the backyard when Graham
spotted him. He'd rushed to the kid's side, grabbing
him seconds before he'd plunged in, and just moments
after *that*, Holly had latched on to Graham's arm in a
rather permanent way.

It was the life Graham had always dreamed of, but
struggled to find. His upbringing was hard, his teenage
years harsh and lonely, and it had taken every ounce of
will to fight his way out. A pretty wife, a perfect son and
a nice place to come home to had still seemed far off.

Until that party.

The first thing Graham did when he moved in was
to have the pool filled. Which was probably the perfect
piece of foreshadowing.

Graham was practical, but Holly liked *nice* things.
Fun things. *Shiny* things. Things that could hurt Sam, or
hurt her, and things that always left Graham wondering
just how the hell the package—that perfect-from-the-
outside life—could be so different from the contents.

Nothing reminded Graham more of that fact than
standing at the end of the street that led into the heart
of that neighborhood. Shiny and nice.

False advertising.

Except for Sam, of course. The kid was heartbreak-
ingly golden. Smart and sweet and full of life. The last
part came from Holly, undoubtedly, while the first two

were prime examples of the simple ability to overcome the odds. Which Graham related to perfectly. And ultimately, that's what broke him. Not Holly's affairs, or alcohol abuse, or the feeling that he was living on the periphery of some could-have-been life.

Graham wanted that kid. He was willing to fight for him, tooth and nail, and when Holly finally came out of her boozy haze long enough to realize what was happening, to see that her shiny doctor husband was going to take away her shiny son, she sobered up. Just long enough to kick him out. Just long enough to make him hurt. And just long enough to get killed.

Graham eyed the fork in the road warily.

One direction led to the Niles home and to Keira; the other went straight to Graham's old place and his bad memories.

Funny that he and Keira had lived so close to one another at some point, but never crossed paths.

Though maybe not so funny, if Graham was being honest. The two years he'd called this area home had been a closed-door hell. He hadn't had much time for making new friends. Between putting in sixty hours a week at the clinic, chasing down Holly at every turn and still trying his damnedest to be a good father to Sam.

Graham ran a hand through his shorn hair. As much as the past was to blame for his current predicament, he really didn't have time for dwelling on it.

He planted his feet in the direction of his former life for one moment, then swung toward Keira's parents' house.

Toward my future.

If I have one.

Three blocks brought him to the correct street, and that's where he switched from a comfortable own-the-place swagger to a don't-belong-here skulk. There weren't many people out, but that wasn't terribly surprising. It was noon on a Tuesday, and the residents were mostly at work.

Graham wove through the backyards, grateful for the owners' preference for shared good-neighbor gates and large hedges rather than sparse trees and bolted fences. They offered plenty of cover.

He didn't know what he'd find when he reached the Nileses' place. Maybe Dave would've taken up residence on the couch—a thought that made Graham's lip curl—or maybe he was just watching the place from some panel van on the corner. Either way, Graham was going to tear a strip off him. The man had jeopardized his hope of keeping Keira alive.

Alive?

That thought didn't just make his lip curl. It didn't even just make him pause. It stopped him dead in his tracks.

He'd been making his plans—a little spontaneous and uncharacteristically reckless—and the resulting moves with the idea of keeping Keira safe. What he *hadn't* been doing was focusing on what it might really mean if he wasn't successful. He hadn't truly considered the fact that her life might be in jeopardy. If she met Michael Ferguson, if Dave somehow put her in contact with him…

Graham closed his hands into fists, flexed them open, then closed them again.

Damn.

Keira would be a witness. She'd become someone who could do something even Graham himself couldn't do—a person who could identify Holly and Sam's murderer on sight. A liability. No way in hell would the cold-blooded killer let her just walk away at the end of it.

Graham moved a little quicker and he didn't slow again until he was two doors down from the Niles residence.

Once there, he stopped and did a careful visual perusal of the perimeter.

It revealed no sign of his cop friend. There wasn't a single car on the cul-de-sac.

So Dave had either left her alone completely, or Graham's instincts were off and he hadn't brought the girl there at all. A niggling of self-doubt crept in.

What if he was wrong?

Moments later, though, he spied a solitary light in the otherwise-dark Niles home. It was like a tiny beacon from behind the closed blinds, quashing any question Graham had about his gut feeling. He knew he was right; Keira was in there, completely unguarded.

Waiting for him, possibly.

Hopefully.

Graham cut through the final backyard that lay between him and the girl, then paused on the other side of the fence. After a quick glance around to make sure no one was watching him—at least not overtly—he grabbed ahold of a low-lying branch on a sturdy tree and pulled himself up. He shoved down thoughts of how ridiculous he would seem if caught—*a grown man climbing a neighborhood tree*—and surveyed the Nileses' landscaped yard. It was tidy, but not manicured, well-cared for, but not overdone. A yard *he* might've liked to have when he lived in the area. Holly had been partial to all things marble and all things floral, and with the removal of the pool, had commissioned an elaborate gazebo.

Yard envy is not *the point of this mission*, he reminded himself and moved his gaze around the lot, looking for ways to get to the house without being detected.

A big tree, much like the one where he sat now, offered ample coverage between the edge of the yard and the fence. Just a few feet from that was a line of shrub, a storage shed, then another tree, which was right beside a wide porch.

The layout of the home was familiar to Graham—his had been larger, but otherwise very similar.

The porch hung from the rear of the house. It was topped by a country-style door that undoubtedly led directly into the gourmet kitchen. Glossy wooden steps led up to the second floor. At the top of those was another deck, this one long and narrow. It would be home to sliding glass doors that would lead into the master suite.

And that's your best bet, Graham decided.

He didn't hesitate. He didn't look around as he moved from one spot to the next. If anyone was watching closely enough to catch his stealthy entrance, he didn't want to see them coming. He'd fight, if he had to, but if he was going to be taken out by a sniper, he'd rather not be looking down the barrel of the gun when it happened.

Graham made the transition from one yard to the

other easily, and no one stopped him as he sidled up the back stairs. No alarm sounded when he found the sliding glass doors unlocked and slid them open. In fact, the only noise he heard other than his own shallow breaths was a tiny squeak as he slipped from the master suite into the hall.

Careful to tread lightly, Graham eased past the requisite family photos that lined the stairwell. When he hit the middle of the steps, he froze.

There she was, straight across the expansive family room. Her head was down, her face pointed in the other direction, and for a very long, very slow heartbeat, Graham feared the worst. His stomach dropped to his knees, violent waves crashed inside his head and, try as he might, he couldn't breathe.

I'm too late, he thought, an indescribable thrum of desperation weakening his whole body.

His eyes closed and he grabbed at the railing to steady himself, unexpected moisture burning behind his lids.

He sank down to the stairs, racked with despair.

Chapter 21

Keira had woken with a start, her heart thumping in her chest and her head pressed into her dad's sports-car-themed mouse pad. It only took her a second to remember where she was and why she was there. The only real question was, what had woken her so abruptly?

Her eyes sought the clock above the mantel.

It was 1:03 p.m.

Three hours in a face-plant. And she didn't feel at all refreshed. She rubbed her cheek, trying to smooth out the little marks left by the mouse pad.

Then the ceiling above her squeaked, and she went still.

That's what woke me, she realized.

Keira knew the sound well. The culprits were three loose floorboards, one right outside the master bedroom, one on the very top stair and a final one, three up from the bottom step. When she was a teenager, her dad refused to fix them because there was no way to navigate through the hall without triggering one, making it next to impossible for her to sneak out—or in. Now, her dad said the squeaks added character to the house. But right that second, all they added was fear.

She cursed her own stupidity.

She hadn't bothered to bolt any of the doors or check any of the windows. And someone with good intentions wouldn't sneak in through the upstairs.

Keira glanced to the other side of the room, through the formal dining room to the French doors just off the kitchen. It was the quickest way out. But the back door had a notoriously rusty handle, which often stuck.

Her eyes flicked to the hall at the edge of the living room. It led to the front door. And straight past the stairs—the only way for the intruder to get to her.

She decided to take her chances with the kitchen.

But she waited a second too long. Before she could move, the final squeaky floorboard sounded, and Keira was stuck.

In a panic, she snapped up the nearest thing she could use as a weapon—an egg-shaped marble paperweight—palmed it, then closed her eyes and waited.

She heard the trespasser hit the last step of the stairs softly, then the pause at the bottom. Keira tensed. Whoever was attached to the footfalls didn't come any closer.

Why is he holding back?

She was afraid to breathe. Afraid to move. And her hand, clasped so tightly around the paperweight, was growing sweaty.

Her fingers wanted to move.

They were going to move.

They *did* move.

And even the slight adjustment drew a sharp inhale from her potential attacker.

Dammit.

Keira leaped to her feet, the paperweight slippery in her palm. She zeroed in on the invader.

He was standing on the bottom step. The relative dark created by the tightly drawn blinds obscured his face and bathed it in shadows.

He took a tiny step toward her.

"Stay there!" Keira commanded, only a slight tremor in her voice.

He paused, but only for a second. And Keira wasn't taking any chances. She drew her arm back and prepared to launch the marble egg with all her strength. It might not hit him, he might duck... It didn't matter. What Keira wanted was time.

She tossed the paperweight and turned to run.

He called something after her, but she ignored it.

Go, go, go!

She wasn't anywhere near fast enough. Strong arms closed around her, pinning them to her sides and lifting her from the ground.

"Stop!" His harsh tone not only demanded attention, it required obedience.

She wasn't going to give him the latter, and she was only giving him the former because she had no choice. And she sure as hell wasn't going to make it the *good* kind of attention, either. She kicked her legs, hoping to hit something—anything—important. He just squeezed her tighter.

"Keira!"

She ignored the fact that he knew her name. "Let me *go*!"

He ignored her, too, and backed up until they hit the stairs. He pulled her to a sitting position, his thick, muscular thighs wide around her, hugging her hips snuggly.

Keira wanted to yell, to holler for help, but her throat was dry, and she was scared that a scream might prompt him to do something worse than whatever he was already planning.

A little moan escaped from her lips. "Please."

"Keira."

Her name, the second time, was spoken much more softly. And finally she recognized the voice.

"Calloway," she whispered, her whole body sagging with relief.

"It's me," he murmured into her hair.

For a second, Keira just let herself lean against him, appreciative of his solidity. But it didn't take long for the heat in her body to rise. It bloomed from each part of Calloway's body that touched her. His inner thighs to her outer thighs. The bottom of his forearms on the top of hers and his chest pressed into her back. Her rear end pushed straight into his—

With an embarrassed gasp, Keira pulled herself away.

Clearly, all it took was the feel of his body against hers to turn her blood into lava and her mind into mush.

Which isn't so bad...is it?

"What are you doing here? You said two days. You're okay?" she made herself ask, trying to calm the blood rushing through her system and failing completely as she took in his changed appearance.

Dr. Graham Calloway.

The title seemed at odds with the man she'd met in the woods, but at that moment, she had no problems imagining him in the role. He'd shaved his beard, revealing a strong jaw and showcasing those amazing lips of his. The clean-cut look suited him and took years off his face. A white T-shirt hugged his thick, well-muscled body, and a pair of slightly too-big jeans hung a little low on his hips. He sat on the step above her, the extra height making him look even bigger than usual. From where Keira was, she had to tip her head up to meet his gaze.

God, he looks good.

He brought his hand up to push back his hair and gave her a clear view of his gray eyes. The want in them burned brightly. Keira's pulse thrummed even harder.

"Will a sliding scale do?" Calloway wondered out loud, and Keira had to struggle to remember what question she'd asked him in the first place.

"Sure," she managed to get out.

He tipped his head to one side thoughtfully. "All right. Three out of ten for having a hard object thrown at my head. Eight out of ten for having found you alive. Two out of ten because I'm a little disappointed that you're finally wearing pants."

Keira blushed, jumped to her feet and smoothed the borrowed pajama bottoms. "Are you just going to sit there?"

"Did you have something else in mind?" he teased.

Keira shook off the innuendo—and what it did to her—and headed straight for the kitchen without turning to see if he followed.

* * *

Graham watched Keira walk away, just because it was a nice view. He waited until she'd fully disappeared down the hall before he rose to follow her.

He felt markedly different now that he knew she was okay. Almost relaxed. He knew it was a bit—*okay, a lot*—premature to be letting down his guard, but for some reason, he couldn't quite help it. Seeing Keira in her own element probably had something to do with it. Even though it wasn't *her* home, it was a home she was clearly comfortable in.

Silently, she filled a kettle. She skirted the island with familiarity, rummaged through the cupboards, found what she was looking for, then set up two mismatched cups with chamomile tea bags. She didn't speak as she worked, but Graham had no problem imagining her humming as she went along, pulling out some kind of loaf from the freezer, thawing it in the microwave, then setting that on the counter beside the tea.

It was nice. Normal. Graham liked it.

So he stayed quiet, too, waiting as she laid everything out. When she was done, he took a small sip of the tea and let the floral flavor lie on his tongue for a moment before swallowing.

Keira climbed onto an island stool beside him, her knee almost touching his. Her delicate hands wrapped her mug, and she shot him an expectant look.

Graham wished immediately that the meeting wasn't about to take a serious turn. He wanted to make her blush again and laugh. He wanted to kiss those lips and drag that hair from its tight ponytail and forget that they were in any kind of danger.

But you can't.

There were other far more pressing matters to deal with. He needed to ask her why Dave had brought her here instead of staying in the resort town. And why he'd left her alone. When he opened his mouth, though, something else entirely came out.

"I'd like to turn that sliding scale into a ten out of ten."

"What—"

Graham didn't let her finish. He put one hand on the back of her head and the other on her chin. She trembled a little in her seat, but she remained glued to the spot as Graham lifted her face gently and kissed her lips. And as light as his touch was, desire surged through him.

Slow it down, Graham cautioned himself.

He trailed a finger down her cheek, then leaned back and smiled.

"Eight," he joked. "Maybe nine."

There was that blush.

Damn.

He drew her close again. He dragged his mouth down her cheek, tracing the curve of it, and the pink spread from her face to her throat. Then lower. He pulled away so he could look at her, so he could admire the arch of her brow and the swell of her breast and see that she wanted him as badly as he wanted her. He wasn't disappointed. Keira's lids were half-closed, and what little he could see of her eyes was glossy with heat. Her chest rose and fell against his enticingly.

To hell with slow.

Graham's grip on her neck tightened, and she gasped. He pulled her forcefully into his lap, making her teeter a bit on his knee, her legs dangling down. Her choice was between holding him tightly and falling to the ground. Thankfully, she chose the former. Her arms slid up to Graham's neck while his arms slipped to her waist.

He kissed her again. Forcefully. Possessively. She opened her mouth, welcoming his exploration. Her hands were in his hair and then they were sliding down his back, then holding him as if he was her lifeline.

"Graham," she said against his mouth, and he liked the way his name sounded on her lips.

"Yes, love?" he breathed back.

"I'm scared."

Fierce protectiveness filled his heart.

"I won't let anyone hurt you," he promised, and he meant it. *Not as long as I'm alive.*

Keira shook her head slowly. "No. I'm not scared for me."

"What're you scared for?"

"You. And us. If there *is* one, I mean. Or could be. I don't want this to be it."

Graham heard the need in her voice, and he had a matching one—an almost painful one—in his own when he answered. "I like you, Keira. More than like you. I have since the second I saw you in that car. That's the real, selfish reason I pulled you out. I wanted to know you. As crazy as it is, I felt like I *had* to. Or maybe I felt a little like I already did. The line is kind of blurred. I don't know if I can promise you a future— hell, maybe that's not even what you're asking—but I can give you now. I can give you honesty. I can give you *us.*"

Her eyes were wide and hopeful. "All right."

Trust, unexpected and almost unbelievable, expanded in Graham's chest.

"I'm not a perfect man," he warned her.

"I know," she replied.

Graham grinned. "Oh, you do, do you?"

She went pink. "I meant I don't *expect* you to be perfect."

When in doubt, go for shock.

"I lit your car on fire," Graham stated.

Keira face went a little redder. "I know that, too."

Graham raised an eyebrow.

"Dave told me," Keira admitted.

"Did he tell you *why*?"

"To cover up the evidence. But he meant it in a bad way. I know better."

Graham swallowed. His throat was raw with appreciation of her understanding, but his heart was dark with guilt at needing it.

"How do *you* think I meant it?" he asked.

"You were buying time. Protecting yourself."

"I don't know if you know this, Keira, but most men don't commit a felony in the name of self-preservation." He was half joking, but she didn't smile.

"I'm glad you're not most men," she said.

He leaned in to give her a soft kiss. "Did Dave tell you anything else about me?"

"Not really."

"But?" Graham pushed.

"I searched you on Google."

"I'll bet *that* didn't have anything nice to say about me."

"I don't believe everything I read."

"But some of it?"

"Not most of it."

Graham closed his eyes for a long moment, but he could still feel Keira's gaze on him. It wasn't judgmental or even assessing. Just patient. She put a hand on his cheek.

"You can tell me," she said.

Graham opened his eyes and nodded. "Holly was wild. Impetuous. A little crazy, sometimes. Her mom died when she was young—just nineteen—and left her a lot of money. Her dad was never able to control her and, believe me, he tried. Screened her boyfriends, put a tracking device on her car, recorded her phone calls, you name it. But she was an adult. At least in the strictest sense of the word. She refused to be reined in. She wasn't even trying. It's just who she was. The baby—Sam—slowed her down for a while. But as soon as she was settled, as soon as *I* was settled…she started up again. Drinking and other men…"

"It's not your fault," Keira said, sounding very sure.

Graham was sure, too. Holly *couldn't* be controlled, and it had nothing to do with Graham. That didn't stop him from feeling guilty about her death.

The truth.

"I didn't love her." The admission came out hoarse, and Graham cleared his throat and tried again. "I didn't love her, but I was a good husband. A faithful husband. And that kid… I loved him more than I've loved anyone before or since." His voice was rough once more, and this time he let it stay that way. "I couldn't let anyone think I had anything to do with his murder. I'd rather die myself. That's why I ran. Why I paid Dave to search for the man who killed them. Why I've never been able to walk away and start fresh, even though I've got the means." He looked at her face and saw the tears threatening to overflow, and his heart broke a little more. "I'm sorry, Keira—"

Her lips cut him off. Her fingers dug in to his hair, then ran smoothly, soothingly, over the back of his neck. She was pouring herself into the kiss, and Graham accepted it. Reluctantly at first, but with increased acceptance. Then with enthusiasm. He met her attention forcefully, his tongue finding purchase between her lips, his hands getting lost in her auburn tresses. She sank into his arms. She belonged there. When she pulled away, Graham felt the loss all over.

Then she spoke, and the loss was forgotten.

"My bedroom is upstairs," she said, her words loaded with promise. "Third door on the left."

Wordlessly, Graham scooped her up and moved at double time to the staircase.

Chapter 22

They were a tangled mess of arms and legs and bed-sheets and sweat. Calloway's muscular, oversize body took up three quarters of the available space. Never before had Keira's double bed in her childhood room seemed so small.

But it's the perfect size, too, she thought as she opened her sleepy eyes and looked over at him.

His face was still peaceful, and Keira was a little envious. A silly grin was plastered on her own. And her mind refused to sit still because it was too full of sweet nothings.

Beautiful.

Incredible.

Amazing.

And the way he said her name. The way he whispered it. The way he called it out, as if there was no one else in the world.

And what he'd said earlier was right. It *was* crazy to feel like this. It would be crazy to feel like this even after a few months. But after only a few days... That pushed it right over the edge. But damned if Keira cared.

She examined his face carefully, memorizing the lines of it in the soft morning light. She liked the thick crest of his eyebrows and the dusting of silver in his hair. Already, the shadow of a beard peppered his cheeks. She liked that, too.

Her heart wanted to burst through her chest with its fullness.

But there was a heaviness there, too. One the allover glow couldn't quite mask.

Because Calloway wasn't safe, and their time together was finite. His hideaway was no longer an option, her parents' house wasn't any better and her own apartment was the first place the man who'd killed Calloway's family would look.

Their only option was to run somewhere else.

"No."

Calloway's statement was soft but decisive. And he hadn't even opened his eyes.

"No, what?" Keira replied.

"I can feel you thinking."

"Someone else's thinking can't be felt," she argued.

He cracked one lid. "Yours can."

Keira made a weak effort to detangle herself from his arms, but he held her firmly in place. She didn't struggle too hard. Truthfully, she was happier to rest her head against him than she was to resist him.

"I didn't even know you were awake," she said as she trailed her palm across his chest.

"Little hard to stay asleep while you're plotting something that's going to kill you."

"That isn't what I was doing."

Calloway eased his hold and rolled both of them to their sides, so they were facing each other.

"No?" he said. "What *were* you thinking about, then?"

"Leaving."

"Leaving?" he repeated, sounding surprised.

"Leaving together," she clarified. "You don't have to find Ferguson. Or risk *your* life. Not if we run."

"Keira…"

"They already think I'm dead," she reminded him. "Dave told me the media was all over the story."

Calloway's expression clouded. "And you're just going to walk away and let it stay that way?"

A lump formed in Keira's throat. "They'll mourn and move on."

"How long will you last? What if one of *them* dies? Will you stay away when they have the funeral? Or one of your parents gets sick or has an accident?" He shook his head, then added in a harsh voice, "You have no idea what you're saying. What you're committing to."

"I don't see what other choice I have."

"You can stay here, and let your family and friends know you're alive."

"And what happens to you?"

He smoothed her hair back from her face. "Are you asking what happens to *me*, or what happens to that *us* we talked about?"

Keira didn't answer him. She *was* worried about Calloway directly. She didn't want the police to catch him or for him to be arrested for a crime he hadn't committed. But she also had to admit—at least to herself—that she was scared of losing him. She was just too embarrassed to make the declaration out loud.

Two short days, and you need this man as badly as you need air.

Even thinking it was enough to make her face heat up.

When she stayed silent, Calloway sighed. "I've spent a long time isolated from the people I knew. It nearly killed me to hear the rumors. It nearly broke me a hundred times. Hiding is the hardest damned thing I've ever done. I would never forgive myself for dragging you into that life."

"I don't care," Keira said, her voice full of residual post-lovemaking conviction.

"You *think* you don't care."

"Don't tell me what I think."

"I wouldn't dare."

Calloway leaned forward and gave her bottom lip a little tug with his teeth. Then he released it and ran a hand over the same spot, sending renewed sparks of desire through her. Keira stifled a pleasure-filled sigh. Calloway's face was determined, his jaw set and his eyes not in the slightest bit tired. And Keira had the distinct feeling that he was trying to distract her. He formed a lazy path from her mouth to her shoulder to her hip, then traced a circle over her sheet-covered abdomen.

Two more seconds of that *and it's going to work.*

Keira grabbed his hand, determined herself. She needed to make him understand that she wasn't going to just let him slip away. He tried to pull his hand out of hers. She held firm. *Take that.* But his thumb was still loose, and it began to move up and down, just below her belly button, and it was far more distracting than his whole palm had been.

She willed herself not to give in to the temptation he presented.

"You've been gone for a long time," she said. "So maybe you've forgotten how to compromise. Relationships are a two-way street, Calloway."

He didn't even blink at her use of the *R* word. "What do you want me to do, Keira? Let Dave take me in? Say the word, and that's what will happen. But there is absolutely zero chance of me allowing you to abandon your life on my behalf."

Keira's stomach dropped. "You can't go to jail."

"I will, if it means keeping you safe."

"I'm not letting you sacrifice yourself for me any more than you're letting me sacrifice myself for you!"

In an unexpected move, Calloway flipped her from her side to her back, then propped himself above her, his biceps flexing with the effort.

"You're a stubborn girl, aren't you?"

"No."

"That blush tells me you *know* you're a stubborn girl," he teased. "I *have* to prove my innocence, Keira. Or we don't stand a chance. Do you know where Dave went?"

"He said he had to take care of a few things." She paused. "Calloway..."

"Yes?"

Keira pulled the sheet over her chest, then propped herself on her elbow, facing him. "Why would he suddenly start thinking you're guilty?"

Calloway's expression clouded with surprise. "Is that what he said?"

"Not exactly. It's what he implied. Or maybe what I inferred. But it was like he was trying to scare me."

"But he *knows* I'm innocent," Calloway muttered.

"He knows it?"

Calloway gave her tight nod. "Dave's the one who found Holly. Hours before I got home."

Keira frowned. "But the papers said it was *you* who found her."

He ran his fingers over the ridges in her forehead. "I thought you didn't believe everything you read."

"I don't. But that's a pretty big discrepancy."

"Lie down with me again."

Keira opened her mouth to tell him no, they had more important things to worry about. But when she caught the pleading look in his eyes, she was powerless to resist. She curled up beside him, her body tucked beside his, her head resting on his chest.

Graham waited until Keira was settled, the soft scent of her hair flooding his senses, calming the thud of his heart.

"If you want to listen, I'll tell you the story," he said, his voice low.

"Okay," she agreed.

And for the first time, he told the full truth, and

shared the hard thoughts that kept him awake for four years.

"Dave and I met in high school. We started out hating each other. We fought, actually, in one of those parking-lot fights, with the crowd of guys egging us on and screaming for blood. God knows what it was about. We both got suspended. Not a first for me, but Dave's dad was a cop, and he was royally pissed off that I was ruining his kid's life. He turned up at my house, demanding to know what *I* had done. When he saw my living situation, well, I guess he took pity on me. Absentee mom. Drunk dad. So instead of giving me hell, he took me home and commanded Dave to take care of me." Graham paused and laughed as he remembered it.

Dave's father was everything Dave wasn't. Hard and decisive on the outside, kind and insightful on the inside. He didn't take anyone's garbage. Graham admired him. Loved him.

"He changed my life," Graham told Keira, curling a strand of her hair around one of his fingers. "He gave me value. Helped me get that scholarship for med school and made me believe I could do it. He died when we were twenty, and I promised him I'd see it through. He even left me a bit of money to help out. But Dave took his death badly, and pretty soon it was me carrying his weight instead of the other way around. Sorting out his fights and saving his rear end every weekend. If it hadn't been for his father's name, I doubt he would ever have made it past the first day as a policeman. He developed a hell of a gambling problem and I was always bailing him out of one debt or another. We went on like that for years, Dave messing up and me picking up the pieces."

"Just like you did with Holly," Keira added.

"Just like that," Graham agreed, then took a thick breath. "Which brings me to the next bit. Things moved fast for Holly and me. Met and married in less than a year. I adopted Sam…and Holly adopted Dave."

"They had an affair?" Keira asked.

"There were things…a pattern, I guess, that took me a while to notice. Money moved from her account on the same day he paid off a car he could never afford in the first place. Every time Holly made a cash withdrawal, Dave would show up with something newer and shinier. A suit. A computer. A vacation in the Bahamas. And he stopped asking *me* for money. Holly got more and more distant. And once, I overheard a very heated conversation between the two of them. Holly was yelling about jealousy and entitlement, and Dave was yelling back about sharing what should never have been mine."

"But you never asked either of them if your suspicion was true?"

Graham shook his head. "I rationalized *not* asking. What if I was wrong? I didn't want to ruin nearly a decade and a half of friendship. Or worse, jeopardize what I had with Sam. So I just started the divorce process on the sly. I hired the best lawyer I could afford, who promptly figured out that we were near to broke. My income and our assets were the only thing keeping us afloat. All of Holly's savings were gone, her investments mostly sold off, her cards maxed out. Which meant I had no choice but to confront her. But I never even got as far as asking about Dave before she flipped out. She threw everything I owned out on the street. Then threw me out, too. Three days later, the cops were at my hotel room door. Holly had drunk herself into a stupor, fallen down the stairs and called 9-1-1, blaming *me*. For the first time in a long time, Dave had to come to my aid. He bailed me out, dropped me off, then went to reason with Holly. Instead… Well, you know what he found."

"That's terrible." Keira's voice was full of the same ache that plagued Graham's heart, but then she spoke again, and her tone was also puzzled. "Why didn't he just report it himself?"

"I told him not to," Graham admitted. "I thought I was protecting him. And what was left of Holly's reputation."

"And that's why he helped you all these years?"

"Yes."

Keira pushed herself up and met Graham's eyes. "But, if he just admitted that he was there first, wouldn't that exonerate you?"

Graham shrugged. "Exonerate? No. Create reasonable doubt? Maybe. Or it might just implicate Dave, and as much as I question his motives at the moment… he's not a killer."

"You know that for sure?"

"I believe it one hundred percent."

"So we're back to wondering why he suddenly changed his mind about you being the good guy."

Graham stared at her pinched-up features and couldn't suppress a smile.

"Is that where we are?" he teased. "I thought we were in bed, getting ready to—"

She cut him off. "I'm going to ask him."

Graham's grin fell off his face immediately. "No."

"Are you telling me what to do again, Mountain Man?"

"This time, yes, I am. Do *not* ask Dave Stark why he changed his mind about protecting me."

"Asking him is the only thing that makes sense," Keira argued. "And you're supposed to be chasing after Ferguson."

"You take priority, Keira. I'll deal with Dave first," Graham said grimly. "He owes me an explanation for what he said to you, and for leaving you here alone."

She opened her mouth as if she was going to protest again, then closed it and laid her head back on his chest.

"Calloway?" she said after a minute.

"Yes?"

He braced himself for another spiel about how and why she should endanger herself. Instead, her fingernail traced his collarbone, then his pectoral muscles, then found the edge of the sheet, just below his waistline.

"What were you saying before?"

"About?" The word came out throaty and full of heat. Now her hand slipped *under* the sheet.

"About what we were getting ready to do in this bed," she filled in.

With a growl that made her laugh, Graham grabbed her by the hips and lifted her over top of him.

Chapter 23

Keira eyed Calloway guiltily. He was definitely sleeping this time, his handsome face slack, his breathing even.

Seduction had never been Keira's strong point, but she'd worked her hardest to wear him out.

Not that it wasn't rewarding for her, as well. Graham was a fierce and attentive lover. And that made her feel even worse.

But there's no way he'll willingly let you out of his sight, she reminded herself.

She felt that little tug at her heart again, pleased that he cared so much. He'd be mad when he woke up and found out she was gone. Furious, probably. But it was worth it, if she could figure out what it was that Dave was after. Because she had a feeling it was more than misguided morals and Keira felt just as protective of Calloway as he did of her. His story broke her heart.

She couldn't help but wonder how much of *his* heart remained in pieces, as well. Every time he said his stepson's name, she heard the pain.

I want to fix that.

She knew justice wouldn't make Calloway whole immediately, but maybe it would start the healing process.

Keira slid her body free from Calloway's embrace, stood up and stepped to the closet. A stack of board games and her mother's rejects—the clothes she couldn't wear anymore but refused to part with—greeted her.

Keira snagged an oversize T-shirt and a pair of leggings, and reminded herself that she wasn't trying to impress Dave with her fashion sense anyway. That didn't stop her from cringing at her appearance as she caught sight of her reflection in the mirror on the back of the door.

Her hair was a disaster, and the wound on her thigh, though held together nicely by Graham's stitches, was still hideous.

She slid on the clothes and patted her hair. Now she looked as if she'd dressed up as her mother for Halloween.

"Nice," she muttered aloud before she remembered she was supposed to be keeping quiet.

Calloway stirred, letting out a noisy sigh, and Keira froze, her eyes fixed to his image in the mirror.

Do not *wake up*, she commanded silently.

He rolled to his side and stretched one arm up, and the bedsheet slid down, revealing a tantalizing amount of skin. Keira's eyes roamed the exposed flesh greedily for a second before she gave herself a mental kick in the butt and opened the door, cutting off her view.

She moved into the hall, wincing as the first telltale

floorboard squeaked. But there was no sound from the bedroom, so she moved on to the stairs.

She went still when a loud knock on the back door reached her ears. Then she heard it squeal open.

What the heck?

With her heart in her throat, Keira tiptoed down the stairs and paused outside the kitchen. Part of her wanted to charge in and tackle whoever was in there. Part of her wanted to wake Calloway for protection.

She steeled herself not to do either.

After all, home invaders didn't usually knock before they let themselves in. Did they?

Her assumption was confirmed when a familiar voice called out, "Keira?"

Drew.

What was he doing here? He wasn't supposed to be back from his business trip yet.

She had to get rid of him before he figured out that Calloway was in the house.

Keira took a breath and stepped into the kitchen. She fixed what she hoped was a surprised—and not guilty—look on her face as she greeted him.

"Drew! Where did you come from? How did you even know I was here? You scared the heck out of me!"

He immediately wrapped his arms around her. "*I* scared *you*? Thank God you're okay!"

She extracted herself from his embrace, marveling at the fact that just a few days ago, she'd been considering pursuing a relationship with this man. She didn't feel the remotest bit of attraction toward him.

"Why wouldn't I be okay?" she asked.

Drew fixed her with a concerned gaze. "Your face is plastered all over the news, Keira."

"Is it?"

He raised a speculative eyebrow, and Keira told herself she needed to rein in the innocence a bit.

"They said you'd been in a horrible accident on the mountain. That your car went over the side of some cliff."

They'd identified her.

This is bad.

Did that mean that Dave Stark had given his official statement, or had his plan been circumvented?

Or is he the one that leaked her name?

Drew closed his hand on her elbow. "Hey. You still with me?"

Keira shook her head and moved away. "I'm fine. I just—I was about to sneak out for a quick cup of coffee. You want to come?"

Drew frowned as if he wanted to say no, and for a second she hoped he would. But then his eyes fixed on something just over her shoulder, and Keira followed his gaze to the spot where she and Calloway had abandoned their mugs earlier. Her pulse jumped.

"You sure you want coffee? Looks like you already had some tea for two," Drew observed.

She forced a laugh. "I guess I was a bit tired this morning when I got in. I made a cup, forgot about it, made another, then didn't drink either of them."

"So you didn't have company?"

"Company?" Keira echoed nervously.

Drew nudged her shoulder. "You know. A guest. Like

me, but who doesn't know where your parents keep the extra key to the back door."

Keira shook her head. "No guests. Unless you're *actually* counting yourself. So…coffee?"

Drew nodded, and Keira breathed a big sigh of relief as he held the door open. She followed him out, careful not to let her eyes stray toward her bedroom window.

When Graham woke, he reached for Keira automatically. As though he'd been waking up beside her for years instead of days.

But a lot can happen in days, he thought drowsily. *You can lose a life. Start a new one. Fall in love. Become something you never thought you'd be.*

His hand slid across the bed, already anticipating the silky feel of her skin under his palm. When his expectation fell through, his eyes flew open. Her spot on the bed was decidedly empty.

Graham sat up and swung his bare legs to the floor. "Keira?"

He waited about ten seconds for her to answer, and when she didn't, he grew irrationally worried.

"Keira!" he called a bit louder.

He snapped up his jeans and T-shirt from the floor, slipped them on without bothering to locate his discarded underwear, and moved toward the door. He cracked it open and paused. The house was ominously silent.

"Hey!"

He made his way downstairs, taking the steps two at a time. The sun was going down, and the main floor was nearly dark. Worse than that, there was no sign of Keira.

Where the hell had she gone?

He stepped from the bottom of the stairs to the kitchen and flicked on the lights. The two nearly full mugs of chamomile tea still sat where they'd left them.

Dread was pooling rather quickly in Graham's gut.

He walked around the kitchen slowly, trying to find a clue that would give him a hint as to where she'd disappeared to.

And whether or not it had been on purpose. Or for that matter...purposeful.

"She could've just needed something from the store," Graham told himself out loud.

The thought eased his mind for a tenth of a second. Then a little white card on the edge of the counter caught his eye.

He lifted it slowly.

"Sergeant David Stark," it read, followed by a phone number in bold.

"Well, that answers that," he muttered.

No wonder she'd dropped the whole ask-Dave issue so easily. She'd already made the decision to disobey Graham's request.

Did you really expect her to obey *you?*

She'd been nothing but a challenge since the second he pulled her from the wreck. Which he liked. Except right at that second. Graham gritted his teeth. Right that second, what he wished was that she was a complacent pushover waiting for him to make the decisions so he could keep her safe.

He paced the length of the kitchen, then out to the living room, then back again, trying—and failing—to find an outlet for his frustration.

He cursed himself for being played as much as he cursed her for playing him.

And play you she did. Like a damned drum.

Of course, his body had been more than happy to let her have her way with him. She fit in his arms so perfectly, it was as if she was made for him. And when she fixed those green eyes on him, her pupils dilated with need, her mouth parted slightly as she exhaled his name…

Graham shook his head. That kind of passion wasn't a ploy. That kind of chemistry couldn't be faked. So, yeah, she might've been manipulating him with sex, but she hadn't been immune to what was happening between them. He was sure of it.

Graham paused on his third run through the living room and ran his fingers through his hair. It really wasn't nearly as satisfying as it had been when it was still long.

He needed something to *do.* Something to occupy his mind and his hands. His eyes flicked around the room until they found the dimly lit computer in the corner.

It had been a very long time since Graham had used a computer. His brief search on the trucker's phone was the closest he'd come to that kind of technology since he went into hiding.

Keira looked you up. It's only fair that you look her up in return.

He smiled a self-satisfied smile. He was pretty damned sure she'd hate the thought of being checked up on.

Drew set down a paper cup in front of Keira. It was chocolate-and-coffee scented and topped with a generous dollop of whipped cream.

"Decaf mocha," he said. "I know it's your favorite."

"Thanks." Keira took a sip, grateful for the way the hot liquid warmed her and for the extra second it gave her to gather her thoughts.

Drew waited patiently as she slurped off the whipped cream. He didn't deserve to be lied to the way she was going to have to lie to him. Another tickle of guilt rubbed at Keira's mind. She covered it with a second mouthful of mocha.

Guilt, fear and desire. Those three things seemed to have dominated her emotions since the second she laid eyes on Graham Calloway.

Drew finally broke the too-long silence. "You want to tell me what happened up there on the mountain?"

She met his gaze from across the table.

He really did know her well. Maybe better than anyone except her closest girlfriends. He'd been a shoulder for her on a few occasions, a great help to her parents on many more. And right that moment, she was selfishly tempted to tell him the truth, even if just to garner his opinion on what to do.

She opened her mouth and then closed it.

It's not your secret to tell.

And letting the metaphorical cat out of the bag would only ease the pressure of keeping it under wraps temporarily. It would expose Calloway in a way that Keira would never forgive herself for.

"I don't really remember what happened," Keira lied softly.

Drew frowned. "You don't remember?"

"I remember the crash. And the cop who drove me home. Everything between is kind of fuzzy."

"The cop who picked you up…did he say anything else about what happened up there?" Drew pushed.

"Like what?"

"Like the fact that when they were searching for you, they found some abandoned cabin that might've belonged to an accused murderer. That before that cop found you, they thought maybe the killer had got to you. They even issued some kind of manhunt just in case."

Keira's vision blurred for a dizzying second and she reached for the table to steady herself. She swallowed, her throat dry. She drank some more of the mocha. It did nothing to ease her parched mouth, and the rush of blood to her head wasn't letting up, either.

Was it a coincidence, or had Dave Stark taken his betrayal of Calloway a step further and exposed him to the press?

Oh, God. Are they still looking for him?

"Keira?"

"I'm okay," she managed to get out.

"You sure?"

"Yeah. I guess the thought of being that close to a suspected killer… What else did the news say about the alleged murder?"

"Alleged? This guy—Graham Calloway—has been on the run for years. If he was innocent, something would've turned up by now. You know, they never even found the kid's body? And apparently he stole some thirty-million-dollar painting from his wife before he killed her."

"He…" Keira trailed off, her thoughts suddenly a jumbled mess. "Did they say all of that on the news?"

"Online."

".I didn't read anything like that. He didn't—" Keira snapped her mouth shut.

"Who didn't do what?"

Dammit. She needed to get ahold of herself. Her tongue seemed to be working faster than her brain. She had to fix that.

"The cop," she said slowly. "He didn't say anything about any of that."

"What *did* he say?"

"To keep to myself. In fact, he'd probably be pretty annoyed with me if he knew I was out in public."

"I bet he would."

"What?"

"It's frustrating when you give someone instructions and they don't listen."

Keira sensed something ominous in his words, but she couldn't pinpoint her worry, so she lifted the mocha up and covered her concern with a gulp.

"I should take you home, I think. Wouldn't want to anger that cop," Drew stated.

Keira nodded, the bobbing motion making her head feel funny. Really funny. Weirder than it had since she'd first banged it in the car accident.

She stood up, bumping the table and sloshing around her mocha. She made a move to grab it, but Drew was quicker.

"You've probably had enough of that," he said.

That struck Keira as funny, and a tinny giggle escaped her lips. "Enough decaf mocha?"

"Mmm-hmm."

Drew slid an arm around her waist and clasped her elbow, then led her from the café to the street. It felt wrong to be in someone else's arms. But she didn't have the energy to pull away. Not even when she noted—rather vaguely—that they were heading in the wrong direction. They walked along in silence, Drew keeping Keira from stumbling, and Keira trying to grasp the elusive warning bells that kept sounding in her head.

They rang even louder as Drew paused in front of an older sedan.

"This isn't your car," she pointed out lamely.

"No," he agreed. "It's not. This car belongs to someone else."

"Who?" Keira wasn't even sure why she asked.

"Mike Ferguson."

A violent shiver wracked Keira's body.

Mike Ferguson. Calloway's *Mike Ferguson. The killer.*

"I don't think I know him," Keira lied.

"Don't worry. You're about to get to know him quite well, actually."

Keira met Drew's eyes, and they didn't look like his eyes at all.

In fact, the man she thought she knew—the one who'd been her parents' neighbor for nearly half a decade, who always had something nice to say about her clothes or her hair, and who mowed her dad's lawn *just so* when they were on vacation—was gone.

If Keira bumped into a man who looked like this in a dark alley, she'd run screaming in the other direction. She wanted to run screaming *now.* But when she moved her legs, they turned to jelly and the sidewalk wobbled. Drew caught her.

"I've thought a lot about what I would do if you ever

fell into my arms, Keira," he said, his voice as dark as his expression. "It's unfortunate that it ended up being like *this.*"

Keira flailed a little, but all she did was send herself into the side of the sedan. Her hips smacked the door handle hard enough to bring tears to her eyes. Drew's grip tightened.

"You should really be more careful."

"I'm careful," she said, her words slurred. "Usually."

"Not careful enough. Not today anyway." His voice dropped low as he went on. "If some killer *had* found you, and he *did* follow you here, he wouldn't have too much trouble getting in. What if that happened?"

"Alleged," Keira corrected, smacking her lips in an attempt to fend off the numbness that seemed to be overtaking her mouth.

"I'm not talking about Graham Calloway now, Keira."

"Who *are* you talking about?"

Drew smiled.

He smiled.

And it was a terrible smile that bared his teeth and turned his face hard. A smile that said, "Me."

Oh, God.

Graham pulled out the chair, straddled it and gave the mouse another click. In minutes, he'd had Keira's name plugged in. Except his search had been almost fruitless. Only two things popped up—a link to her social media and a brief mention in a local paper.

After a swift perusal of the first, and a read-through

of the second, he felt as if a few hours with her had taught him more than the virtual world ever could.

So much for the magic of Google.

Then Graham frowned. Hadn't she said Dave told her that her accident was all over the news?

He tapped the keyboard again.

Keira Niles. Car accident.

Nothing.

Keira Niles. Rocky Mountains.

Even less than nothing.

Car crash, Rocky Mountain Resort.

Nope.

Maybe his search was too broad. Maybe her story hadn't reached anything national yet.

Graham racked his brain as he tried to recall the name of the local paper.

Derby Reach Gazette?

He typed it in and the computer autocorrected it to Derby Reach Post, and Graham added her name once more.

"Nothing," he muttered to the empty room. "What the hell is going on? I know she wasn't *lying*."

He was as sure of that as he was of the fact that her feelings for him weren't phony. So if she'd been telling the truth... Graham's fierce worry came back, stronger than before.

He pushed the chair back and, two seconds too late, realized he wasn't alone in the house anymore.

"Dave was the one lying to her," he said.

As if on cue, Dave's voice came from behind him. "I'll tell you what you want to know, Graham, if you agree to come with me.

Graham jumped to his feet two seconds too late and spun, prepared to throw a punch straight into his disloyal friend's face.

Unfortunately, the other man had a pistol levelled at his chest.

For a long moment, Graham stared at the weapon and seriously considered whether or not to jump him anyway. He took a step in the other man's direction, and Dave cocked the pistol.

"I wouldn't move again," Dave cautioned. "Not suddenly anyway."

"Are you really going to shoot me, Dave?" Graham demanded coolly.

"I'd prefer not to," the other man replied. "But I'll kneecap you if I have to."

"What *do* you want, then?

"The same thing you do. To make sure Keira Niles is safe."

Graham shot Dave a disbelieving look. "You've got a funny way of showing it."

The policeman made an exasperated noise. "I've done everything I can. I took her off the mountain. I gave her strict instructions to stay home. I'm here now to—"

Graham cut him off. "Where is she?"

Surprise registered on Dave's face. "She's not here?"

"I thought she was with you."

"Me? Why would she be with me?"

"Because she wanted to ask you why you stopped helping me. Because she's stubborn as hell. Because I found *your* business card on the counter, and now she's gone."

"I wish she *had* called," Dave replied with a head-shake. "She was supposed to, if you happened to walk through the front door."

"I didn't come through the front door," Graham muttered. "Where is she, Dave?"

The policeman lifted the gun and used it to scratch his forehead. "Motivation."

"What?"

"Mike Ferguson's guy...he must've followed us. Stupid of me, I guess. I took the man at his word."

Graham's blood ran cold. "You're actually working with him."

Dave didn't respond to the accusation.

"I'll take you to Keira," he offered instead. "But I'm going to need you to put on my cuffs."

Graham snorted derisively. "Like hell."

"We don't have time to fight about this."

"Then give me the gun." Graham shrugged. "Why would I even believe you know where she is?"

"What's the alternative here, Graham? You think I'm going to have you slap on the cuffs so I can drag you to *jail*? Think about that for just one second. Your rear end is *my* rear end. If I turn you in, it'll either come out that I've been helping you, and the justice system will take me down, or it *won't* come out, and Ferguson will take me down instead. At least this way, we both stand a chance." Dave paused and used his free hand to pull a set of handcuffs from his pocket. "I know that the second I let down my guard, you'll beat the hell out of me."

"I'll beat the hell out of you if I even *think* you're letting your guard down."

Dave sighed. "Cuffs, Graham?"

Graham grabbed them from the other man's outstretched hand. He held them for a second, feeling the rift between the importance of his past and the importance of his present widening. If he put them on, he might very well be sacrificing himself to the man who killed his wife and son. If he didn't put them on, he might never get a chance to save the woman whom he was undoubtedly falling in love with.

Already fallen in love with, corrected a voice in his head, and he gave the voice a mental nod.

Yes, he'd already found that crazy, can't-live-without-her feeling.

And he knew what it was like to have no chance at all to save someone he loved.

It wasn't really much of a choice at all. He slid the cuffs to his wrists and snapped them shut.

"Show me they're secure," Dave ordered.

Graham lifted his hands and tugged them apart hard enough to bite punishingly into his skin.

"They're secure," he replied coolly.

"Good." Dave tucked his gun into his belt and stripped off his jacket. "I'm going to hang my coat over the cuffs, and we're going to take a walk."

"A walk?"

Dave shook his head. "No questions, unless they're about the weather or the Derby Reach Cardinals. You're going to stay on my right side—my gun side—just a little bit in front of me, but not so far in front that it looks forced. Got it?"

"Baseball, gun side, best buddies strolling through the neighborhood. Got it," Graham agreed.

And as Dave led him through the house and out the front door, Graham realized he didn't even have to ask where they were walking to.

Chapter 24

Keira didn't even know she'd passed out until she was already struggling to pull herself into consciousness.

And wakefulness was unpleasant enough to make her wish she was still asleep.

Her eyes burned when she fought to open them. Wherever she was, it was dark, but that did nothing to relieve the sharp stab behind her lids. In fact, the rest of her hurt just as badly. Her head throbbed. And her throat ached and her wrists were on fire.

She was seated, but the chair dug into her shoulder blades and into the backs of her legs, too. She tried to adjust her body to ease some of the pain—*any* of it—and failed miserably. She was completely immobilized. And starting to sweat.

Where was she? What had Drew done? And *why*? Dear God… What about Calloway?

She might've cried, if she'd had the energy to do so.

"Water?"

The unfamiliar voice cut through the panic building up in her system. Abruptly, consuming something liquid was more important than being free, and she croaked out an assent.

"Please."

A cool metal rim reached her lips, tipped up, then drizzled a stream of water down her throat. Keira sucked it back thirstily, and it was pulled away far too soon.

"It's the sedative," the voice told her. "It'll make you crazy thirsty like that. But you don't want to drink too much, either, or it'll just come back up again."

"A little more?" Keira pleaded.

The unseen man sighed, but he did lift the water to her mouth again, very briefly.

"Good enough," he said. "In a few minutes, I'll turn on the lights, but the sedative will have given you a wicked headache, too, and the light will exacerbate it, I'm sure. In the meantime…are you as comfortable as can be, considering the circumstances?"

Keira wasn't sure how to answer. The speaker's question was genuine sounding. Almost kindly. It was the voice of someone's grandfather offering a child a sweet treat. But he clearly wasn't there to rescue her.

"Ms. Niles?"

"I've been better," she whispered hoarsely.

She could hear the shrug in his reply. "I suppose you probably have. Maybe we *all* have."

"Are you going to cut to the chase, or just keep stringing her along?" snapped another angrier voice.

Drew.

"We can do things my way, or you can leave," the first voice answered him in a restrained tone, then turned its attention back to Keira. "Should we try the dimmer?"

He didn't wait for her to answer. There was a click, and the room was bathed in a low, almost tolerable light. Keira squinted against the watering of her eyes. She was in a formal dining room, pushed into a corner away from a heavy wood table. And two figures stood in front of her.

The first was the new Drew—his expression set in a cruel scowl.

The other was an older man whom she didn't know, but who looked vaguely familiar. Even in the dim light, Keira could tell that he was a cut above average and he suited his voice perfectly. His gray hair was thick and styled, his suit well tailored and his skin ruddy in a just-returned-from-the-Bahamas kind of way. He offered her a smile.

"Okay?" he asked.

"Okay," Keira agreed, her voice still burning like fire.

"You know Mr. Bryant," he said pleasantly. "But I don't think we've had the pleasure. I'm Councilman Henderson."

Councilman Henderson.

Keira's mind made the connection quickly. This was Calloway's father-in-law. The local politician with the wild-child daughter and the high ambitions and the reputation that needed protecting.

"You recognize my name, I see," he observed. "So

that makes things a little bit easier. What I'm hoping is that we can make it *all* easy."

"Easy, how?" Keira wanted to know.

"Talking to her is a waste of time," Drew interrupted.

"If you weren't perpetually tired of wasting time," the older gentleman stated, "the painting would be in my hands and Holly would still be alive. I've told you before, there's doing things. And then there's doing things with finesse. Wouldn't you agree, Ms. Niles?"

"Finesse didn't bring you the girl," Drew retorted before Keira could answer. "I did."

"No," the other man argued, still sounding patient. "Whatever drugs you fed her brought her here. And I'm damned sure asking her nicely would have sufficed."

"You think *asking* her would have worked?"

"The girl is clearly in love with Graham and there's not much a girl won't do to protect the man she loves."

Keira opened her mouth to argue, but couldn't do it. *In love with him?*

The realization made Keira's pulse race again, this time joyfully. Yes, she *did* love him, in that fast-and-hard, head-over-heels way that people wrote songs about. Everything about Calloway sang to her, made her thrum with life. The accident, the rescue…all of that had sped up the process, but there was no doubt in Keira's mind that the feelings were genuine. The very real likelihood of death intensified it all the more. And it made denying it impossible.

"I do love him," Keira said, hearing the truth of the statement in her voice. "And I'd lie to protect him. But I don't know what you're talking about."

"You'd lie," Drew snarled. "But would you *die*?"

Keira's reply was defiant. "Yes."

"Good."

He lunged at her, his hand drawn back for a blow. Keira braced herself, but he didn't make it close enough to hit her. Henry Henderson's fist closed on the back of Drew's collar, and he dragged the younger man back so forcefully that he fell to the ground with a thud.

"You fail at *every* task I give you," Henderson said, his voice betraying emotion for the first time. "You have no patience, no fortitude, no redeeming qualities. None. Now get out, guard the door and give Ms. Niles and me a few minutes alone."

Remarkably, Drew didn't even argue. He just pulled himself to his feet and slunk from the room. Henderson waited until the French doors were closed, then pulled out a chair from the table, seated himself and crossed his legs. When he turned his attention back to Keira, he was completely calm once more.

"Sometimes my sons forget who works for whom. My apologies," he said softly. "Now, where were we? Oh, right. Asking first certainly wouldn't have hurt. Ms. Niles, Graham Calloway has something I want. The man has been pouring his heart and soul out to you for days. He's either told you what I want to know, or he'll come here to rescue you and tell me himself. It's a win either way."

Keira barely heard what the man was saying. Her head was too busy trying to wrap around his first sentence.

His son.

No, not his son. His sons. *Plural.*

And Keira had a sinking feeling she knew who the other one was.

She needed to warn Calloway.

She stole a glance at Henry Henderson. He'd snapped up a newspaper from the table and turned his attention to what appeared to be a crossword puzzle.

Good.

Keira's hands twisted behind her back in search of a vulnerability in the rope. And after just a few seconds of trying, she found a loose spot, no bigger than her pinky finger. She just barely managed to keep from letting out a relieved cry.

She looked at Henderson again. He face was placid, as if he had no care outside of what word fit into fifty-one down.

I've got one for you, Keira thought. *What's an eleven-letter word for "drawing one's attention away from something"?*

D-I-S-T-R-A-C-T-I-O-N.

Keira closed her eyes for one second, dug her pinky into the loop, then opened her eyes again and asked, "What makes you so sure Calloway will come for me?"

Henderson blinked at her as if he'd completely forgotten her presence. Which she was damned well sure he hadn't.

"Pardon me, Ms. Niles?" he said.

She was also damned well sure he'd heard her the first time.

"There's a chance he won't come."

Henderson gave her a considering look. "Does he love you?"

Keira's face warmed. "I don't know."

Henderson shrugged. "I guess it doesn't matter. I believe he'll come, love or not. He'll feel responsible for you and obligation is a huge part of Graham's makeup. But if I'm wrong—which *is* a rare occurrence—I do have another ace or two up my sleeve."

The loop widened under Keira's attention.

"Like what?" she asked.

Henderson shook his head. "I think that's enough divulgence for the moment."

He went back to his crossword.

Dammit.

She had to keep him talking.

"What makes you think he even has this painting that you want?" she persisted. "He might not have it at all."

An amused smile tipped up the corner of the older man's mouth. "He has it."

Henderson took another sip of his drink and scratched something else onto the newspaper.

Keira had worked her finger in up to her knuckle already, and on the other side, she'd found another loose piece.

"How do you know?" she persisted.

Henderson folded the crossword in half, set it on the table and placed the cup on top.

"He had thirty-two million reasons to keep it," he told her.

It was Kiera's turn to blink slowly, and she had to force her fingers to keep working.

"Dollars?" she asked.

"That's right."

"But…"

"But what? You thought he was nothing more than

an everyday hero, motivated by a general care for the well-being of mankind?" Henderson shook his head. "I'm afraid not."

Keira wiggled her wrists. There was definitely some extra room now.

"If Calloway had a thirty-two-million-dollar painting, and he cared so much about the money, why was he living in a shack?" she asked. "Why wouldn't he sell it?"

"He's greedy, not stupid. The first thing I did when my daughter died was to report it missing."

"The papers didn't say a word about it," Keira pointed out.

A few more inches, and at least one hand would be free.

Henderson smiled again. "They wouldn't."

"Why's that?"

"Because I didn't report it to the police."

Keira tugged a little harder on the rope and feigned confusion. "Why not the police? Wouldn't they be the best people to track it?"

"I'm afraid not." His tone was patronizing. "If a wanted criminal is going to sell a thirty-million-dollar painting, it's not going to be through the appropriate channels. The people I reported its theft to are the kind who monitor the darker side of things, Ms. Niles. People like your friend Drew."

"Drew?" she repeated.

One final little yank, and Keira felt the rope drop behind her. Quickly, she tucked her feet together under the chair to cover up the dangling evidence.

"The wannabe art thief," Henderson clarified.

"Well. That explains his wannabe expensive taste." Keira forced a laugh as she tried to take a casual look around.

The vase in the center of the table.

It was big and painted blue and probably worth more than a month's worth of rent. But it also looked breakable. Into small, sharp pieces, preferably.

She'd have to find out.

Chapter 25

The house didn't just rest on top of its little hill. It loomed. Forbidding and hideous in its austerity.

It was the biggest one on the block—the one that all of the other houses in the neighborhood were modeled after. It wasn't that much older than its surrounding homes, but the lot was double the size. It was clearly designed not necessarily to stand out but to rule over.

Holly had told Graham that her mother had built the home, then given the rest of the property to her father to develop. A billion-dollar gift before the woman passed away and left everything else—the house, her fortune, her summer house overseas—to Holly herself.

Opulence.

It left a sour taste in Graham's mouth. It was one of the reasons the police believed he'd killed her. Killed *them*. Holly had spent the money—nearly every penny—and Graham, who had grown used to the *op-ulence*, was thrown into a rage.

The only thing left was the money in trust for Sam. The only way for Graham to get to that was to get rid of both of them.

Graham's jaw clenched involuntarily at the theory.

Money meant nothing to him. It never had, really. He'd gone into the medical field to help children who couldn't help themselves. He'd married Holly to help Sam.

But he'd wound up helpless, and the day he'd walked in and found Holly's body and Sam's blood…it was seared painfully into his memory.

The sirens had been close before Graham heard them.

Too close.

He'd known he ought to get up, slip out of the house and pretend he hadn't been there at all. That he hadn't received the frantic phone call from Dave, hadn't come home from the motel and hadn't walked in on the dev-astating scene in the front hall of the home he'd shared with his wife and stepson.

Instead, he tore through the kitchen, bending down to open each low cupboard, calling out in a reassur-ing voice.

"Come out, come out, wherever you are!"

Where was the boy?

It was the only thing that stopped Graham from flee-ing. He thought the boy had to be hiding somewhere, terrified. But where?

His heart had constricted as he moved past his wife's

still form again, taking the stairs two at a time and forcing himself not to look back.

He might not have loved the woman the way he
should, but in a million years, he would never have
wished for something like that.

You tried to revive Holly, he'd reminded himself. *You
really did. But you needed to find Sam.*

She'd been gone long before he got there. Blood loss.
Or the fall down the stairs. Even with his medical ex-
pertise, Graham couldn't say what had ultimately killed
her.

Sam.

A crushing anger pushed at the corners of Graham's
mind at what his stepson had witnessed.

He *had* to be a witness.

Graham couldn't even begin to accept the idea that
the boy might've met the same fate as Holly. He loved
the boy too much. Like nothing else in the world.

"Sammy!" he'd called as he'd opened the boy's bedroom door.

The usual assortment of Transformers and Lego and
art supplies were strewn throughout the room. Graham
saw none of them. The only thing that held his eye was
the bed and the dark circle in the center of it.

No. Oh, no.

Graham knew blood when he saw it. It covered his
hands and chest now, just as it covered his vision.

"Dr. Graham Calloway!" The cold, commanding
voice had come from the doorway. "Hands where I can
see them."

Numb, Graham lifted his arms and placed his palms
on his head and turned around slowly.

"They're dead," he'd said to the officer in blue. "Holly and Sam are dead. You're too late."

The later-damning statement was out before he could stop it. It was also the last thing he'd said in that house the last time he'd been inside.

Until now.

"Am I going to have to drag you in there?" Dave's question forced Graham back to the present.

"No," he replied, his voice betraying more than a hint of the overwhelming, emotional drainage he'd experienced on that day four years earlier.

"Let's move, then."

"Are you going to uncuff me first?"

"I can't do that."

"Level with me," Graham said tiredly. "Are you taking me inside *just* to hand me straight over to Mike Ferguson, or are you taking me inside with any hope at all of saving the girl I love?"

The hesitation in the reply betrayed the truth even before the words did. "It has to be both."

"That's not even possible."

Dave shot a worried glance up toward the house. "I didn't have much of a choice here, Graham."

"There's always a choice."

Dave's face clouded with anger. "I know you think the past four years have been hard for you, and you only. But I lost something that day, too. Some *things*."

Graham rattled his cuffs emphatically. "What do you think *you* lost, Dave? *Your* freedom?"

"As a matter of fact, I did lose my freedom. Every person on the force knew about our friendship. I've never been promoted, never been given a second look for anything."

"You're blaming that on me?"

"My entire career was stalled when Holly died."

"Your entire career was stalled the second you started it, Dave," Graham snapped. "If I hadn't been there to bail you out of every bad thing you did, you'd be a two-bit criminal instead of a two-bit cop. Oh. Wait."

The other man narrowed his eyes. "I've made some bad choices, but I'm trying to make the right one now."

"By cuffing me?"

"If I don't cuff you, we don't get in. It's as simple as that."

"And what next? We get in there and you say you have to hand the keys to these cuffs to Ferguson because it's just that simple? Will you hand him the gun he uses to shoot me, too, and then blame *that* on simplicity?" The last question came out at a near yell, and Graham took a breath and tried to calm himself. "I thought you loved her, too."

"I did love her. Can we stop talking about this and go inside?"

Graham shook his head. "I don't think so. Not until you explain to me why you turned on me. Why you're helping the man who murdered Holly."

"He's not who you think he is."

"Now you're defending him? Dammit, Dave. You *loved* her. In a way that I couldn't. I never held that against you. I never even tried to stop it. So why do this?"

"It wasn't like that with Holly and me," Dave replied softly.

"You don't have to lie about it."

The other man exhaled loudly. "She was my sister."

It was the last thing Graham expected to hear. "Your what?"

"My sister."

"You don't have a damned sister."

"I don't anymore. But I did."

"Explain," Graham ordered.

"I don't think you really want to hear about it."

It was true. Part of him *didn't* want to hear. He didn't want to know what Dave was using to justify his actions. He didn't want to be asked to have any sympathetic feelings for anyone involved in Holly's and Sam's deaths. And he was sure that's where Dave was going with this.

He pushed past the desire to shut down.

"Explain," he repeated coldly.

Dave sighed again. "When my dad died, he left you cash for college. And even though you weren't his kid, I got it. You had a bond and I respected that. But he left me a different kind of legacy, Graham. He left a letter, confessing that he wasn't *my* real father at all, that my mother had an affair with a local politician. He didn't tell me his name. And I wasn't supposed to tell anyone that I knew. But it ate me up. Every waking moment, I thought about it. About who he might be. You remember how I was when my father died."

Graham *did* remember. He'd blamed the downward spiral on the senior Stark's death. It had made sense.

"How did you find out it was Henry?" he asked.

"Not long after you met Holly, you introduced us, and… I just knew it was him. Something in his eyes, his stance. It reminded me of myself. And he didn't even deny it when I confronted him."

"So you did what, blackmail him?"

"Not at first. I just threatened him with a lawsuit. He threatened me back. He said he knew people who would make me wish not only that I wasn't his biological son, but that I'd never been born at all. And I believed him. Completely."

"So Holly was a weaker target?"

"Not exactly."

Graham was growing impatient. "Stop being so taciturn, Dave. It's not helping either of us."

"Things got worse for me. The man I always thought of as my father was dead. The man who was my biological father threatened to kill *me*. So I did what I always did. I gambled away more money. I kept going until I owed my bookie tens of thousands. Until one of them— Mike Ferguson—sent someone after me."

Graham's anger reared its head again. "You knew him *before* he killed them? You—"

Dave cut him off. "I didn't *know* him, Graham. I never even saw him. I owed him money. And I told you that you didn't want to hear this."

Graham gritted his teeth. "Go on."

"The man he sent was named Drew Bryant, and he didn't even ask me for the money I owed Ferguson. Instead, he told me he was my brother. Mine and Holly's. Another affair, another son," Dave said bitterly. "Henry took the term 'sow your wild oats' to an extreme, I guess. Drew convinced me that Henry owed us something. He'd been working for him and knew of a better way for us to get some money."

Drew Bryant.

He couldn't be Keira's boyfriend-potential Drew.

But he has to be.

"No coincidences," Graham muttered, then said a little more loudly, "After that, you went to Holly."

"After that, we went to Holly," Dave agreed. "She didn't even hesitate. She started paying us right away. Took the cash out of the bank that same day."

"And you were more than happy to take it."

"I owed money, Graham. A lot of it."

"So you thought it was okay to blackmail Holly?"

"We didn't *have* to blackmail her. She gave me the money willingly. She was thrilled to have brothers."

"You bankrupted her!"

"No. I paid my debt, thanked her, then didn't take a cent more. I told Drew I was out, and he agreed. So I kept my nose to the ground and washed my hands clean of Mike Ferguson. I paid my own way for a year," Dave explained. "But Drew kept taking money from her. I had no idea. Not until he came to me and told me she'd run out, and that he was planning on stealing the painting. I wanted to warn her. I was too late."

Bile rose in the back of Graham's throat. "Always about the money."

Dave looked as though he was about to say something else, but the door to the house where Graham once lived swung open, and a well-dressed, furious-looking man stepped onto the front veranda. He motioned angrily at Dave and Graham.

"Do I need to drag you in *now*?" Dave asked, displeasure clear in his inquiry.

Graham stared at the man on the stoop.

"Is that him?" he asked roughly.

If it was—if that was the man responsible for Holly's death—Graham wouldn't have to be dragged in. Just the opposite. It took all of his self-restraint to not run at the man, knock him down and wrap his throat with the chain on the cuffs and demand answers. Under the coat, he flexed his hands.

"That's Drew Bryant," Dave said. "Holly's brother, and mine."

"Where's Mike Ferguson?"

"Inside."

They moved forward together, and when they reached the porch, Drew Bryant gave Graham a dismissive once-over.

"This is the husband?" he asked, his tone as derisive as his expression.

"You know it is," Dave replied.

"I expected you to be more…impressive," the other man said.

Likewise, Graham thought, but he made himself stay quiet, assessing in silence.

He wasn't tall, but he wasn't short, either. His clothes were nice and his hair was tidy, but there was nothing remarkable about him at all. Graham couldn't see whatever it was that made Keira consider him boyfriend material, and he didn't know if that was a relief or not.

"Ready?" Dave prodded.

"Let's go," Graham replied grimly.

He started to step to the door, but Dave put a hand on his shoulder and muttered darkly, "He's not Mike Ferguson. But I bet you're going to wish he was."

Chapter 26

Keira waited until Henderson had immersed himself back in the crossword puzzle before she heaved herself to her feet and dove for the vase. Henderson reacted quickly, leaping up from his chair and pushing Keira away from her intended target. But her hand still managed to bump it, and she sent it rolling.

As the vase lumbered along, flashing blue on brown, Keira used the momentum given to her by Henderson's shove to propel herself under the table. When the older man bent down to grab her, she kicked out one bare foot, smacking him solidly in the forehead. He fell to his knees, but came at her again immediately. She struck him once more, this time in the chin. When he lunged a third time, Keira grabbed ahold of two chair legs and forced them together with as much strength as she could muster. They put a temporary barrier between her and the man hell-bent on getting to her. When he tried to shove the chairs out of his way, Keira gave one of them a push. It clipped Henderson in the eye, and he finally fell back, his hand on his brow.

"Drew!" he hollered.

And Keira thumped the chair forward again, harder than before. This time, the blow was hard enough to send him flying. He righted himself and shot her a furious glare.

"You little—"

Whatever he'd been about to say was lost in the sound of the vase hitting the hardwood floor and shattering.

Keira covered her eyes as the shards flew around her. She counted to three in her head, hoping that would give the porcelain enough time to settle, then opened her eyes in search of a big enough piece of vase to use as a weapon.

But Henderson was a step ahead of her. He already had a pointed chunk of porcelain gripped in one hand and was crawling toward Keira.

For a second, she was frozen to the spot, mesmerized by the gruesome sight in front of her.

Little pieces of blue flecked Henderson's face and around each of them was a dot of crimson. A bigger slice had jabbed into his shoulder, and from that, a steady stream of blood oozed.

He paused on the other side of the chairs.

Move!

It only took Keira a heartbeat to obey the command in her head. She scurried back, hit the wall behind her, then moved left, bringing herself closer to the door.

Bits of blue porcelain scraped underneath her as she slid along the floor, and she ignored the way they dug at her.

Three more feet.

But Henderson was nearly on his feet again and almost as close to her as she was to the exit.

Keira snapped up a piece of broken vase and held it out in front of her as she grabbed the door frame and pulled herself up.

"You might as well drop it. I'm bigger than you and stronger than you. I'm not afraid of hurting you. And I will," Henderson said, and Keira marveled that he somehow still managed to sound calm in spite of his threatening words. "I'm going to overpower you in seconds."

"And you're going to lose an eye in the process," Keira retorted.

"We'll see."

As he jumped toward her, the French doors flew open, and Henderson took advantage of Keira's momentary surprise. One of his arms closed around her, pinning her arms to her sides, and the other came up to press his own shard of sharp porcelain directly into her jugular.

Graham stared in horror at the scene in front of him, the truth unfolding in his mind.

The gray-haired man—covered in abrasions and looking like a poorly aged thug—was absolutely someone he knew. Well. And he had Keira in a death grip and showed no signs of letting her go.

He's inches away from cutting her throat.

"Henry…"

"Mike," the man corrected. "Ferguson. At least as far as this little scenario is concerned."

Graham's stomach caved in; his head boomed with the revelation.

His father-in-law was a well-respected member of the community. A city councilman, with power and influence, and a reputation sullied only by Holly's exploits.

And a murderer.

Graham's mouth hung open, a dozen unable-to-be-articulated questions on the tip of his tongue.

Then he realized the answers didn't matter. Not right that second anyway.

Graham recovered from his momentary inability to move and strode forward, forgetting his cuffs, forgetting the two men on either side of him, forgetting everything except Keira and her safety.

"Stop!" his father-in-law commanded.

A little bead of blood formed under the point he had pressed to Keira's neck, and Graham paused. There was a responding shuffle from behind him, and he quickly found himself grasped by Drew on one side and Dave on the other. He made no attempt to throw them off. All of his attention was on the girl and the man who held her.

"Let her go," Graham said, not bothering to acknowledge his captured state.

"Unlikely," Henry replied.

His voice was full of the scorn that had characterized him so well over the two years Graham had been married to the man's daughter. Graham paused, taking stock of the situation. He knew Keira was being used, not just as bait now, but also as leverage. He knew also that he was faster than the older man and he was sure he could incapacitate the two men who held him.

But can you do both things quickly enough and effectively enough to win?

Maybe, maybe not.

Henry probably wouldn't kill her, given a choice. It would take away that bit of leverage he had. But if he felt as though he didn't *have* a choice...

There was a click behind him and Graham knew he'd wasted too much time thinking about it. One of the two men holding him had cocked a gun.

"It's aimed at *her* head, not yours," Henry said. "Confirm that for me, Ms. Niles."

Keira's eyes lifted to a spot behind Graham, then she met his eyes and inclined her head. Just that slight nod was enough to draw more blood from her throat.

"Stop." Graham was pleading and he didn't care. "Don't hurt her."

Henry smiled. "Are you going to offer to take her place?"

"Yes," Graham replied right away.

Henry's smile widened. "I'd like to say I expected something less cliché from you, but it would be a lie. It's just the kind of bleeding heart offer I *would* expect from you."

"Because I care about something other than money and the public eye?"

"Because caring is your weakness. And that weakness is what got you in trouble in the first place. It's what made you marry my daughter when you should have stayed away and what got you accused of murder. It's what's going to make you give me what *I* want now."

Graham balked at the derogatory simplification of his personality. "I'm not giving you anything."

"Then I'll kill her," Henry replied with a shrug.

Graham forced himself to sound unmoved by the statement. "Like you killed Holly and Sam?"

His father-in-law sighed. "That was an unfortunate accident."

Graham's jaw clenched at the man's casual dismissal of the loss of life, as did his stomach. Before he could speak again, the man with the gun interjected.

"I'll shoot her," he offered. "Maybe in the hand, just to show you how serious we are."

"If you hurt her, I'll have no reason at all to help you," Graham snapped.

His father-in-law sighed. "Drew. I don't want you to shoot anyone at the moment. And, Graham, you should know by now that I never place all my bets on one number."

"You took every other thing from me," Graham countered.

Henry opened his mouth, but suddenly, Keira was alive in the older man's arms. She threw an elbow into his stomach and stomped down on his foot. Henry released her with a grunt and dropped the shard of porcelain to the ground. He reached for her, but Keira was too fast. She darted across the room and reached Graham just as Drew fired off a wild shot.

"I told you *not* to shoot in here," Henry snarled.

"You said not to shoot *anyone*," Drew corrected.

The older man strode toward the younger one, and Graham decided now was the only opportunity they might have to run. The one thing between him and the door was Dave. He met the police officer's eyes.

"Hit me," Dave instructed, just loud enough to be heard.

Graham didn't have to be told twice. He pulled his still-bound hands together and rammed them into Dave's gut. As the smaller man fell to the floor, he dropped the keys to the cuffs and Graham snagged them.

Graham grabbed Keira's hand and dragged her through the French doors and out into the hall. He was glad to see nothing had been done to change the decor in the home. Everything was exactly as he remembered it. Including a large, heavy table positioned against the wall just outside the dining room. Swiftly, he got behind it and pushed—with considerable effort—so that it blocked the doors. Then he clasped Keira's hand once more and set off at a run without looking back.

Chapter 27

Keira raced to keep up with Calloway as he tore through the large home with easy familiarity. They hit the front door in moments, but once they were there, Calloway paused, glanced through the curtains and shook his head.

"Henry's got a man out there in his car," he told her. "I can see him from here."

"Out the back, then?" Keira breathed, her throat still raw.

"Probably just as risky."

Behind them, she could hear the thump of the three men as they fought through the small blockade.

"I've got an idea," Calloway said.

He yanked on her hand, and they moved from the entryway, through the family room, then paused at the bottom of the stairs.

"C'mon!" Calloway called loudly. "The master bedroom!" Then he put his hand on her shoulder and leaned in to whisper, "Wait here."

He thundered up the stairs, two at a time, his feet hitting the steps, loud and hard. When he reached the top, he turned around and tiptoed back down. Without asking permission, Calloway slid his arms around Keira and lifted her from the ground. In complete silence, he carried her into the kitchen.

Moments later, the bang of booted feet and deep voices carried through the house.

They're free.

But Calloway ignored them as he set Keira on the countertop.

"Just a sec," he murmured.

Keira watched in amazement as he crouched low, found a loose floorboard, lifted it, then reached into it. With a heave, he pulled on something inside and an old-fashioned trapdoor squeaked open. Calloway held it up.

"In," he commanded. "There's a railing on your right."

Keira didn't bother to argue. She stepped down into the darkness, her hand finding the railing immediately. She used it to guide her all the way to the bottom of the stairs. As she reached the floor, the light above her cut out, and the door clicked shut. In seconds, she felt Calloway reach her side. They stood there wordlessly, shoulder to shoulder, for a long minute.

"Wine cellar?" Keira finally whispered, just to break the silence.

"Man cave," Calloway corrected, just as softly.

He moved away briefly, then there was a click, and a blue-and-yellow neon sign came to life in one corner.

Vaguely, Keira was aware that her surroundings were similar to those of Calloway's hidden cabin. Wood panel walls and rustic decor.

Mostly, though, all she was aware of was Calloway.

It had only been two hours—maybe three—since she'd seen him. It seemed like a lifetime. She had to feel him. Touch him. Breathe him in and hold him there.

She slipped her hands around his shoulders, molded her body to his and tipped her face up expectantly. Calloway didn't disappoint her. He pressed his palms into the small of her back, pulling her impossibly closer, and tilted down to push his lips into hers.

Calloway's mouth was perfect. *He* was perfect. Perfectly imperfect. Perfectly *hers*.

For the duration of the kiss, the world disappeared. No crazy past haunting them, no violent men hunting them.

The men. The brothers, she remembered, and pulled away reluctantly.

"Dave Stark and Drew—the man I thought I was running to—they're *his* sons," Keira said in a rush. "And Holly's brothers."

He cupped her cheek. "I know. Dave explained it."

"So you were right," Keira added, "About there being no coincidences."

"Sometimes I wish I was wrong," Calloway replied grimly.

He kissed her once more, then moved across the room toward a raised, blank space on the far wall.

"That's just panel drywall," he said. "I sealed up a

window, and it's still there on the other side. It comes out in the side yard."

"You want to break through?" Keira asked. "You don't think they'll hear it upstairs?"

"It's probably our only chance."

Calloway had already snagged a hammer from the tool chest. He angled the claw under the drywall and pulled at the points where the nails had been hammered in. It was a nearly silent endeavor, and in just a few minutes, he'd freed a quarter of the drywall. When he paused to tap the edges, several pieces of the chalky material crumbled away.

"Not too bad," he stated, sounding pleased.

The second half was even easier. The loose bits on the side Calloway had already pried off seemed to have compromised the structural integrity of the one he was taking apart now. It only took a few moments for the whole thing to come down.

The windowpane was covered in grime, and the latch squealed in protest as Calloway forced it back.

Keira sent up a hurried prayer that it would open in spite of its worse-for-wear appearance, then watched anxiously as Calloway put both hands on the glass and pushed. It resisted for only a second before it flew to the side, sending in a waft of fresh air.

Keira inhaled deeply.

"I'll go first," Calloway told her. "Then I'll help you through."

He grabbed the edge of the dirty sill, his biceps flexing as he pulled himself up. He went out quickly, then jabbed his hands back through.

Keira let his warm hands close on her wrists and

drag her up. For a relieved moment, they stood toe-to-toe in the window well. It was short-lived.

Henderson's deep, calm voice carried through the air. "And here I was, thinking you might actually get away."

Keira looked up. All three men stood staring down at them. Drew's eyes were full of muted fury. Dave's were almost apologetic. And Henry's...they were bright with anticipation.

"This is it, isn't it?" he asked, sounding nearly gleeful.

Calloway didn't answer, and Keira though that was a bad sign for them. And Henderson seemed to take it as encouragement, too.

"Should we go back into the house?" His question was far too pleasant.

Calloway clearly thought so, too. "Are you giving us a choice?"

"Not even a little bit," Henderson told them. "Back the way you came."

They all slipped through the window—first Drew, then Keira and Graham, then Dave and finally Henry Henderson.

Once they were in the basement, Graham stood protectively in front of Keira. His father-in-law took a slow look around the dim room.

"Amazing," said Henry. "My wife *built* this house and I had no idea this room was down here."

"Maybe there was a good reason for that," Graham retorted.

Henderson shot him one of his usual impassive stares. "Yes. I'm sure there was. She probably planned on using it as a place to hide her wine. She was rather fond of it. Just like Holly."

"You have no right to say her name," Graham growled. "You lost that right when you took her life."

Henry sighed. "It was never my intention to harm her physically. It wouldn't have happened if Drew had taken care of incapacitating her properly in the first place."

Drew spoke up. "How was I supposed to know she had such a high tolerance for prescription drugs?"

"So you're blaming the murder on him?"

Henry shrugged. "Partially. I pulled the trigger because she got in the way. All I wanted was the painting. It was rightfully mine. But my wife somehow deemed Holly a better choice."

How the other man could be so blasé about the murders of his own daughter and his own grandson—murders the man had just admitted to committing himself—was completely beyond Graham.

"Speaking of the painting…" Drew piped up again.

Without bothering to think about the consequences, Graham turned and swung a fist. He hit Drew straight in the face and the other man collapsed to the floor, his eyes rolled back in his head and blood dripped from his nose.

His father-in-law took a quick step toward the unconscious body, but Graham was faster. His hand shot out and caught Henry straight in the throat. He backed the older man to the far wall.

"Are you going to *do* something, Stark?" Henry asked.

The policeman shook his head. "I'd rather not."

Graham smiled coldly. "Do you know what that is behind me?"

He watched as the man's brown eyes—so like Holly's, so like Sam's—traveled up and went wide as they found the framed piece of art, sandwiched between a Budweiser ad and a Rolling Stones poster.

"That's it," Graham said. "The thirty-plus million-dollar painting you killed them for, you sick son of—"

"Just her," Henderson corrected.

Graham went still. "What the hell does that mean?"

"I didn't kill Sam," Henry stated casually.

"That's a lie," Graham replied in a hoarse whisper. "I saw the blood."

"There was blood," Henry agreed. "Lots of blood."

"Sam is dead."

"He's not. If you let me get my phone from my pocket, I'd be happy to show you."

Graham wanted to tell the other man where he could shove his phone, but a small part of him filled with hope. He tried to fight the burgeoning emotion. He failed.

"Show me."

He loosened his grip just enough that the other man could reach into his coat. He pulled out a smartphone, held it up and punched in a pass code. In moments, a picture flooded the small screen.

A little boy with perfect blond curls and oh-so-familiar brown eyes. He was bigger, and not really smiling in the carefree way Graham had always remembered him. But…

"That's impossible," Graham breathed.

He couldn't take his eyes from the photograph.

"You know it's him," Henry said.

It was. Graham was sure.

"How?" he asked.

"The kid took a through and through," the older man explained. "Holly's second bullet. Went through her abdomen and nicked Sam in a pretty big artery. And you were right about the blood. Way more than I thought one small person could lose. Drew and I bandaged him up pretty tight, took him to a retired doctor I knew. Saved the kid's life."

"Why would you hold that back all these years?" Graham asked.

"What good would it do to tell anyone he was alive?" Henry countered. "Besides which, it made the police search for you that much harder. And I thought the guilt—or the desire for revenge—might get to you eventually. Bring you home."

"Where is he?"

"Close."

"Take me to him," Graham said.

"Let me have the painting, and I will."

"Sam first. We can come back for the painting."

Henry sighed. "Fine."

"Get Drew's gun, Keira," Graham ordered.

She'd been silent, letting the scene unfold, and now she shot an uncertain glance toward Dave.

"He's not going to stop you," Graham assured her.

Dave nodded, and Keira moved. But Graham had misjudged the other man's alertness, and as Keira's hand almost closed on the weapon, Drew sat straight up, twisted and pulled the girl forcefully into his lap.

"Put him down, Calloway. Or I'll shoot the girl," Drew announced coldly.

"He'll shoot me anyway," Keira stated.

Graham's heart squeezed. He couldn't lose her. He couldn't lose Sam again.

"I have to take the chance that he won't," he said. "I love you too much."

"I love you, too," she whispered back.

Drew snarled, "Enough!"

Graham's arms fell to his sides, and Henry shoved past him, his hands already reaching for the painting. But as he moved, Graham's foot shot out. The older man stumbled, straight into Keira and Drew. The gun flew from Drew's grasp. It discharged loudly, and a *riiiiiip* echoed through the basement.

"No," Henry gasped.

Graham's eyes followed his gaze, straight up to the painting. To the brand-new bullet-sized hole that adorned its center.

And Graham smiled.

Epilogue

Five Weeks Later

"Do you think the smoke has finally cleared?" Keira asked, unsure if she was hoping for a yes or for a no.

Graham seemed to sense the flip-flop nature of her question.

"Maybe," he replied. "Maybe not. We can wait here awhile longer. Your work said to take the time you need, and I'm not in a hurry, either."

He uncurled himself from the brand-new, built-for-two rocking chair on the front porch of the old log cabin. He stretched, wide shoulders flexing in a way that made Keira's blood heat up in spite of the chilly air.

"Is he asleep yet?" she wondered out loud.

Graham smiled, that same silly, dopey, love-filled

grin that he always grinned whenever Sam was concerned.

"I was just going to check," he told her.

Keira watched his back as he retreated into the cabin, admiring the view.

My Mountain Man, she thought affectionately.

He was almost always at ease now that his father-in-law was behind bars. His own name had been officially cleared, too. Dave was let off with a slap on the wrist. And Sam… He'd spent four years shuffled between nannies, with—thankfully—little direct contact with his grandfather and the man's underhanded activities. He was as serious a kid as Keira had ever met, but he smiled a little more every day. And twice this week, Keira had heard him drop the word *Daddy* when referring to Calloway.

No, she decided. *I'm not in a huge hurry to get out of here.*

Graham peeled back the curtain to the closet-turned-tiny-bedroom and gazed down lovingly at his kid. His living, breathing kid. He'd never get tired of staring at that perfect little face. He was so glad that Sam had been spared the darker parts of Graham's father-in-law's life.

Graham's heart swelled, gratitude and awe nearly overwhelming him as it did almost every time he took stock of his life.

Accused murderer. Redeemed father. Loving husband.

Well, soon-to-be husband, if the ring in his pocket worked like he thought it would.

"Calloway?"

Keira's soft voice made him turn.

She'd stepped into the cabin, dropped her jacket and stood in front of the blissfully small bed they shared every night in nothing but one of his T-shirts. His favorite outfit.

"Sam's okay?" she asked.

"Perfect," he replied.

Keira smiled. "Like always."

"Like you," Graham teased, happy when she blushed.

He walked to her, wrapped her in his arms and kissed her thoroughly, just to make the pink in her cheeks brighten even more.

"Hey," he murmured when he pulled away. "Can I ask you something?"

"Anything."

He dug his hand into his pocket, yanked out the little box and balanced it on his palm. "On a sliding scale... how happy are you that you drove into a snowstorm, got rescued by a mountain man and almost got killed by a corrupt politician?"

Keira's eyes lit up. "Ten out of ten!"

Graham grinned and kissed her again, secure that fate was well in hand.

* * * * *

Three months ago...
When I'm done, you're going to beg me for the pain.

Chloe Pascale struggled to open her eyes. She blinked against the brightness of the sky. Trees. Snow. Cold. Her head pounded in rhythm to her racing heartbeat. Shuffling reached her ears as her last memories lightninged across her mind like a half-remembered dream. She'd gone out for a run on the trail near her house. Then... Fear clawed at her insides, her hands curling into fists. He'd come out of the woods. He'd... She licked her lips, her mouth dry. He'd drugged her, but with what and how many milliliters, she wasn't sure. The haze of unconsciousness slipped from her mind, and a new terrifying reality forced her from ignorance. "Where am I?"

Dead leaves crunched off to her left. Her attacker's dark outline shifted in her peripheral vision. Black ski mask. Lean build. Tall. Well over six feet. Unfamiliar voice. Black jeans. His knees popped as he crouched beside her, the long shovel in his left hand digging into the soil near her head. The tip of the tool was coated in mud. Reaching a gloved hand toward her, he stroked the left side of her jawline, ear to chin, and a shiver chased down her spine against her wishes. "Don't worry, Dr. Miles. It'll all be over soon."

His voice… It sounded…off. Disguised?

"How do you know my name? What do you want?" She blinked to clear her head. The injection site at the base of her neck itched, then burned, and she brought her hands up to assess the damage. Ropes encircled her wrists, and she lifted her head from the ground. Her ankles had been bound, too. She pulled against the strands, but she couldn't break through. Then, almost as though demanding her attention, she caught sight of the refrigerator. Old. Light blue. Something out of the '50s with curves and heavy steel doors.

"I know everything about you, Chloe. Can I call you Chloe?" he asked. "I know where you live. I know where you work. I know your running route and how many hours you spend at the clinic. You really should change up your routine. Who knows who could be out there watching you? As for what I want, well, I'm going to let you figure that part out once you're inside."

Pressure built in her chest. She dug her heels into the ground, but the soil only gave way. No. No, no, no, no. This wasn't happening. Not to her. Darkness closed in around the edges of her vision, her breath coming in short bursts. Pulling at the ropes again, she locked her jaw against the scream working up her throat. She wasn't going in that refrigerator like the other victim she'd heard about on the news. Dr. Roberta Ellis. Buried alive, killed by asphyxiation. Tears burned in her eyes as he straightened and turned his back to her to finish the work he'd started with the shovel.

Don't miss
Grave Danger *by Nichole Severn,*
available February 2022 wherever
Harlequin books and ebooks are sold.

Harlequin.com